TO: E
ENJOY!

Grey
Justice

Frank J. Kopet

Clip art by Public Domain Vectors,
Mardigann & johnny automatic

FJKAY Production Department
2018

Whatever you can do
Or dream you can do
Begin it
Boldness has genius
Power and Magic in it
Goethe

Grey Justice
is dedicated to
my best friend
my life companion
my beautiful wife
Marie

Grey
Justice

ONE

Emma's wailing cries and supplications reverberated within the hallways of Belvedere Manor. Though her incantations were muffled and incomprehensible, both Mary and Jessie understood: they too experienced this evil.

"Dear God, I think they're doing Emma," Jessie whispered.

"Shush," Mary scolded.

Jessie, with eyes opened-wide, mouthed a soundless urging, *"Please — let's go."*

Mary, shook her head in repudiation, then with newly instilled determination, approached those sounds of human anguish. While Emma's appeal for mercy grew louder Mary's resolve to intercede quickly evaporated. She knew who and what immorality existed beyond that closed door. In futile resignation Mary lowered her head in shameful defeat. She could not help Emma.

Both retreated from the horror within room A122.

***

The assault started when Emma Joslin received her second sponge bath of the day. Unlike the earlier routine, rushed and basic, Gail began to apply a scented-oil. As Emma's body absorbed the emollient, its fragrance awakened her memory; her heart pounded in nervous anticipation. She closed her eyes in an attempt to block out the inevitable wickedness. When Jack entered her room spewing suggestive erotica, she knew both hungered to satiate their lascivious desires. It was at that moment Emma cried out those supplications for mercy.

***

Jack Tridon, the lead nurse of Belvedere Manor's A Wing performed his duties in a manner that first fulfilled his gain, then his self-satisfaction, and eventually attend to the needs of the residents. The long stressful days at the Manor, never exhausted Jack's boundless energy. When away from the confines of Belvedere, he offered most of his free-time to the community. Good-guy Jack, an imposing man standing at six-foot-three, ever ready to support a civic function, never failed to be where the important, the affluent people gathered.

For Jack, socializing came easy. He could adjust his demeanor to the immediate company. Being extremely gender sensitive, Jack spoke to women with an eloquent graceful voice, then wooed them with his cunning charm. Women of every age loved him. As for the guys, he bonded immediately. Being a sportsman with some, a businessman with others, he always presented an image of a quiet-toned gentleman. Jack's bearing and unobtrusive panache made him a man's man. And yet no one sensed the deep malice embedded within the body and soul of Jack Tridon. That handsome, lovable friend to all lacked a conscience; Jack could not differentiate right from wrong.

***

While the residents and workers of Belvedere chose to avoid Jack, Gail Summun became his shadow and in turn assumed an automatic extension of his authority. Gail enjoyed this unwarranted quasi-power with its subsequent domination of the staff. Although she relished that control, she cared more for the subjugation of the Manor's residents. In consonance with her assumed second-in-command position, Gail did have an authoritative, albeit a very feminine appearance.

Standing at five-foot-ten with a svelte figure of proper proportions, Gail highlighted her femininity with professionally colored and styled reddish-blond hair. An application of subtle cosmetic make-up augmented her need to look natural. Her appearance never varied because she always wore the old out-of-vogue nurse's uniform, white from top to bottom, sans the cap. Her blouse, opened at the collar, and when tucked into her short tight skirt, fit perfectly to her body. The white nylon stockings along with white leather shoes completed Gail's presentation of total purity. A duplicate of the outfit hung in her locker, just in case any part of her clothing became soiled.

Gail loved that uniform. When passing a mirror she would, with voyeuristic joy, stealthily gaze at her reflected image. The stolen peek of the woman dressed in a solid white outfit gave her a tingle of excitement; that initial exhilaration amplified as she roamed the facility. Simple swishing noises of her short tight skirt against her nylon stockings drove her higher into a sexual reverie. Past erogenous physical contacts danced through her mind. The thoughts grew into uncontainable desire; an urgent need for intimacy; a longing to touch and feel; a want to dominate another woman's body. As for men, she had zero need for their affection.

***

Gail's sexual demands started simply. Satisfying all the basic needs of her charges meant, at times, very personal contact. When a very subtle touch of a sensuous area went unchallenged, her contact became more deliberate, quickly escalated into aggressive fondling and ultimately into a sexual encounter.

She continued with her solo assignations until Jack noticed a room with a closed door; a violation of one of his many special rules. He yanked it open with authority and caught Gail molesting a female resident. Gail paled with fear. With her clothing in disarray, she backed away from her victim anticipating Jack's admonishment. She waited, wondered why he hesitated. Without a word of rebuke his stern stoic face slowly changed. His glaring eyes maintained contact; he began to laugh. Jack using a rotating hand motion encouraged her to continue. He closed the door. Within moments, they both were ravishing the woman.

***

Jack and Gail regaled in the primal savagery of their first ménage a trois assault. However, the mere reliving of those explosive sensual moments did not satisfy their growing desires. Encouraged by management's complacency, they traveled from room to room sampling the delights or disappointments each woman had to offer. The highs and lows of these subsequent attacks did not matter. It was the anticipation, the act, and then the celebration by retelling how they achieved satisfaction made them hunger for more. Their insatiable lascivious cravings became a constant nightmare for the women of Belvedere Manor.

***

Jack's devious mind assessing the potential tumult from their first attack generated a trail of falsified records. However, he surmised managers of the Manor would soon hear about their malfeasance. Jack chose, at an impromptu meeting, to leak the news to Belvedere's director. An unusual hallucinatory problem existed within the wing: women truly believed they were sexually active. Mild sedatives seemed to relieve the symptoms. Receiving an atta-boy response made it an easy topic for the weekly managers' meeting.

Speaking with zero emotions, Jack cited his thorough investigation, finding the accusations unwarranted he administered some prescribed medication to relieve the resident's anxiety. He reported a few more similar incidents at subsequent sessions. Jack suggested the sexual thoughts seemed to be infectious.

The series of oral complaints, all documented as unsubstantiated, allowed management to classify the events as minor mental anomalies. In addition, Jack offered them a logical solution by administering pre-ordered medications, when necessary; and controlling any viewing of sexually explicit television programs.

***

As predicted, reports of additional assaults came very quickly. The residents, knowing the staff could not help, pled their plight with anyone who would listen.

Visitors hearing the horrific stories demanded immediate action; many wanted to call the police. Their instant anger subsided after listening to a quiet-voiced manager telling them the real-story: some residents lose their sense of reality; they start to believe their dreams. The visitors also learned that the Manor's files contained many reports very similar in nature. All incidents were thoroughly investigated and shown to be unfounded.

They apologized for interfering and leave believing they, as responsible people, did their duty.

It didn't take very long before the residents understood that any complaint, if they dared to make one, would be buried.

***

Mary Archer an intelligent eighty-two-year-old woman, now trapped in a body that failed her, worked her entire life as a dedicated teaching professional. She taught the elementary grades; it gave her daily contact with exciting youngsters, and they became her family. The years flew by. Retirement stole away the joy of teaching.

Although Mary needed the help of a full care facility, her optimism never waned. She knew a life of joy and happiness was still possible, even in a weakened body. She could tolerate the missing happiness and tried to cope. It was the horror within Belvedere Manor that became morally and physically unacceptable.

***

Mary and Jessie rolled down the empty hallway. They turned into the recreation room and espied four women, randomly distributed within. Each sat in muted silence. They appeared to be frozen in place. Mary deliberately brushed by each stimulating them from their self-induced trance, then signaled to gather around her. Initially, they hesitated, waiting to see who responded to the unusual invitation. Once the migration started Mary indicated they should pull up very close to her.

"I guess you all know about Emma," Mary said. A few nodded in agreement.

"You also know that no one cares. That means we have to start helping ourselves." Some in the group stunned to hear Mary speaking in a normal voice stared at her in consternation. She's violating Jack's orders: *"The recreation room must, at all times, be a quiet room. No talking allowed."*

They remained wide-eyed and mute. Being sisters in this sadistic world meant everyone within this circle experienced the cruelty of Jack and Gail's desires. Jessie glanced behind her. Seeing they were still alone in the room, stirred up some courage and said, "How about poor Emma? She's hurting real bad and for a long time now."

"Thank you Jessie. We have to do something," Mary said.

"Oh Mary, stop dreaming, everyone thinks were loonies," Karen said.

"You're absolutely right! Most visitors think Jack's a saint. He's a saint and we're demented," Mary said in a low voice. The group having difficulty hearing relayed the message.

The stolen conversations released them from the pall of a muted existence. Their spirits rose and each felt an élan realizing they were behaving like normal people. Mary felt them bond — each needed the other. These forbidden words were beginning to meld them into an entity.

Sharing thoughts of possible salvation disappeared when some showed their fear and serious doubt. It started with Doris: "Mary, anything we try to do will only make things worse."

"How can it get any worse?" Mary asked. "Look at us, we're abandoned by the world and have to live with these psychopaths. And everyone knows how we are abused." She said while pointing and waving her arms. "They all know, and they won't help us." Some nodded in understanding. "We have to begin protecting ourselves," she continued. "And — if we can, we must punish those who have hurt us. We . . ."

"Y o o o o u." Jack said dragging out the word for effect. His one-word admonition achieved its intent. The women lowered their heads. "I want all of you to be quiet," Jack demanded. "Nice and quiet or you," Jack said as he stabbed his finger in Mary's direction. "Or you and the rest of your old cronies will go flying back to your rooms. Yeah back to your rooms and into bed." He continued pointing at Mary and then towards the others. "A bunch of sleepy-time pills will be your lunch and supper," Jack bellowed. He looked for their reaction. When all remain submissive, he strutted towards the center of the room.

Everyone maintained the lowering of their heads, acting contrite and indicating that they heard the voice of their master. Jack scanned the room. Looking at each of them, he tried to burn his will into their minds. Jack turned, walked around the group, and after failing to stare directly into the eyes of any of the women said, "Break this up — and I mean now." He grabbed Sara's chair and pushed her towards the window. Others quickly moved away hoping to avoid Jack's rage. "And keep your mouths shut. Got it?" The chastised woman nodded their acceptance. Jack strutted around the room and left as suddenly as he appeared.

Mary waited for a short while. Defiantly, she summoned them back into a circle. Timing became critical since Jack could return at any moment. Showing signs of fatigue Mary said, "We have the right to protect ourselves.

We can use our God-given right to sit in judgment of people who harmed us, or hurt any of our brothers and sisters. We can testify and determine their guilt. We can impose a just punishment." Mary stopped for a moment pulled in a deep breath and continued, "I know enforcing a sentence is a problem. We must believe somehow and at some time our judgments will be – a punishment will happen." Mary looked at the befuddled deathly-quiet group of women. She, shaking her head in dismay, left the circle.

Disbursing quickly, a few began to whisper their thoughts; others moved away in silence. Mary sensing she had to continue signaled for all to return.

They sheepishly pulled in around her. Mary asked if they understood what she was trying to tell them. She felt their fears; their nodding heads conveyed understanding. Mary believing she had their silent approval, sat up tall and said, "I, Mary Archer, convene the court of our Belvedere community."

The stress of the moment made her pull in a deep breath. As the air expelled in a rush of anxiety she said, "I ask, each of you, if you are willing to sit in judgment? Show me your acceptance by a thumbs-up."

The impact of words declaring their involvement in an insurrection stunned them into a frozen silence. All of their eyes locked in a unified stare at this woman who was launching them into certain disaster. A few broke contact and silently moved away. A low-level mumbling began as some tried to ramp up their courage to participate in this unwelcome danger.

The light tapping by Mary on her chair, barely audible, yet sufficient for some to hear, signaled that they should continue. Eventually, each nudged another until they all were warily attentive.

Mary glared at the woman furthest away. Using her right hand, pointed at her, thrusting up her thumb as a clue to what she expected. The woman procrastinating for a brief moment slowly responded. Mary nodding at her acceptance continued her pointing towards each of the other women. The routine broke with Sara. She held up her hands in surrender, shook her head and mouthed muted words, "I can't do this!" She looked around for sympathy. No one offered any solace. With tears streaming down her face Sara gave a feeble thumbs-up. Continuing in turn, all voted their commitment. The simple procedure took its toll. More tears began to flow.

Many were too far away to hear, and yet Mary sensed she had to hit them hard. She spoke in a loud authoritative voice, "Think of the horrors. Think of what you suffered." Mary jabbed her index finger towards individuals within the group and demanded, "You, and you, and you be ready to tell your story. We want to hear everything they did to you. We must hear so that this court may judge and punish them." Mary, with heart pounding, silently prayed that no one outside of this room heard her. She added in a quiet voice, "We will begin our work tomorrow."

For a few seconds, the women remained transfixed. Mary's last words were so loud and overwhelming they were certain it would bring immediate disaster. Needing to escape this new self-inflicted danger, all, save Mary, quickly retreated from the recreation room.

Now alone, Mary suddenly realized that the world around her seemed surreal. She felt different. The room seemed different, and then it registered. It wasn't the room.

Her courage and defiance pierced through and ripped away her blinding veil of fear. A subtle smile crept onto Mary's face. The joy of hope flowed into her heart; tears of happiness welled in her eyes.

TWO

The moment it jangled its intrusive alert, the Director of Belvedere Manor glanced toward his phone. Though he was in the throes of pitching the attributes of the Manor, Sal Manfassi merely offered his guest a barely perceptible smile before reaching for the handset.

"Good morning," he said brusquely.

"Hey grumpy, I've got one for you."

Sal laughed and said, "Hey Tina. How are all of my dear friends at Memorial. . ."

"Yeah, yeah, we love you too. Let's talk business."

"Okay, I can do that." Sal lifted his hand, extended his index finger indicating he needed another minute. His visitor waved her hand in understanding.

"He fits your profile. And, believe it or not, he'll be ready for delivery by Friday morning."

"That sounds interesting."

"Come on Sal, stop kidding, I know you can make room for a unique client."

"Tina we're very close to our maximum," Sal waited a short respite then quickly added, "I'm certain I can do something to accommodate you."

"Accommodate me?" Tina chuckled, "In case you didn't hear me, I'm telling you this guy's a prime candidate."

Sal looked at his visitor and knew she was absorbing his part of the conversation.

"Of course, course you're right, Tina. Only professionals, like yourself, have that special sensitivity to recognize those who can use our medical expertise and of course our special capabilities within the A Wing." He offered his guest a big smile. "I assume you will take care of the transportation."

"We're just like Tony's Pizza. We deliver. Hey Sal, why are you talking crazy this morning? Ah, let me guess. Umm, I bet you've got someone in the office who's judging your proficiency as a manager," Tina snickered.

"You are absolutely correct in your assessment. Can I call you back within — oh, let's just say a little bit later?"

"Wow! Very impressive," she laughed. "Since it is very apparent you're tied up. I'll call Milo."

"Now that is a wonderful suggestion. Please do that," Sal responded curtly.

"Okay. Now, get back to your visitor before you lose him. Or is it a cute little her?"

Sal chose to ignore her intuitively correct comment and said, "Tina. I thank you very much for the call, bye." Without waiting for a reply, he returned the handset to its cradle.

"Sorry for the interruption. That phone dominates my life; it rings, and you witnessed it. I'm programmed to answer. I'm not trying to justify my rudeness; in my world every call has its own sense of importance. We at Belvedere try to give our hospital-clients immediate service." His guest smiled her response. "So, please tell me a little more about your mother?"

"Mom has health issues and she can't — and now she can't do a lot of things without some help. I feel like a horrid daughter that I'm not able to be there for her. We've talked about a live-in nurse's aide — I feel I have to look at all the options. Guess you've heard this story before."

"Mrs. Turner, all of us at Belvedere Manor know and appreciate the stress any major health issue imposes on the entire family. Please believe me; we know what you're going through — and how you feel." Sal suppressed an urge to smile. "Before that phone call, we were talking about the Manor and now, just a guess, you're wondering about the A Wing."

"You're reading my mind."

"I've been helping people for a long time, and I appreciate your need to garner every nugget of information."

"Thank you for understanding."

"Each wing, in the Manor, offers a different type and level of care. When we greet a new resident, we assign a wing and a room based upon the client's need. Our staff of managers is very experienced. They examine, with great intensity, the myriad of reasons why an individual seeks our professional care. Some require special medically driven amenities, such as high-tech bedding. Then there is a broad variety of unique physical, medical and psychological treatments. Most require a critical and timely dispensing of their vitally important pharmaceuticals. I must emphasize that each facet of care, day and night, seven days a week, is extremely important."

"This full-time care has to be expensive."

"Not really. If you break down the costs, we are very competitive. However, and I must emphasize, if required, we examine the individual's ability to handle the financial aspects of their case. That's another vital element of our business. I'm sure it doesn't apply to you so I won't bore you with those details." Sal stopped for a moment, leaned forward and then started again. "I'm very happy we're having this talk. It helps me to do my job knowing a family member is deeply concerned about their Mother. I know this is very difficult for you." Sal cocked his head, gestured with his arms as if offering a hug. "Now about that A Wing; we use that part of our facility to house some of our long-term patients. Many of these folks remain bedded all day long. A few are mobile. However, none of them, and I do mean none of them will ever live an independent life." Sal looked towards his quest. Fearing he was beginning to lose her, added quickly, "They are important to us. They are part of our family and we offer them our love and care. From the little you've told me about your mother she will not be housed there. She will be with others who are alive and enjoying the amenities of the Manor. Your Mom will find new friends and enjoy life."

Sal's words seemed empty and lacked conviction. Although she wanted to know more, Mrs. Turner wished the man would just shut down his pitch of love. She blew out a breath, albeit very slowly releasing some of her anxiety and asked, "Can I tour your facility? I'd like to see the various wings."

Her walk-in visit started with a simple request for some information and now expanded in scope. Sal's face fell into a frown. Mrs. Turner looked at the man seated in front of her. She sensed his change in demeanor and wondered if she erred in considering Belvedere Manor as the ideal place for her mother.

Sal, caught between wanting to finalize Tina's offer that meant acquiring a new client, knew he had to get back to snaring the potential business sitting before him. "Absolutely," Sal said with a surge of enthusiasm then continued, "This facility is open to all visitors. I mean legitimate visitors, not a bunch of sightseers. And that is, of course, within the normal visiting hours of 2 to 5 and 6 to 8." Sal stopped and tried to give the appearance of a confident man who could relieve her heavy burden. When Turner did not respond nor offer any thoughts he continued, "Do you think you will be visiting very often?"

"When I can — when I can, I will visit in the evening. I guess that is what most people do?"

"Yes, yes that is what most working folks do. However, we do have a group of people who prefer to visit during the afternoon. We also have church folks and fraternal groups that come in and socialize, play games and do that sort of thing. People are always coming and going. This is a busy place, busy place."

Sal arose from his desk and said, "Well Mrs. Turner let's take a walk and show you this wonderful home. Again, you understand we don't allow visitors at this time of the day. Mornings are an extremely intense time. A lot must be accomplished in a short period."

Since his visitor didn't offer any comment, Sal continued: "This facility consists of three wings. These are parallel to each other and separated by courtyards. This design allows almost every room in the facility to have a large window glowing with natural sunlight." They turned a corner, and Sal continued. "This passageway is about half-way down each wing. It's a great step saver." Turner remained quiet and merely nodded her head in understanding. "This area houses the guest reception area, administrative offices, pharmacy and the physical therapy room. The kitchen, laundry and some maintenance rooms are located in the back building."

"It seems efficient." Danielle Turner offered.

"Each wing is self-sufficient. They have their own dining room plus a recreation room and a nurse's control station. That allows independence, flexibility, and gives us redundancy in management capability to take care of emergencies. Let's go to our left and head towards A Wing. Any questions so far?"

"No, no questions — well, I, I do have one question. During your phone call, you mentioned being at maximum capacity. Do you have room for us?"

"Ah, I'm happy you asked, and the answer is yes I do. We have a beautiful private room in the C Wing. Please understand it is available now — it may not be vacant very long," Sal smiled as he led the way into A Wing.

***

As Mary Archer made her way towards the recreation room, five additional residents trailed behind. Then, after entering and making certain they were alone, whispered their hellos and how-are-you-doing. Mary gave them a moment before signaling to move in closer to her.

"Before we start, I want to offer a prayer. Please join hands."

The women moved in allowing each to touch or grasp a neighbor's hand. With heads bowed in reverence each also peered up towards Mary to hear or see what she was saying. After pulling in an anxious breath Mary prayed in a low clear voice: "Dear Lord. Dear Sweet Lord, please guide us and help us. Please help us to protect our community from evil; evil that is torturing your children. We seek Your strength to drive this horror from us. We cried out to those around us for justice, and those cries were suppressed. We shouted out to those who could help us, and our pleas went unanswered. All civilized people have abandoned this community, and we in our utter desperation seek thy help. Although we are weak -- alone — we promise You — we will work hard and try to protect our brothers and sisters. We beg You to bless this group with Your wisdom. We ask for Your strength to help us to do our duty. We also humbly ask for Your forgiveness; forgiveness for our thoughts; forgiveness for our actions. Amen."

They quickly broke the circle whispering among themselves their understanding of the offered words. Quiet prevailed, as most felt the burden of a task they did not understand; confusion abounded. They had big concerns about potential trouble. And trouble would come just by gathering and talking. Knowing anything they did clouded their future, someone murmured, "Even Mary's prayer asked for forgiveness for our thoughts and actions."

All in unison turned towards the voices of people entering the room. The noise motivated a few women to wheel quickly towards the window; others proceeded towards the opposite doorway, hopefully away from any possible trouble. None of them traveled too far since all wanted to listen to the intruders.

"This is the recreation room for our A Wing. As you can see we have some of our residents relaxing and enjoying the facility. Let's continue to the Nurse's Station just beyond the rear door," Sal said as he tugged on Danielle Turner's arm.

"Oh my," Danielle said while looking across the room. "Can it be? Is that woman — that woman over there, is it Miss Mary Archer?" Turner pointed towards Mary and started to move in her direction. "Miss Archer was my eighth-grade teacher. Is it okay to go over and talk to her?" she said in an excited voice.

Sal paled hearing the woman mentioning Archer's name. Jack's fabricated reports spun within his head; Mary was involved; the lucrative business of A Wing had to be protected. Sal reached out, grabbed Turner's arm. "Yes you're right she's Mary Archer. You may want to talk to her. Some residents don't want to be bothered by visitors. You're welcome to try. Please do not say, or do anything to get her upset." Sal still clung to the woman thinking how to restrict her then said, "Before you go, I want you to know she has a problem with reality. She may let her imagination go on. How can I say this? She may offer thoughts that are — are a little unusual. Please be gentle and I beg you, respect her privacy."

"Are you telling me she has a mental problem? Now, that's hard for me to believe. She was always on top of everything."

"Time takes a toll in many different ways. And again, if you must talk to her, please be gentle and understanding."

As they walked towards Mary, the other residents retreated, just a bit, shying away from the big boss and his companion. Mary held her place, sat up defiantly and stared at the woman walking towards her. She appeared familiar — Mary did not recognize her.

"Hello Miss Archer. It's Danielle." Mary did not respond just looked at her quizzically. "I was in your eighth-grade class." She laughed a little and said, "That was quite a few years ago."

Mary suddenly recalled her old student and smiled. "Hello Danielle. Yes, I remember you. I think about all of my students. The best part of my day is spent recalling the fun I had with my children." Mary chuckled a bit and then said, "I recognize that little singing you have in your voice. You've gotten a wee bit older. Yes, you are my Danielle."

"How are you feeling Miss Archer?" she said while searching for something to talk about.

"How am I feeling? Well, well let's say I'm here because I have a few problems. I will also say things could be better." Sal Manfassi glared at her, and she received his message to shut up. "Let's talk about you. My students were my life, and I love every one of you. Please tell me. Why are you here? To visit with me, I hope?"

"I'd love to visit. Right now Mr. Manfassi's showing me the facility. My Mom — Mom is, well she's not able to take care of her-ssself." Turner's stuttering surprised her. She had not stuttered in many years; her anxiety surged; she then said, "It's been a fast process. She's getting worse and Mom's starting to acknowledge the fact she needs help."

"That I can understand," Mary said sadly.

"So, here I am looking into the possibility of Mom becoming a Belvedere resident. So far, from what I have heard and seen I believe she could be happy here." She stopped her nervous rambling, took a breath, and said with feeling, "Have you been here very long?"

"Far too long; it seems like an eternity and I often wish the Good Lord would call me," she said while looking at her former student.

"I don't like to hear you talk that way Miss Archer. You always taught us to be happy and to look forward to the new adventures of every day."

"Yes, that's true. Life is an adventure. In here, we carry a very heavy burden, and I want to tell you about it — if you come and visit with me," Mary said as she glared at Sal with hatred in her eyes.

Turner missed Mary Archer's contemptuous gaze towards Sal Manfassi and answered, "I'll come. After Mom is in and settled, I'll definitely visit."

Sal Manfassi heard the commitment from Turner and knew he had to finish the tour. "I know your time is running short Mrs. Turner. Let's continue. Bye Mary," Sal said as he squinted with his eyes in a non-oral message for her to keep quiet.

"Well, Mr. Manfassi, we just started the tour, and I've found a friend. Things are looking brighter all the time. Why is she in this Wing?"

Sal ignored the question and busied himself by moving a resident out of the doorway. They walked away from the group towards the hallway of A Wing. After they passed through the rear door, the women looked at one another and wondered what just transpired. The group slowly maneuvered towards each other.

"Who was that?" Jessie asked.

"See the power of prayer. That young woman was a student of mine, and she will come back and visit. Let's all hope she's the one who'll help us," Mary said pointing to the departing visitor.

Manfassi and Turner were far out and away from hearing when Mary gestured to the women to gather. They made a tight circle. Mary leaned in and whispered, "Back to business." She boldly raised her voice and said, "Yesterday we formed our court. Are you all ready to begin?"

Mary glanced at each of her associates. She felt the uneasiness of most yet believed she could overwhelm their uncertainty by showing some fortitude. "With the help of our Lord, I Mary Archer, charge Jack Tridon with the crime of felonious assault. As all of you know he brutalized my body in every way imaginable. When it began I shared those horrid details with all of you; repeating them now will only increase the pain. So, here and now I proclaim before you and the good lord that I am giving a truthful testimony that Jack Tridon is guilty and must be punished."

Mary remained quiet while the accusation passed slowly through the group. Their tears flowed. They shared each other's pain. Some did not hear everything that Mary said, intuitively understood. They recalled the brutality and again suffered the cruelty of the nursing staff. Each felt alone and the deep shame of forced sexual participation tore at their hearts. Some wrung their hands in despair; others cried with sobs of regret. Eventually, the sting of Mary's accusations sank into their souls. They dried their tears and supplanted their sadness with a determination to fight. Mary waved to come back. Hesitantly, they moved towards each other.

Now regrouped Mary said, "Since our time is precious we must compress our testimony. I swore an oath, and his crimes against me are sufficient for condemnation. In my mind, all of us must share the burden to convict."

Mary slowly recited a litany of abhorrent sexual transgressions all the while rotating her gazes towards each of her companions. Her unblinking eyes transmitted her determination for them to understand their participation. Some bowed their heads in an attempt to make the ugliness go away.

"Look at me," Mary demanded. "Hold up your hand to affirm his guilt." Though a few were slow to respond, they all confirmed the verdict.

Mary knew she had to finish quickly and said: "We the court of our community presented the testimony of many victims and have judged Jack Tridon to be guilty of horrendous crimes." Mary scanned her contemporaries for any reaction. They merely remained mute and stared at her.

Mary then continued, "I now proclaim that since Jack Tridon has been found guilty of crimes against our society, he must be punished. He must suffer the maximum penalty of death. His execution shall be at the earliest time possible and in any manner convenient to our community. The formal proclamation of this judgment and the resultant penalty shall be given to Jack Tridon at the moment of his death." Mary dumped the words in one blast and then looked at her friends as a wave of incredibility flowed slowly from one to another.

Then two of the women, when they understood what Mary said, displayed a look of horror. They shook their heads vigorously; they refused to accept the burden and backed away. Both turned from the group. They did not respond to subtle calls. Fostered by years of living within the law, they had to reject Mary's insanity. Killing was against the law; everybody's law; God's law.

Mary understood the conundrum; their world churned out of control, and now they talked about an execution. Mary approached the closest one and said, "If he came to your room and wanted to use you again would you kill him if you could? Or would you just let him do his will; or maybe he and Gail . . ."

"Stop it! Stop! Mary you're making me relive the worst days of my life. Why don't you just let me be? We are asking for more trouble and oh my God, I don't know what. . ."

"Sara, look at me," Mary pulled on her chair and said, "We are not asking you to do anything other than to convict and determine the proper punishment. How the punishment is accomplished is something that has to be resolved. Maybe, the state will wake-up and do something. We are trying to maintain our sanity. Take a moment and think about what you have gone through. Don't you want to stop him? Don't you want to punish him?"

"Yes," Sara said wearily. "Yes I do. God help us."

The loud voice blared and resonated within the room. "STOP THIS NOISE. How many times do you have to be told? Mary you're getting to be a real troublemaker. Am I getting into that thick head of yours?" Jack bellowed as he came into the room. He stared at all the women in turn and tried to impress into them his strength and power.

Mary recognized the difficult circumstance; this was the second day he caught them. She immediately offered, "I apologize to all in this room and especially to you Doc Tridon. I know how you care for our well-being, and I am just thoughtless in making noise. Please forgive me. At times, I just don't remember where I am and just ramble on. Again, I ask all of you to please forgive my rudeness," Mary said in as contrite a voice that she could manage.

"I hope you're serious in this matter. I talked to you yesterday." He stopped and walked to Mary. He pointed his finger within an inch of her nose and said, "If I catch you again you're dead meat. You'll lose your recreation room privileges; lose it for at least a month if not more. Got it?" Jack yelled.

Mary lowered her head down as in deep remorse and nodded a reply. She watched as Jack backed away while surveying the room, then turned and walked out. She waited to see if he would pull his stupid trick of coming right back. Sure enough, he returned, strode through the recreation room, looked around, and then departed by the back door.

Mary wheeled to the other dissenter and said, "Want to reconsider?"

"Let's get that S O B," Karen said with a determined voice.

Mary put her index finger up to her lips asking them to be quiet. She could not lose what she accomplished and had to take the risk. She signaled for them to come closer. She had to solidify the proclamation of his guilt and sentence. "We must vote the sentence. Since this is a capital crime with a capital punishment, I believe we must be unanimous in its imposition. If you vote for the sentence, give a signal." She pointed at each and all, in turn, responded with a thumbs-up. Mary looked at the doorway, took an audible breath and said in a firm voice, "Jack Tridon, tried and shown to be guilty of serious crimes, is hereby sentenced to death. His execution will occur at the earliest time possible."

The women broke away from one and another and quietly meditated upon their actions. Some smiled determining they just played a silly game. They had fun talking and believing they were in control. Others trembled in fear hating the circumstances that brought them to this conclusion. Mary stayed firm in her intentions. She wanted to continue. Getting this far, took too long; she feared Tridon's sense of danger. Mary again waved for attention pulling them back together.

"I accuse Gail Summun of crimes against our community. She, a woman, was evil because of her sexual actions with us. Her nakedness applied to our bodies is a horror that makes me shiver. Her odors are forever in my nostrils. Her taste is forever in my mouth. We have to stop her. We have to punish her. She shared Jack's crimes and so shall she share his punishment of death," Mary said as she looked at her companions with determination.

The women glanced from one to the other, some with questioning eyes, and then a nod of the head at the understanding they were talking about Gail. Some mouthed the word 'Guilty'. Others pointed their thumbs upward without Mary asking for a verdict.

Mary could not lose this moment. She needed all of them. Each and every one had to acknowledge Gail's crimes. At the same time, she did not want an emotional rush to judgment. Although Mary feared a possible return of Jack, she had to slow down the process.

Mary asked if anyone wanted to offer vital specifics. Doris shook her head and said, "Everyone here knows Gail forced us to perform abnormal sexual acts. We too have the taste and smell of this woman burned into our memory. Let's get on with the vote."

Mary pointed at each to make the verdict personal. They all convicted Gail, guilty, of multiple counts of forced sexual crimes. Mary nodded her assent. She declared Gail guilty and sentenced her to death.

The women backed away. Some shuddered and rubbed themselves indicating they felt a chill. Others took tissues to their eyes and blew their noses as their bodies reacted to the sadness of the past hour. A few kept looking at the now separated group and probably wondered what in the world did they just do.

One of them said, "We're a bunch of old fuddies who are fantasizing about who we are and what we can accomplish."

"Oh Well! I guess what we did was better than trying to get a group together for a bingo game," Jessie whispered to Mary.

"Don't fool yourself Jessie. We held a legal court of the isolated, democratic community of A Wing. All the people, in our area, who are capable and of sound mind were at our session. We have the authority and moral right to protect ourselves. That's what we did and shall do. How? I don't know. What I do know, we continue to suffer horrible pain and mental anguish, because of those two. I guess that's not totally true. You and I both know there are others in this Belvedere organization hurting others. This is just the beginning. When we finish with Jack and Gail then who knows what we'll do. Please remember to pray for our community," Mary said as she started to roll towards her room.

As Mary proceeded down the hallway she thought, *"Jack and Gail, we no longer fear you or your possible actions. It is you who will taste fear. It is you who will soon stand before God almighty and tremble as you are sent to your eternity in Hell. With the help of the Good Lord, we will soon find a way to escort both of you to your final reward."*

THREE

For those who dared to take it, the money was always there. Sal Manfassi thought he knew how, and while managing Belvedere Manor with a wondrous cloak of legitimacy, he continually dipped into the never-ending sources of funds. He subtly maneuvered his legitimate company into the world of illicit business.

The slide into the slime moved quickly, and he chose carefully to make certain anyone joining him could and would walk close to the line of legal limits. And when necessary to cross that line boldly and enter the very profitable arena of white collar fraud.

Sal's management team understood the risks. They salivated at the thought of unrequited financial rewards and followed his lead with passion. He in turn made them peerless. He presented them to the business world as highly respected professional managers while he taught them how to become an uncompassionate group of thieves.

Sal gently tapped the end of his pen for attention. "Okay Milo, let's hear the monthly financials."

Milo began by ticking off various elements of the corporation and inundated them with extraneous details.

"Cut the crap Milo," said Sal. "You do this every month. We're not interested in the minutia. Get to the bottom line. Come on, how are we doing?"

"It's all here, Sal. It's the complete story," Milo said as he turned his electronic pad for all to see.

"Beautiful — great — right — we know you can run the operation." Sal implored his skilled manager. "Please the . . ."

"I got it. I got it, say no more." Milo smiled.

The growth of their individual holdings remained strong. The accounts were meticulously maintained, plus Milo integrated the shady elements of their business giving it a glow of legitimacy. He even paid taxes making the team feel secure believing they were beyond anyone's challenge, including the ever watchful Internal Revenue Service.

"Congratulations on another successful month. We're heading for a great quarter. I applaud all of you for performing difficult tasks in this demanding business. If we can maintain this pace, we'll have a wonderful year. Anyone have any questions on the financial data?" Silence around the table gave Sal the impetus to continue. "Okay, now remember, we have a State review coming up next week. I hope we're ready. Let me modify that, we have to be ready for the State pigeons when they come in for their plucking." Sal laughed at his choice of words. The lack of reaction to his weak joke plus the dour facial expressions of his team prompted Sal to end the meeting.

"George let's go to your office," Milo said. "You were very busy while away on your holiday. How's twenty-three half-hour sessions sound?"

George Faulkins, a private contractor who covered the physical therapy requirements for the entire facility, stopped and stared at Milo.

"Whoa, does that fit Milo? I'm only here three days a week. You're making me a little nervous."

"You worry too much. Who's going to add up the numbers? The dummies just push the paper into the system and by simple magic their computer issues a nice credit directly into our account. Relax. Do you think I would do anything to get us into trouble?" George looking glum didn't answer. Milo continued, "I know how far we can go and believe me, we're not there yet. You do your thing, and I'll do mine. Okay?"

"All right — all right, let's do it," he said with trepidation.

"The forms are right on top of your desk. Just sign 'em and leave 'em, okay? I have to get ready for a new guy coming into A Wing. How about that George? You're going to have another new client."

***

Milo now back in his office picked up the phone and hit a speed dial number. "Hi Tina," he listened as she chatted and then asked, "Can you give me the scoop on the new resident? You know the one you and Sal talked about."

"Sure thing, give me a second to pull the file. You're going to like this one," Tina cooed.

Milo pondered the moves he had to make to accommodate a new client. "*Joey in A124 is ready to become fertilizer,*" he said to himself. He guessed Joey had a month or two at the most before he left Belvedere's care. *"We can move Joey into B. He won't care."*

"Here we are: male, age 62. He's had minor emergency abdominal surgery; hospitalized for six weeks because of complications; he's weak and still bedridden; single and no known family in the area; some assets and the social worker is working with his affairs. That's about it."

"That makes him a very interesting client."

"Absolutely and I believe he will require a long, long, very long time to mend while in your fine care." Tina chuckled and asked, "Did I do good?"

"Better than good, you did an excellent job, my dear Tina. When he arrives, we'll evaluate his condition and then see what category of finder's fee you deserve."

"That's something I'd love to discuss, and perhaps we can have a nice talk the next time we meet. In the meantime his file will be ready any time you want to pick it up. Or, it may make more sense for us to send it with the patient. Yah, that's what I'll do. Send it with the patient."

Tina now lost in her thoughts hung up her telephone without waiting for an answer. She jumped out of her chair, strode to the elevators then repeatedly jabbed at the call button while waiting for the next up-car. "They should have a special elevator for the staff. Wasting our time like this doesn't make sense," Tina grumbled to herself.

An elevator, filled with people, opened its doors. The passengers moved in closer allowing her to enter. Tina refused to cram in. She waved them off with a blunt, "No thank you."

Leaving the passenger elevator area, Tina decided to use the one dedicated to transport patients, bed and all. An empty up-car arrived almost immediately. She sauntered in with authority and rode up to the sixth floor. Tina walked past the nurse's station and proceeded directly to the room of the soon-to-be-discharged patient.

"Mr. Termine. Mr. Termine, are you awake? Hello, can you hear me?" Sam Termine opened his eyes and stared at the intruder. "Ah! There you are," Tina continued. "I have good news for you. You're well enough to leave here and go to a wonderful place to rehabilitate. The Belvedere Manor has a nice room for you. Believe it or not you'll be moved later today," Tina said in a light and happy voice. "Can I do anything for you before you go?"

Sam Termine, with tired eyes, gazed at Tina. "What'd you say?" Hearing her words again still had no meaning. He wished everyone would go away and let him rest.

Tina satisfied that she conveyed her message left the room and stopped at the Nurse's station. "Hi, you can kiss Sam T good bye. We were lucky to get him a bed at Belvedere. I want him ready to go by eleven. Transportation will be here so you make certain he's ready." Without waiting for a response, she turned, walked away, and said, "Look out world, Tina Morris is on the move. Everyone please note and kowtow as I pass."

***

The ambulance arrived on time, and as required the EMTs went directly to the sixth floor. "Hi! We're here for Mr. Samuel Termine — and from what we're told, a batch of paper. I looked into 606 and guessed that's the guy," he said to the floor nurse.

"You're half right. You found Mr. Termine. As to travel, he's not going anywhere until we get a release. Did you check with the office?"

"Dispatch said Tina Morris ordered the trip. Ah hell, give me the damn phone," the EMT demanded and received an immediate cold stare from the nurse. She backed away from the counter and put her hands on her hips and offered him a quiet challenge.

"Oh! I'm sorry." The nurse still didn't respond, and he continued in a contrite voice, "May I please use your phone? This has been a rough day."

Saying nothing, she merely handed him the telephone and waited.

The EMT quickly understood her muted body language. "Again, I'm sorry. What I really need is Morris' number." he said as he gave her an I-give-up sign with his hands.

The EMT punched in the numbers, waited and said, "Ms. Morris this is EMT Peters. The nurse says he ain't ready to go." He waited for the response and then said, "Well that's great, if you've got his release I can . . ."

Tina said, "I didn't say I had anything. Relax. I need about an hour. Go, have a cup of coffee."

"Sorry Ms. Morris, we can't do that. You'll have to reschedule. There's another pickup at Mercy. The boss tried to do you a favor and squeeze this one in. Can't wait, we got'ta go."

"Mr. oh-what-ever-your-name is I can have things ready in a half-hour. Just sit still for a while.'"

"Not possible. Sorry, I can't wait. I'll call my office and give them the news." Tina tried to interrupt. The man simply said, "Bye."

Moments after the EMTs started down the hallway the phone rang. Picking up the receiver the floor nurse heard Tina screaming, "Are they still there? Hold them. It is your responsibility to keep them there until I can finish my paperwork." The nurse did not say a word. She gently replaced the handset back into its cradle and walked away smiling.

"Better make sure Mister Termine has a dinner and breakfast order. Looks like he is going to be with us for another night," she said while walking past the dietitian's office.

Tina cursed at the dial tone and slammed the phone into its cradle. She ran down towards the ambulance entrance. When in view, she yelled to the guard, "Don't let the Carrier Ambulance guys go. Hold them." She reached the guard's station and continued, "They've got to take a patient today. If you don't keep them here you'll be sorry." She left as quickly as she arrived.

The guard, concerned by her demeanor, called the head of Security. "Captain, got a little problem with Ms. Morris. She wants me to detain an ambulance crew. I ain't doing it on her say so. What's your take on this?"

"You can't restrain any properly behaving person from leaving the building. When you see him simply ask if he can wait for a while. If he chooses not to, just tell him to have a nice day. Don't sweat it. You're doing a fine job. Other than that, is anything else going on?"

"That's my only problem. Thanks to you, I don't have a problem. Thanks again Captain."

Tina worked at a frantic pace pulling together the set of documents needed for the release. She called billing and then the Social Worker and continued right down her checklist. Some were already in place. The other few responded to her demands for instant service. Tina smiled with satisfaction knowing they yielded to her unreasonable requests.

With her binder now filled, Tina sauntered down to the ambulance entrance and boldly approached the guard. "Where are they?" she demanded.

"Where's who?" he asked in a faux innocent tone.

"You know who, the driver; the ambulance for my patient. That's who."

"Oh, those guys, they left more than an hour ago."

"I told you to keep them here. Why didn't you hold them? You ignored my very specific directions. You are apparently incompetent in performing your duties. This is going to be your job. Do you realize you cost the hospital a lot of money because of your inability to follow orders?" The guard glared at the raging woman and wisely remained quiet. She continued her tirade, "Do you know they will charge us for the incomplete run? We should take it out of your pay. I'm going to make a full report of your incompetence and negligence." She stared at the man and waited for him to humble himself.

"I did my job Ms. Morris. I checked with the Captain, and he gave the word. If they got'ta go, I can't hold 'em."

"This place is loaded with idiots. No wonder they're always crying about money. With people like you working here, we'll go broke. You'll be hearing from me," Morris yelled to the guard who tried to maintain his dignity.

Tina returned to her office grabbed the telephone and keyed in the number to Belvedere. "Milo, the stupid system got us again."

"That sounds like our new client's not coming today? Or does it mean, not coming at all?"

"He's coming. Don't worry he's coming. It's just going to be delayed until Saturday. The ambulance guys and then security screwed up. This world is loaded with incompetents."

"Tina, take it easy and no sweat. Saturday will work out just fine. I'll have to give up part of my day off. Believe me it's not a problem."

"Now that you mention it, I believe I too will have to work overtime to clear up this mess. The Hospital won't be happy paying the overtime. Seeing that it's needed to cover the shortcomings of others they should be thrilled. I'm right, right?"

"Anything you say Tina."

"In fact, I think I'll have to accompany the patient to make certain he's properly transported, especially on a weekend. We can't tolerate any further complications. Milo I'll be there Saturday; let's aim for mid-morning."

"Sometime in the morning it is. Maybe we'll have the place to ourselves and have a little fun. Don't work too hard," Milo laughed as he ended the call.

***

Danielle Turner sat opposite her mother and held both her hands. "Mom we have to talk."

"Oh! I can't remember the last time you held my hands like this. This must be very serious. You look pale. Are you getting sick?"

"No Mom, I'm fine." She hesitated for a moment took a deep breath and said, "I talked to Doctor Juliano. You need more attention than I can give you." She paused and continued when her mother didn't respond. "When Bob and I go on a business trip, you know you'll be all alone. That's not good."

"So what's the answer?" Florence Danzell asked.

"We have a day nurse coming during the week. She's been great, and you liked her. Having her here gave us the experience of what it costs to have this kind of help."

"Yes I do like her and she's been very helpful. I also like the women who come when she can't. So what's the problem?"

"They're very, very expensive and we only have them for eight hours and just five days a week. The cost for twenty-four hours is enormous. We can't afford it."

"I don't like the sound of this," her mother blurted. "So what does it mean?" She stopped and then with an anguished voice, "Oh my God. You're getting ready to put me away?"

"I've been in agony for weeks. I talked to Reverend Dugan. I talked to our accountant. And, you know I talked to Doctor Juliano."

Florence Danzell yelled at her daughter, "You talked to everyone except me. Why didn't you talk to me?"

Danielle distressed by her mother's very angry outburst said; "I love you and want the best for you. I looked to everyone who could give me information. This is very difficult for all of us."

"So what has everyone decided is the best for me?"

"Let me tell you what I did this morning," Danielle offered.

"Apparently you did not go to work. Now I'm keeping you from your job. I wondered why Bob was home, now I know. Let's get on with it."

"I met with Mr. Sal Manfassi, the director of Belvedere Manor."

"Oh God, you are serious." Florence put her hands to her mouth in horror and began to cry.

"Please, I want you to be healthy and happy. This is the only way to take good care of you." Danielle now in deep despair could not look at her mother as she spoke. She turned when she heard her very weak voice.

"Can't we afford to bring in help?"

"No. Oh, we could do it for a while — then everything would be gone."

"I have plenty of assets."

"You can afford the cost of Belvedere Manor. You can have a beautiful private room. Plus you'll have the around the clock care you deserve. They're good caring people who know how to . . ."

Florence Danzell not allowing her daughter to finish talking, interrupted, "You visited this place without my knowledge. And now you want me to give you my approval. I can't do that."

"Mom . . ."

"Let me finish. I will not give you my approval. I will accept your decision. If you want me out of the house, then I will go wherever you want to send me."

"Mom . . ."

"So do it," Mrs. Danzell said as she crossed her arms in defiance.

"We have to Mom. It is the only way I know that will allow us all to survive."

"So when's this supposed to happen?"

"Tomorrow morning."

"Oh my God! Can't we wait a few more months?"

"I talked to Doctor Juliano, and he agrees you need proper care — now. We can't wait a few more months. For your own health, we have to do something. Mom, please help me to help you. In your heart, you know I want to do what is right." Both were quiet and then Danielle added, "It will be tomorrow morning."

Danielle stayed with her mother for a while and both remained silent. The weight of the decision crushed them both. Danielle looked at her mother shook her head in despair and then went to the telephone.

***

Sal fiddling with the papers on his desk answered within moments of his phone ringing.

"Hello Mr. Manfassi. This is Danielle Turner."

"Good afternoon Mrs. Turner, how can I help you?" Sal said greeting his potential client with a happy voice.

"It's been a tough day — I've made a decision. I want to move my Mom into your care. She needs the attention I believe your people offer," she said with resignation.

"One of the most difficult decisions a loving daughter has to make. You're doing the right thing. We'll take excellent care of your Mother. Remember you're close enough so you can visit very often."

"I know and that's a primary reason why I chose Belvedere Manor. There's an additional minor consideration, and that's Miss Archer. It felt good to see she's a resident. Mom knows her. Perhaps they can develop a good friendship."

"Have you discussed this decision with your mother?" Sal asked.

"I did. It was a very difficult conversation. Mom doesn't want to leave her home. I'm still shaking from our talk."

"People don't like changes. A serious change like this can look frightening to anyone. That's why we're special. We know how to make the transition a pleasant experience," Sal said trying to sound upbeat.

"I hope so. I'm going to need all the help I can get."

"Well, I'm pleased to hear your family will be part of our family. You know we'll treat your Mom with the best we offer. And, you're absolutely right about knowing others in a new environment." The Mary Archer connection whirled in Sal's head. "I hope you understand we have to move slowly to get your Mother integrated into a happy routine. Folks coming in need settling-in time. We'll work with you and your Mom to be certain she has a lively social life."

"A lively social life, those are great words to hear. Mom hasn't had much of a social life in the past few years."

"Your Mom will be residing in C Wing, in that nice private room, you saw on our tour. I held it for you. You know the demand for this facility is very high and rooms are not vacant very long."

"I appreciate all of your efforts. I know this is the right decision," Turner said as she sought the reassurance from Mr. Manfassi.

"Stop thinking about it, stop punishing yourself. Your love for your Mother is why you have to do this. You're doing the maximum a person can do by getting the best care available."

"Thanks. I have to keep reminding myself I can't provide the care you can and this is what is best for Mom. Please tell me I'm not putting Mom away."

Sal ignored her last provocative words and said, "We can arrange for transportation or did you intend to bring Mom in yourself."

"I want to drive her myself. We'll take a short tour of the neighborhood. Can we come in tomorrow around mid-morning?"

"I'll be here. I believe you told me she was a tea drinker. I'll have a hot pot of Darjeeling in my office, decaf of course. You'll be greeted with a mini-tea party."

"Mom will like that. I'll bring some scones from Maxwell's Bakery. Those are a favorite of hers."

FOUR

"What can you tell me about the new woman: Florence Danzell? Do you think we can squeeze in a few extra billings?"

"Not yet. We've got to go slow with this one." Sal paused for a moment and then said, "Yeah, Milo. It could be a problem. She's not my concern. It's her daughter. The woman lives no more than twenty minutes away. She'll probably want to get her nose into everything."

"Is Danzell a good addition?"

"In a traditional sense, I think so. We'll soon find out."

"Did you meet her?"

"No — only met the daughter. She walked in, all alone and a day later, bingo, here we are. This is going to be an interesting morning."

"Need some help with the admission?"

"I can handle it. Oh, and they know Mary Archer?"

"That's not good news."

"She spotted her in the rec room. Says Archer was her eighth-grade teacher, sashays right in, and says hello. And get this: Archer doesn't remember her. Then said she did. Maybe she did — or maybe not. Archer's a very devious woman."

"Oh yeah, she'll take advantage whenever or where ever she finds it. I'll talk to Jack. We have to control Mary."

"Milo, I think we need a break from this place. We're getting paranoid. Florence Danzell could be a quiet angel, zero trouble to the staff."

"Vacation yeah, as for zero problems, I don't think so. You've got a premonition, and I say let's go strong. Isolate and clamp her right away."

"Relax, easy my friend. First let's meet our newest guest."

"Too bad she didn't come in with the daughter."

"Milo, forget it. We'll be okay. If she's a pest I'll take care of it." Sal ruminated for a moment and then said, "Let's try to maintain a separation between these two admissions. There's no sense in a bond forming just because they're coming on the same day. They may feel a little sympathy for each other."

"Not from what I heard — she may be spunky, Tina tells me the guy's out of it."

"You're still tight with Tina?"

"With her, I should get hazard-duty pay. She's very competent in one way and an absolute psycho in another. Her recommendations are solid. She does her homework. When we're alone, she thinks she owns me. Every part of me is hers," Milo said as he shook his head in a phony indication of being unhappy.

"Come on Milo, you know you enjoy your little sessions. Didn't you tell me they were therapeutic? Is she wearing you out?"

"Go ahead and laugh. Someday you will see me a bag of skin and bones. Then who'll help you run this place," Milo said while pointing his finger at Sal.

"You're right. When you're with Tina, we have to make sure you get enough liquids. Yeah, get yourself a nice case of bubbly. Get the best you can find, and charge it to the place."

"A case of Dom Perignon?"

"No Milo. I'm not talking about that foreign junk plus alcohol's not good for you." Sal laughed and continued, "I'm offering you some really nice root beer or ginger ale. It has to be name brand stuff. Not that super-market junk." Sal bellowed a laugh and thumped Milo on the back. "Some guys have it made and all I hear is moans, groans and complaints."

"You want to change places for a week or two. Then maybe you'll see what I do to keep this place moving."

"I don't want to take away any of your pleasures." Sal looked out the window and said, "We've got company. I think the Danzell woman is here. I'll meet them in the parking lot. Good luck with Mr. X."

Sal walked briskly through the building, out the front door and waved an enthusiastic greeting. "Hello, and welcome to Belvedere. I'm Sal Manfassi, and you must be Mrs. Danzell. It is so nice to meet you — and on such a beautiful morning."

Sal helped Mrs. Danzell into her portable wheelchair and gave a wink to her daughter as a sign he thought all was going well. "May I offer you some of our hospitality in my office? It'll give me a chance to tell you all about how hard we will work to make you happy."

"How can you talk about my happiness on this day? I am not happy to be here and there is nothing you can do to change that. I'm being wheeled to what is apparently my final domicile, if anyone can call a place like this a home. This is what we used to call an Asylum. You put people in places like this when they are unable to do things for themselves. Some people can stay at home. Their family takes care of them. Not me. I'm put away." She ended by folding her arms across her chest and challenged anyone for an answer.

Danielle paled at the long angry outburst, sighed with a deep breath, and in a barely audible voice said, "Let's go to your office Mr. Manfassi. Introducing Mom to some of the wonderful features of the Manor is an excellent idea." She took firm control of the wheelchair and while pushing her Mother into the facility tried to work out her frustration.

Walking to the entrance seemed to take forever; it gave Danielle an opportunity to reinforce her determination. The moment the Manor door opened she felt her bowels churn. Her knees weakened as fear took charge of her resolve. Sweat poured down her back. She felt lightheaded and wanted to run away from this moment. After they were through the doors and into the hallway Danielle said, "Is there a women's room I can use?"

"A visitor's lavatory is just down the hall, on the right. You can't miss it."

"Thanks, I'll be right back."

Sal took charge of the wheelchair. "We'll go the same way. There's not much to see before we get to my office. Do you know any resident in our establishment?"

Sal smiled when he heard her answer, "No I don't. All my friends live at home, or live with their families."

***

Danielle Turner suffered a case of instant diarrhea. She felt all of her life liquids abandoning her. Adding to her discomfort, her blouse, soaked with perspiration, stuck to her back. Within seconds she finished her bodily purge, redressed and while washing her hands looked into the mirror. She shook her head in disbelief and spoke aloud to the pale sweaty image looking back at her. "Well you sorry looking daughter, are you up to this? Okay, remember this is the only way, and it has to be done. It has to be done." She stopped, lowered her head and breathed in deeply and said, "It has to be done. I've got to do this. It's for Mom's health and safety, right?" Turner wiped her face with a damp paper towel and blurted, "That's a load of bull; it's because you don't have the money to do it any other way." The dehydrated and saddened woman finished by combing her hair then walked slowly to Sal's office.

***

Sal felt the piercing stare of Mrs. Danzell. He broke eye contact by getting up and going to a table that held two carafes and a collection of China cups. "I have coffee and freshly brewed Darjeeling tea. May I pour you a cup of hot tea Mrs. Danzell?"

"I could use a little tea, and Darjeeling sounds civil. I take mine black, no sugar, and I hope it is good and hot."

"I like to use these thermally insulated carafes. The manufacturer advertises that any liquid remains hot for at least twelve hours. Now please note. I have two carafes.

This one's dedicated for coffee — and this one's strictly for tea. I believe the oils in coffee fuses to the lining. It's very difficult to remove. Therefore, one for tea, and one for coffee, and the two should never be mixed," Sal said as he offered the cup to Mrs. Danzell.

"I wish I was elsewhere enjoying your tea. Do you always serve tea, in good China, to all the residents?" She asked as she looked up to see his reaction to her question.

"I only wish we could. However, just as we all do at home, we have sturdy plates and cups made out of a nice synthetic material for daily use and attractive stainless steel utensils. Now, Mrs. Danzell, you didn't use your good China and silverware every day, did you?"

"No."

"Tell you what. If you ever feel a need for a good pot of tea, just give me a call. I'll break out the bone China, and it'll be a party for you and me. How's that sound?"

Before she could answer, Danielle Turner entered the room. "Sorry I took so long." She approached her mother and reached behind her to remove a bag and said, "Mom I bought some Maxwell Bakery scones. I tied it to the back of your chair, and you didn't even know it was there. Would you like one with your tea?"

She looked at her daughter and then over to Sal Manfassi and said, "I could not get that scone down no matter how hard I tried. And I know if I did, it would come right back up."

Sal, ignoring her response, started his normal talk about the facility. He tried to sound as upbeat as possible while watching the daughter, already very pale, continuing to wilt. This guilt trip had to end. He waited patiently for Mrs. Danzell to sip a little of her tea and when the moment seemed appropriate he offered, "Let's take a tour and show you how this facility runs." Sal came around to Mrs. Danzell, took the almost full teacup from her hands and started to wheel her out of the room.

***

Tina Morris arrived within minutes of Florence Danzell and her daughter. She immediately entered the facility, went directly to Milo Drew's office without waiting for her client. "Hi handsome, it's me?" she said before entering.

"Come in, come in. You're right on schedule and if you look out the window you'll see your mister what's-his-name is also here."

Tina gave a quick look, shrugged her shoulders and plunked down into a chair. "Yep, you're right. They're here."

Milo started toward the doors and said, "Wait here, I want to see the EMTs . . ."

"Screw the EMTs. Let them wait," Tina said grabbing Milo's arm. "Ah, you stay right here. I'll show them where to park." Tina stood in the hallway gave a quick hand signal indicating to come to the office, then held up her other hand showing them they had to wait.

***

"Hey guys, please move a bit," Sal said as he tried to leave his office.

"Sorry Sir we don't mean to be in the way. We're waiting on where we're supposed to transport this gentleman."

"Well I can help you there. He's assigned to A Wing. It's to the left. Mr. Termine goes to room — what room is it?" Sal asked as he passed Milo's office.

"A124," Tina bellowed as she came sauntering out. "Mr. Termine goes to A124," she repeated while pointing the proper direction.

Danielle, now in the hallway asked, "Did I hear you correctly? Did you say Termine? I went to school with a guy named Sam Termine."

"He's Sam Termine. I doubt very much that you two went to school together. He appears to be much older than you." Tina looked at Danielle Turner, gave her some body language indicating she should accept her input and asked, "Are you a new client?"

"Yes. Well, it's my Mom's first day."

"Let me introduce Mrs. Danzell and her daughter Mrs. Turner. Ms. Morris is associated with the Memorial Hospital, and Mr. Milo Drew is our Operations Manager. They're in today to take care of the gentleman going down the hall." Sal smiled at the group hoping they would disappear.

"Mrs. Danzell, you are a resident of the finest healthcare facility within the state. I know because I visit all the homes throughout the area. You will be happy here," Tina said as if ordering the woman's happiness.

Florence Danzell looked at the woman with steely eyes and growled, "After visiting, you can go back to your own home. Try staying here for a few days. Have you ever had the feeling of finality? Do you know what it means to say this is it? There is no more. I doubt it. You come and then you go. You see only what you want to see."

The shock of hearing the old woman's aggressive response made Tina back away. She sucked in an audible breath in anticipation of another onslaught.

"I too want to welcome you Mrs. Danzell." Milo said trying to ease the tension. "Our staff will do everything they can to make you feel comfortable. Please call me, anytime, and I will help you with any problems that may develop."

"See even you" She said pointing a finger directly at Milo. "You're telling me I will have problems," Mrs. Danzell pouted. She sat with her arms locked across her chest.

Sal pushed Mrs. Danzell away knowing these two could not compete with the quick-witted woman and said, "Milo. I think your new client needs you. And we should continue with our tour. Milo, please see me before you go home." He turned and said, "Bye Tina."

***

"Mrs. Philips, this young lady is Mrs. Danzell. She is our newest resident."

The nurse came out from behind her station. "Welcome Mrs. Danzell. I'm Jen Philips." She took Florence's hands and caressed them. "I'm the floor nurse for this weekend. You'll be seeing me all day today and tomorrow."

"Thank you dear. If you only work weekends, I'm guessing, it's because you have children, and you're a full-time mother during the week. Am I right?"

Smiling the nurse said, "I know you and I will be friends. You already know much about me in just a few minutes. You're right. I have a girl four and a boy seven. My husband takes care of them during the weekends."

"Thank you for giving up your family to take care of me. I will try hard not to make your burden any heavier than it is."

Jen pushed the wheelchair down to her room. When she tried to enter, Mrs. Danzell held out both arms and stopped the motion.

"I want to say a prayer before we pass over this threshold. Please put up with me for just a few moments." She bowed her head and silently prayed, *"Dear Lord, please take care of all who enter this home. We are weak and need your strength. We need your wisdom to help determine right from wrong. My mind despairs because my body is failing. I pray the feeling of evil in this place is not true. I pray if there is evil here I am made strong to fight it. I pray I am here to do your work. Please show me what it is I can do before I am called to come to you. Amen."*

***

"Thanks guys, we can take it from here," Milo told the EMTs as he raised the bed's side rail.

The men rolled their gurney out of the room muttering to each other, "Hope these idiots take care of that guy."

"Those two are more interested in each other than getting him in bed. It's awful quiet in here. Where's everyone?"

***

"I've got some time before the lunch crew comes — care to join me for a little fun and frolic. Room 130 is available." Milo took a smiling Tina by the hand and led her down the hallway.

The sign on the door to room A130 read:

"DO NOT ENTER — CONTAMINATED PREMISES"

Milo pushed the door open, made a small bow and invited Tina to enter and said, "Enter my lovely woman and enjoy the treats this room is about to offer. In order that we maintain the cleanliness within, we must remove all of our clothing and, at all times, maintain extreme close contact to each other."

"The room's contaminated!" Tina protested.

"Don't believe everything you read. I posted that sign. If it spooked you, it will give us all the privacy we need. Don't need locks on the door, just a little psychology will keep it closed. That makes everything a little more exciting to think that well, maybe someone just might try to peek and see what's in this room."

Tina entered, started to disrobe, and asked, "Any hangers in the closet?"

***

"The two of them are still down the hallway. I don't think they went all the way to the kitchen. Maybe they're in the vacant room," Mary said to her roommate.

"Weekends sure draw the dregs of society into this place. At least we get a little break from Jack and Gail."

"Be careful, you never know when they pop in. I want to meet the new one."

"Mary, please don't get us into any trouble."

Mary indicated with a finger to her lips to be quiet, waved a small goodbye and rolled out of the room. Looking both ways, Mary scooted out and quickly entered room A124. A name on the footboard read: "Samuel Termine — Dr. Carl Lunkens". After gazing at the sleeping man, Mary wondered if she knew him. "Samuel, Samuel Termine — you awake?"

Sam opened his eyes and glanced at the woman next to his bed. He said nothing in reply while returning to his stupor. She tried again to talk to him. He still did not respond. Backing away Mary rolled to the door and listened for traffic. When satisfied she started back to her room, then heard a door close.

"Where are you going?" Milo asked.

Mary gazed up at Milo. "Isn't it time to eat? I thought I heard someone say to come to lunch." She looked at him sweetly and asked, "Can you push me to the dining room?"

"It's a little early. Where are those aides? If you heard someone, they're probably around. Tina, care to push Miss Archer to the Dining Room?"

"Don't have time Milo. I've got to run. Can you meet me tomorrow and discuss the finder's fee? I'm thinking about a nice dinner and then who knows?"

Milo ignored Mary and followed the scent of Tina down the hallway.

"You got caught and slipped right by them. Mary you live a charmed life," Jessie said.

"Come on Jessie, let's go have lunch."

FIVE

Florence Danzell could not sleep. Alone, in a strange room made this Saturday night long and difficult. She looked towards the darkness, reminisced while she tossed and turned throughout the endless night. The despair she felt during the night yielded with the awareness of dawn signaling the start of a new day. Pale streaks of light played along her bed. The stillness of the long night broke gently as the motions of the morning activity gave off their distinct sounds. She looked out into the hallway and could hear and see people walking by. The air moved with the activity and whiffs of various scents floated into her room. The strange odors attacked her senses; a chilling tension grabbed hold of her body.

An aide entered, deposited a breakfast tray on her bedside table, lowered it to the proper height then maneuvered it towards Florence.

"Good morning," Florence said to the smiling young woman.

"Good morning," she sang in reply.

"My name's Florence."

"Good morning," she repeated with a gesture sort of implying the greeting exhausted her command of English.

"Thank you dear. I enjoyed your smile."

"Good morning," the aide resounded as she left the room.

Florence removed the dome covering her breakfast. A strong scent of institutional food hit her. She felt nauseous, turned away allowing the feeling to pass. Hoping for some warmth, Florence grasped the cup of water with both hands. It felt cold. Putting a finger into the tepid liquid confirmed her initial reaction. With no evidence of a tea bag anywhere on the tray she lowered her head and closed her eyes.

The morning sun now beaming into the window allowed her to feel a comforting glow. The soothing rays of the sun mellowed the weariness. Florence fell into a welcomed sleep.

"Mrs. Danzell. Hello Mrs. Danzell," she said touching her gently.

Florence stirred, looked about trying to focus. Suddenly, she realized where she was and tried to recognize who entered her room. "Oh, Jen? You're Jen Philips. Am I right?"

"Good morning. You have an excellent memory Mrs. Danzell."

"Thank you young lady. My friends call me Florence."

"Well Florence, you haven't touched much of your breakfast. Anything wrong?"

Pointing at the cup she said, "Its tepid water."

"Eat a little of the solid stuff and I'll be right back."

***

Harry Benas entered the facility, walk directly towards Sal Manfassi's office. With his head spinning to and fro, Harry, satisfied that no one was in the hallway, entered Sal's unlocked office.

Harry Benas, Belvedere's Nursing supervisor, a proven workaholic dedicated the bulk of his time to his job. His efforts yielded a smooth-running facility with a great history of providing proper care for most of its residents. Harry enjoyed having a quasi-legitimate place to manage. He enjoyed working with his staff. He also took pride in enhancing the health and wellbeing of the B and C Wing residents. As for A Wing he deliberately separated himself from the difficult daily decisions. Since Jack Tridon wanted that responsibility, Harry allowed him to usurp his authority.

A nice quiet Sunday morning suited Harry. Once he started his thievery, it became his monthly routine. He moved knowingly and quietly about the office, sat down at Sal's desk, reached under and pulled out the computer keyboard. He pushed on the power button and sat back waiting for the system to come alive. Sal's computer had access to all the files on Belvedere's network. Each segment of the facility generated and maintained files necessary for the proper management of their sector. Anyone could review, maintain, add to, or change their files, provided, they had the correct passwords. Harry acquired the magic keys to this computer by simply watching Sal while he struggled trying to learn how to operate the system. At that time, while he mastered the monster, Sal appreciated Harry's help. However, while attempting to become competent, Sal unwittingly gave away the security of the entire system.

The computer screen glowed with information. Harry demanded the accounts payable section and scrolled to a company named HBC Industrial Supply. He keyed in the screen asking for new data and then expertly entered items showing an invoice for $435.76, a phony bill for supplies delivered during the past month. He offered a small discount of 1% for payment within thirty days and chuckled as the system accepted his input.

Harry verified the system shut down properly and looked over Sal's desk. Everything appeared to be as he found it. He exited the office, entered the general office area and walked over to the lockable, albeit unlocked, file cabinets. He opened a familiar drawer and quickly thumbed to his specific file folder. The HBC Industrial Supply file contained a collection of invoices. He added the newest one, in proper chronological order.

***

To Harry, the staff members, working the weekends, were very special people. He hired them, knew they were extremely competent and they needed the extra income. Their dedication and skills gave Harry an opportunity to uncover and correct problems missed by his regular overworked staff. He walked down the hallway, entered C Wing and immediately spotted the duty nurse.

"Good morning Jen. How's the world treating you?"

"Hi Harry. Checking up on us?"

"You know better than that. You do a super job. I'd be lost without you guys."

"Sounds like a great time to ask for a raise."

"The only raise you can get around here is, oh you know the old cliché. So tell me how's it going? Any problems?"

"We have a new resident. She could use a little company." Jen pointed towards her room.

"She's in 325?"

"Yep. Name's Florence Danzell. I'm making her a decent cup of tea. If you can wait a second you can take it with you."

Harry with the cup in hand, knocked on the doorframe and waited for Florence to recognize him.

"You may come in," Mrs. Danzell said in a timid voice seeing the strange man.

"Hello. My name's Harry Benas, I'm the Head Nurse."

"Good morning Harry. My name's Florence Danzell, my friends call me Florence. Are you my friend or my jailer?"

"Ah look, I bear a gift of friendship. This fair maiden, is a cup of steaming hot tea," Harry said as he dumped the tea bag and then offered her the ungainly mug.

Florence examined it and felt its warmth and then gazed at the man. "A finer gift cannot be found. Thank you. I need this more than you'll ever understand." She sipped the hot beverage and said, "Earl Grey!"

"You're a tea drinker. You know there are a few of us around here who enjoy a good brew. Every once in a while, I get the kitchen to boil some water — just for me."

"If I could I would," she said sadly.

"Ah, that is a nice offer. Thank you. Florence, you can count on sharing my brew. Remember it doesn't happen very often. My days are extremely busy. We seldom have time for the good life. When I can, I'll share it with you." He waited, when she didn't answer, Harry Benas said, "Okay?"

"I'm sorry, yes, more than okay. My very close and special friends call me Flo."

"I hope I can reach that level, Florence."

"You've already brightened my day. Thank you Harry."

"It was my pleasure dear lady. Enjoy your tea while it's hot."

Harry left the room, walked to Jen Philips and said, "She's putting up a good struggle. I think she'll be all right. Good move with the hot tea."

"Thanks Harry, I try to be human. I hear there's a new resident in A Wing. What's the prognosis on him?"

"Tough case, he's been in the hospital a long time. We think he'll be here even longer. Have you seen him?"

"I don't have time to roam. I have my hands full. And, I don't need anything else to do. That's a difficult wing. How're Jack and Gail holding up to the pressure?"

"Jack's a dynamo with endless energy. He's giving a talk this afternoon. Can you believe it, it's a Sunday and Jack's talking to a woman's club?"

"Most guys will be watching the big game. What about you? It's Sunday and here you are," Jen chided.

"Here I am and here I go. Enjoy what's left of the weekend, and again you're doing a nice job," Harry said as he turned to leave.

"Thanks," Jen said laughing and waving a good bye.

Harry walked through and checked on the staff in B Wing. After a few brief words, he was on his way to A Wing.

The nurse in A Wing, a temporary employee exhibited unusual anxiety. "I've reviewed all the residents," she blurted.

"That's great. I think you know what's needed. Just continue doing your job. Forget I'm here. I just want to look around. If you have a major problem however . . ."

"No problems, none at all," she said with a fluster and walked away.

Harry smiled, went directly to Sam Termine's room and peered in. The man stirred. He walked in. "Hi. I'm Harry. How are you doing?"

"Okay, I guess. Feeling very woozy. Where am I?"

"Belvedere Manor. We're a complete healthcare facility."

"Does that mean I'm getting better?"

"Absolutely. You're in a great place staffed with some wonderful people. They'll take care of all your problems."

"Sounds good to me. I've been out of touch with the world." Sam tried to turn and winced with pain. "Ow! That hurt."

"Take it easy. We have stuff to take care of that pain."

"Thanks. It's comforting knowing good people are trying to help me."

Harry lowered his eyes and spoke in a soft voice, "Stay in bed. Get your rest." He began to walk away, stopped, turned towards him and said, "Take care."

***

Milo awoke, glanced about realizing the woman next to him was Tina Morris. He leaped out of bed and felt his head pounding with the pain of a wild night of booze and music. His stomach groaned rebelling against the abuse it received. He shook the bed as he sat down hard. "God, my gut hurts. My head's killing me. Got anything I can take."

Tina turned over, looked at the disheveled and naked guy sitting right next to her. "Milo, this is not the proper way to wake up your princess. You have to hold me and cuddle me and say sweet words," she said as she extended her arms to him.

The blanket dropped away exposing some of her nakedness. Tina extended her arms. Milo slipped over to her. She held her arms up towards him. He could not resist and joined her.

***

"There I bet your headache is all gone," Tina cooed.

"Tina, I'm so weak my body doesn't have the strength to hurt. You sure have the formula for curing the common hangover."

"There's no end to my talents," Tina said as she toyed with his uncombed hair. "I had a great time. Did you enjoy the evening?"

"What evening? You mean we packed all that into one night."

"When are we going to do this again?"

"Tina, I'm a married guy. Once in a while I can get away -- I have to make a call."

Milo reached over and grabbed his telephone. He punched in his home number. "Hi sweetheart." Milo grimaced as he received the blast he expected to hear and then said, "You knew I was going out with business associates. We drank a lot, and I knew I shouldn't drive — and maybe kill myself." Milo again waited until the end of the lecture. "I feel fine now and I'll be home as soon as I get cleaned up. Love ya."

"That was really sweet. I like that. I'm a business associate."

"Yes you are — you're a real honest-to-goodness business associate. In fact let's talk business. The new client appears to be a good prospect, and we want to reward you. How does two hundred sound? Pretty good huh?"

"You spent more than that last night."

"You were super happy the last time we gave you a hundred bucks."

"That was last time. You know you got a super bargain. I didn't understand the value of what I do. Now I do."

They sat on the bed, ignored their lack of clothing as each tried to understand the other.

"What are you trying to tell me?" Milo asked with apprehension.

"I want a share of the long-term benefits you guys get from my efforts. A little up-front money isn't right."

"Exactly what do you want?"

"I deserve a piece of that extra-special income -- every month."

"What extra income?" Milo stammered and flushed at her words.

"Stop it, you know, I know, because you showed me. Don't you remember about two months ago we . . ."

"All right, all right, I got the picture. Spell it out. What are you expecting?"

"A little love note wrapped around an appropriate amount of pure cash," Tina said smiling and then continued, "Then, you deliver it here to my apartment. I can count it after we have a romp or two in my beddy-bye."

Milo got up, started to dress, changed his mind and said: "Mind if I take a shower?"

"You know where the towels are, and some disposable razors. They're on the top shelf."

Milo quickly showered and dressed. Tina remained naked.

"I've got to go."

"No breakfast?"

"Food, ugh, not the way my stomach feels." Milo made a motion to leave turned and said, "You know I have to talk to Sal about your demands?"

"It's not a demand. I made a business proposition. Think of the benefits — for both of us."

"Better get dressed, Tina, you might catch a cold standing around like that."

"I like to be this way -- just for you. This is part of that something special for both of us," she said as she turned around and held up her arms to display herself. Tina rushed up and threw her arms around him and held up her pouting mouth. "Got a good bye kiss for me?"

SIX

"Sorry guys. I know I'm late — I had a rough weekend." Milo sank into his chair and glanced around the room. "Hey, you know it was business. Entertaining Tina is a tough job." A few started to laugh. "Come on, don't laugh, I didn't get home until Sunday afternoon. And, my head's still killing me.

"We don't want to hear about your headache. Did you settle this fee nonsense?"

"I Didn't." Milo waited for a reaction then continued, "She wants something every month."

Sal threw his pencil down on the table in a rage. "And that's blackmail."

"Not in her mind," Milo said.

Harry Benas pushed his chair back and in a nervous voice said, "Why are we making this a problem? Give her whatever she wants."

"No Harry, we can't do that. She'll never be satisfied. What I recommend. We . . ."

"Wait a minute," George Faulkins interrupted. "Giving that woman anything was a big mistake. I say we quit, right now.""

"Getting cold feet George?" Milo sneered.

"You better believe it. I've always had bad vibes — going to jail doesn't fit my lifestyle."

"Milo, you were going to recommend something." Sal said while smiling his encouragement to continue.

"Flip it around. Let's blackmail the blackmailer."

"Can't any of you see what's happening?" George said. "We're diving into the sewer."

"I didn't mean -- what I should have said, let's record her extortion. Put a video camera in my office. Hide it somewhere so she can't see it. I'll bring her in on the pretext we intend to pay. She'll blabber, and we'll have her."

"You've got a devious mind. Anyone got anything better to offer?" Sal queried.

George stood up. "I still don't like any of it. It stinks. It smells."

"I asked if anyone had a better idea." Sal chided.

"You want another way? I'm with Harry. Pay the woman. Pay her and make him the last one — for a long time. . ."

"George, I . . ."

"Hold on Sal, I'm not finished," George said angrily. "I recommend we use our talents and get this Termine guy up and out of here fast. When he goes, the payment stops." George backing away from the table turned towards the window.

"Carl, Harry, do you have anything to say?" Sal asked.

Doctor Carl Lunkens and Harry shook their heads indicating no.

"When can you be ready?" Sal asked Milo.

"She wants an answer by Wednesday," he lied. "If you guys can cover my work here, I'll take care of Tina."

"That was a nice speech George. But no one's going to push us around. Milo knows her better than any of us. We'll do it his way. Okay guys? Okay George?" George answered by shrugging his shoulders in defeat. "Milo, do what's necessary. If you need anything, let me know."

Sal tapped his pencil on the table. "Alright, back to business. Next subject is Sam Termine. He came in pretty weak. Got an opinion Doc?"

"If he's typical and I believe he is, he can be long term within a month. Sal, why are you asking me? Tridon knows how. He's done it before." The Doctor twisted uncomfortably in his chair. He knew his intent to maltreat was a violation of the basic oath he took when he became a medical doctor. He just condemned a potentially viable man to a life of total dependence. He felt a small tinge of guilt. His only solace: he knew he wouldn't have to meet the man.

***

Sal noticed George remained seated after the others quickly disbursed and asked: "Okay what's bothering you?"

"I want to plead my position one more time. Get legitimate in all Wings. Stay that way until we can sort out what we are doing. My gut's telling me we're running into a disaster. Making a few dollars is one thing. Now we're planning to blackmail a woman. That's a felony. That's big time in jail."

"I hear you George. Here's how I see it. I perceive this Tina problem to be purely business, and my intuition says to go along with Milo's plan. You have to remember he has first-hand knowledge and knows the woman better than any of us. You may consider this action to be blackmail or extortion. I believe the confrontation with Tina is a business negotiation. It's a difficult negotiation that needs some special tools."

"Are you willing to spend time in jail for Milo's business tactics?" George asked.

"No one's going to jail for what we're doing, Milo's a genius. He has us covered with a blanket of legitimacy. If he says he can contain Tina, then I believe him. And, you should too." Sal got up from his chair and walked over to him. "Relax my friend, we're in this together, and I'm not afraid. Relax. Go and get a cup of coffee."

***

Lani, though small, was a very strong woman. She knew how to care for patients without hurting them or herself. Sam Termine, strictly by reason of his room number, became her responsibilities.

Approaching Sam with caution, she lifted his covers and saw his toneless body. Muscles were practically nonexistent. Bandages couldn't hide his extremely thin torso. This man needed a lot of medical attention. It also meant an instant increase in her burden.

When touched, he winced with obvious discomfort. Lani hesitated. Sensing his pain, her compassion urged her to forego her native patois and speak English. She looked about hoping no one else could hear. "Where do you hurt?" she asked in a quiet voice.

"Mostly here."

Lani tugged the bed cover back. He lay still. Goose bumps formed on his bare legs. He started to shiver. Lani quickly recovered him and asked, "Is there anything wrong with your legs? Can you walk?"

"I've been in bed for a while. I really don't know how long. Oh woman, I feel so tired."

"I'll try to change your bandages — and clean you. I am sorry if I cause you any discomfort."

Lani worked as gently as possible, dressed him in a clean institutional night gown, and lifted him into a wheelchair. He needed a pillow to prop up his head.

"You have to move around to get better. Your muscles are — they need exercise. Are you willing to try?"

"I'll do whatever you think I need. Right now, I feel very tired."

Lani whisked through the bed change then squatted in front of Sam. She had to nudge him from his slumber. "I'll hold your feet see if you can push back." He felt her pressure. He responded as best he could.

"What's wrong?" Sam asked.

"Not walking made them weak. You have to move as much as possible. Don't just sit in that chair, move your feet around. Push down into the floor, when in bed, use the footboard. Push hard. Kick the covers. Point your toes toward your head. Move every muscle you can." Lani worked with his feet and moved his legs and urged him to push against her motions. Time was their enemy. Lani had to stop. She lifted him back into his bed. "I have to go. I'll try to see you again. Work some more and try not to sleep."

Sam nodded his understanding. He dosed off as soon as Lani left the room.

***

Sam blinked and tried to clear his bleary eyes. He felt a hand upon his shoulder and heard, "Sam, wake up, can you hear me?"

Sam turned towards his visitor. "Hi, I think I'm dreaming."

"No you're not dreaming. I'm real."

"I mean I think I'm back in school and seeing my teacher. You're Miss Archer, right?"

"And you are Samuel Termine."

"Miss Archer," Sam swallowed and repeated, "Miss Archer it's wonderful to see you again." He reached out with his hand.

"I can only stay a few minutes. If they find me here I'll be in deep trouble." She turned, looked around and then said, "Please listen to me. You are in a very bad place. The people here are evil, and they will hurt you. Why are you here?"

"I was in the hospital."

"What's wrong with you now?"

"I don't know. The nurse said I should exercise."

"Which nurse?"

"A little black woman."

"Lani? She talked to you? She spoke English?"

"I only saw one person today. I guess she's the one, seems to be a very nice lady."

"Lani works hard."

"I'm so confused. Maybe — maybe I am dreaming all of this."

"No Sam, you're awake. I have to go. I'll try to see you as often as I can. Just remember what I said. This place is not what you think it is. Try to keep alert and help yourself to get better."

***

Sam looked around his room, saw he was not alone and waved to the man in the next bed. He merely nodded his head in response. Sam closed his eyes and disappeared into a quiet fogged existence.

SEVEN

The rays of a beautiful sunny day danced about his room. Its cheer held little meaning for Sam. Today like the day before merely added to a continuum blur of time. Sam's mind and body failed to fight the drug-induced stupor.

His breakfast arrived and, as usual, it remained on his table until the steward made rounds returning it to the kitchen. Sam never noticed the rush of feet or the clamor of stacking trays.

***

Lani whisked into Sam's room, placed his lunch on his bedside table and gently touched him. "Sam, please wake up." She nudged him harder. He remained in a stoic calm. Lani reaching in pinched his nose for a brief second. He reacted to the lack of air with a gasp. "Wake up. You have to start helping yourself."

Sam stared at his tormentor. He recognized Lani. While she commanded his bed to change its shape, she encouraged Sam to ride the action into a sitting position.

"That'ssh a hell of a way to wake up a guy." Sam said slurring his words.

Lani smiled and spooned up some of his food and offered it to him.

"I'm not hungry. That stuff looks terrible."

"You have to eat. Eat everything they give you. Then maybe someday you can leave this place." She placed the spoon into his hand and said, "You're not helpless. Feed yourself. Try moving around." She pushed his bedding into place. "They keep me very busy. I can't stay to feed you. Now eat."

"Tastes terrible."

"Are you moving your feet? And legs? Pushing on the bed?"

"I don't know. Can't remember. Maybe I do. I don't know. Maybe sometimes when I'm half awake." Sam shook his head in an attempt to clear the fog and continued, "Which doesn't seem to be very often."

"Work hard, stay awake, and eat everything. Taste doesn't matter; you need food." She turned and walked out of the room.

Sam played with an item trying to determine its origin. He brought a morsel to his mouth, sampled the gooey consistency, drank a little milk, closed his eyes, and fell asleep.

***

Gail and Jack continued with their rounds going from room to room with robotic like motions. They observed and checked the status of each of their charges. Then they entered Sam Termine's room.

Jack stood at the rail of Sam's bed. He eyed the immobile man while noticing his grayish tone and shallow breathing. Sam did not respond to Gail nudging of his arm. Jack, using both hands, grasped and shook Sam violently. Sam opened his eyes. Jack expelled a breath of exasperation, turned to Gail and said, "This guy's out of it. We have to cut back on the meds."

"How much?" Gail asked her mentor.

"What's he on? Let me see the chart." Gail spun the computer cart around. Peering into the monitor Jack said: "Three times a day, has him wacked out. Make it two."

It took a moment for Jack to input the medication change. Then, with an animated flourish, he tapped in the initials of Carl Lunkens.

***

Before Danielle reached the last step, Reverend Dugan opened the parsonage door. "Thank you for coming. Please, let's go to my office. We can chat in private."

Danielle Turner, surprised at the eager reception, followed Reverend Dugan. He immediately turned right, passing through a pair of opened French doors and entered the frugal parish office. He offered, and she sat in a chair next to the minister's desk. "You thanked me for coming. I'm the one who should offer you our appreciation. Thank you for your help. This has been a very tough time for my family."

"I know. I've seen it before. It can be very difficult for you — and your family." The pastor waited for a moment before continuing, "Your mother just made a major lifestyle change." He paused, took in a deep breath and said, "It does not remove her from our flock. My concern for the souls of all of our brothers and sisters remains strong where ever they may reside."

"Reverend Dugan you asked me to come in to talk about Mom. Is there a problem?" She quickly added, "Why couldn't we talk over the phone?"

"Oh, it's not a serious problem, as yet. In fact, we want to avoid a problem — and you can help us."

"We? Us?" Turner queried.

"I received a telephone call from Mr. Manfassi. He's the gentleman who managed the admittance of your mother to Belvedere Manor."

"Of course, I know Mr. Manfassi. Why is he calling you about Mom? Why didn't he call me?"

"I visit often and sometimes conduct a short service for the residents. When I do it's usually on a Thursday afternoon. Sometimes I have a conflict, and I have to cancel. I try to do my best. Mr. Manfassi's a great guy. He'll take excellent care of your family."

Danielle grimaced, stared at her pastor and wondered why the sales pitch. She waited for the man to answer her question. Dugan seemed to be pondering his words. Danielle couldn't tolerate his delaying game. She demanded in a strong voice, "You did not answer my question." The pastor's eyes widened as Turner's instant anger showed. Danielle quickly added, "Tell me what the man said."

"Tell you what he said, oh yes. Yes, he told me your mother was going through the typical blues of a newly arrived resident. He's seen it before. Yes, he's seen it before and knows she will be fine." The man tried to swallow; his dry mouth betrayed his anxiety. He wiped his arid mouth with his hand and said, "He thinks you can help her. Help by letting her fight her battle alone — of course with their staff."

Danielle stood up and looked down at the man. "What's that supposed to mean?"

The Pastor blinked at the rush of aggression and quickly added, "He believes it would be best for your mother if you did not visit her. Not visit the rest of this week. Of course, he meant only the weekdays. By the weekend, it'll probably be okay." The Pastor began to perspire. He squirmed in his discomfort.

Danielle shouted: "He wants to isolate her from her family? That's ridiculous. Are you sure that's what he said?"

"Oh, please don't take offense. I didn't mean to give you any distress. We all want to help." He looked down at his desk and added, "It's not isolation. It's already Tuesday, and I'll be there on Thursday. I'll talk to the staff and make certain your Mother comes to the service. Please believe me, Mr. Manfassi, and his people will take extra care to get her happily acclimated; and of course, deeply involved in many activities."

Danielle still standing put her hands on the desk and leaned towards the man and bellowed, "Reverend I don't like it. I think it stinks. What about Doctor Juliano? Is he part of this?"

The Pastor, seeking some time to think, opened a desk drawer and pulled out a tissue. His nervous gestures continued as he needlessly wiped his very dry mouth. His voice, barely audible, betrayed his anxiety as he asked: "Are you going to cooperate with this reasonable request?"

Turner sat down. With a sign of frustration, she combed her hair with her hand and looked up at the ceiling then finally offered, "You should have asked me for my schedule before telling me not to visit my mother. I have an important business trip. I should be traveling right now." She then quietly said, "That's part of my problem. Business is bad. It's not coming in; we have to go and find it. This is an absolute must trip. I couldn't visit anyway."

"Shall I call your dear husband?" the Pastor asked in relief.

"I'll tell him. Bob will be happy to hear he's not wanted."

"You're getting very angry, and that's not healthy."

"Yes Reverend I am angry. You can do all of us a big favor and tell Manfassi from now on he calls me to talk about Mom. Do you understand me, Reverend?"

"I will convey your feelings when I visit on Thursday."

"I have another question; do you ever look in on Miss Archer?"

"Ah, Mary Archer, she was always such a vibrant and intelligent woman."

"Was? Was? What are you trying to tell me?"

"The years have not been kind to Miss Archer. Her body is failing her, and her mind is . . ."

"Reverend, please tell me what you're implying."

"Well, you know people who are infirm just sit around and watch a lot of television. The stories offered during the daytime are rather ugly and very sexual. When the mind starts to lose its hold, people begin to imagine they're part of what they are watching. Before long, they start telling stories that are, well, are at times very weird. I'm sorry to say Mary Archer, she — she at times, loses her sense of reality."

"Who told you this?"

"I witnessed it. I've had conversations with her and, well, it's hard to believe she can say such things. She's not the only one. It's very sad to see. Miss Archer, she and some of the others fantasize about circumstances — circumstances that are very gross. Of course, we know that none of their babbling is true."

"You investigated?"

"That's my job. I make certain my flock is properly cared for. I must tell you Mary's stories were without foundation. And again, she's not the only one. It seems to be contagious with many others falling into the same problem. It is very sad."

Danielle Turner sat stunned and shook her head in disbelief. "Thank you for your time and concern. I'm sorry I talked a little rough. This is a difficult time, and I truly appreciate everyone's help. I feel like running over to Belvedere and — God, I'm being pulled apart." Danielle wiped her sweating brow. "Please, Reverend Dugan, tell Mom I said hello, and we love her."

"Yes, yes I'll do that. Have a successful trip and we'll pray for your safe return."

Danielle again thanked the Pastor, shook the man's hand and left the parsonage. She entered her car, opened her case, pulled out a tablet and entered a note: *Call Doctor Juliano.

***

Lani rushed down the hallway, looked around before dashing into Sam's room. She nudged his arm and asked, "Are you okay?" As with Jack, Sam did not respond.

"If you can hear me, I will be here early tomorrow."

Sam stirred a bit, adjusted his position and continued with his clouded slumber.

EIGHT

Lani arrived twenty minutes before her starting time, just so she could see her new patient. Sam, though unmoving and apparently still in his daze responded almost immediately to Lani's touch. She leaned into him and softly said, "Good Morning. How are you today?"

"Hi," he said while blinking his eyes into focus. "Guess I'm okay. I ate some of my dinner last night. I don't remember the last time I did that."

"Great. Did you enjoy the food?"

"Tell the truth I don't know what it was. It didn't have much of a taste. I ate it anyway."

"Let's get you cleaned up and ready for the day. Are you trying to move around and working those muscles?" Without an oral or physical response, Lani got the message. She withdrew the covers and examined his bandaged body. "Still hurt?"

"Yeah, I feel very stiff. Looks like I could be here for a long time."

"I wish I knew — I just don't." Lani cleaned Sam with a sponge bath, dressed him in fresh bedclothes, and said, "Please try to stay awake and enjoy a good breakfast. I'll be in to see you later. Okay?"

"Good breakfast?" Sam smiled, nodded his approval, while trying hard not to close his eyes.

***

Florence Danzell, up and out of bed for hours, felt the morning dragging into another day of solitude. The absence of her family played hard on her and she yearned for familial contact. Checking off today, Thursday, on her planning calendar, she noticed that her daughter promised to visit on Saturday. There were two more days to go before a visit. Reading books and writing letters consumed the week to date. Now the walls around the room seemed claustrophobic. She had to escape from the drudgery. Florence wheeled out of her room, albeit hesitantly, and into the hallway. She espied the floor nurse working at her station. "Excuse me. Can you tell me if there's anything of interest going on in this place?"

"Do you have the weekly bulletin?"

"Well that sounds like something I should have. May I have a copy?"

The sullen nurse looked around her desk, found the small stack of undistributed calendars, and without a word, handed one to her.

Florence Danzell tried to ignore the rudeness of the nurse yet felt the sting of another unnecessary indignity. She turned away, scanned the sheet and spotted a 2:00pm religious service. It was scheduled for the recreation room. A simple note on the chart showed a name: Dugan. "Could this be our Reverend Dugan? Can't be two Dugan ministers in this area," she thought to herself.

Florence retreated to her room. She tried to fortify herself combating the feeling of loneliness. Going to the religious service seemed to be the most important thing she had to do today. The hours dragged on. The noon meal proved to be a culinary dud.

"It would be so simple to put a little imagination into the preparation and presentation. I wonder if they would let me into the kitchen and show them a trick or two," Florence said to the silent aide who retrieved her tray. A smile, the standard reply to all queries, came quickly and Florence merely returned her gesture with a simple wave.

***

Milo needed two days to buy and install two miniature video cameras. Aiming the devices to cover the vital parts of the room was easy. An attempt to hide them from a casual visitor took a few iterations of various positions before he gave up on being able to secrete them. Now he had to rely on Tina's attention to be on the greed in her heart and not on the decor of his office.

It didn't take very much of an effort to convince Tina she should visit Belvedere Manor. Telling her she was part of their team, and they had to discuss important business matters created visions of that extra income she demanded.

Milo sat in his office. With his door wide open, he busied himself with normal duties, while waiting for his visitor. A gentle tapping on his doorframe was the first alert then he heard a singing greeting, "Good morning Milo. It's nice to see you're here and just waiting for me."

Milo jumped up, moved from behind his desk to envelope her in a gentle hug. "Hi, come in, come in," he said while guiding Tina to a seat. Milo retreated behind his desk, sat down, and surreptitiously triggers on the video system. His subtle motions went undetected. He winked and smiled allowing a few extra moments for the equipment to begin recording. Then like a serious businessman he looked directly at her and said, "Well, good morning Tina. Would you like some coffee?"

"Keep the coffee for now. Let's talk business. Okay?"

"Okay. What can I do for you today?" Milo said hoping Tina would get a little chatty and commit herself.

"Oh aren't you the sly one. Cut it out Milo. You asked me to come here, right? Let's get on with it. Saturday, you do remember Saturday?" She glared at him and added, "And you know what I want."

"Just a second." Milo got up and closed the office door. "Okay, now what were we talking about?"

"M – o – n – e – y," Tina said spelling each letter.

"Right, money, you want us to pay you for your services."

"Oh, come on Milo, enough with the jokes."

"Tina, I paid you a finder's fee to transfer a client, which, by the way, we cannot do, and since I did, it was not an expense item for Belvedere. I, your old pal Milo, gave you a couple of dollars out of my own pocket."

"Why would you do that?"

"Why? Because I like you. I wanted us to be friends."

"And you expect me to believe that?"

"The truth is the truth. We are friends, right?"

"A lie, is a lie, is a lie. Doesn't matter to me — hey Milo why did you call me?"

"You are a very important person to our business. We need you for what you do."

"Thank you."

"Talking like this helps in understanding how we can aid each other in doing the best job we can."

"Yeah Milo, I like that. And setting up a monthly payment process for unique clients . . ."

"Whoa, are you . . ."

Tina interrupted him in turn and said, "Hold on, hold on, let me finish. Since this is new to both of us, I'll forgive any payments for the previous ones. Let's start with this Sam guy then it'll be a one-time slug of cash, on delivery, plus a few bucks a month for any new resident."

"What is your idea of a slug of cash?"

"Oh, I was thinking about five hundred?"

"Ouch, that's a lot of money."

"No ouch, this is business. However, since you seem amenable to my new business proposal, let's make it — hmmm — how about three."

"You want me to give you three hundred dollars, then a monthly fee for every new resident you send us?"

"Yeah, I like that, start with three hundred, and I'm certain we can arrive at a decent monthly number."

"Tina, you're performing a vital function for us and for the Hospital. Our business needs your support — where do we go from here?"

"Get the money, then you can take me out for a grand lunch. We can have a nice chat and just dally away the afternoon. "

Milo opened his desk drawer, withdrew a metal box, took out a small package of bills and counted, albeit very slowly. "Twenty, forty, sixty, eighty, and another twenty

makes one hundred dollars. Three hundred is impossible."
Milo collected the small pile of bills and passed it to Tina.

"One doesn't do it. I need at least two." Milo
nodded, counted out another hundred and placed it atop
the first hundred.

"Thank you. See that was easy. As for the monthly
fee, I'd like to set the next collection date at the first of the
month. I'm thinking about twenty-five bucks per client is
reasonable. Maybe there should be a minimum, hmmm —
got to think on that. Yeah there should be a minimum of
say a hundred." Tina got up and started towards the door.
"Although it's a little early, I'm ready for lunch, how about
you, Milo?"

Milo reached under his desk, shut down the
recorder and said, "Sit down Tina. There's something of
interest you have to see. Take a peek at this." He spun his
computer monitor around. "I need a moment." He picked
up the phone and said, "Play number one."

"Who are you talking to?"

"We're going to see a little movie."

"Oh, Milo, have you got some dirty movies today?"
Tina laughed as she waited for the signal to come through.

"You're right, dirty movies. Just watch."

Tina jumped out of her chair. "What in the — what
is this all about?"

"Well you said you like things simple. And it is very
simple. What you just did is called extortion. We recorded
your demands with a few witnesses right next door."

"Milo, it's not just me. We're in this thing together.
You don't dare show this to anyone."

"Not so Tina. We have all our bases covered.
Belvedere Manor is squeaky clean. You're the one that's in
deep trouble." Milo stood up and walked around towards

her and sat on the edge of his desk. "However, we can be reasonable."

"You are — I hate your guts. I'd like to slit your throat. Then seeing Sal in the doorway said: "You too."

"Ms. Morris you've just committed a felony, and as you saw, we have a video recording. You also threatened Milo with bodily harm, and I witnessed that. I strongly suggest you listen to Milo," Manfassi said.

"You and Milo — and the rest of your band of thieves have been cheating the insurance companies — and the government. I can . . ." Tina stopped when Sal interrupted.

"You've said enough. Listen to Milo. We have an offer. If you don't want it, I'll call the police. Do you understand?" Sal said and awaited her input.

Tina looked at the men, frowned and shook her head in denial, then said in resignation. "What's the deal?"

"Very simple: give back the two hundred bucks and there are no more finder's fees. We also get to choose first on all potential clients; and believe it or not, that's it."

"That's it huh. Everything's for you with a load of grief for me." Tina pondered then relented. "I want that video before I leave."

Milo picked up the phone punched in a number and ordered, "Bring in the recording."

Harry walked into Milo office and handed him a USB stick. "Is this what you want?"

Milo said, "Tina. I want to show you the label. This is the recording. Look, now I'm putting this thing into a tiny envelope." Milo withdrew an envelope from his desk, inserted the USB drive, pulled off the seal protector and closed the envelope. "See the address. This sealed envelope will be sent to our attorney. He will have instructions to forward the envelope to the State Police in the event you cause a problem, any kind of a problem, for Belvedere, or for any of us. And you better not quit your job for at least a couple of years."

Tina lowered her head in defeat. "I thought I was part of the team and just hoped for a piece of the spoils." She raised her head and stared at Sal Manfassi and said, "I can't fight you. However, some day I will be back. This is not a threat this is a promise, a promise I make to the both of you." Tina turned and glared at Milo for a few moments and then hurriedly left his office.

***

Florence waited in vain. Arriving at the recreation room early she hoped the good Reverend would be at the service way before the announced time. He sauntered in a mere one minute before 2:00pm. Then without looking at his scanty congregation, immediately began the ritual.

The minister mumbled through the service in a bland unemotional manner. He opened his Testament, randomly selecting a reading. It didn't reflect the season nor did it offer a theme for the day. His rambling approach added confusion to an already undefined message. The man appeared lost in his thoughts as he spouted a series of 'Thou' and 'Shall'. To Florence, the rite lacked meaning or substance. Though it only lasted a total of twenty minutes, on occasion he stopped talking, as if in deep meditation. Then he flipped through some pages of his holy book and started babbling again before offering a final blessing.

Florence stunned by the man's demeanor stared at him and thought: "Why is he here?" She shuddered. She felt an instant revulsion and huge need to confront the minister. "Has he changed? Have I changed? Or did he always have one face for the parishioners and another façade for . . ." She suddenly broke off her thought and lurched towards the man.

Reverend Dugan never looked into the eyes of those seeking his solace. He finished his service, turned from the people and began to stuff his briefcase.

Florence approached and said, "Good afternoon, Reverend Dugan."

He looked down towards the strong voice and responded, "Good afternoon. Oh, Mrs. Danzell it's you. I noticed you within our congregation," he lied. "Did you enjoy the service?"

"No — I — did — not," she said in a slow deliberate voice. "Is this the way you offer the scriptures for these unfortunate people?" She looked at him as his mouth hung open in surprise. "If anyone needs to hear the good words of the Lord, it's the souls who were here today. We came to hear and receive the comfort that the bible offers. You," she said pointing a finger at him. "You failed in your sacred duty. Worst of all you cheated us out of an opportunity to feel the warmth of our beliefs." She then wagged a finger in his direction and said, "Don't you ever come in here again and offer such a weak uninspired performance. I can't even call it a message."

"Was it that bad?" the chastised Reverend Dugan asked.

"Bad? It wasn't bad. It was awful. We need hope. We need reasons why we are here. We need encouragement for why we are suffering — and what it all means. Why do you bother coming?" She didn't give him time to answer continuing, "It would be best if you invited someone to come in your stead. Even an inspired lay person could do a better job."

"Mrs. Danzell, you're upset because you're here. Please accept my sorrow that you are . . ."

"Reverend Dugan it's not me; it's you. You made me angry. I'm still the same woman I was before I came here last Saturday. My body may be a little weaker — my mind is still intact." She wheeled up close, looked up into his eyes, and said in a low threatening voice, "I strongly recommend that you examine your conscience. Are you doing the Lord's work? Or are you just going through the motions to satisfy your calendar?"

"Mrs. Danzell, I . . ."

"Good day Reverend." With those words, she spun her chair, started to leave the room, quickly turned and added: "Say hello to your dear wife."

NINE

Sam spent his first week at Belvedere Manor in a chemical stupor. Even in this short period, with some nutrition and exercise, his strength began to return. Lani's determination and vigorous efforts yielded these positive results because she forced him to eat his food; she coaxed him to use his weakened muscles. Her initial gentle motions quickly turned into aggressive movements and Sam's emotions churned. He despaired, tried to tolerate the pain caused by the movements yet relished the thought of walking again.

Lani pushed and pulled on his legs while working against his resistance. She urged him to stand; then shuffle into position while she maneuvered him towards a wheelchair. His arms always showed some strength. However, he had to hold onto Lani when his legs didn't cooperate.

"You're looking better. I'm happy to see you're starting to stay awake. Before, when I moved you around, you tried to sleep. It frightened me. Now I think I know why."

"Why?"

"I looked in your records. At first, they gave you a lot of drugs; then not so much." Lani continued her work as she talked, "I don't think you need those pills. I know they are strong. Very sick people need them; people with terrible pain. Do you have any pain?"

"I don't feel anything. Most of the time I'm numb."

"I am sorry. What little I know, if it was me, I wouldn't take any more."

"Don't take my medication?

"It's a drug. It doesn't make anyone well it just blocks the pain. I see what it does to people. Please trust me, you don't need it. It only makes you groggy; then all you want to do is stay in bed. You should be awake and work hard to get stronger. You have to do exercises. Do you understand what I am saying?"

"I can handle some pain."

"Then don't swallow any more. When they give it to you make believe you're sleepy and take it from them. Or try to hold it in your mouth and wait until they leave. Then spit it out."

"You want to help and I appreciate it. Here's where I get very confused. If the Doctor wanted me to exercise wouldn't he send someone to help me? Again, I know you want to help — and you are . . ."

Lani interrupted him. "Doctor? There's no Doctor. Look at me. I'm your friend, and I'm telling you this is a very bad place. They don't want you to get well. They are terrible people and want to use you to make money." Sam tried to interrupt her. She held up her hand and continued, "Just listen to me. Try as hard as you can to get out of here and as soon as possible. I have seen what they do. You are young and can regain your health; have a long life. And, you will not need this wheelchair if you help yourself. I have to go now. Work those muscles. If I can I will be back."

Lani left Sam sitting in the wheelchair. He felt sleepy, started to drop then shook his head and tried to fight the urge to sleep. *"What's happening? God, she says I'm going to end my days here. Is she right?"* Sam ruminated.

***

Mary entered Sam's room quietly; he didn't notice her until she was right in front of him. She whispered. "Sam, it's me, Mary Archer." Reaching towards him, she held his hands. "I'm so happy to see you up out of that bed. How are you feeling?"

"A little achy, I feel very tired all the time, in fact, if I could I would get right back in bed."

"Oh Sam, I'm so sorry to see you're here." A tear began to well up in her eye, and she said, "I can't stay too long. I'm going to be blunt. As I told you before, you're in very deep trouble, and you have to get out of this place. These people are animals and want to use you. Soon you and your body will be worthless. They're feeding you powerful drugs -- not to help -- to cripple you."

Sam looked at her and said: "This is a health facility they're supposed to be getting me back on my feet. I don't get it. You're trying to scare me. Why? Miss Archer I haven't seen you in years. Why are you coming back into my life this way? I'm tired and hurting. I don't need this kind of talk. Please go away."

Mary looked at Sam. The tears started to flow from her eyes. She knew he needed good medical care, and with it could be a viable human again. Mary dried her eyes.

Then put her whole body into as tough a stance as her condition allowed. She pointed her finger at him in her old teacher's way of driving home a lesson. "When you were my student you listened to me and learned. Did I ever do anything to hurt any of you? No! If anytime in your life you need to listen, it's now. I know it's very difficult to hear and understand while you're drugged. Sam you must trust me. Trust me like you did a long time ago." She stared at him hoping he absorbed her words. When he did not respond she said, "Are you listening to me? Don't you believe I want to help you?"

"I'm so confused. What do you want of me?"

"I want you to believe what I'm telling you."

"And I really want to," he said as he put his hands to his hurting head.

"Sam if I could I would put a torch to this place. I can't. Maybe I can light a fire under your rump and get you out of here."

"I've never seen you so angry."

"It's frustration not anger."

"Look at me. What can I do? I'm in the worst shape in my life. Why are you so frustrated with me? What have I done? What do you want from me?"

"I want you to trust me and stop taking the medications. Skip one dose and you will understand. Gail will be in here any moment — I've got to go." She pushed away and rolled to the door. Mary looked up and down the hallway, sensed it was a good time to leave and wheeled out and across to room A123.

Sam gazed at the vacant doorway. He shook his head trying to comprehend what just happened. He lowered his head in deep thought and slowly closed his eyes.

***

Gail entered his room and touched his arm. "Sam, wake up, time for your meds." Gail poured a small quantity of water into a tiny plastic cup and handed it to him. She reached over to her cart, grabbed a paper cup with a tiny white pill and emptied it into his hand. "Okay, down the old hatch," she said as she put the medication into his mouth. Sam pictured Mary Archer pointing her finger. He recalled Lani's words. After pushing the drug under his tongue, he sipped a little water, nodded his head and handed the empty cup back to Gail. She tossed it into the cart's waste bag, turned and left the room. Sam worked the pill from under his tongue and spit it into his hand.

"Now why did I do that?" Sam mumbled.

***

It felt strange to be sitting in the wheelchair. Without the drug controlling his mind, the stimulating visits by Lani and Mary Archer kept him awake. He looked around his room and then towards his roommate.

Pushing on the wheel, once he released the brake, he found it easy to move. His roommate seemed to be asleep. Sam moved in closer and read the two names on the end of the bed: "Charles Whitson – Dr. Carl Lunkens."

"Mr. Whitson, are you awake? Hi I'm Sam Termine."

Charles Whitson turned his head a little more and looked directly at Sam. He indicated for him to come closer. When Sam was as close as the equipment allowed, Whitson whispered, in an extremely weak voice, "Trust and believe your friends."

Before Sam could respond he heard Lani reentering the room.

"It's good to see you're awake and moving around," she said happily. "I guess your arms are working okay. Are you stretching those muscles in your legs? You can't keep them still. You've got to move those legs."

"It's hard. They don't feel right."

Lani bent down and took his right leg and began to massage it and move the joints. "I wish I knew more about this. All I really know is you've got to keep the muscles working. You have to help yourself at all times. Point your toes; lift your knees; rotate your foot. Tomorrow, I'll get you up early, and then you will be in that chair most of the day. Okay?"

"Is there a physical therapist in this place?"

"There is one thing you have to remember: you are in the A Wing. I beg you. Please don't ask them for anything."

Sam reached down into his chair, retrieved a messy tissue holding his meds. He handed it to Lani and said, "Please throw this away."

Lani took the little lump of wadded tissue and said, "Thank you for your trust." She smiled, waved a good-bye and quickly left.

***

Sam's mind spun with rehearing the voices of Lani and Mary Archer. He tried to think through all possible reasons for his predicament. His concentration broke when strange sounds penetrated the room. Listening he judged they came from the adjacent room and strained to hear. People were laughing and yet he thought he heard someone crying.

***

"Sam! Sam! Ah, there you are. Name's Jack Tridon. I'm in charge of this wing. How's everything?"

"Jack. There is . . ." Sam started to say.

"Whoa. Wait a minute. I told you what I am. I guess no one told you who I am. I am THE man and YOU, as a resident, will address me as Doc Tridon. Doc Tridon! Do you understand?"

Sam stared at the large man in front of him and decided to play along with his game and said, "I am sorry — my mind is not very clear. I didn't mean to offend."

"That's all right. You're new here, and I'm a very forgiving person. You just have to learn who's who. Again, how's everything?

"Okay I guess. May I ask you a question?"

"That's why I'm here. Shoot."

"Will I get any physical therapy? I want to be back on my feet."

Jack looked at Sam Termine and said, "Oh my! Looks like you have more problems than we thought. You received at least three sessions this past week. Just by asking that question shows me you are having some short-term memory loss. That's got to get into your record."

"I had three sessions? This week?"

"Let's not dwell on it; it'll only make you upset. Did you receive your medication this morning?"

"Yeah, a nurse gave me a little white thing. Took it with some water. What's it for?"

"That's great stuff. It makes certain you don't have any pain. You don't feel any pain, right?"

"Thank you. I don't have any pain."

"We take good care of our residents. Just do what we say, and you'll be fine. What's my name?"

"Doctor Tridon"

"Now, now, there you go again. You didn't listen. It's Doc Tridon. Got it?"

"Thank you Doc Tridon. What did we say happened last week? I'm sorry, I feel so groggy. Maybe if I get some rest I can remember." Sam closed his eyes and let his head drop. Jack Tridon smiled leaving the room fully satisfied with his work.

Sam opened his eyes when he thought it safe. "Son of a — Miss Archer's right. I'm wallowing in a pig sty," he said talking aloud to himself. "Legs move and I mean move."

TEN

Sam began his second week at Belvedere with the drug-induced fog slowly dissipating. Other than the normal aches of healing plus an occasional sharp stitch jolting his system, he felt fine.

Every waking moment was another opportunity to stress and flex his arms, legs and torso. Whenever fatigue set in he rested for a while and then started again. The simple conditioning exercises, subtle and unobservable did the job intended.

Per his plan, the nights were sleepless, exciting and very rewarding. Once the facility became quiet it allowed those simple daytime exercises to expand in motion. Rather than stress and flexing he pumped the air with his right leg, and then his left leg as if riding a bike. The stimulating exercises sapped his limited energy forcing him to rest frequently. Eventually exhaustion took its toll. He closed his eyes and fell asleep.

***

The morning crew arrived, quickly performed their cleanup rituals, then pulled Sam, still asleep, from his bed and plunked him into a wheelchair. Their fast actions startled him into awareness. He realized they had him out of the bed.

Sam yawned out of his grogginess, reached down and massaged his legs. The muscles felt thin; he wondered if they would ever be strong and viable.

Concentrating on his need to exercise Sam did not hear Mary Archer entering his room; his peripheral vision spotted some movement. He turned towards the door. She was coming to him with a finger placed on her lips.

"Shush. Just listen. It's good to see you're awake. Just nod your answers. Are you taking medication?" Sam shook his head to indicate no. "Do you believe I am telling you the truth?" Sam nodded yes. "Are you eating all of your food? Do you get enough to eat?" Mary rattled off the questions, and Sam nodded or shook his head to the probing questions. She left before he could say a word.

***

Mary Archer remembering Danielle Turner telling her that her mother, Florence Danzell would be a resident of Belvedere wondered if she really came. If so, Mary wanted to find her. The Danzell family, were a potential link to the resources of the outside world. Locating and talking to Florence, was paramount, regardless of the risk.

She had to avoid Jack while checking the other wings. He could be anywhere in the building. Mary moved with caution.

The fastest way to the other wings utilized the center passageway. Being the most convenient also made it the most visible. By design, anyone at the nurse's stations could monitor the traffic, if any were there.

Since all the nurses distributed medications at the same hour, the dosing routine, being a set standard, the entire staff followed its beat. Mary judged, at this moment, they should be moving from room to room.

Leaving A wing and entering the B wing occurred without incident. She rolled towards and peered into the B Wing recreation room; not seeing Florence Danzell, she proceeded on.

Mary gasped seeing a nurse working at the B station. She did not recognize her.

"I don't know her, and she doesn't know me. Just keep going girl," she thought to herself.

Mary maneuvered through the corridor between the B and C wings. She saw the unmanned C Wing nurse's station. Getting to the recreation room required her to enter the C Wing hallway. For a moment, Mary hesitated then boldly wheeled directly into the unoccupied room aiming towards the furthermost corner. Feeling somewhat safe Mary believed someone would have to enter a short distance to see her. She could only wait a few more minutes before retreating. Her anxiety spiked seeing Florence Danzell enter and then turned to leave.

Mary called out, "Don't go."

Florence Danzell spun back and said, "Hello, I didn't see you."

Mary grimaced at the loud greeting and waving her arms indicated Florence should come to her. Meeting her halfway she said, "Hello Florence."

"My goodness it's you: Mary Archer. I am so sorry to see you're here. I am thankful I know someone in this -- this place. How are you doing?

"We have to talk."

"Oh, yes. It's been so long. We have a lot of catching up. Where is your room?"

"I'm in far wing. We must talk — there is little time."

"Oh Mary, I think we have all the time in the world."

"Florence, Belvedere is an evil place."

"Evil? What do you mean by that?

"I shouldn't be here. Please just listen."

The woman looked at Mary, questioned the sanity of her old friend while answering hesitantly, "Okay."

"Please I beg you, promise me you'll not act upon anything I'm going to tell you. It is very important that you understand what's going on; it is equally important you don't start running around trying to be a hero."

"You're scaring me."

"I didn't mean to frighten you — you can't help us by not knowing."

"You're so serious and mysterious. It's apparent you're afraid of something. I meant it when I said you're starting to scare me."

"You have a very dynamic daughter. She could create an unbearable repercussion. I need your promise?" Mary, in a non-oral questioning motion, twisted her head slightly looking for her response.

"Okay, yes, I do promise to keep secret anything you tell me. Under one condition: you have to let me help."

Mary recited the entire litany of sexual abuse of the women, the crippling of the residents, and suspicions of other frauds within the facility. She spoke with rapid-fire words. Florence totally mesmerized, merely listened.

"And that is the God's honest truth."

"Oh Mary! How? This can't be real. The people here look normal and honest."

"That is precisely part of the problem. Most of the facility, C wing and B wing are well managed. They look clean; they have everything that a person needs; the staff does anything required to run a normal operation. Now that you're a resident of C wing, I can guarantee you will receive excellent treatment; care with all the respect and love that's possible. That's where it ends. Our wing, the A wing is the wing from hell."

"Why?"

"Because they know they can. Just take a good look at the residents in your area, then at our people. There's a crucial difference in our profiles; and very simple to recognize. Almost every one of you has some contact with folks on the outside. You have a normal life with visitors, receive mail, and get telephone calls. I know some have smart phones, tablets and computers. The outside world is linked to them in various ways. Now for the ugly truth about the people in the A wing: we're all alone. None of us have any dependents. We have no family. No visitors. Believe me Florence; it makes a big difference in who and where you're located in Belvedere."

"Don't the ministers, church groups and social workers visit the A wing?"

"Sure they do. When they come in, they're brainwashed and told we're mentally incompetent. They've heard it so often when they come in they listen to us, smile, and pat our hands like we're children. Then they ignore anything we may say. All of us know, by experience, if we speak to a visitor or cause a problem we're punished."

The punishment is cruel. At times, it's physical. The worse is being forced into bed-rest for weeks. You can't get up. It is torture to remain in your bed and get stiffer than you already are. That's the easy stuff, it can get worse."

"Oh Mary you're making everything sound so terrible."   "It is terrible. And the people who manage this facility are shrewd. They know how to control us; and control any visitor from the outside."

"Couldn't you get your Doctor to help?"

"No! We have a very bad Doctor, and he's part of the staff. Oh Florence they've been at this a long time."

"How about our Reverend Dugan, has he heard any of this?" Florence asked thinking she had a solid connection to solve everything.

"That man? Of course he has and it goes into his ears and merely rattles around his empty brain. He is worthless. Dugan comes here just about every week, and never hears, smells, or sees anything unusual. Belvedere's perfect with that hypocrite."

"Is that why you didn't come to the Thursday service?"

"I can't stand to look at that man. He's glib with words, lots of talk without substance. Believe me when his time comes, he will get his toes singed at the gates of hell."

"I went to the Thursday service. He babbled. I tried to listen to his sermon. It had no substance, no meaning. He did not deliver a message. I gave him my opinion of his awful performance."

"It's not only him. They're all alike, some far uglier in their actions."

"What you told me is too serious. I can't keep my promise. I have to talk to my daughter. I know I promised.

I know she can do something. My daughter will do what I ask of her. She knows a lot of people."

"I know you believe in her — and in the people she knows. They can't fix this evil. Others have tried — tried and made things worse."

"I know Danielle can help."

"Of course she can. And some day your daughter and outside help will be welcomed. Right now, we have to wait. Okay?" Mary said as she got closer to Florence and held her hand.

"Florence, a promise is a promise. They'll run circles around Danielle. They'll make her and everyone she brings in look very foolish. And she won't solve this problem."

"She can bring in the police."

"Florence, you promised!"

"I just heard some terrible things and I can't just sit still. If you don't want our help, why did you tell me?"

"I felt you had a need to know. Please believe me we have to wait for the right time."

"Why isn't this the right time? Oh, Mary this is crazy."

"It is crazy. Look into my eyes and tell me you will keep your promise."

Florence Danzell stared at Mary. She tried to understand. Mary appeared calm; her demeanor didn't fit the tragic story. Florence began to think and said to herself: "If all of this is true, why isn't she over wrought and demanding help? Perhaps this is a fabrication. I better wait before asking Danielle for help."

"Florence, please answer me. Are you keeping your promise?"

"Yes, of course I will. Is there something I can do right now?"

"Okay there is something. Can your daughter bring me some protein bars? Athletes and weight lifters eat them to bulk up their bodies. There's a man in our wing who needs help. He has to build up his strength, so he can get out of here. I think they're expensive, and I don't have much money. Don't know how I can pay you back." Mary lowered her head in the shame of begging.

"When you worked, teachers weren't paid very well. Don't be concerned about a few dollars. Mary — this problem needs more than protein bars. I want to do something about . . ."

Mary interrupted her, "I know you will help, and we need you. Just do a lot of praying right now. Sorry, I've been here too long. I have to get back without anyone seeing me. Can you be here, next Saturday, about the same time?"

"Yes, of course. Mary, I've already learned, a whole week is a long time in this place."

"Please, Florence, do it my way. I really have to go."

"How do I get the bars to you?"

"No problem, just have your daughter walk to room A123 and drop them off. No one will stop her. They fear visitors in our wing and will be happy to see her go. And I'm out of time."

The horrors churned within Florence. She, believing everything Mary told her, could not fathom the perpetrations, and the lack of authoritarian response made her shake her head in disdain.

Mary peered out of the doorway and heard. "Hello, can you help me?" Mary froze and waited. "I'm looking for room B223. Can you point the way?"

Expelling an audible sigh of relief Mary said, "I can do better than that. If you can push me, I'll get you right where you want. It's not visiting hours. How did you get in?"

"I dropped off some baked goods. Its nice stuff left over from our fund-raiser. I couldn't get in the front door, so I went around and through the back doors. The people in the kitchen let me in. I thought it would be okay if I went to see my friend. Are they going to toss me out?"

"Just act like you belong. Pushing will help, sort of gives you a legitimate reason to be here. Go right on down this corridor. See we're approaching the B wing. Could you go a little further, and take me to the A Wing recreation room?"

"My pleasure."

As they entered the A Wing, Mary saw Jack sitting at the nurse's desk. He watched them go by while scrutinizing the stranger. Failing to place her, he said aloud: "Not good having strangers walking around," he pounded his desk with fury.

Mary, hearing Jack's vocal exasperation, smiled and said, "We're almost there. Thank you dear, for the ride. Now all you have to do is just go back the way we came and turn left at the first hallway. The room you want is on the right about halfway down."

"Who was that?" Jack demanded as he rushed towards Mary.

Mary, feeling a sense of relief, turned towards her antagonist, and said: "I'm sorry. We're you talking to me?"

"You know damn well I'm talking to you. Who was that?"

"Don't use that kind of language. Now, who are you talking about?"

Jack, with hatred in his eyes, glared at Mary. She knew her taunts had tested his limits and still said, "Oh, if you meant that woman who just left here, I don't know her name. She wanted to know where the B wing was, and I showed her. You wouldn't want her roaming around this wing. Now would you?"

"You are a troublemaker, always on the edge."

"Extending a little kindness to a lost soul is a virtue. Try it sometime and you may get to like it," Mary said smiling a motherly smile. Jack glared, shook his finger as a threat, then turned and walked away.

***

"I got'ta go," Sam said seeing Lani entering his room. "Can you help me to the bathroom?" Wordlessly, Lani maneuvered him towards the toilet, entered and with gentle subtlety helped him to stand, lower his pajama, and to sit on the commode.

"This is a great incentive to get better. I've got to be able to drop my own drawers and act like I'm human. Sorry to be a burden to you."

"Work hard and your body will work with you. I'll be back in a few minutes," Lani said as she closed the toilet door.

He sat quietly. The opposite door opened and nurse's aide looked in. She apologized: "Sorry." While the door was open, for that moment, he had a chance to look into another room, a room similar to his.

Lani knocked and asked, "Are you finished?" She entered before he could answer. He nodded a yes. With a few very fast motions, he was back in the chair, getting his hands washed and then wheeled out of the room. "Today you will eat your dinner in the dining room. Please be very quiet. They do not like talking."

"What?" Sam glanced up at the woman and said, "You've got to be kidding?"

"Just watch, listen and learn. Know where you are before you say anything."

The small dining room had eight tables and a few chairs randomly set. Lani wheeled him up to a vacant table. He gazed around. The décor, cheerful and pleasant made it a very nice room. A large picture window allowed the sunlight to come in while offering a beautiful view of the courtyard. And yet the room felt eerie. A scattering of people sat motionless with heads bowed staring into their table.

Mary, entering the dining room on her own power, had an entourage of Jessie and four other women following her, albeit each went to different table. Mary pulled up next to Sam mouthing a quiet hello. Sam smiled.

To him, the deathly quiet made the room appear to be populated with zombies.

"Good afternoon ladies. It's nice to be up and enjoying a meal with all of you," Sam said trying to sound as cheerful as possible.

"Please Sam, no talking. When they come in . . ."

Before she could finish her warning, she heard Gail: "Mary, you of all people should know the routine. Why are you making all this noise? You know the rules: your friends and neighbors need peace and quiet."

"Right and I tried to explain your rules to our new resident . . ."

"How many times do I have to tell you? Mind your own business. No one needs your help in running this fine establishment." She moved closer to Sam and said, "Well, I see you're up. I'm very, very surprised. You should be in bed, not here."

"I appreciate your concern, thank you. Right now, I'd rather be up. Now about these rules, can I have a copy?"

"You don't need anything. Just accept the fact that we maintain absolute quiet in this area. You should remain silent, like the rest, and in doing so will not disturb anyone. Got it? No more talking, do you understand?"

"No — no, I don't understand. If you think it makes everyone feel better, I will try to be quiet — as quiet as I can be."

Gail stared at him contemptuously and then gazed about. All heads were down; no one wanted any recognition. Gail still steaming about Sam's arrogance, stopped at the far end of the room. She turned looked towards him pondering her next move.

An aide wheeled in a large tiered cart stacked with trays of food. The cart had an institutional an all-in-one appearance. Each rectangular gray colored tray, with little compartments separated by ridges, held different items of food. Sam peered at each while being transported to its recipient noticing a large variation in items. Upon receiving his, he stared at the meager offering shaking his head in dismay.

"Can't I have something that's a little solid?" Sam asked the aide.

Gail sprung from her lair yelling, "This is the last time you will be told. Maintain the decorum or I will assume you finished your meal — finished and I will escort you to your room."

"I only asked for some solid food."

Gail, red with anger, yanked Sam's chair away from the table. "I see you are not interested in eating. That's a shame with such good food going to waste."

"Wait, wait. I'm sorry. You have to give me a chance. I'm new here."

"You had your chance. Maybe this is the lesson you need. You're going back, right now." Gail pushed the chair roughly and exited the dining room.

Mary watched Gail move Sam then said to the frightened women, "Give me something from your tray. Put it into your napkin; scrape off the soppy gravy, quickly so we can feed this poor man."

Mary wheeled from table to table, and just as she received the last bundle Gail returned and said, "What're you doing?"

"I'm going to my room. Don't feel up to it today. Thanks for your concern."

Gail's eyes followed her then turned towards the remaining women and said, "I gave up my Saturday to be with you, and I receive nothing, only aggravation." Then Gail examined their trays, noted the missing food, and commented, "It's about time you people ate most of your dinner."

***

Mary saw Sam, sitting despondently -- in bed. She pulled up close. He tried to offer a happy smile.

Placing the napkin packages on his table, she said: "Eat as much of this as possible. We will give you all the food you need to get well. Please trust me." She reached over and placed his water container on the tray table and said, "You also need liquids. Drink water and lots of it." Before Sam could answer her she was gone.

Gail's crude response to his foray into the dining room awakened his sense to fight. Mary Archer delivering food amplified the message: eating is a necessary means of getting stronger. And Belvedere didn't care if he ate or not.

As he nibbled on some meaty morsels, he noticed a woman entering and sidling up to his bed. She put two slices of buttered bread on his tray and left without saying a word.

Utilizing the bread Sam made a sandwich by piling on a mélange of mystery items supplied by Mary. As he chewed he mumbled, "If I only had a nice cold bottle of beer."

ELEVEN

Although some pain persisted, he knew he made the right decision to discard the medication. Sam felt alive and felt the strength in his arms and legs returning. The fleeting interaction with the residents encouraged him while the conflict with Gail instilled a stronger will to survive. He desperately wanted to live, to walk and most of all to be a normal person.

Sam wiggled out from under the bed covers and began his exercise routine. The efforts continued through the night. He worked and rested and then worked some more. The nighttime became his friend; he reveled in his newly found verve to recover his health.

The exercise routine consumed all of Sam's thoughts. The time seemed to pass too quickly. Light of daybreak throwing streaks of sunshine into his room meant Lani would soon be at his side saying, "Good Morning"

***

"Good morning beautiful lady," Sam said with a smile.

"Ah, someone is feeling better. Are you ready for another wonderful day?"

"I don't know about that. Lani, your kindness to me is pure love. I've been thinking about you and what you said."

"What did I say that has you so happy?"

"About doing exercise and helping myself. I want to stand up and walk. Walk out of here and go home. Lani, I have to trust somebody and young lady you are it. Will you continue to help me?"

"It's Sunday. This is one of the best days of the week because the devils don't usually come in. I say usually because sometimes they're here and cause trouble. Just be careful, remain alert, and try to obey their stupid rules. We learned a difficult lesson. They didn't like seeing you in the dining room."

"That's a tough one. I enjoyed being with the folks."

"My fault, I made a big mistake. I'm sorry. Forget about the dining room. It is better that you stay here."

"Okay."

"Please don't let any of the staff, not even the cook, know that you're getting stronger. Never let them see you standing or walking. You have to make them believe you're still very, very weak. Fool them and then work hard. It won't be too long. When you're ready you'll just walk away."

"If that day ever comes I want to take you out to the finest restaurant around here and treat you to a five-pound lobster dinner," he said laughing.

"I will be honored to have dinner with you," she said demurely.

"Lani, you're a very intelligent woman. And I sense well educated. Can you tell me a little about yourself?"

"My home is Jamaica. I came here two years ago. It's very difficult to try to start a new life. Companies don't want to recognize my education. I had to work somewhere, so my cousins, they work here, helped me to get this job. They told me to hide my education and especially my ability to speak English, or I wouldn't be hired."

"That means your supervisor has to speak Jamaican and English."

"She speaks English and Patois, our native dialect."

"And she has to be a cousin."

"All Jamaicans are family."

"Lani, I'm very lucky to have you as a friend."

She presented a Mona Lisa smile and said, "Do you know Belvedere Manor has the authority to make all decisions about your health and finances."

"No — I guess someone had to. I was out of it for a long time. How do you know?"

"My people are all over this place, and we know how to listen. The managers think we don't understand what they're saying. They talk all day about anything and everything. We share what we hear at the end of the day."

"What do they say about me?"

"I'll tell you if you promise not to get excited. Just listen. Okay?"

"Sounds like you're going to tell me some things I won't like."

"Perhaps I shouldn't say anything," Lani said looking at him for a signal. She wanted to continue and hoped it would encourage him to fight for his health.

"Please — I won't do anything stupid."

Lani gazed at the man and said, "The apartment you rented is no longer yours. They cleaned it out. Took all your personal things and put them in a storage area down in the basement. Your computer and camera were given to Sal Manfassi's son."

"My computer and camera are in some kid's hands. He'll ruin them. I'll . . ." He stopped when Lani backed away and put her hands on her hips. "I'm sorry — please."

Lani came closer and continued, "Those items do not exist on the inventory of your possessions. We know because they talk and laugh. You don't own a computer or camera. You had a truck. . ."

Sam interrupted her and said, "Had? Had a truck?"

"You're getting excited. Do you want to hear what I know?

"Yes -- please go on."

"Your truck is used by the Belvedere staff for running all kinds of errands. It's used every day and usually parked in the back. This is the way they do things. After a while, what records they have will show all of your possessions are worthless and everything will just disappear."

"Son of a bitch — they're a bunch of thieves. Doesn't anyone watch this place? They're all . . ."

"I'm telling you, to protect you, not upset you. Do you understand? You must work hard to get well. Get well and then get out of here." She waited for Sam to answer and when he remained quiet with his head down, she said, "You can buy computers and cameras. You can't replace your body."

Sam slowly pulled up his head and gently said, "You're right, I'm sorry. I shouldn't talk to you that way."

"I've heard those words before. If you translate them, it's difficult to understand why son of a female dog is so bad. We have some Jamaican words that are not very nice," she said smiling her acceptance of his apology.

"What about my pension?"

"Your pension is sent directly to them and goes right into their account. They're supposed to give you some money for your personal use. It's so you can buy candy or toothpaste. You will not see any of it."

"How about my disability payments?"

"It's the same thing. They have complete control. Please, whatever you do, don't ask about your finances. Just act dumb. That's what they expect of you. They want you to be docile and most of all not cause any trouble."

"I did ask about physical therapy. Doc Tridon told me I'm getting some therapy and I must be losing my memory."

"They lie and cheat and do anything to make money. Physical therapy, X-rays, and drugs are very expensive. These items mean big money and extra income for them, especially if it's not supplied. Your name and many others are invaluable. A few extra names and hours of service get lost in large and complicated invoices. For their scheme to work, you are important. They have to keep you here, here, and incapacitated.

"Are my medical records kept at the nurse's station?"

"Yes."

"Does it have the details of the treatments that I supposedly received"

"That is one of the things they do well; keep records whether real or not. Get your feet working and then some night go and see." Lani finished her duties and waved a goodbye.

***

"Did you go to church this morning?" Florence asked as her daughter and son-in-law walked into her room.

"Wow! What a wonderful greeting, I guess you had a nice morning. How's it going Mom?"

"I've been in this place a little over a week and missed two Sunday services. You have your health and two good feet. The least you both can do is go to church for all of us." They looked at each other and did not know how to answer the challenge. She continued, "How was your trip?"

"Mom, we have to tell you about the dinner party we went to last night," Danielle said trying to change the subject.

"That's your excuse? You're away all week and then go to a Saturday night party. You stayed out late, had a wonderful time. Why couldn't you get up to go to Church?"

Danielle walked up to her mother and gave her a kiss on the cheek and started to wheel her out of the room. "Let's change the environment and maybe we can get you in a better mood."

"Nothing's wrong with my mood. How long are you staying today? Five minutes, or perhaps stretching it to six minutes."

"Mom, I'm sorry we're trying -- let's go back." Danielle said. "We brought some scones and a thermos of green tea. And look, I brought some of your China cups."

After Danielle cleared a space on the top of Florence's chest of drawers, she poured the brew into the cups. "No sugar, right?"

Florence took the cup and slowly sipped the beverage and closed her eyes in delight. "Wonderful taste and such a subtle aroma; you know green tea is great for the stomach and digestion. God only knows we need it in this place."

Danielle placed a scone on a small china plate and placed it in front of her mother. Florence picked up the treat using a napkin. She gently wiped away the small crumbs, held the small plate in her hand and lovingly felt the surface. "This dish witnessed many good meals and family enjoyment. It feels so good holding it and touching it. I love the feel of its texture." She looked up at Danielle and said, "Thank you."

Danielle and Bob talked nonstop giving all the details of their business trip. Florence sat in silence staring into space. She felt a distance growing between them as their days of travel and work took on an unreal image. She could not relate to their enthusiasm. Her mind drifted to the conflicts within Belvedere. Mary Archer's unbelievable story haunted her.

Danielle sensed her mother's disinterest and said, "Well, guess we'll be on our way. Need anything special?"

"No. No, thank you. Just come and visit with me whenever you can," Florence said sadly as she watched her family leave. Moments after they were gone, she hit the arm of her chair and said, "I forgot to ask for the protein bars."

***

As usual, immediately after the noon meal, Mary Archer and her companions went to the recreation room.

Entering as a group, each woman went to a separate section settling into her own trance. Before long, many of their heads bobbed with sleep claiming their minds. Mary's brain still churned full speed ignoring her companions and thought about the future. Things were changing, and the changes were positive. Florence Danzell, Danielle Turner, and now Sam Termine were again in her life. She knew she made a mistake talking to Florence and definitely told her too much. The only thing she could do now was pray that Florence kept her promise -- and wondered how the Danzell family could help.

"Mary you're too quiet. You're going to get us into trouble. I can feel it," Jessie whispered as she pulled next to her.

"Jessie, we are in trouble. Please don't give up hope. I know someone will help us."

"Oh Mary, I'm so afraid. Forgive me for being so weak. They have control over my body and my mind and dear God, I fear for my soul."

"These devils may possess our bodies. You should always maintain your mental health. Don't ever say they control your mind. Do you understand me? Look at me. Do you understand?"

"Mary, I need your friendship. Please always be my friend."

"You did not answer me. Do you understand?"

Jessie began to weep and merely nodded her answer and disappeared into her solitude.

***

Jack Tridon walked into the recreation room and looked about with satisfaction. "Good afternoon ladies. I'm pleased to see you all looking so fit and content on this beautiful Sunday. This is such a peaceful room."

Mary looked at the man and nodded an acknowledgment that he entered the room.

Jack left as quickly as he came.

TWELVE

"When are they coming?"

"Nine," said Milo. He grinned recognizing his boss's anxiety. "Relax Sal, from what I know it's going to be the same group; they're a bunch of robots. I think it'll be just like last year."

"Happy to hear you're so confident. Are we ready for them?" Sal asked nervously.

"Absolutely, stop worrying. Here's a copy of our schedule," he said and pulled a blank sheet from his folder. "This morning we'll have a leisurely tour of our wonderful facility. Around noon, we will go out and have a great big expensive lunch. By early afternoon, we'll still be enjoying a fantastic meal. Before we all realize it, it is late afternoon, and we're still munching and chugging — everybody's happy. I'll recommend we come back — they'll want to call it a day. Tuesday we . . ."

"Alright Milo, I got it. Just remember, these people can cause a lot of grief; we have to be careful. How many are coming this time?"

"As I said, I think it's the same hungry four. God, they sure can eat and drink. I think I'll take a little walk around for a last minute look-see." Milo got up, stretched and gave a big audible yawn and said, "Want to join me?" Sal shook his head no and pointed. Milo turned, paled when he saw a man at the door. "Hello — may I help you?"

The visitor thrust out his hand and said, "Paul Tolski! We're a little early. I assume that's not a problem for you. This is my first visit here. I believe you know the rest of my team."

Milo stunned by the sudden appearance of the State audit team wondered if they heard any of his conversation with Sal. He remained frozen in place while his mind raced and fought for control.

Sal sprung off of his chair and said, "Of course, of course it's not a problem. We're here twenty-four hours a day, seven days a week — and you're always welcome. I'm Sal Manfassi, and this is Milo Drew. Milo is our operations manager, and I'm the director. Come in. Come in." The visitors crowded into the small office standing behind Paul Tolski.

"I would like to introduce my team," Paul said.

"That's not necessary, Mr. Tolski. We are very well acquainted with Ms. Valley, Ms. Gannet and Ms. Routell. How are you folks?" Sal said as he went to each and offered his hand. "I can't believe it's been a year since your last visit."

The three women, with their eyes darting about nervously, watched as Sal went from one to another.

"Come in and relax. Would you care for some coffee or maybe tea?"

"No thank you. I would like to get started. That is if you are ready. We have a lot to do, and I want to be certain we cover all aspects of our audit. It's my guess, if we stick to my schedule, we should be done in about three days. If needed, we can be here, another day or so, or as long as is necessary. None of us want that of course — it's still an option."

"Okay, well, we'll work with you. If we . . ." Sal started to say when Tolski interrupted him.

"I appreciate that. Thank you. I do have an agenda detailed by topic. There are no time allocations, so we'll have to take each item, one at a time, and give it its due." He reached into his portfolio, retrieved two copies and gave them to Milo and Sal. The entire audit team remained standing. "Let's review what's expected and perhaps you can alert the various people we'll be interviewing."

After a quick scan of the one-page agenda, Milo challenged Tolski and said, "This is a lot different than previous audits." Tolski's grinning smile disappeared. His body language emitted a powerful visible message. Milo recognizing his faux pas asked: "Any flexibility in this?"

Tolski waited a moment, spoke through a tension-clenched jaw and said: "No! Absolutely not, we will go through every single item as outlined," then added sarcastically, "do you have a problem with my schedule?"

Sal's adrenaline surged after listening to the brief, albeit contentious conversation and said, "No, no, we don't have any issue with your agenda. Milo likes to optimize everything. Mr. Tolski, we're here to support you. We'll do it your way and only your way. Just tell us what you need, or who you need. Tell us what and how, and it's yours. Our time is dedicated to this visit.

"That's good. Now . . ."

"Mr. Tolski," Sal interrupted. "We do have one priority that cannot be overwhelmed by your audit." The emphatic 'not' came out with authority, and he continued, "Our number one priority is the proper care of our residents. They come first, and we must not at any time interfere with their routine. You will work the audit around their normal day. I cannot allow them to be upset by anyone. Do you understand?" Sal finished his challenging words by smiling and waited for a response.

Mr. Tolski looked at his adversary. He understood Sal's position was irrefutable; he decided to get out of the discussion gracefully. "Of course, please understand we're here for the same purpose. We, my team, want an assurance that all residents are properly cared for. It's a pleasure to know you are very protective of them. Please notify your staff that we're here on a non-interference basis. Non-interference of the resident's routine that is."

"We're ready to start. Give us your opening prayer and then let's do it." Sal smiled at his joke while looking into the poker face of his visitor.

Paul Tolski ignored Sal crude comment and said, "Could you arrange to have some simple sandwiches brought in, fast food burgers will be fine."

"We made plans for lunch. Just to take a break from the tedium. It will . . ."

Paul interrupted Sal. "Sorry, no thank you. Please feel free to luncheon where you wish, our team will be eating alone. I hope you don't mind. For us, it'll be a work-while-we-eat session. As for time, we'll need no more than thirty minutes for lunch." He withdrew his wallet and from that a twenty-dollar bill. Please take this to cover the cost. If it's more, I insist you inform me of any difference. I'm sorry to trouble you. I need a receipt for any charges."

Sal, with consternation in his eyes, looked towards Milo and said, "Let's get to it."

"We require a quiet place to work. Is there anywhere we can put our things and sit down?" Paul Tolski looked around the crowded office then glared at Sal.

"What kind of hosts are we Milo? We haven't even offered our guests a chair. Tell you what. I'll dedicate my office to you, and your folks — for as long as you are here. How's that sound?"

"Will we interrupt normal business activities if we use your office?"

"Nothing that can't be handled by others on the staff," Sal said with confidence.

"Settled, we'd like our sandwiches brought in about noon. Now I would like a private meeting," Paul Tolski said as he started to move towards Sal's desk.

"Of course, just give me a minute. I can give you a clean desk," Sal said scooping up his papers shoving them into a drawer. He scanned his office looking for items needed to be secured from a bunch of snooping eyes. When satisfied he pulled keys out of his pocket and locked his desk with a dramatic motion. "I'll send in a couple of chairs. Anything you can think of before we leave?"

"Thanks for your hospitality. Where will you be, so we can call you when we're ready?"

"Milo's office is right next door. Any idea how long you'll be in session?"

"We'll come when we want you," Paul Tolski said in a commanding tone while ignoring the question.

***

"Who in the world does he think he is?" Milo asked in frustration. "What're we going to do now?"

"First thing, don't panic. I thought this could happen one of these days. Let's live with it. Just try to anticipate whatever he throws at us. Remember we're fundamentally clean in B and C." Sal took in a deep breath and puffed it out in frustration. "Get someone to cancel that lunch reservation. Look on the bright side. We're saving a bundle by not taking this gang to the trough to pig out," Sal said with a snicker.

"Did you look at his agenda? If this turkey goes line by line, this audit could take three weeks. Did you notice the women were very nervous?"

"Oh, yeah, and that's good. They may not be a team. He could be a loner; maybe he doesn't know how to delegate. If we play this right, we may earn the best audit report the State's ever seen. Then again . . ."

"Look at the first item. He wants to review the entire list of residents. We're almost at capacity. That's one hundred and thirty nine people."

Sal jumped up hearing the woodpecker staccato on the door. The glaring eyes of Paul Tolski greeted him upon opening. The man immediately questioned, "Did you look over the agenda?"

"Yes we did. And that first item indicates you want a list of residents. Is that right?"

"I want to review more than a list of residents. I intend to exam these folks personally — and from many different angles. First, I assume you have an alphabetical run off. I want to see that. Second, I want to go to the financials of each and then onto their health records, etcetera."

"Wow! Okay, we have that information. It will take a bit of time to pull them together. These files are in many different locations." Sal said in exasperation.

"I don't want you to gather them. I want to go where they're located. I want to see how they're developed. If you have source data in hard copy I want to see how you store and maintain them. I want to speak to those who receive, use, and maintain them."

"The computer will give us all of this info. Here just sit down and I'll show . . ."

"Mr. Drew you don't seem to understand. I don't want to see processed data. I want to see how it was processed. The only computerized print out acceptable at this time is the alphabetical list of residents. Can you run that off for me? I need a working copy for each member of my team, plus a copy for the master file."

"That I can do, however, what I'm going to print should satisfy you. It'll have more than a listing it has . . ."

"Mr. Drew, you have a computer. Why don't you use its power and just give what I require, a listing of the residents? We have an agenda, and I don't need complications. Can you comply or does someone else in your organization know how?"

"I can develop anything you need. Give me a few minutes to rewrite a section of code. I'll delete any extraneous information and print an abbreviated list."

"That's just fine. We'll be waiting in the office. Thank you."

"Is there anything you want to work on while we're waiting for Milo?" Sal asked.

"Not the way things get done. We have an agenda and I intend to follow it precisely."

***

"Going to be a tough week," Milo said as he worked with the computer. Within minutes he accessed the abbreviated data. The listing looked good on the monitor, and the laser printer quietly produced a high-quality document. Milo gave it to Sal. He looked it over and nodded his approval. Milo quickly inputted the request for seven more copies and watched as the machine automatically complied. "I'm keeping one of everything we give him. Do you want to follow the action?"

"Yeah! And let's be with him at all times. Keep notes, this guy's a complete unknown. If we stay together we may be able to figure him out. Don't rush right in with these lists. I want to test his level of patience." Sal sat down and placed the small pile of paper on his lap.

They waited fifteen minutes and looked at each other, and Sal smiled. "Think he's at the boiling point? Maybe he . . ." The knock on the door was even more vigorous than before, its rattle reverberated into the room. "Come on in."

Paul, while strutting into the office asked, "Are those the lists we require? We've been waiting a long time."

"You're just in time. I checked them, and they're exactly what you required. Five copies, right?"

"That is correct thank you. We'll review them and get back to you shortly; and perhaps have some questions." Paul left with the lists in hand and closed Milo's office door.

"So far, this is a crazy audit. I guess all we can do is sit and wait. How about pushing the door open, I need some air."

***

This time Paul knocked gently on the frame of the opened door. "Mr. Manfassi, could you join us now. We're ready to discuss the first agenda item. Our review took a little longer than we expected. I assure you, we did a thorough job."

Milo and Sal entered the office behind Paul. Paul sat in Sal's chair and indicated they could sit down with a wave of his hand. Two of the women jumped up to yield their chairs. Sal and Milo stood waiting. "Now this list you gave us. Could you sign it with a certification that it's current and accurate? Our files must be crisp."

"Milo is an officer of this corporation, and he can authenticate any document he generates. Have you altered the list in any manner? You're shaking your head no. Have you marked up the document with notes?"

"Well yes. . ."

"We can't certify an altered document. And I guess you all have made some kind of notation on your own copy." A quick survey of the team validated his assumption. "Okay, well, that's not a big problem. We'll generate a fresh list, certify it and then photocopy that so we can retain a record for our file."

Paul felt the rebuke and looked at his team. They lowered their heads in a false attempt to look busy. "Alright if you must, now let's discuss . . ."

"Before we continue I would like to comply, fully, with that certified list. It is important to us that we remain current with your requirements. Please bear with us for a moment. We'll be right back."

Both left the room and Milo said, "You're trying to drive him up a wall."

"No I'm not. I wanted to know who he is, and now I think I know. He's a phony paper-pusher. The man's incompetent. He doesn't know a thing about performing an audit and probably has a political Godfather who got him transferred into this job. And those women know he's a problem. They're not going to help him. He wants paper. We're going to set him up so he'll leave here with reams of paper. I believe that will keep him happy. This is going to be easier than previous audits. The old audit teams were gluttons. This one has a dunce for a leader. Milo, our state taxes are at work, isn't it wonderful?"

Sal gave Milo his copy of the list. "Cert this one so we can get right back to him." Milo scrawled his signature at the bottom of the last page of the document then thumbed back through the earlier pages, initialing every one. His impression tool, squeezed over his signature, finalized the certification. He looked towards Sal for approval. Sal merely shook his head in rejection. Milo got the silent message. He embossed his initials on every page. Sal took the document and flipped the pages, not to ensure its accuracy, merely to consume some more time.

Looping from Milo's office into Sal's, with the formal document in hand, they saw Paul sitting and looking out the window. "Hi. May we come in?"

Mr. Tolski waved their welcome. He reached out to take the list.

"We certified it as current and accurate; also protected Milo's signature by embossing it with our company seal. Notice the deep impressions. What do you think? Does it satisfy your needs?"

"Oh yeah, I like that. If we can continue to perform like this, we're going to enjoy this audit."

***

"I heard Jack talking to Gail. State people are in the building," Jessie said.

"Did they say anything else?" Mary inquired.

"Something about an audit, with a new man, and others were here before."

"Did they say anything about our wing? Come on Jessie. Think. Tell me everything before you forget."

"Oh! Oh, you're making me nervous. He said they'll visit us this time and everyone should be medicated to quiet down the troublemakers, and you know who he means."

"I guess I do. Let's hope we get a chance to talk to them."

"Don't say we. Mary, please don't say we."

THIRTEEN

The audit team moved through Belvedere Manor like a military unit. They went in lock step behind Tolski who followed Sal and Milo. For two days they examined files while ignoring the facility around them. They reviewed orders for office supplies, menus for the meals, purchase orders for the kitchen needs, orders for pharmaceutical supplies, and schedules for social activities. Anything that generated a piece of paper received equal scrutiny. Tolski demanded copies of some and took every precaution he deemed necessary to acquire samples of data from every source. All copies made for the audit team received that official certification: an authorized signature encircled by an embossed seal. Ecstatic with the size of his growing file Paul Tolski glowed with satisfaction.

The intense routine of searching for, examining and collating data satisfied Paul; his team did not share his enthusiasm. They remained silent participants. Paul ignored the complacency as he concentrated on the task then scribbled comments in his ever present notebook.

The Belvedere files were open to the audit team and Paul, a good ferret for data, knew how to get at the details of the facility. In a very brief time he gained substantial knowledge of their day to day operations. Sal and Milo gave and showed him everything he asked for exposing their entire operating philosophy. Sal, believing in Milo's ability to maintain clean records, enjoyed watching a fault-free audit.

Paul's confidence in Belvedere's management began to soar. The tremendous package of data validated his growing confidence.

***

At this stop they were in the kitchen area monitoring the processing of packaged and raw ingredients in preparation for a meal. The experienced crew smiled knowing a collection of eyes followed their motions while the basic food items became the menu designed for the day's consumption.

Whiffs of yeasty bread baking eased the tension. The state team relaxed their steely stares, and each began to wander. Paul, although also affected by the wondrous baking aroma, continued his dogged inspection of labels; he happily noted that every item tracked with the planned menu.

Tolski ignored his team roaming aimlessly about the kitchen and withdrew a purchase order from his stack of certified documents. The order for fifty pounds of freshly ground beef indicated it was delivered. Milo acknowledged the receiving date as accurate and led the way towards the cold food storage area. Upon opening the walk-in refrigerator Milo pointed to the five huge rolls of meat.

Paul, not satisfied viewing it at a distance, walked in. Milo, showing confidence, merely waited outside the chamber. The frosty label on the bulky package confirmed the contents were on hand and ready for use. Touching the package, he felt the cold unfrozen meat yield to his pressure.

Sal smiled watching Milo going through the faux antics of assuring the refrigerator was secure.

"My team needs to sample your food. Is it possible to prepare additional lunches and serve it — in your office?"

"It will be our pleasure to have you as our guest. I suggest we do that tomorrow. It is a bit late today, and I doubt if the kitchen's prepared to add four more delicious meals," Sal answered and looked towards his visitor for comment.

"Tomorrow's fine. Of course, we'll pay for the meals. Please review my calculations to be certain we're reimbursing you an acceptable amount."

"I'm confident you have the right figures. Milo, please substantiate Mr. Tolski's offer."

Milo took the paper and admired the detailed work, especially the comprehension Paul Tolski had of his operation. The man knew how to audit the paper trail.

Being a number's guy, Milo had to acknowledge the auditor's efforts: "Well done Mr. Tolski. You are very thorough. This isn't the way I would tackle the assessment. I really like your approach." Tolski smiled his appreciation of the compliment.

"How are we doing with your agenda?" Sal asked.

"We've been through the resident's documents. Their personal and financial data appears to be in order. And this facility, based on our findings, is under excellent control. Plus, I have sample copies of the data I need for my complete review back at the office. So far, I am very pleased."

"Happy to hear those words," Sal said with a big smile.

"However, as you know, that's only a portion of our agenda. We must look at the medical records, much more of the physical plant, and we're looking forward to those personal interviews with the residents."

"The individual medical records are maintained where the action is, on the floor," Milo said with pride.

"Isn't this data globally computerized and available?"

"Not required."

"The government requires all data . . ."

"I don't mean to interrupt. Our MD set up the recording system and according to him we are one hundred percent compliant. I'll make a copy of his correspondence."

Sal and Milo coached their MD to create a system that gave them the minimum necessary and yet a computerized efficiency within Belvedere. The system did not have access to the Internet. Or more importantly, to them, the outside world did not have access to selective records at Belvedere.

"I'll need that. I see computers everywhere. With Wi-Fi available each should be talking to another, right?"

"That's right. However, since we choose not to do it that way, we don't have a system-wide Wi-Fi."

"Why not?"

"Security, safety from hackers, privacy issues, and I can go on. It's a good system. That computerized record is kept near the resident. Of course it is instantly available for the entire professional staff, if deemed required. So, if anyone needs a copy, they ask the staff to reproduce the one from the floor. It is dated and only good for historical information."

"And it's not globally available, within Belvedere?"

"Right, as for the other supporting records, like schedules and billings for services, those are in the general office area."

"I'll need a little time to create a list of medical records we want to examine. I'll call when we're ready," Paul said.

"I would like to offer you the services of our Head Nurse to aid in your selection. He knows everyone and can tell you who's who and what their problems are," Sal said.

"Thank you that would be helpful. Canvassing the range of medical service that is required within this facility is going to be a big job." Paul started to walk away and said: "I would like to go back the long way around so I can see a little different activity."

Milo and Sal watched as the audit team left and when they were far enough away Sal asked, "Did Harry make up his list?"

"He did B and C and asked Jack to do A. Sal I have to give you a gold star. Paul thinks you're really trying to help him. What a great guy you are Mr. Manfassi!"

"No time for this Milo. We all can have a good laugh when these people are gone. While he's here, Tolski's a dangerous guy. Get him to say bye-bye really fast. Let's move it a bit; we have to stay with them."

***

Mary and the usual group of women, each sitting in their designated place, ate their noon meal in total silence. Their seating, assigned by Gail, with an adequate distance away from another, precluded any casual conversation. The silence, broken by loud voices in the hallway, prompted all, in unison to look up.

Mary, assuming the audit team was in the area, placed her utensils on top of her partially consumed meal and rolled into the hallway. She saw the visitors stopping at the nurse's station and for that brief moment thought she had a chance. Mary exaggerated her motions showing the wheelchair poised a heavy burden. She moved slowly and when near the group puffed a breath of feinted exhaustion — and stopped. Mary timed it perfectly; she thought she had an opportunity to meet them.

From the moment she exited the dining room Jack Tridon saw Mary. He followed her movements and knew she was too close. "Gail, please assist Miss Archer. We can't let our residents struggle."

Gail understanding the message expertly grasped Mary's chair and began to push her down the hallway. "Let's go dear," she said in a sing-song voice.

"No, no, I only wanted a drink of water. I haven't finished my meal. Please take me back to the dining room and bring me a glass of water," Mary said loudly with a smile for everyone in the group.

Gail acknowledging Mary's trap, searched in vain for any other choice other than responding to her request. Feeling the flow of anger generating a slight flush, Gail knew the audit team watched and waited for her reaction. Jack recognizing her conundrum, made a head motion that, in essence, said: "take her back to the dining room." The team observed with interest the interplay between the resident, Gail and then Jack. Everything stopped while Gail tried to get control of the moment. Mary took pleasure at the forced smiles her tormentors presented. Before Gail reacted Mary said, "Hello everybody. Are you here to visit with me?"

Sal, trying not to glare at her, responded quickly, "Not today Miss Archer, Not today."

Gail, regaining some of her composure began to wheel her away. As a last chance to engage, while Gail moved her away, Mary gazed into the eyes of the visiting women. Failing to get any response Mary folded her hands into her lap not enjoying her ride back to the dining room.

"Don't forget my water dear," Mary said with a motherly voice.

"You'll get something that's equal to the trouble you're causing. And that's a promise," Gail whispered as she left.

FOURTEEN

Judging by his huge pile of paper Paul surmised any normal person would say he did a super job. Believing Belvedere Manor was a great facility, wasn't relevant, Paul having a published agenda, had to complete the audit.

"If at all possible I want to finish today. There are two major issues remaining: first we need to taste samples of today's noontime meal, and second to interview a representative number of the residents. Since it's too early to eat I'd like to tackle the interviews. Let's see. You have the capacity for 141. However, we know you're not full. With 139 clients, you're almost there. Mr. Benas gave me his recommendations — in my estimation, it is insufficient. I believe we should interview at least 10 percent or about fourteen people. I think we should choose four residents per wing or a total of twelve. Yes, that's what we'll do, twelve people."

Sal stood up and said, "Twelve is a lot of interviews. Talking to a dozen people, at fifteen minutes to a half an hour each, is a four to six hour task, plus you'll need a little time for record keeping making this more than an all-day affair. Is that what you have in mind?"

"I don't think the interviews will take that long."

"Most of our residents enjoy visiting. You may ask a simple question like acknowledging their name. What you'll get in response, from some, is a long debate toying with the question. They'll smile and drag out an issue until . . ."

"Ah, I get it, thank you. Hmm, I do want to finish this morning. We'll need the afternoon to complete the file. I guess twelve is too many. Let's make it three people per wing, and I'll try to hold it down to about twenty minutes per."

"Paul, as you already know, we want to help you. I'd like to suggest we cut it down to a couple of people per wing. Why not pick one man and one woman? Although we do have more women than men, it will give you good insight as to the wellbeing of the residents," Sal offered.

Paul turned to his team for a reaction to the suggestion. They responded with enthusiastic nods of approval.

"Okay! Two it is. Let's start with the A wing. Our documentation is in alphabetical order. Do you have a listing by individual wings?"

"We'll generate one for your records. As an expedient, I suggest we use the charts at the nurse's station."

***

Milo ducked into his office and phoned an alert to Jack. He didn't need to. The chattering of people walking down the hallway gave Jack the signal. It was his turn to play the game. When they arrived, Jack looked up and said "Good morning."

"Jack. This is Mr. Paul Tolski, Ms. Valley, Ms. Gannet and Ms. Routell. Oh, I'm sorry. Didn't you all meet yesterday?" Sal, grinning, turned away from his guests and said, "Mr. Tolski is finishing up his audit and wants to interview some folks. They would like to choose one man and one woman."

"How can I help?" Jack said smiling.

"May I see your charts?"

When Paul moved into the nursing station, Jack slipped away from the computer console allowing Sal access and said, "It's kind of early and most residents are still in their morning clean up. I hope you don't mind a little mess and in some cases the immediate area could be a bit odiferous."

Paul Tolski concentrated reviewing the names while they scrolled by, then indicated his two choices.

"Okay, this way folks," Jack said as he led the group down the hallway.

Contrary to Sal's prediction, the first woman Paul chose to interview refused to communicate. She didn't respond to his greeting nor answer any of his questions. Turning her head when he spoke she remained aloof and ignored him.

"Sal, help me out here."

"This is a difficult wing. It has many troubled people. Our dear Clara is always contentious. Today she's decided to be mute. Sometimes she talks and then sometimes she clams up and ignores us. She is typical of a lot of folks in this area. They can look and act perfectly normal, when you try to talk to them it's another story."

"Give me an example," Paul said.

"Oh, they make up silly stories. They say things like they're in their family home. Paul let me tell you that's the easy stuff. Sometimes the stories are extremely troublesome and pretty horrible. We've heard them accuse this dedicated staff of abuse and maltreatment."

"Oh, that's sad."

"It is very sad. Our staff works hard to give them great care, and it hurts them to hear the accusations. Our team puts in a tremendous amount of energy and is difficult to watch the residents continue to degrade physically and twice as hard to see them go mentally. Of course, we address the fantasies as best as we can."

"Hopefully without using a lot of the state's resources."

"Our professional staff works hard to soothe them. Jack lets the fabrications roll off of him like no one else can. The nurses before him used to leave in tears. It's a tough job, and it takes special people like Jack to do it."

Paul made some notes in his journal. When finished he gave Jack a knowing smile of approval.

"This man, Sam Termine, let's try him. Your chart indicated he's quartered in room A124," Paul said.

"Mr. Termine is our newest resident," Jack said. "He requires substantial pain medication; I don't know how he will respond to an interview."

"Thank you for your insight. I'd like to see him anyway." Paul continued walking and entered Sam's room.

Lani stopped refreshing Sam's bed and stared at the intruders. Jack saw Sam was sitting in a wheelchair. "You can finish later," Jack said dismissing Lani.

Some of the team backed away from the crowded doorway giving Lani space to retreat. Then everyone surged into Sam's room.

"Good morning Mr. Termine, my name's Paul Tolski and I'm with the State audit team. May I ask you a few questions?"

Sam scanned the people in his room. "Why are there so many of you? I can hardly breathe. I don't care where you're from. Just get out of here. Leave me alone."

Jack blanched at the aggression and started to approach Sam. Tolski noticing Jack's response said, "We apologize if we're disturbing you." Paul turned towards his team. "Please do as he asks." Then facing Sam said, "Would it be okay if it was just me?"

"Not a good idea," Jack offered.

"Jack it's not a problem. If Mr. Termine says okay, it's fine by me. What say Mr. Termine? Okay everybody out except Mr. Tolski," Sal said without waiting for Sam to respond.

The group shuffled out into the hallway. Sal closed the door holding Jack by the arm while escorting him away from the audit team. He whispered, "Relax, it'll be fine. We have to play it their way."

"Mr. Termine, we didn't mean to disturb you. Our purpose is to help and make certain all regulations are in full compliance. I understand you're new to this facility. Is that correct?" Paul asked in a gentle voice.

"Do you really want to help or are you just putting in your time to get a paycheck?"

"Wow! That's a knuckle cracker. Let me see if I can answer very simply. I'm here first as a person who loves people and second because I need a paycheck. At least, I want to think that." Paul waited a moment then added:

"Your first shot is right on. This is a job, and a good job plus I get a good buck for what I do. At times it's stressful requiring a strong effort. I try to give my employer an honest day's work."

Sam glared at the man and said, "So many strange things going on here. I'm cynical of the whole world at this time. I don't know who to believe, who to trust?"

"You can trust me. I have no allegiance to Belvedere Manor. My job is to make certain you're getting what you're paying for."

"That's one problem right there. I'm unable to pay the full freight and the State's carrying most of the load."

"Whoa! Stop and think about what you said. You're a taxpayer or were when you worked for a living. Any money paid to this establishment, for your care, is coming right out of the taxes that you paid. It's yours and mine and everyone else's. In the big picture it all balances out."

"What big picture?"

"Everybody pays a bundle for taxes. Then the State pays for roads; pays for education; pays for police protection. The State also pays for the supplemental costs of healthcare. It's a long list."

"So your point is: I don't drive. Therefore, I don't use the roads; don't go to school; I don't go out where I need police protection. What I do need is help with healthcare, right?"

"Very perceptive, you're the taxpayer, and you're my boss. I'm here to help, if you will only work with me."

"Ask away."

Paul ran through his list of standard questions about the routine of the facility and made copious notes. He then said, "One final question. Is there something troubling you?"

Sam looked at the man and thought this individual may just be the answer to solving the problems at Belvedere. He looked at Paul and said, "We're treated like animals. More like prisoners. We can't talk to one another. Food is used as a control. Bed rest is used as a punishment. People are tortured."

Paul looked down at the man and asked with a serious voice, "Have you witnessed any of this?"

"No! No, I've heard about it from others," Sam stammered.

"Well then tell me. Who are the others?"

"I don't think I can tell you right now. I've opened my mouth so let's say it is my problem. Keep the others out of it."

Paul put his hand up to his face and rubbed his chin. He appeared to be in deep thought. He continued to massage his face in an attempt to delay any reply to Sam. Then Paul Tolski asked, "Do you take any medication?"

Sam remained quiet and said to himself, "Oh boy! He thinks I'm looped by drugs, and I'm in la-la-land. I've said too much. This ain't going to work. I've got to backpedal."

"Mr. Termine, are you with me? Do you take medications? Hello Mr. Termine, You seemed to have drifted off. Can you answer me?"

"I'm sorry. Yeah I do. They give me a painkiller, once or twice a day. I can't remember exactly. The stuff makes me groggy, and I sleep an awful lot."

"Thank you, Mr. Termine. You've been very helpful. Try to work with your healthcare providers, and I'm certain they'll have you in tip-top shape very shortly. I'm finished with my questions. Do you have any questions for me? "

Sam shook his head without giving an answer. Paul Tolski quickly left his room.

"How did it go?" Sal inquired.

"I'm satisfied. Tell me is it common for the residents to have negative feelings about the facility and its personnel?"

Sal looked at Paul and said in a quiet fatherly tone, "Because of their problems, sometimes it's their age, isolation from family and friends, or strong medications they take, we become their jailers, and torturers. The food we serve, or perhaps don't serve, is viewed as a weapon. This is a tough environment for working professionals. Did you hear any words to that effect?"

"Hmm. Thank you for your help," Tolski said without answering his question.

***

Mary watched the audit team standing outside of her room. She believed one of them was still in a room because of the way the group remained in the hallway. The large group chatted among themselves; she could not hear their conversations. They were very close. Being in bed, she knew she lost a chance to talk to them. The group suddenly became quiet. Mary heard Sal's bellowing voice, and then they all drifted away.

Jessie looked at her roommate and said, "Thank God you were in bed. Lord knows how much trouble you would make for all of us if you were up."

"Jessie, I love you like a sister and want you to be happy. I will not rest until we can live in peace, and I hope it's soon."

***

They set a fast pace walking towards B wing. The interviews there were brisk and uneventful. Residents had the appearance of proper care and looked basically content. They were not at all like those in A wing. Even though the facility was almost identical in physical appearances, there was something different. Paul's gut roiled with consternation. He wanted to do a superb job, and everything seemed great until that interview with Sam Termine. Paul had his notes, and he would write it up as it happened. They moved on.

"This is C wing. How are you doing with time?" Sal asked hoping to finish with the interviews. "How about a quickie walk-through, these wings are all the same?"

"Don't think so. My notes said we would do two residents per wing, and that is just what we will do," Paul said testily. He looked at Sal and then Milo and thought: *"Everything was great — up to now. What are you guys hiding from me? Why are you rushing me?"*

"As you prefer — the nurse's station is again situated in the center of the wing." Sal walked quickly and ahead of the group in an attempt to speed up the process.

"Who's the newest person in this wing?" Paul asked.

"That's easy. It's Mrs. Florence Danzell. She's in room 325. Is she your choice for an interview?"

Before answering Paul looked over the files. He wished for more time and more interviews. He wanted to make the right choice and hopefully uncover any problems. The newest one seemed the way to go. "Yes, I'd like to talk to Mrs. Danzell."

"Do you have anyone else in mind for your second interview?"

"You pick the male for me and let's go see him first."

The interview with the man in C wing went fast and problem free. It became obvious they choose the perfect individual as a spokesman for the place. The interview only fortified Paul's feelings that they were steering him. Then the group proceeded to Mrs. Danzell's room.

"Good morning. May we come in? I'm Paul Tolski from the State, and these are my associates." He introduced the entire team and then said, "Of course, you know Mr. Manfassi and Mr. Drew."

"My goodness, so many visitors and all at one time, it would be nice if you each took a turn and visited for a while. Please tell me why you're here."

"We're performing an audit and part of the procedure is to interview residents. May we have some of your time?"

"Audit away," she said in jest.

Paul asked all the basic questions, and Florence answered truthfully. These answers made the facility appear efficient and proper. He closed his notebook and casually asked, "Do you have any questions for me?"

"Did you interview other people while you were here?"

"Yes I did. Two in A wing and two folks in B wing, and a gentleman down the hall."

"Did you believe everything they told you?" Paul reacted to the question with a quick snap of his head. He felt the question like it was a hard fist to his body. Florence then said, "Or did you classify some of their information as coming from some loonies?" She stopped and looked at Paul and then quickly added, "Please don't answer that. I think you would have to lie, and that's a serious sin."

"Mrs. Danzell . . ." Paul started to talk and Florence stopped him.

"Please leave. Your interview is over, and you all are making me tired." She turned her chair away from them.

Paul looked at the team, shook his head slowly walked out of her room.

"This has been an intense three days," Paul said. "I want to thank you for your cooperation. You and your staff have supplied all the information I required." Sal tried to interrupt him; Paul put up his hand and continued, "Just let me finish. Everything appears to be in order, and I will submit a favorable report."

"Speaking for all the fine folks of Belvedere, we thank you. This is a nice way to end the morning," Sal said.

Paul's stomach ached. The unusual interviews with the new residents made him lose his appetite, and he knew his team did not want to eat a Belvedere lunch. They would welcome any escape. "I have a change to our agenda," Paul declared. "If it doesn't upset your staff, I would like to return to the galley and merely sample some of the food in process."

"We can do that," Sal said.

"I will pay you for what we ordered."

"That's not necessary. No dinners, no costs."

"Thank you." Paul turned to his team. "Let's do a cursory survey of the menu items."

The audit team, now exhibiting broad smiles, nodded their approval.

Upon entering the area, they roamed as a group, stopped at times to peer into a steaming pot, nodded their satisfaction then moved on. As for Paul, with his digestive system rebelling and the heat and humidity of the cooking area amplifying his ill feelings he remained close to the entryway. Perceiving his reluctance to participate as an indicator to speed up the process, they ignored most of the food preparation, walked through the area and quickly returned.

"Please extend our thanks to your chef. The food looks delicious, and I'm certain the residents will enjoy their meals." The audit team followed Paul as he walked down the hallway.

"I don't think you missed an item on your agenda. Is there anything else we can do for you?"

"No thank you. We need a few minutes, and we will be on our way. There's one thing that's bothering me. It's the sadness of some of the people. Is there any way we can help them?"

"We put in a lot of extra effort helping those folks. Every single day our professionals work on that problem. You're very observant. Thanks for your concern."

"When I get back to the office I'll ask how others handle similar situations."

After the State audit team exited the building Sal and Milo peered out the window to make certain they were off the premises. "How about that, we did it," Milo said.

"Come on Milo, think about it. We just lit a time bomb. This guy's not done. He's a paper freak. And that kind is never satisfied until all the elements have closure. He left with a bunch of questions. And Florence Danzell put him on a bad guilt trip. We have not seen nor heard the last of Paul Tolski. I have to make a phone call."

Sal went to his office and immediately punched in a number without using a reference. He waited and then said, "Hi. This is Sal Manfassi I'd like to talk to the man."

"My old friend Sal, I knew you'd call. Paul's quite a character isn't he?"

"Oh, he's a real winner. There may be a problem . . ." Sal reiterated the details of the past few days, voiced his concerns, and ended his soliloquy with: "And getting back to why I really called. When are we taking the gals out for a night on the town?"

"Don't worry about Paul. I'll take care of him. He has to learn how things get done, and as you said, first things first, getting together sounds great. You name the time and place and we'll be there. Hey, I've got a call coming in. Stay in touch and don't worry."

Sal replaced the phone and leaned back in his chair and said, "That's covered. Now Milo let's try to find what's with our guy Termine."

FIFTEEN

"I never heard of protein bars. Are you sure she doesn't want pecan bars?" Danielle Turner asked her mother.

"Danielle, I have excellent hearing, and I know what she asked for. Will you please go to a Health Food Store? Or maybe the supermarket handles them. Just ask for protein bars. I'm certain somebody will know. Will you do that for your mother please?"

Danielle tried to parry off her mother's plea and started to say, "I talked to Doctor Juliano and . . ."

"Did you hear me? I asked you to do something. To do something for me and you just push my words away and start to talk about Doctor Juliano."

"I'm sorry Mom. My mind's working overtime. Of course, I'll try to find those candy bars -- tell me has Doctor Juliano been in to see you? He told me he was going to drop in and give you a quick physical."

"He was here and I sent him on his way. I don't need another physical and you, and Juliano know it."

"You've been through some stress these days, and we want to be certain you're okay."

"Maybe my body is breaking down — my mind's able to handle anything this world throws at me. I need someone to respond to my simple wishes. Danielle I still need you."

"So now I'm a delivery girl."

"You are who you think you are. I think of you as a loving daughter who is concerned about her mother. I hoped that if I asked you for a simple errand, you would take it as a pleasure to help your mother. It may be the last thing you ever do for me. Do you want to do it with a grudge or with love in your heart?"

"Mom, you know I love you and want only the best for you," Danielle said in complete resignation.

"And I love you," Florence said and offered her arms for a hug.

Danielle came over, gave her a hug and kissed her mother on the cheek. "Why does Miss Archer need these pecan bars?"

"Protein, protein bars! Please get it right, they're protein bars!"

"I've got it. Protein bars. Why do you need protein bars?"

"We're starting a track team and want to get into shape. Oh Danielle, just humor us with this simple little request. It gives us the chance to communicate, and it adds a little excitement to our lives."

"Candy bars add excitement?"

"They're not candy bars. They're a source of essential nutrients. When do you think I can have them?"

"As they sing in that nice little musical —
Tomorrow, tomorrow," Danielle sang, giving a poor
rendition of the Annie song. She began to chuckle.

"You know that's the best part of our family. We
always find a way to laugh."

"So tell me, if I find some, what then?"

"Not if, you'll find them. When you come in, just go
to Miss Archer's room. It's A123. About the same location
as my room except it's in the A wing."

"That's too complicated. When I come back, I'll
come right here; then we both will go to see Miss Archer.
How's that sound? Maybe we can visit with her for a while.
I'd like to talk to her; see what's really going on."

Florence looked at her daughter and felt a chill of
apprehension and said, "That sounds very nice. Yes, I think
I'd like that."

"I'll go shopping later this evening. As for another
visit, I hope to see you within a couple of days, for sure by
the weekend," she said while giving her mother a goodbye
kiss.

***

"What do you think Termine said to Tolski?" Milo
asked.

"I don't know. Tolski looked perturbed and yet if
you remember, he said everything was okay. Let's go visit
our Mr. Termine and find out what happened." Sal gave a
come-on wave to Milo and proceeded out of his office.

"Look at this place. It's well maintained. It's clean
and quiet. We've made a wonderful facility for our
residents. The State has to be super satisfied."

"When different people come in, who knows what
they see. In the government, big promotions come from
publicity and scandal," Sal said. He then began to murmur,

"Tolski! Tolski! Who are you? What do you want? We know you loved your reams of paper. You got that, was it enough?"

***

Sam, while sitting in his wheel chair, looked out the window. His roommate having the prime location, Sam had to look across the man's bed to see the outside world.

Sal stopped at the doorway and said, "Anything of interest out there? A lot of different birds fly onto the property."

"No. Just daydreaming and getting mesmerized by the beauty of the sunlight. The more I look, the dopier I get."

"That's nature's tranquilizer at work," Milo chimed in.

Sam knew why they were here. They wanted a critique of the auditor's visit. He pondered his predicament for a moment before deciding he had to return to what they wanted: a massively drugged patient. "Maybe — I think ninety-nine percent of my condition is a reaction to meds. I'm always falling asleep right in my chair. It's kind of scary. When I wake up and don't know where I am."

"We would not give you anything to hurt you. Of course, anything we administered is meant for your wellbeing. How are you feeling?" Sal walked closer to Sam and peered into his eyes.

"Okay, I guess, confused most of the times. Right now, I'm very sad. I don't know why," Sam answered with words he believed they needed to hear.

"Does our personnel treat you properly?" Milo asked.

"Personnel? Oh, you mean the aides, the nurses?"

"That's right."

"They come and go. They keep me clean. My room's nice and neat. This place smells good too with whatever they use." Sam knew they didn't want to hear any complaints.

"You had visitors earlier and seemed disturbed. Everything okay now?" Sal asked.

"They overwhelmed me, just too many people and all at once. Some smelled of smoke and I hate cigarette smoke. The smoke made me feel claustrophobic, and I felt like I was being smothered. The room started spinning. I felt a little nauseous. Did I hurt anyone's feelings?"

"It wouldn't matter if their feelings were hurt. It's your health we're concerned about. You did the right thing. I wish I knew about your aversion to cigarette smoke. We wouldn't allow them to enter the building let alone your room. Milo make note of Mr. Termine's comment and let's establish a policy about secondhand smoke. I know what he means about residual smoke," Sal said while making gestures showing his deep concern.

"Did Mr. Tolski bother you?" Milo added trying to show his concern.

"Was that the man's name?" Sam tried to appear droopy and then added, "No, not at all. He seemed to be a nice guy. He just asked a lot of dumb questions. I don't even know why he was here. Do you know what he was trying to do?" Sam said as he gave a big all-American yawn.

"What sort of problems did you talk about?"

"He didn't tell me about any problems. What problems should he be asking about?" Sam asked as naively as he could.

"I don't know of any." Sal answered. Then he couldn't wait any longer and asked directly, "I wondered if you had any problems."

"My only problem is that I'm here and not able to take care of myself. You folks have seen a lot of patients. Tell me, do you think I'll ever get well enough to be on my own again?"

Sal looked at Milo and said, "Listen to him. He's almost on his feet, and he wonders about getting better. Mr. Termine you're practically out of here. It's up to you and good old Doctor Lunkens. You take care and get some rest. Let us know if you need anything."

A moment after Sal and Milo left the room Sam gave them an obscene gesture with his arm. He sank into his chair and mumbled, "You lying S O Bs, and who is Doctor Lunkens?"

***

"Make certain he keeps taking the drugs. He looks too lively to me. Ask Lunkens if he can tolerate something super strong. Termine's a smart cookie. I want him to be a non-problem."

***

Sam waited a few minutes and rolled to the door. He looked out and then up and down the hallway. With no one around he slowly ventured outward and safely into the hallway. He aimed towards the recreation room, carefully peered in and saw a group of women at the far end. He recognized Mary Archer, moved quickly towards her and said, "Hi, Miss Archer. I'm trying to get around on my own and . . ."

"Shush. You can't talk in here either. You're disturbing our tranquility." Mary turned to make certain none of the staff were in the room. "Go to that corner and wait for me."

Sam, shaking his head in disbelief, obediently went across the room. Mary followed him. "I'm happy to see you up and moving about. Are you getting the feel for this hell hole?"

"Maintaining silence is an annoyance, how can I see the bad stuff?"

Mary looked around again and when satisfied said, "You want to see for yourself? Tomorrow at approximately 10:00am you will hear sounds coming from room A122. That's Emma's room. She's a very dear lady who is bedridden. Her roommate is worse off; she can't communicate." Mary again checked and whispered, "A horrible violence — oh we don't have time for easy words. Forgive me. Very simply, Jack rapes Emma."

"What? Oh God! Miss Archer that's crazy."

"You're in line with everyone's reaction. We're crazy."

"Oh, Miss Archer, that's a tough one to believe."

"I know. Sam, you don't have to believe me, go and see for yourself." Mary again looked about to be certain they were still alone. She then continued, "Even worse, whenever Gail is on duty she participates in her own ugly fashion. They're so bold they do everything in the nude."

"Now how do you know that?"

"How do you imagine I know? See all the women over there. They know what I know."

"Miss Archer what are you telling me . . ."

"Every one of us in this room felt their sting and suffered the pain of their lust. We're all scarred by those two devils. We had our turn and now they're defiling Emma. The poor woman is going out of her mind."

"Let's talk about you, Miss Archer. You said Jack raped you. Did I hear you right?"

"You heard me. It was worse than rape because the two of them made us do horrible things. The tastes of their bodies are burned into us. I can't spit enough to clear them from me. They know more ways to violate a person than I ever imagined. They are evil, evil people."

Sam looked at his old teacher and said, "I am so sorry I — I . . ."

"Oh Sam, say no more. It's so unfathomable it becomes too difficult for any sane person to understand. This is a very bad time in my life. There was a time when I thought about men, marriage and a big family. Time went by — I enjoyed my job, and my students. The fantasy of getting married, living a family life got pushed far into the background. I guess it could've been fun — it didn't happen. What I'm trying to tell you: before him -- before him I never had sexual intercourse. During my entire being, my body never received a man. When Jack — it was — it was very painful. I was in agony — and he laughed. They both hurt me and they laughed. I was in a tortuous hell. After that I cried for a very long time. I went into a bad depression. They drugged me. It didn't help because I cried right through the medications. I cried and cried. The other women wanted to help me. At first I couldn't talk to them. I felt a deep shame? I was ashamed of what happened."

"I don't understand. Did you scream and shout for help? Or after, did you accuse them? Did you go to the administrators of this place? What about the authorities?"

"Oh, so many questions. Of course, I screamed for help. No one came. Right after, I reached out to many people in an attempt to get help. They listened, showed outrage then nothing." Mary put her head down showing her despair. She sighed and let out a deep breath of frustration. "Then they ravaged every woman in our area."

"Why didn't you all get together and complain as a group?"

"You would think that would be the way to get results. We tried. It didn't work. You have to understand, Jack is the all-American Boy. Everybody believes whatever story he tells. And part of that tale is we're all classified as demented or subjected to hallucinations."

"What about the men on the floor? Are they also abused, you know sexually? What about me?"

"Jack is strictly out for women. His appetite is insatiable. Gail is also strictly for women. She likes other women to do things to her. Use your imagination, or go see for yourself."

"How can I see? Don't they lock the door?"

"None of the doors lock. You can't even lock the toilet." Mary drew in a deep breath and again heaved a big sigh.

Gail walked up to the entrance of the recreation room. She looked at the women at the far end. Everyone appeared to be quiet. She left as quickly as she came.

"Never know when that witch flies in on her broom. Always be cautious. She didn't spot us this time."

"Why . . ."

"You shouldn't be here. Go back. If you need validation, visit Emma before you return to your room. Talk to her; get the feeling of her absolute fear of dying. She believes she is continually committing grievous sin with the devil. The poor soul believes that when she dies, she will go right to Hell. She is in torment and is still being physically abused. Sam, you want proof? It's right next door to you. Tomorrow morning, about ten, listen very carefully, and you can hear them."

"Why at ten?" Sam asked.

"Think about it. By ten everything is supposedly in place. The aides are either in the laundry or helping in the kitchen. If any are in this area, they know not to open a door that is pulled shut. Any closed door is sealed with fear. Jack's drummed it into every aide who ever worked this wing. Leave a closed door alone. Everyone's afraid of Jack. He knows he's in control."

"If I leave now, will I be allowed to go into Emma's room?"

"No, of course not, you'll be stopped! You have to sneak in. If they catch you, just act dumb and confused. Ask for help to your room."

"I'm going to try." Sam said as he slowly rolled out in the hallway.

Mary returned to the group giving them a thumbs-up signal. Receiving the message each nodded in approval. Sam may be the man who will help them.

***

Gail turned the corner from the end corridor and saw Sam in the hallway. She picked up her pace and walked towards him. Her voice reverberated within the hallway as she yelled, "You feel strong enough to be moving around like this?" She caught up to him and grabbed his wheelchair. "You're too weak for this. You belong in bed." He felt the surge as she propelled him into his room. She spun him around so he faced her. "And you're just a really lucky guy, because I'm going to get you a new goody. Most of the time it's taken with a meal, I think you need that treat right now; don't go away. Understand?"

"Oh, I understand," Sam muttered. "It's just what I need: some more pills."

Sam closed his eyes. A few moments later, he heard Gail reenter his room.

"Open wide," she said placing the medication directly into his mouth. "Come on, swallow, and drink all of this."

Sam maneuvered the pill under his tongue, drank the water as ordered and handed the empty cup back to her. He lowered his head staring into the floor.

"Someone will be here shortly. They'll get you into bed. And that's where you will have a delicious supper." Gail patted his head and said, "Now aren't we nice to you?"

The moment Gail walked out Sam disgorged the pill into his hand and wheeled into the toilet. The moistened medication needed a soft flow of water to carry it down the drain.

Sam noticed a small trace of light coming from the edges of the opposing toilet door. He listened; not hearing anything moved closer. Placing his ear on the door caused it to open, just enough so that he could see in. Peering into the quiet room gave him confidence, although he rolled in very slowly. Two people were bedded — neither paid any attention to him.

Sam moved deeper into the room. Glancing at the nameplate on the footboard of the first bed he read: "Emma Joslin," The woman, fully awake and staring up at the ceiling remained very still. He pulled up close to the bed and said, "Hi, Emma. I'm Sam Termine. I'm your neighbor."

Emma turned towards him and gazed at him with dark sad eyes. "Oh Sam, I am so afraid. Can you help me? Can anyone ever help me?"

"Of course − if I can − I'll help you. Tell me, why are you afraid?"

"I fear death. Not because of dying -- I fear what awaits me. I am a horrid sinner − I sin − I have no way to salvation."

"Can I call a minister or priest to help clear your conscience?"

"They cannot help me. I'm possessed by the devil. He and his dark angel force me to live in continual sin. I don't have the strength to stop. They use my body and I have to do terrible things for them. I pray, and I pray, and God does not answer my prayers. God has abandoned me. He has abandoned me because of my sins."

"Emma, you are wrong. God hasn't left you. He's here. I'll pray for you. Please believe me Emma, together we shall exorcise this devil. You have to trust me. I promise you; while you still live you shall be freed from this evil. God will welcome you into his paradise."

"Dear sweet Lord, I pray you are right. My mind has not as yet abandoned me. I feel good with you here. You must be a good man. Please don't go. If you leave I know I will sin again. I will add to my horrible burden of a blackened soul."

"Emma, I can't stay. I'm so sorry for your pain. Believe me Emma, I will be back," Sam said as he quickly returned to his room via the shared toilet.

***

"So far everything Miss Archer told me is true. I've got to get out of this zoo," Sam murmured to himself.

An aide entered Sam's room. He waved a welcome and yielded to her efforts to change his clothes. She worked quietly and efficiently and within moments, he was in bed. When the aide tried to draw up the covers he shook his head. She left the room. The covers remained at the foot of his bed.

Alone and unencumbered by the bedding he began to exercise his legs. He pushed on the end board feeling a limited measure of strength. He pointed his toes, pulled up his knees.

Sam's promise to Emma tortured his conscience; he had to find a way to help her.

SIXTEEN

"*Okay! I can play your game. You want me in bed. I'll stay in bed. Stay in bed all day, sleep and get some good rest. Then the night will be mine,*" Sam said to himself.

Having placed his trust in Lani, discarding all drugs allowed Sam's body to purge their earlier effects; his mind recovered its clarity. Sam's strength also returned faster than he thought ever possible. His muscles responded beautifully to the stretching and simple exercises. Returning to health became Sam's clandestine battle within the confines of Belvedere Manor.

His routine usually worked. Now, when Sam tried to sleep, he failed. Closing his eyes he reflected on the various ways he learned to relax. His mind drifted; his muscles lost their tension. His breathing slowed down; his body sank into the mattress. Sam began to envision himself again practicing Tai Chi. He opened his eyes very slowly; he thought about the wonderful feeling of wellbeing while practicing this soft martial art. The daily sessions had lasted for years — then he stopped.

Sam had a great Tai Chi teacher. He and everyone in the class felt a sense of accomplishment. Her students were diverse, an unusual mixture of age, gender and ability. The odd mixture of people didn't matter. They all worked hard absorbing her lessons with equal vim.

Sadly the classes ended when an enticing job offer wooed her away from the area. Some tried to maintain the group and encouraged each other to reinforce what they already learned. Without a designated leader, problems developed when opinions clashed as to the-right-way to perform. Unable to resolve the numerous conflicts ruined the harmony stifling Sam's enthusiasm; he stopped practicing.

Sam reflected on the joy of the past. Those were wonderful days, and he realized he desperately needed that Tai Chi discipline and concentration. The moves were beautiful. If he started, he thought he would remember. It would augment his simple stretching and exercise.

He tried to recall the various forms with the associated breathing and mind control. It came slowly then flowed back. Just rethinking and mentally reviewing the basic motions gave him a feeling of confidence; he knew what he had to do.

The light of the day passed. Sam sat up in his bed, looked at the clock. It showed 10:20pm. Then as quietly as possible, he lowered the rail of his bed cringing when upon reaching the bottom it made a clanking sound. The hallways remained very quiet. His thin legs moved easily over the edge. Dangling them there for a moment, until he gained some self-reliance, led him into swinging them back and forth. He aimed his toes upward and downward, rotated his feet until they pointed towards each other and then away. The stretching exercises Lani suggested had worked its magic. He felt confident. It was time to try to stand.

Sitting on the edge of the bed with the floor still about twelve inches away from the bottom of his feet gave Sam a tinge of panic. He closed his eyes and took in some deep breaths. The floor looked even further away when he reopened his eyes. It appeared to be too far. He had to find a safe, simple way to get out of bed.

Sam pulled his legs back onto the bed. He inched his way towards the middle, rolled onto his stomach, rotated so he lay sideways while wiggling towards the edge. With both legs dangling, he pushed lowering his feet to the floor. The tiles felt cold as his toes touched. The bandaged part of his body still resting on the mattress began to ache. *"No pain, no gain,"* He said to himself as he gritted his teeth.

With most of his weight now on his feet, there wasn't any indication of a problem with his spindly legs. He, very slowly, raised his body. While holding onto the bed rail for support Sam allowed his legs to absorb his total weight. The effort made him feel slightly nauseous; clammy hands held onto the bed railing. Sucking in a few deep breaths eased the roiling of his system.

The cold floor penetrated into the soles of his feet. Then a simple push on the bed rail had Sam standing upright.

Standing achieved only part of his goal. Removing one slippery hand from the bed rail he rotated his body, very slowly by the shuffling of his feet. *"One little step at a time,"* he muttered. The motion, easy and feeling natural, proved he had a good sense of balance. Plus his legs had sufficient strength to support him. Although he surmised he had to maintain contact with the rail it gave him needed assurance. Using mini-steps he traveled towards the end of the bed. The excursion took its toll. Feeling extremely tired didn't matter; he wasn't finished. Sam made a simple turn and repeated the movement.

***

The many nights of stretching and exercise proved their worth; Sam could walk, albeit aided by the bed rail. His confidence soared.

Sam placed both hands on the rail then moved outward extending his arms until he was about twelve inches away. Opening his hands, his fingers unclenched remained in contact while his thumbs slowly moved away. The movement formed ideal Tai Chi hand circles. His open hands, still leaning on the rail, turned inward, slid towards each other and stopped when within an inch of touching. His hands and arms now formed the beginning of another circle. Sam felt the effects of the Chi energy. He pulled a very deep inhale through his nose and sensed his body expanding with each breath. Exhaling, deliberate and slowly through his mouth, emitted a barely audible "*foooo*". Sam adjusted his feet by alternately shifting weight and moving them apart until both were at shoulder width. Tucking his chin made his head erect; his shoulders relaxed.

Sam began to recall the precise Tai Chi posturing. Now confident with his balance, he continued by lifting his hands. They floated upward and stopped when reaching the height of his chest. His arms and hands maintained the beauty of a circular form while he assumed a meditation stance. Sam's eyes picked an imaginary target beyond the wall. He stared at it, and then the serenity arrived. His vision closed down into a tunnel of fog. He looked. Saw nothing. The meditation stance working its miracle allowed his body to feel a wonderful sense of peace; his mind acknowledging the splendor of the moment.

Sam broke his trance. The joy of the accomplishment filled him with a desire to continue. Now filled with conflict, Sam returned to his bed, stretched, and felt his body relax. Knowing this outing was only the beginning, he had to continue. The night still offered time.

Now remembering the Tai Chi routines, he yearned to work through the classical moves. Sam wanted to perform a set filled with exacting precision. Buoyed up by his earlier success, Sam rolled and slipped to the floor. He stepped away from the bed, stretched, relaxed and stretched again. His body responded as he pulled in breaths of air charging his lungs. Controlling his breathing, Sam expunged the air with a slow deliberate release; then assumed the grounded Tai Chi starting position.

Using the moves he learned years ago, at first, his balance wasn't perfect, yet adequate. The pace he set, slow and deliberate required a totality of concentration and body control. He moved slowly; he began to perspire.

Sam recalled and performed the exercise through eight, albeit somewhat compromised, moves. His hurting body blunted the precision demanded. The subpar performance did not matter. Every exercise, regardless of accuracy, offered him an opportunity to release the flow of Qi energy within the meridians of his system.

Sam stopped, assumed a mediation stance grounded to the earth with arms up and chest high. His arms, legs and hands formed those critical circles. With breath slowed Sam stared into the void before him. A wonderful feeling of peace again purged his uncluttered mind. After an unmeasured amount of time, when ready, he broke the trance and bowed.

Feeling energized Sam crawled into bed; his body, moist with perspiration, began to relax. Checking the time, Sam realized he worked about four hours. A new worry penetrated his joy. Did he overdo it? Will the night's activity hurt him more than help him? Though his thoughts pondered the questions, he responded orally, *"This is the only way. I've got to keep moving."*

***

Sam couldn't rest while reflecting upon Mary Archer's story about his neighbor Emma. From what she said, they go at it around ten in the morning. That he had to see.

Sam again got out of bed, very carefully, and navigated towards the toilet. The ambient light within the room proved adequate. Now able to see he opened the toilet and entered. When he closed the door, the extreme dark forced him to reopen it, just a crack. Then pushing on the opposite door met with complete resistance. To lessen the tension he tugged on the knob and slowly turned it open. The door moved easily; he pushed, very gently, until it parted about a quarter of an inch. Sam peeked in and knowing the layout saw the closest bed: Emma's bed.

Sam had to find some sort of an obstruction; something that would stay in place keeping the door slightly ajar. As a norm in his room, the toilet door always showed a small opening. If it was the same for Emma's no one should notice.

Upon returning to his room, he searched his table and then his roommate's.

Locating a stub of a pencil gave him some hope.

Sam, abandoning his cautionary style of walking returned to the toilet. He knew he needed some sort of adhesive to keep the pencil in the jamb of the door. He saw the soap dispenser. A simple push on the lever caused a burp while emitting a white stream into the sink. It felt gooey enough. He dabbed a little in the frame of the door. The pencil stayed in place. He tugged the door, very gently, until it met the impediment creating a three-inch gap. That large a space could attract attention. He only needed about a quarter of an inch. Sam retrieved the pencil and bit it in half. The soap tasted terrible; he spit into the sink rubbing his mouth on his sleeve. Placing the thinner piece back into the door's jamb allowed the door to remain open a tiny bit, more than adequate for his voyeurism.

***

Sam checked the time: 4:36am. With daybreak still hours away he felt tired. He didn't need any pills to fall asleep.

SEVENTEEN

The constant clamor of the morning crew penetrated the veil of Sam's comforting slumber. It also warned him to be wary. Though sleep now failed him, Sam kept his eyes closed; he controlled his breathing and tried to meditate.

Gail dragging her medication console spun it around viciously and deliberately slammed it into Sam's bed. The sudden contact, muted somewhat by his hanging blanket, surprised him, yet he remained unmoving with his eyes closed. Gail, bemused by his apparent stupor reached in yanking back his threadbare sheet. Sam did not respond. She tapped him on the chest.

"Wake-up my sleeping beauty. Come on let's have another bite of the apple."

Sam opened his eyes, blinked a few times, turned his head and pretended to focus on his tormentor. She pulled him up into a sitting position placing a water cup in his hand.

"Okay droopy-drawers open up; open your mouth and show me those pearly whites."

Sam thought he had prepared for this kind of an onslaught. It was Gail's shrieking voice assaulting his senses that made him feel the danger; his heart thumped with fear. Gail shoved a tablet into his gaping open mouth.

"Come on. I don't have all day," she demanded.

Sam took a sip of the water. Gail's eyes followed his moving hands; she didn't see him push the medication under his tongue. Tossing his head back, he faked the downing of the medication by swallowing a big gulp of water.

Gail retrieved the empty cup and sang, "Good night." She, having nothing for Mr. Whitman, pushed her cart from the room.

Sam spit the pill into his hand, reached over the bed rail and deposited the saliva laden drug in the hanging urinal.

***

Explicit orders, citing Sam's current health and future wellbeing, now demanded total bed rest. That order required aides to change his bedding, wash him, feed him, and dress him in clean nightclothes all the while Sam remained in bed. That part he could tolerate. He followed their motions and wordlessly moved as needed. It took extreme fortitude for him to use the portable urinal and the ever present bedpan. Even though the toilet was a mere few steps away, he had to play their game.

Lani tending to him at times sympathized with his plight. She too could not violate the bed-rest order. It was cruel and physically debilitating. She wished that she could just scoop him out of that prison and give him his freedom.

They could keep him in bed; they couldn't stop her from offering loving care and encouragement.

"You're still very skinny. When you move, I feel some strength in your body."

"And that's thanks to you."

"To me, you feel cold. Do you need another blanket?"

"No, what I really need is a pair of socks."

"Don't go away," Lani laughed as she rushed out of the room and walked down the hallway.

She waved a hello to her friends as she pushed open the laundry doors. Some offered a smile, waved back and then continued with their chores.

"Socks, men's socks," Lani said, trying to talk above the noise of the washing machines and dryers, then pointed to her feet.

One of the women nodded in acknowledgement, walked towards the wall of large dryers and the sorting tables. She searched the various piles of freshly laundered clothes found a matching pair and handed them to Lani. The heat of the drying cycle warmed her hands.

Lani pocketing the socks felt their warmth against her body. She expressed her thanks by blowing a kiss.

"Think these will fit?" Lani asked Sam.

"Where did you get them?"

"A nice guy wanted you to have them," she said laughing.

***

At 9:00am with the entire place dead quiet, Sam still feeling groggy. He tried sitting up shaking his head in an attempt to dislodge his weariness. Fidgeting around, sucking in deep breaths all proved to be feeble attempts to remain awake. He dare not fall asleep. The clock moved slowly. As it approached 10:00am he felt a surge of trepidation. His heart beat rapidly; apprehension and fear tried to take charge; his bowels rumbled.

Sam's sweaty hands grasped the bed rail, lowering it quietly. If Mary Archer's story had any merit, then Gail and Jack should not be roaming the halls. They were the only ones who cared if he violated the order of bed rest. Pushing down the covers and shoving the tray towards the foot of his bed eliminated any impediment for a fast out and in.

Surveying his path, he planned his movements to minimize motions and noise. Though the weariness still stole some strength, he felt ready.

A few minutes before ten o'clock he heard the groan of door hinges. The door to Emma's room closed with a solid thud. Whoever entered her room did so with authority and with little concern for the noise. Sam's heart pounded; he could hear his pulse. Opening his mouth, Sam took in and expelled gulps of air. Within a few moments, he could be an eyewitness to an assault; an assault by people who were in complete control over every aspect of his life.

Gentle sobs from Emma's room broke his reverie. He heard her stifled cries. Though the sounds were barely audible, Sam thought he knew what they were and who was making them. Then he heard the guttural grunts accompanied by other compelling din. It offered some validity to Mary's accusations. To be certain, Sam had to see this tragedy.

Last night's activity brought back his sense of balance. The days of stretching and strain produced sufficient tone needed for this venture. Sam slid out of his bed safely. He pulled on the toilet door opening it slowly and as quietly as possible; a gentle push while holding the knob made it close sans noise. The toilet now lit by the faint glow of light from the opposite door allowed him sufficient visibility to move with confidence. His feet, shrouded in borrowed socks, moved soundlessly towards the screams of torment -- and sighs of gratification.

Sam got as close as possible making certain he did not touch that door; a door held ajar by a pencil sliver. He held his breath, peered into the room and the shock of the atrocity made him shudder. His eyes, now tearing, lost their focus. Anger welled within him. He fought the urge to take immediate action. Knowing he did not have the strength to rescue this poor woman from her agony, moisture ran down his face.

Sam shaking with hatred brushed away his tears. He watched Gail and Jack dominating poor Emma with neither of them showing any empathy for the poor woman beneath them.

Gail's sexual appetite, quietly consumed her victim while she ignored Jack violent attack with his torso and head in constant motion. Sam stopped breathing when Jack turned towards him. He remained motionless until Jack again twisted away.

Sam, within the darken room, retreated by feel. His door opened easily. Then he decided to minimize any hinge noise by closing the toilet door in a very fast controlled manner. Though he eliminated the squeak the motion created an air pressure against the opposite door forcing it to open a few inches.

"Who's there?" demanded Jack.

Sam ran to his bed, crawled in, and pulling the covers up tight, feigned sleep. In his haste to settle in, he forgot the bed rail; it remained in the down position.

Pondering his fate, he believed he should ignore this stupid mistake by merely mimicking a sluggish doped up bed-bound patient.

That little creaking door made Jack, and Gail, instantly abandoned their fantasy. Jack, while still naked, jumped from Emma's bed and entered the toilet. He pushed on Sam's door and looking into the room could only see the two men in their beds. His anger spiked; he felt trapped. Jack didn't dare to enter the room knowing anybody in the hallway could see into Sam's room. No matter how angry he felt, he didn't want to expose himself.

"Someone wants some big trouble. Get dressed and let's look around," Jack ordered.

Gail responded to his urging by carelessly tugging on her clothing. "What's your guess? Who are we looking for?"

"You look like hell. Good God woman you're losing it. We've got to remain in control, and the first thing is to appear normal. Fix your clothes and comb your hair."

Gail stung by Jack's comment finished her grooming by using Emma's brush and comb. She wiped her lips clean of the brilliant red lipstick. Now satisfied with her appearance, she turned towards her victim. Emma realizing the torment of the day was almost over remained in her propped up position. Gail flipped Emma onto her back, grabbed the extra pillows tossing them to the floor. Emma remained passive allowing Gail the freedom to do as she pleased. With a few rough motions, Gail wrestled Emma's arms in her nightgown, pushed her back and pulled the single garment to the woman's feet.

The slime from Gail and Jack remained on Emma's body; she knew it would permeate her clothing; it wouldn't dry for a long time. That moisture would be a newest reminder of her living in sin.

Gail still seething in anger pulled up the bed rail with an unnecessary force. It made a loud 'clang' when it hit the top.

***

Jack now fully dressed entered Sam's room, walked towards his bed and immediately noticed the position of the bed rail. "Wake up you son of a bitch," Jack bellowed.

A cold chill hit his body the moment he heard Jack's voice. He resisted the urge to respond to the aggressive command. Sam held his breath, then slowly rolled his head up, just off the pillow, and looked at Jack with semi-opened eyes.

"I said wakeup."

Sam generated some saliva within his mouth and forced it out of the corner of his mouth. "Good morning," he said as he tried to present himself as a person in a drooling stupor.

"You're not fooling me. Sit up and talk to me."

Sam's heart raced. He ignored the command to sit up and remained supine. "Ah it's Doc Tridon. Good morning — good morning," he repeated and attempted a weak smile.

Jack pulled back the covers and went directly to Sam's feet. He held both up. They were clean. He felt them, and they were warm. With a show of disgust, Jack dropped Sam's feet back onto the bed.

Jack didn't look far enough. Sam's dirty socks rested under the base of the covers. Sam guessed right; the man would search him. Jack jerked the bed rail into its up position. "I think you're going to be a big problem. We should get rid of you," Jack threatened then turned and walked out into the hallway.

Sam tried to return to his pretense of sleep; the stimulation of the events robbed him of his plan. His breathing, fast and labored, remained high as sweat poured from his body.

Jack's final words were evil and menacing; their intent extremely clear and Sam felt very vulnerable.

***

Sam guessed the fast footsteps were Gail's as she ran down the hallway.

***

Mary saw them leave. She noticed Jack's unusual demeanor. A scowl of anger replaced his normal happy mood following a tryst. Another difference: Gail and Jack didn't leave together. Mary knew something happened. This was the first time she ever saw Gail a little messy and disheveled. Then Mary's concern turned towards Sam. She told him about the attacks now wondered if he exposed himself while trying to spy on them. Mary peered down the hallway. Not seeing anyone she rolled across and into Sam's room.

"Did you hear them?" she whispered.

"Yes. I heard them — and I saw them."

"How did you . . .?" Mary started to ask. Sam stopped her.

"How long has this been going on?"

"With Emma, they went back to her about two months ago," Mary said and then added, "Over a year with me — and the others."

"And you notified the authorities?"

"No, not directly, when it started with Jessie, we talked to Mr. Manfassi. That complaint didn't go anywhere. We tried different approaches we told the visiting ministers — and priests. We talked to the women in the office."

"Why don't they believe you?"

"Belvedere needs Jack and Gail; they protect each other, and we are easy to control. Their story is so simple. We're very sick people. And now all of us are viewed as old sexually frustrated women who constantly dream up new fantasies."

"Will they believe me if I tell them what I saw?"

"Sam, we were raped and they didn't believe us. Do you think that for one moment anyone will believe you? Never! In fact, you'll make it worse for all of us if you tried to get outsiders involved."

"How can it get worse? Emma's in a deep depression, and they're hurting her. When's the next time?"

"It's whenever they want. Jack goes in alone when Gail has a day off. He's a lot quicker when he's without her."

"Miss Archer I promise you somehow I'll stop them. I'll work hard and get out of this place and then come back with people who will help."

"You can try. It won't work Sam." Mary pulled up very close and asked, "Did they see you?"

"I don't think so. I got a little careless. Jack came into my room. He thinks I know what's going on."

"It'll be bad to have Jack on your back. He'll make your life even more miserable than it is. Please be careful."

"I'll be alright. My concern is for you, for you and Emma."

"Sam, I know how you and others can help. Stopping them won't be easy. I can't stay here any longer, take care my friend."

Mary quickly wheeled out of Sam's room knowing she left a distraught and physically exhausted man. She also knew this limp pile of skin and bones could be a Phoenix; a challenge to the evil within Belvedere.

EIGHTEEN

Tolski stared at the report sitting in the middle of his desk. He knew it was deficient because it lacked his analysis on information he considered vital. Those comments he heard from Mr. Termine and Mrs. Danzell needled his conscience. He wondered if he failed to find some latent problem. His first inclination was to sign the formidable report and forget anything else. It didn't work. His inner voice wouldn't let him. Paul pushed the report away, left his desk and walked to the office of the department manager. He poked his head past the opened door and asked, "Can I see you for a minute?"

"Sure, what's on your mind?"

"It's about my visit to Belvedere. There's . . ."

"I know what you're going to say. Some of the residents tweaked your conscience. Manfassi called yesterday afternoon and clued me in on the interviews. He told me who you talked to and gave me histories on their physical status including a detailed rundown on medications. Am I getting close to your problem?"

"Right on target," Paul said in resignation.

"Paul, you just completed your first, very first, audit. I gave you one of the best so you wouldn't have any real issues. Please don't screw it up. Okay?"

"I hear you. Sorry I bothered you."

"No problem. I know you want to do a bang-up job, just don't get involved with a lot of nonsense. Some residents, although they're nice folks will say anything to lock you into a conversation; they'll feed you a load of kooky ideas. Most of them are okay. A few are a little — ah you know what I'm trying to say," he said laughing. Tolski smiled and nodded. "Now get out of here and let me get back to work."

***

Paul sat behind his desk trying to recall exactly what he heard from Sam Termine and Florence Danzell. The man's words were most troubling. Since neither of them actually witnessed anything, he decided to do what he should have done before he ran the audit: review the previous year's report.

"I'll wait for it thanks," he said to the sullen guy on duty. The archives clerk remained seated. Paul then said with authority, "I need it now." The clerk looked at him stoically, rose from his chair, reconfirmed the name and year of the required file and plodded off disappearing into the maze of shelves.

Returning in a shorter time than Paul anticipated, he thanked the clerk for this proficiency. Anxious to see who performed this audit, he opened the file, scanned the title page.

He stared at it, and it glared right back. His department manager performed the audit.

Paul, now back in his office, retrieved his own file, removed the Termine and Danzell interview notes, tore them up into small pieces and let them fall like snow into his wastebasket.

Tolski sucked in a deep breath and mumbled, "I personally didn't see anything at Belvedere. I guess I'm just a doubting Thomas. This audit is finished." Paul signed the forms and gave them to the departmental secretary for transmittal to his supervisor.

He took his file, filled with certified documents, and dumped it into his opened cabinet.

***

The State audit agency did not approve anything. Using a negative concept they worked to find reasons for disapproval of a facility. Always believing a latent deficiency could exist, a blanket approval would automatically accept that deficiency. Therefore, Belvedere Manor would receive a letter stating the recently performed audit had zero deficiencies. It also indicated they can operate for another year provided they continued to follow all rules and regulations. It basically meant: don't screw up.

***

In the A wing, Gail and others maintained the bed-rest order for Sam Termine. Thinking the numbing medications made him robotic they deposited subsequent doses into his hand and he palmed the pills while swallowing some air with a gulp of water.

Sam didn't have to feign his need for sleep. His fatigue, totally normal for a guy doing nightly exercises, provided the proof to Gail that the prescribed drugs worked.

Jack and Gail smiled whenever they walked by seeing Sam in a deep sleep.

***

When Sam's meals arrived, he stirred with a nudge, ate what they offered and quickly returned to his slumber. The daylight, along with its ambient noise, slowly dissipated into the quiet of the night.

Sam, like a Dracula, stirred when the facility went dark. Now 9:00pm, the halls were deserted. He rose from his bed, slid to the floor and performed some preliminary Tai Chi stretches. He moved with newly gained confidence and felt the excitement of the pending activity throughout his body.

The night nurses never made rounds in any wing. All residents, according to the charts, were properly medicated and asleep. Grossly understaffed, they seldom found a reason to walk the halls.

Sam peered out the doorway. Looking both ways he didn't see anyone. Returning to the center of his room, he began an exercise. Even though he felt the pinch of the bandages on his upper torso the occasional twinge of pain proved tolerable; his meditation-in-motion flowed smoothly.

Sam dug deep into his memory trying to recall the minutia of the first set. A little hesitancy at first the moves transitioned into a flow with controlled precision. His ability to perform encouraged him to continue into the next stage. The tentativeness disappeared. His breathing matched the cadence and then varied against the pace of the physical action. With graceful motions he advanced through the complete routine.

The Tai Chi exercise had all the aspects of hard martial arts. The potentially damaging consequences of brutal motions reverted into something beautiful when dampened and performed with finite exacting control.

Sam moved with the required deliberate unhurried pace. He danced a powerful routine placing a special emphasis on his breathing. The Chi energy he sought awoke within his midsection. It flowed and radiated out into the extremities of his body.

Sam was healing physically. He was healing mentally.

The movements felt wonderful. When he finished he assumed a meditation stance — and held it. The pose worked. His body relaxed into a peaceful calm.

Sam slipped out of the stance, albeit very slowly. A moment later, he climbed back into his bed. For a moment he felt relaxed then the horror around him broke the tranquility. It brought him back to reality. He thought about the atrocities.

That horrific event pierced through his peace. His anger flared.

Sam again got out of bed and repeated his Tai Chi exercises. For now, Tai Chi was all he had.

***

Sam buoyed by his ability to get up and move around, decided it was time to get bold and do something beyond his room. He went to the doorway and this time stepped out. Acknowledging it was a careless move he instantly froze and looked about. With no one in sight it allowed him a sigh of relief. He entered the hallway and then crossed over into Mary Archer's room and quietly strode towards her bed.

"Miss Archer, are you awake?"

She responded by opening her eyes, "Sam? Is that you Sam? What time is it?"

"It's a little after two. Sorry to wake you," he hesitated for a moment then added, "We have to talk."

She reached out and grasped his hand. "Thank you for coming. And thanks to the Lord, you're getting well. When did you start walking?"

Sam, ignoring her question asked, "Miss Archer, what can I do?"

Mary heard the anxiety in his voice and said. "I thank God for sending you to us. We so desperately need help. We need you Sam. There're so many of us here who want to escape from this horror. You know we can't do that. We can't run, and we can't fight. Heaven knows we've asked. No one, and I mean not one soul, answered our call."

"I told the State auditor, there was trouble. He listened, scribbled something, and walked away.

"You spoke to the state people?"

"Yeah, he kind of listened and as I said he walked away. Then they came to see me."

"Who came?"

"Sal and Milo, they were fishing for what happened with the auditor."

"Sam, visitors don't want to hear about our problems. We only have each other."

"Miss Archer you wanted to tell me something."

"You have to promise . . ."

"I learned my lesson," Sam said.

"Okay. Abandoned people — people like us, can bond together to protect themselves. We did that right here at Belvedere." She waited for Sam and when he remained quiet she said, "Do you follow me?"

"I guess."

"When I said protect, I meant we can't fight off their aggression. We're too weak."

"With me here, that's changing."

"I hope so — Sam, there's more. We have a need for justice. Even though their abuse has been horrible, our action has to be in a civilized manner."

"That's why we have a police department and a court system."

"You are absolutely right. That is exactly what we did. We paneled our own jury, tried and convicted them."

"You have an underground court with a judge and jury?"

"For those who know, it was visible. Our sessions were held right under their noses."

"What's it accomplished so far?"

"Nothing, absolutely nothing — as you witnessed the attacks are continuing. Mentally, we're preparing ourselves. We're getting ready for very strong action."

"Oh Miss Archer, you gals are mush in the hands of any one of them. All they have to do is blow on you, and you will fall over. What actions are you talking about?"

"Sam before we talk about that, you have to see more of what's going on in this wing." She hesitated and then asked, "Do you know what plans they have for you?"

"I think so. Keep me here for a while. Milk the insurance. Steal from the government programs."

"No! No Sam. You've got it all wrong. It's not for a while, its forever. They intend to keep you here, in Belvedere, by crippling you. They'll make you permanently dependent on them for care.

"How do you know this?"

"You can see what they've done. Just go and look into room A120," Mary said and sat up in her bed. "Sam what's more important is for you to go look at your own records. They're in the computer at the nurse's station. Read about the wonderful treatments you're getting and not responding to." She paused for a moment and added, "Go see your records. Then you will know you're in the battle of your life."

Sam patted Mary's hand and said, "Okay, thank you — I'm tired and there's not enough time to try tonight. I'll see you tomorrow night, if it's okay with you."

"Of course it's okay. Sam please — be — careful."

NINETEEN

"Hi Mom!" Danielle Turner said as cheerfully as she could muster. "How are you doing today?" She gave her mother a kiss on the cheek and before her mom could reply added, "I brought those energy bars you asked for. Kind of expensive if you ask me."

"Oh Danielle what am I going to do with you. Well thank you anyway for the effort -- you know I asked for protein bars."

"Sorry, it's the best I could do. The people in the health food store told me they thought you probably meant this kind." She handed the box over to her mother and said, "If you could only see the people running the store you wouldn't want any part of the stuff they sell. All of them look emaciated and in need of a good meal." Florence examined the box, and Danielle continued; "Now I've done my part. It's your turn. Please tell me why you want these?"

"Danielle, I told you, we're trying to help someone get well. Come on let's go see Mary."

"Mom, this facility supplies all the nourishment any resident could possibly need. Please I beg you. Please don't get involved. You could be doing more harm than good." She sighed and then preached, "It isn't right to offer food supplements. We don't know anything about their physical -- or other problems." Danielle Turner pouted and waited for her mother's reply.

Recognizing her childish posturing, Florence said, "Oh hush! You sure can get into a snit over little things. Let's just go and find Mary." She thought for a moment and then added, "She's probably in the recreation room."

Danielle, pushing her mom with determination, walked briskly through the hallways and corridors. All areas they passed were quiet; no one was in the A wing recreation room. Undaunted Florence Danzell directed, "Okay, let's try her room. It's A123, and I think just around the corner."

Gail heard the visitors, looked up from her desk, and demanded, "Are you lost?"

"No, we know where we are going. Thank you." Florence helped to propel her chair past the station and towards Mary Archer's room.

Gail rushed passed them. "We don't allow visitors in the resident's rooms."

"Young lady, I don't know who told you such a thing; that is utterly ridiculous. Please move out of my way." Gail held her position. "Alright, since you persist in this stupidity let's call Mr. Manfassi and discuss this absurdity." Florence spoke in a loud defiant tone. She glared at the woman blocking the hallway.

Gail recoiling with the rebuke said, "I'm sorry. I didn't mean — it's just Mary and Jessie need additional rest. They prefer to be left alone. I'll be happy to tell them you were here."

Mary hearing the commotion peered into the hallway and said, "Hi Florence." She turned towards their antagonist and said, "Gail if we're interfering with your work — we'll go to the recreation room."

Gail flushed and stammered, "Mary! You must go back to bed. The Doctor says you need extra bed rest."

"Oh, I think you're confusing me with someone else. Goodness knows we have some people who need loads of care. Better check your records dear. Come on Florence."

Gail reddened as the group paraded past her. They entered the recreation room and immediately retreated into a corner. "Better talk fast Florence. The wicked witch will be back with a vengeance."

"Here's a box of energy bars. Danielle bought these when she couldn't find the protein kind. I think there are eight in the box. Will she let you keep them?"

"If she finds them, they're gone. We have a few ways of making things invisible."

"Why do you need a supplement?" Danielle asked.

"They're for our newest guest. He needs to get his body in shape as fast as possible and escape this nightmare."

"What nightmare?"

Mary ignored her question and asked, "How often do you visit your mother?"

"On weekends," she answered showing some embarrassment.

"Danielle that's not good enough. You have to be here every day for the next two weeks."

"Miss Archer, not to be impertinent, what I do is actually none of your business. I take . . ."

Florence Danzell interrupted her daughter and said, "Haven't you learned yet when Mary Archer tells you something it is for your own good. There's a deeper meaning to all of this. Mary's right and I like that idea. You should visit me every day."

"Oh, Mom, that's a tough one. I've got some business trips planned. Please tell me what's going on. Both of you, and I mean both of you, are hiding something. If there's a problem, a nightmare problem, I know I can help."

"Everybody has problems. If you want to protect your mother, then the answer is very simple. You can be a big help to her, and all of us, by being here for a very short visit every day. Vary the time of your visit. Just by your walking through this place shows everyone you care. And when you can, please bring some solid food, bring some nice fried chicken, or a rare steak sandwich. Please no hamburgers or make-believe roast beef. A chicken leg and thigh are enough. A juicy steak sandwich from a restaurant would be great. Use your imagination."

Danielle listened, grimaced and looked at her mother with pleading eyes and asked: "What's going on here? Please tell me."

"Danielle is it so much to ask? Please visit often and do this little chore for your mother. Don't ask any more questions, alright?"

Danielle indicated her frustration by throwing up her hands in an I-give-up gesture then said, "I will be here tomorrow; and Mother, I'd like some answers, answers that make sense."

Mary ignored Danielle's posturing and said, "Bring the food in an inconspicuous package. Thank you." She leaned towards Florence and whispered, "Can't talk now. I'll come to your place tomorrow around the same time." She pulled back and said, "Danielle thank you for your help, especially accepting our eccentric behavior. These energy bars will be useful." She looked towards the hallway. "I know Gail's waiting for me. You folks go and have a nice visit."

Mary watched them leave, waited a few minutes and then wheeled right into the awaiting Gail. "Jack's not going to like this. You better plan on spending a lot of time in your beddy-bye."

Mary fluffed and played with the sweater covering the box of bars. She looked up at Gail and said, "Don't be mad with me. I didn't invite them. Didn't you notice how quickly they left?"

***

Danielle, shaking her head in consternation, pushed her mother and asked "What's going on with Miss Archer?"

"Nothing's going on. All she said was to visit often and bring some delicious food items. I know you will help."

"Absolutely, whatever Mother wants, Mother gets." Florence remained stoic. "Is everything else okay?" Receiving a mere nod of her head as an acknowledgment to her question wasn't typical of her mother. Danielle reacted with a shiver as they approached her room.

Danielle offered a goodbye kiss then an extra-long loving hug. She left the room walking with stern determination to the main corridor and directly to Mr.

Manfassi's office. Looking in she saw the casually dressed man. "Got a minute?"

"Always have time for a member of the family, even on a Saturday. How's Mom doing?"

"That's what I'd like to talk about." Danielle sat down staying on the edge of the chair. She leaned towards Sal and offered, "She's acting very strange, and I'm getting concerned. Has the staff reported any problems?"

"All new residents suffer a mild case of anxiety. Some handle it very well. Others go into various forms of depression. We're very sensitive to these initial reactions. People do crazy things like believing they must be a caretaker of their neighbors."

"This is Mom's problem?"

"As I said most new residents go into a minor depression. Many float over it and settle right in; a few people require a little assistance. I think a little simple medication for your Mother may be necessary."

"What kind of medication?"

"Oh, nothing exotic, I'll ask the nurse to review your Doctor's orders. This kind of a problem is anticipated, and admitting Doctor always a write prescription and authorize to medicate as needed."

"So you have seen something? Is this why you called our minister?"

"Yes — on both counts. We thought time would take care of her distress," Sal lied as he gazed up towards the ceiling. He pulled his head back, stared at Danielle, and said in a soft serious tone, "I'd like to hear what happened. Your observations are very important. Sometimes a family member picks up on a deeper problem quicker than we can. Please try to recall everything that occurred. Little things can be important."

Danielle told Sal about her mother asking for special energy bars. She related their meeting with Mary Archer and her strange behavior going into detail about the request for extra food including the mysterious shroud covering its need. She also mentioned the encounter with Gail and questioned her demeanor.

"Oh, please don't bring any special meals. That's one reason why we didn't want you here during the first week," Sal fibbed. "People want to spoil their family with guilt food. They feel guilty leaving their loved one here. As a solace for their conscience, an easy way to compensate for their failure is to bring in something to eat. Please remember it is our responsibility, Belvedere's responsibility to monitor the diets of the residents. On occasion, a little food or candy from a visitor is fine; sometimes it helps with morale. Little things are okay and are of no concern. Substantial food items, like steak and chicken legs, can be a serious problem. Let me give you an example. You have a good set of teeth and enjoy chewing on a nice piece of meat, so do I. We had a resident, a guy without teeth, trying to eat a chunk of solid meat. His relatives, thinking they were being generous, brought it in. The man loved the taste, broke off a big piece and started to choke. Our nurses saved him using a Heimlich maneuver. That was not a fun day."

"I can only imagine."

Sal continued, "And another concern is the proper type of food a recuperating — or an elderly person, can digest. Are the nutrients balanced? Is the fiber content adequate? Did you know we monitor and measure the nutrients our residents consume? Sustenance is a very complex subject. If you look into the dining room, at any mealtime, you will see a large variety of items being served. That diffuse selection is professionally designed to assure proper nutrition is served to every individual. Outside interference is a huge danger to many of our folks. Get the picture?"

"I got it. It didn't sound right to me, and I'm glad we talked."

"I'm happy I was here this morning. Understanding dietary concerns can save us, both of us, a lot of grief."

"Thanks for your time and advice." Danielle said then added, "I do want direct involvement with my mother. Please no more calls to ministers."

"No more calls and I have your number," Sal said sheepishly.

"Will you ask the nurses to look in on Mom?"

"As soon as you leave I'll do what's necessary. We will make your Mom comfortable."

"Thank you." Danielle started to leave, turned back and pleaded, "Please — take good care of my mother." She left the building grimacing while walking out. Danielle didn't enjoy this visit and yet had a sense of satisfaction knowing that talking to Mr. Manfassi was the proper way to avert potential problems.

***

Sal waited a few minutes to be certain Danielle Turner cleared the area then picked up his phone. "Milo, before you start whining I know its Saturday."

Sal's serious tone intimated they had a problem. "You want me to come in?"

"No, no, it's not necessary. I came into the office today and believe it or not, I had a visitor: Danzell's daughter. She told me, her mother and Mary Archer, were getting chummy. And both of them were acting a little odd."

"I don't like that."

"They asked her to sneak in food; and won't tell her why. Getting friendly with Florence Danzell and her daughter isn't good." He stopped for moment and then continued, "I thought we had a loner in Archer. Why did we put her in the A wing?" Sal didn't allow Milo a chance to answer. "She was a grammar school teacher. We should have anticipated old students bumping into her."

"Sal, she retired years ago. It appeared that . . ."

"Right, right," he said in frustration. "Now she's causing trouble. Ahhh!" he said in disgust. "Jack's not in. Can you find him?"

"Did Gail show up?"

"Oh yeah, I know she's in. That's another problem. Gail had a run-in with Danzell's daughter and I heard all about it. God she's dumb."

"What'd she do this time?"

"Treat an important guest like . . ."

"Like a resident," Milo said laughing.

"It's not funny."

"No it isn't. I'll call Jack."

"Milo, first things first, this Archer and Danzell link is serious. We have to control it. Make certain you tell Jack to tone down the rough stuff. We're supposed to be businessmen not a bunch of sadists. Do you understand?"

"When we gave Jack control, he did his part. He's generated a lot of profit, for all of us." Milo puffed and added, "I know he has his macho needs — how he runs that wing — everything's worked doing it his way. The guy doesn't respond very well to micro-management."

Sal heard the hands-off words and blasted, "In this case, Jack will be micro-managed — now get him on the phone. Have him call me. I need to talk to him."

***

Sal keyed in the page system. Gail, recognizing his voice reacted by instantly reaching for the phone. "Hi, did you page me?"

"Yeah, thanks. I'm looking for Jack. Is he coming in today?"

"That's what he told me. When he does, do you want to talk to him?"

"Yeah I do. Until he does I want you in my office." Sal hung up the phone without waiting for a response.

As the loud disconnect hit her eardrum Gail pulled her head away from the headset. She slammed her phone into its cradle and mumbled, "You're going to pay for that pain Mister Big Shot." Gail pushed some papers around her desk looking for a pencil. She grabbed a pad and an elusive pencil hiding beneath a stack of papers.

The thought of a meeting, and the possible benefits of working with top management, eased her anger. It made her quicken her pace. She arrived at Sal's office, entered without a customary knock, walked right up to his desk and said, "Hi Sal." He didn't respond. She ignored the snub, sat down and asked, "What's up?"

"You tell me what's up. What's with Mary Archer and the Danzell woman?" Sal bellowed.

Gail paled hearing the challenging words. She lost all of her bravado, wiggled a bit to sit on the edge of her chair and offered, "Sal it's . . ." She, sensing someone behind her, stopped talking.

"Hi. I just got into the building," Jack said. "When I saw Gail going into your office, I thought maybe I could be of some help."

Sal pointed to a chair. "Oh I bet I know. It's about the Archer woman, right?" Jack said while closing the door.

"Sit down Jack. We've got a problem." Sal looked directly at Gail and said, "Gail we need you on the floor." She didn't move and Sal continued in a dismissing tone, "Thanks for coming in."

Gail clamped her lips tight, glared at Sal and then towards Jack. Jack stared back and made a sudden head motion towards the door. The non-oral gesture spoke louder than any shouted words. Reddening at her dismissal, Gail arose, walked out of Sal's office slamming the door closed.

Jack pulled his chair closer to the desk and said, "Sal you don't have to tell me, I know Gail's a problem. It's something that needs fixing."

"We have a bigger issue, and its name is Mary Archer."

"I've noticed that she's feeling a little restless. She's been a bit chatty lately. What's she done that I don't know about?"

"Talking to Florence Danzell, she's our new resident in C. Danzell's daughter came to see me. She dumped a story of strange things happening. They were asking her to bring in a lot of food. She doesn't know why, and apparently they won't tell her."

"Does she believe we have a nutrition problem?"

"That's why she wanted to see me. She doesn't know what to believe. I told her this was a typical reaction of a new resident. And that her mother has some anxiety and minor depression."

"What about Mary Archer?" Jack asked. He sat waiting and assuming Sal would let him do the job his way.

"What do you recommend?"

Jack smiled knowing he still had control and said, "She can't have visitors. We have to break Archer from this nasty habit. Sedation is a good start. Plus it'll be easier to control her if she's isolated. I'll move her into a single. We can switch her with Gertie in A126; she's out of it and won't notice a thing. Jessie, Mary's roomie, is easily intimidated. We'll make certain she keeps quiet."

Both turned towards the ringing telephone. Sal picked up the handset and listened. Milo spoke nonstop explaining his failure and venting his frustration at not finding Jack or Harry at home.

"Milo if you would shut up for a minute, Jack's in my office. I'll put you on the speaker."

Sal reiterated his conversation with Jack and asked, "do you foresee any problems Milo?"

"No. I just wonder if we're doing enough."

Jack smiled at Sal while he talked to Milo. "Of course not, she was naughty and needs a little spanking, then sent to bed for a long time. As to possible sedatives, I've got the right stuff. Lunkens set us up with all the meds the floor needs."

"What do you mean by spanking? Are you going to get rough?" Milo asked.

"Hey Milo somehow I've got to get her attention and a little pain at the proper time works like magic. She's no different than the rest. How any stimulation is applied is dependent upon her reaction. I'm not going to drop her drawers and give her a few pops if that's your concern. That's not my style." He laughed as he envisioned his last statement. "I'll do my part. Are you going to contain Florence Danzell?" Jack asked as he rose from his chair with a swagger of authority.

"We'll do something. Drug her up a little. That's what her daughter expects," Sal said. "What say Milo?"

"I think it would be best to keep the C staff out of the loop. I'll have Lunkens come in and take care of it. She'll be in lullaby land very shortly."

"Milo it's Saturday. He's probably on some golf course. We've got to control the problem right now," Sal demanded.

Milo, sensing Sal's urgent tone, asked with a bit of anxiety; "Jack, can you give her something?"

"If you can keep the C nurse busy, I'll visit Florence with her new medication," Jack said with a big grin on his face. "I'm certain her Doctor ordered something to quiet her nerves." Jack rose from his chair and said, "First Archer."

***

Jack walked quickly to take care of business. Gail waved from the nurse's station. He signaled for her to join him. Gail followed at his fast pace and entered Mary Archer's room. Mary wasn't there. "Where is that woman now? Gail, do you have control over these people or what?" he yelled then turned quickly hearing Mary exiting her toilet. "Oh! There's our little troublemaker."

Mary paled as she looked up at the angry man standing over her. She knew she had to pay some sort of a penalty for her violation of the rules. She tried to steel herself from his wrath. Jack swung his right hand and slapped Mary hard on her left cheek; before she could react, he hit her again on her right cheek with his other hand. The second blow, equally hard to the first, made her and her wheelchair spin hitting the wall. Her face began to glow; she felt the pain and heat of his assault.

Gail caught his arm before he could strike again. "Too much on the face, people will notice. Let me finish all of this with a little female gentleness."

Mary withstood his fury and did not cry from the pain she felt. She didn't give them the satisfaction of knowing the severity of the anguish and humiliation they inflicted. Her face showed the finger marks of Jack; her cheeks were puffing up and in need of immediate attention to lessen the damage. Jack grabbed her chair, twisted it aiming it at the door. He wheeled her down the hallway to room A 126. "Get some ice. I'm switching her with Gertie."

Jessie witnessing the assault shook in fear. She turned her chair towards the window, closed her teary eyes and shivered while waiting for a penalty she did not understand. The fear and anxiety made her shout a silent howl of horror. Her mouth opened wide in a soundless screech that she alone could hear. The terror demanded a scream; her fear squelched the sound. Her mouth slowly closed, and her eyes bulged out without seeing. The tears of normal sorrow began to flow, and her skin chilled as she waited for her punishment. Jesse shook with a fear of uncertainty.

Jack, with high energy determination, made the room change by tugging their beds into the other's location. Mary now resided in A126. Jack exhibiting his disdain for both of these women ignored their personal items and left them behind.

Mary with reddened face sat tall and defiant as Gail applied a couple of ice packs. The thermal shock drove spikes of pain into Mary's cheeks; her head throbbed in agony and cascaded her into a state of hatred she never felt before. She looked up at Jack with non-blinking eyes. Jack glared down at Mary and said, "Strip her, completely, and get her into bed."

"Getting her naked is okay." Gail moved towards Mary and cooed, "I need to show her some special affection — seeing her in such pain — has me — it has me turned on." Gail worked quickly and asked, "Do you mind if I take a little break?"

Jack laughed, walked out and closed the door. The moment the door closed he swung it open, popped his head in and said, "Before we forget, you better write-up her fall from bed; make note of our excellent treatment. You can also cite the room change as a special safety measure taken to assure her well-being. And be certain to keep her nude. I want all of her clothes out of reach and placed somewhere — oh I don't care, just somewhere, not here. No more roaming for this one." Jack started to leave and said, "I want you to attend to her at all times. No aides in this room. She talks to you or me, period. I'll cover for the rest of this weekend. Make certain you tell me if you're not going to be here."

***

Jack returned to Sal's office and said, "One down and let's take care of Danzell. Want to join me?"

"Do you have the medication?"

"The same stuff we always use. If we pull her charts I'm betting Lunkens convinced her doctor to give us the option to use it — if needed."

Sal left his office to lure Jen Philips away from the area. Jack left a few minutes later and walked towards the C wing. With no sign of the charge nurse, Jack entered Florence's room, walked up to her and said, "Hi, your doctor, Doctor Juliano ordered some special medication."

Jack gave her the pill, with some water, and waited for her reaction.

"Juliano didn't say I needed a new prescription. Are you sure?"

"Dear Lady, I came today, on my own time, just to make certain you received this. I believe it has to do with your digestion. Are you having trouble with gas?"

Florence paled. She did develop a little upset system generating a lot of flatulence. She took the pill and downed it with a sip of the water.

"Please drink it all. It will help your problem. Oh, and it may make you drowsy. Tell the nurse when you feel tired."

TWENTY

At 2:00am, with everything extremely quiet, Sam peered out the doorway then dashed across the hall. He stayed against the wall while inching his way towards Mary's room. Entering quickly, he approached what he thought was her bed, reached in and gently touched the reposing woman.

"Miss Archer," Sam whispered

"My God, what are you doing here?" Jessie gasped.

Sam reeled back realizing he erred, asked: "Where's Miss Archer?"

"She's moved," Jessie said and then pointed, "126." Hoping to shroud herself from harm, she tugged her covers over her head. "Go away. Go. I don't need any trouble."

Her plea, barely perceptible, achieved some results as Sam with a growing consternation, merely patted the lumped up bedding and whispered, "I'm sorry. I don't mean — I'm going now."

Not knowing the accuracy of Jessie's information, if she was wrong, it could be disastrous. Luckily, Jessie didn't scream due to his intrusion. He could not afford to take any chance that others wouldn't mimic Jessie's docile manner. Talking to Mary Archer could wait. Examining his records at the nurse's station now became his top priority.

Sam backing away from Jessie's bed turned and quietly exited her room. After checking and confirming the hallway remained empty Sam hugged the wall as he walked towards the nurse's station. While passing three rooms, with their doors agape, he heard some sounds slumbering residents; then saw the dimly lit control center. He darted behind the counter and went directly to a darken screen of the area's monitoring system. The power switch glowed. He wiggled the mouse, and the computer came alive. The password for the workstation, inputted hours ago, and never logged out, allowed Sam the freedom to access all data.

After a few false starts, Sam located his file. Reading and concentrating on the information became difficult as he continually looked up in fear. He wished for the safety of his room. He knew the opportunity to obtain any data could disappear any moment. His palms ran with sweat; his breathing labored as tried to digest the facts.

Once he understood the format Sam marveled at the enormity of his records, especially since he only arrived a few weeks ago. One of the records he sought, Physical Therapy, showed Doctor Lunkens ordered therapy 'to restore his ability to function normally'. Sam enjoyed reading it since it seemed generous and a wide-open prescription for any therapist to apply his skills. Then came the entries made by a person named George Faulkins. It indicated Sam had a half an hour of therapy on a variety of days since he arrived.

Sam scrolled down to the section on x-rays. Ten x-rays were logged. They required images of two arms and one leg because of a 'fall from bed'. In sheer disgust, he aborted the site and though tempted did not shut down the computer. Sam had seen enough. The sweating continued; he became light headed thinking about his records with fraudulent entries.

A woman's voice pierced the quiet. Sam heard the intruder talking. Judging by the single voice conversation he assumed she was using a cell phone and had no regard for the sleeping residents. Her loud and agitated voice started and stopped with the heated debate. Each outburst had a finality tone that appeared to settle the call's issue only to respond again and again with equal vigor. Her conversation ended with a loud goodbye. Then her footsteps became softer as she walked further away.

Sam retreated to his room, climbed into bed and pulled up the covers. He pondered on the records, especially the drugs. Not recognizing the names or their intended purposes, Sam didn't know the form, or if he actually took them. Perhaps many of these are also part of the inflated record of his care. His mind swirled with the what-ifs of the drugs knowing some had to be the kind to keep him on his back.

So far, he's confirmed everything that Mary Archer told him. Mary, Jessie, Emma and probably many other in the wing, including him, are part of a money making scheme. He froze as he again heard the squish of the shoes.

Whoever walked the halls stopped a distance away, perhaps as close as the nurse's station. It could be a nurse; it could be anyone, including another resident seeking free use of the telephone. The voice sounded like a woman's. For him it was difficult to hear and discern. As the subdued talking droned on and on, Sam wondered why, since the staff never roamed before, why tonight?

*****

The morning sun began to filter into his window. Dawn changed to morning with a suddenness that made his stomach churn. Then the chatter of the morning crew signaled the awakening of Belvedere Manor. Sam kept his eyes closed, stayed in his bed while the newly arriving people stomped in the hallways.

Sam feigned sleep as the aide came into his room. Since Lani did not work on Sundays, a total stranger walked towards his bed. Sam felt this was the wrong time to play his game of being a sleepy head. The woman had a task to perform; working with her would be easier for both. With Sam's cooperation, she did her chores in a rapid and efficient manner then went on her way to care for others.

*****

Breakfast, delivered by the fleet motion of an aide, rested on his tray-table. The food didn't smell good; it didn't look good and with his newly found appetite failing him, he pushed the spoon straight into the large bowl of oatmeal. It stayed right in place. With a feeling of disgust he gave the tray a vigorous push. The entire table moved away.

He laid back into his bed and closed his eyes. The peace he sought would not come as a constant rattling noise kept him awake. Sam's head rose off the pillow. He looked around to see the source of the annoyance. The din seemed to come from across his room. He saw the enfeebled Mr. Whitson, his roommate shaking his bed rail. When he had Sam's attention, he pointed to his food tray and then pointed towards Sam's tray. The message was very clear. Sam smiled, nodded his head and said, "Mr. Whitson. I thank you. I'm acting like a moron and letting them win. Thanks for the jolt."

As much as Sam wanted to eat the gooey tasteless food, it wouldn't go down easy. Chewing the oatmeal didn't help. Taking a big gulp of water began to dilute it. He swallowed a little bit at a time. When a loud burp erupted, he grinned with satisfaction.

His pillow didn't feel right. Sam tugged it into place, pushed into the middle to form a little nest, laid back and tried to find some sleep. His moments of peace evaporated when he heard; "Enjoying the food Mr. Termine?" Jack entered and walked to Sam's bed. "Open your mouth, time for your medication." Jack waited until Sam sat up and opened his mouth. He placed the pill far back on Sam's tongue. It was impossible to retrieve. Sam had to swallow the poison with the offered cup of water. "Open again," Jack demanded and then checked to be certain he had consumed the pill. "Now you can go and visit the land of Nod."

Sam turned over. He pulled the covers up nice and snug and settled in to sleep away the drug.

***

Danielle entered the building with an authoritative demeanor and went directly to her mother's room. She stopped at the door when she saw her mother in bed. A quick look back into the hallway showed no one at the nurse's station; the place looked deserted. Danielle expected Sunday afternoon at the Manor to be alive with visitors, people all over the place. She never anticipated this level of quiet.

As she waited in the hallway, Jack Tridon walked towards her. Danielle upon recognizing him said, "Excuse me, I'm Danielle Turner. My mother is in room C325. She's in bed...."

"Ah yes! Mrs. Turner I know your mother, and she's just fine. She's been very busy with all the activities around here, and I guess she's tuckered out," he lied. "Why don't you sit in her room and take it easy? Or if you like, we will certainly tell her you visited."

"Isn't there a floor nurse in this wing — on a Sunday?"

"Absolutely — she's taking a break, and we cover for one and another," Jack fibbed. He knew Jen Philips called in sick; they weren't able to get any other coverage.

"I wasn't going to stay very long. I'll leave this magazine," Turner said as she walked towards her mother's bed and decided to awaken her. "Mom, hey Mom, wake up it's me, Danielle" she said while shaking her. Florence opened her eyes slowly and then closed them again in a sense of non-recognition. "Come on Mom wake-up. I want to talk to you." Being a very light sleeper, she always awoke to the slightest touch or sound. Danielle then recalled Sal Manfassi's words: "they would medicate her."

Seeing her mother drugged beyond awaking, Danielle felt a surge of anger rushing into her system. Her breathing became deep and intense; she had to do something to fix whatever they did to her mom. Now sweating profusely, feeling helpless, Danielle needed professional help. She knew Doctor Juliano wouldn't work on a Sunday. Even the brusque male nurse disappeared. "Mom I know you can't hear me — I promise you'll never be treated like this again. I'll call Juliano first thing in the morning. He'll fix this problem. If he can't I will." Danielle suddenly realized, although she began her soliloquy with a whisper, her voice ramped up in volume to beyond normal. No one responded to her rant.

***

Danielle Turner's gut churned. She felt guilty leaving her mother. Before she left Belvedere, Danielle needed to talk with Mary Archer. She walked briskly towards the A Wing. The moment she turned into the corridor, she ran right into Jack.

"Hi, again, looks like you're lost? Come on I'll show you the way out."

"No thanks. I was going to say hello to Mary Archer before I left."

"Mary's not up to having any visitors today. It wouldn't be right to disturb her. Of course if you were a family member — that makes a big difference," Jack smiled as he drew the lines of authority.

"I understand. Please tell Miss Archer, I will visit when she feels better."

"And I'll do everything I can to keep you out of here," Jack said when she was way beyond hearing.

"Mom's in bed. Mary Archer's in bed. I sure hope this is a coincidence, and they aren't connected. I wonder if I can get Doctor Juliano today," Danielle jabbered to herself as she walked out of the facility.

TWENTY ONE

The medication Jack forced into Sam exerted its power; he slept through the day; he had no memory of anything happening on this Sunday. Missing all subsequent nourishment, other than the meager breakfast, yet absorbing the potent medication made him fall into the abyss of a drugged day.

Sam looked at the clock, and it showed 10:20. Though dark outside, the hallway light emitting an eerie glow bled into his room. A sudden urge to urinate hit Sam. He reached for the urinal suspended on his bed rail, fumbled with his underpants then realized they clad him with a diaper. Ripping them off with a driven anger, he made it in time before the flow of relief.

Dressing him as if he was already an incontinent patient was a strong message. He forced himself, albeit a little unsteady, to maneuver out of bed.

The moment his feet touched the floor, Sam while still holding the rail, began his stretching exercises. This time he felt like he was moving in slow motion. Feeling a little more secure he freed himself from the handhold while performing a complete set of stretches. Starting out very hesitantly Sam ended the preliminaries by flowing into a smooth routine akin to meditation in motion. Pleased that he could recall the steps, even under the spell of the drugs, he began to integrate the proper breath control. The yin and the yang of the practice worked its marvel.

It was just past midnight. He should have sufficient time to visit Miss Archer, if he could find her.

Sam peered into the hallway. Not seeing a soul in either direction he waited to break the uncertainty.

If Jessie's was right, Mary was now in the room adjacent to his. Although it may be closer, they were isolated by a solid wall.

Sam moved out quickly into the open hallway. Since most of the doors were notorious for having squeaking hinges, this one proved to be no exception. He entered, by quickly opening and closing Mary's door with a pair of squeals.

Sam couldn't see very well and delayed any motion allowing his eyes to acclimate to the partial darkness. The moon glow drifting in through the window gave the room a little ambient light.

"Miss Archer, Sam — are you awake?"

"I heard you coming in."

"Thank God it's you. Jessie told me — I had my doubts."

"Jack moved me."

"Why are you in this room -- with a closed door?"

"I met with Florence Danzell — and with her daughter. They didn't like that. Now I have a terrible fear for Florence's safety. I hope her daughter has a mind to look out for her."

"Danzell? Danielle? They were here?" Sam got close to Mary and though dark, he saw her swollen face. He put out his hand to touch her cheek and felt the warmth of the welts. He pulled back hoping he didn't give her any more pain than he guessed she received. "Who hit you? I have to know."

"Yes Sam, I agree, you should know everything. Jack hit me. He did it with a violence I never felt in my life. The pain on my body is nothing compared to the pain in my heart. I never imagined anyone could do this."

"Jack? You said it was Jack?"

"Yes, yes, Jack hit me. He slapped me twice. Oh Sam they were so — so hard. My head and neck still throb." She stopped and sobbed, "What followed was in many ways a lot -- Gail she — Gail violated me."

"I'll get those . . ." Sam spit out his threat as he could feel the pain and sorrow in his dear friend Mary Archer.

"Sam, stop it." Mary interrupted.

"No Miss Archer, I want to get out. Then get you out of here, I . . ."

"Oh Sam, if we leave who is going to protect all the others."

"We'll get help to clean up the place."

"What kind of help? You yourself talked to the State people and what happened? Nothing, absolutely nothing happened. And you know why? I'll tell you why. It's because they're very smart. Smart and well connected and no one believed you." Mary's voice got stronger as she spoke. "Sam we're isolated. People on the outside won't help us. We're alone and have to do what has to be done."

"What are you talking about?"

"Do you remember the other day? I told you about our session; we held a trial. Jack and Gail were measured to the standards of normal decency. They were convicted of rape and sodomy. It was unanimous."

"You convicted them? You convicted them with whose law?"

"Our law, our law and we were all witnesses. We were victims and witnesses."

"And I saw what they did to Emma. So what? Who's to punish them?"

"We will. We determined their penalty. We will enforce that punishment."

"What punishment?"

"Sam, we condemned both of them to suffer the pain of death." Mary struggled to sit up. She pulled the covers up to her neck and slumped back into her bed.

Sam moved to help her to sit and said, "You're not making sense. They didn't listen to your complaints. Now you expect some authority to kill someone? Just because you want them punished?"

"No Sam we know we can't do that. We imposed the sentence and we, all of us, have to do it. We have to punish them." She stopped her emotional outburst and sighed. Mary drew in a deep breath and began again; "Our mental health means nothing to them. We're looked upon as a physical commodity. Sam, you are part of their phony income scheme. They are evil, evil people."

"Miss Archer, right now I don't care about them stealing money. I do care about you. I care for people like

Emma. I don't know how all of this happened I just want all of this to end."

Mary and Sam sat quietly. She reached out and held his hands. Each appeared to fall quietly into deep thoughts and prayer. The stillness reduced their tension and then slowed their rapid breathing. Eventually Mary stirred, broke the false calm and said, "Thank you for coming to see me. Your visit gave me strength."

"Can I do anything for you? I mean right now, before I leave. My mind is spinning with what you told me." Sam pulled away from Mary's bed and said, "I'm sorry — you know I can't stay."

"Go. You're a good man. Get out of here — and pray for us."

"Before I go, I will make you a promise. This horror will be fixed." Sam squeezed Mary's hands confirming his vow.

TWENTY TWO

Danielle Turner checked her watch as she waited impatiently for that magic hour. Doctor Juliano's office staff had to be in the office. Before Danielle made her call she allowed a few minutes past the hour. Feeling elated hearing the receptionist voice she sank into despair when the woman said: "I'm sorry. Doctor is with a patient. Would you like to leave a message?"

Danielle, reiterating her need to talk to the doctor received a bland response, "I'm certain he'll get back to you promptly. Do I have the proper number to reach you?"

The receptionist definition of promptly turned out to be three o'clock in the afternoon. Even after that long wait Danielle had to wade through the controlling wickets. "This is Doctor Juliano's office calling. Are you Mrs. Turner?"

"Yes, I am Mrs. Turner. Please. I need to talk to Doctor Juliano." Danielle waited longer than she perceived normal. Her mind wandered and she thought. *"Line up and be ready to talk to the almighty. We can't waste the man's time."* When she heard Juliano's voice she instantly switched to her normal self and gracefully responded, "Thank you Doctor for returning my call. It's about Mom."

"Of course, is she ill?"

"I don't know."

"Belvedere always calls me when my patients need attention."

"So they haven't called you."

"No — please I have a very busy schedule."

"A few days ago, Mom was talking a little crazy. I think you know she met an old neighbor. Actually, the woman was my eighth-grade teacher, Mary Archer; she's now a resident of Belvedere. The two of them are . . ."

Doctor Juliano interrupted her: "Please, what's the problem.

"Mom was with Mary Archer and both were talking about mysterious problems. Neither of them gave me any details. Then they asked me to bring in special food — and to visit every day."

Doctor Juliano, growing very impatient, barged in, "Your mother can eat everything and anything whether it's cooked there, or you bring it in. And you say your mother wants you to visit often. That sounds pretty normal to me. Is there anything else?"

Danielle, feeling uncertain, said very hesitantly, "It was the way they were talking to each other. It sounded very weird. When I left Mom, I talked to Mr. Manfassi." She took a deep breath. "He told me it was a common occurrence for a new residence to let imaginations take charge; alluding to the stress of entering a different environment." Danielle waited for a moment and when

Doctor Juliano remained mute she continued, "He said you prescribed some medication to help her over the trauma of moving into a full care center."

"Mr. Manfassi gave you a straight and extremely accurate answer. It happens to just about every person we admit. Yes, I did prescribe some mild sedative and other typical medications for them to use, as needed." Juliano suddenly realized what he said. Drugs may have been dispensed without his knowledge. His voice trailed off and then continued very softly, "They are professionals. I'm certain they apply their skills with care."

She picked up on the change in the Doctor's tone. "When I visited yesterday my mother was very sleepy. I've never seen her that way. I couldn't get her to stay awake."

Juliano replied in a consolatory manner, "She probably didn't sleep well ever since she arrived. Your Mom is stressed, extremely tired, and then she takes something to relieve her tension. Chemistry calms the mind; and the body finally gets the rest it needs. You too would be droopy eyed and then sleep for a long time under the same conditions."

"Is it your opinion what I witnessed is normal?"

"Yes, it is absolutely normal. Belvedere nurses are very special people. They always reach for the telephone if they suspect a problem. Believe me they're not bashful when it comes to calling for help. Your Mother is in a fine facility. It's staffed with folks who are trained and are dedicated to give excellent care."

"Then you're not concerned?"

"More than that, as I said before, I am confident in the establishment's ability to care for your mother. Remember I recommended Belvedere." Juliano knew Danielle would persist. Since he wanted to end this conversation, he offered, "If it gives you any comfort, I can drop in to see her; just to confirm she's acclimating to her new environment."

Danielle grinned knowing she squeezed out a commitment said, "Thank you. This guilty feeling is getting to me. Your visit will probably help me more than Mom."

"No problem. I'll schedule — hmmm — let me check my calendar. Okay, I can be there on Wednesday. Wednesday morning — that is if no emergency develops."

"I wish it could be sooner -- again thank you." Danielle waited for a moment wishing the man would reconsider. Juliano remained silent. "I'll meet you there. Perhaps together we can get Mom, or me, on the right track."

"Danielle, your mother IS on the right track," he said emphasizing is. "I should be at Belvedere around ten to ten-fifteen. Okay?"

"Wednesday at ten is fine. Thank you again Doctor."

***

After the Monday morning business meeting ended, Milo returned to his office, settled into his seat, leaned back and stretched out his arms to relieve his tension. The ringing of his telephone broke his satisfying stress-relieving motion; he picked up the handset. "Good Morning, Milo Drew."

"Hello Milo — Tina." She waited, when he remained silent she added, "I hope you haven't forgotten the sound of my voice."

"Hello." Milo said in a cold tone. "What can I do for you?"

"This is very difficult for me. I'm more than a little embarrassed — I'm sorry. I became someone who . . ." She stopped, cleared her throat with a gentle cough, and said,

"Well it wasn't me. I want to apologize to you — and to Sal for my behavior."

"Don't know what you are talking about. Do we have a problem?"

"You still like me?" she cooed.

"What's not to like? How can I help you?" Milo said in a business-like tone.

"Be my friend again. We had a lot of innocent fun," she said with a laugh.

"You have always been my friend. Implying we're not friends is a real mystery to me," Milo lied.

"I can be even more mysterious if we can get together. There are some potential clients we can review, if you have some time. Some are very interesting and could be available, no strings attached."

"Are you sure your name is Ms. Morris?"

She laughed coyly and answered seductively, "No, you have it all wrong. My name's Tina."

Milo reacted to the sensual tone by squirming in his chair. He asked invitingly, "Tell me, what's really on your mind?"

She waited briefly and then said sweetly, "Got your interest have I? Well, I'd like to visit sometime this week." Tina anticipating an instant invitation asked, "Today okay?"

"Sorry, forget today and tomorrow. I can squeeze you in, if it fits your schedule, on -- hmm let me see -- how about Wednesday."

"Milo those are such nice words. I love the thought of a squirmy squeeze," she laughed and added, "Wednesday's okay with me too."

"Wednesday it is. Please, not too early — does midmorning sound about right?"

"Good and I'll even bring something for you to munch on," she said with a giggle.

"No need. Tina I have another call coming in, got'ta go, see you Wednesday. Okay?"

"Okay and thanks Milo. See you soon." When the dial tone buzzed in her ear, she too broke the connection. "And I'll bring something to get your attention," she sneered.

Milo walked into Sal's office, plunked down in a chair without an invitation and said, "She's baaaack. Guess who I just talked to?"

"No time for games Milo," Sal said gruffly. "Who are we talking about?"

"Our favorite extortionist: Tina Morris. She's all lovey-dovey and wants to make up. Claims she's seen the light and in the error of her ways. She's coming on Wednesday to make a peace offering."

Sal glanced up at his office manager and asked, "Is she Greek?"

"What? Oh yeah, beware of Greeks bearing gifts. That's not her. She played a ridiculous game, lost big time and now she's hurting."

"And you believe Tina wants to kiss and make up? The woman's no-good Milo. Let her go."

"Sal, we can use her. I can control Tina."

"And you miss her."

"And I miss her."

Sal reached for his wallet, withdrew a bunch of bills and said, "Milo, you don't miss her, your miss her femininity. Here," Sal said offering Milo some money. "Go get yourself some professional physical release."

"Thanks for the offer. I don't need it. I've got my own private stock."

"Tina Morris is trouble, big time trouble. I want to be with you when she's here. Do you understand? I never liked her and now I don't trust her. And one other thing, I thought you were fed up with Tina's sexual appetite."

"Sometimes you don't know how good you have things until they're gone. Sal, I'll be the first one to call you — when we talk company business."

"And how long do you need to take care of personal business?"

"Ah! Time has no meaning when one's in paradise." Milo laughed as he left Sal's office.

***

"Good morning Mary. I'm here to make your day as pleasant as possible. I hope you had a good night's sleep because I feel a deep need," Gail said as she entered her room. "I enjoyed your company so much the other day. I just couldn't wait until we had some more time together."

Mary glared at her tormentor, turned her naked back to Gail and waited for the pending assault.

"Isn't that cute? You want me to play with you. That's good because I have some ideas that will make you feel a new sense of ecstasy," she said as she whipped off the covers and fully exposed the woman. "I have more good news for you. Jack decided that I should dedicate my fun time to you. He will service Emma all alone. Doesn't that make you just shiver with delight?"

Mary felt the woman sidle next to her. She trembled anticipating another session of perverted horror. It seemed like an eternity before Gail satiated her desires and left Mary's bed. Judging by the rustle of clothing she surmised Gail was dressing. Sighing deeply Mary waited for the woman to leave. With the blankets remaining at the foot of the bed, she felt cold, and yet did not dare to reach down to cover her nakedness.

Gail, now fully dressed said, "See how much fun we had, Ta-Ta until tomorrow." Gail opened the door allowing it to remain ajar for a voyeuristic moment. Gail waited for Mary's reaction, and when none came, closed the door with a laugh.

Mary wearily reached down, drew the sheet and blanket up to her chin and prayed, "Please dear Lord, God of mercy, please help us all."

***

Jack left Emma's room with his hair tousled and his clothes in uncharacteristic disarray. "Looks like you had as good a time as I did. My guess is you had a romp with a woman from the wild-wild-west," Gail said.

"I had a chance to try a few new moves. When you're with me, I have only half of a woman. You know I think Emma sort of enjoyed it." Jack smiled then said, "I have to admit I missed your coos and sighs. Have your fun, solo, for the rest of the week. As for Saturday, let's have a real double yahoo."

"You're on. You know I may even get a little daring and get a taste of you," Gail said and gave Jack a wink.

***

When Sam heard Gail and Jack talking about the assaults of Mary and Emma, he clenched his hands into fists and felt the stress within his body. "I've got to help them. I will help them. I will help them." Sam kept repeating the words until they became a mantra — it did not release the steely grip of his tension.

***

Sam, deep in thought, seeking any way he could to aid his neighbors, didn't see Gail entering his room until he heard her say, "Time for your medication. I can see this stuff is really working. Don't you feel better?"

"I'm numb. I sleep all the time."

"You look terrific. Another few weeks of bed rest and you'll be fit to run a marathon."

"Thank you for your excellent care. Although I'm groggy most of the time, believe me, I know what you are doing."

Gail looked at him quizzically, then smiled and glowed thinking his words were a compliment. Realizing she misconstrued his intent he continued, "I sincerely hope that someday I'll be able to treat you to some special things. Something very unique because I know you deserve recognition for what you do," Sam said in a deep voice.

"Now, now, I don't look for favors, though that was a very sweet thought." She gave him an angelic smile that couldn't hide the evil emanating from her eyes. "I love using my skills for the benefit of my patients."

"Miss Summun the result of your work is all around us. As I said, some day you will be recognized for what you've done. That I promise you," Sam said and then immediately added, "And I hope and wish that I'm the one to convey that reward."

Entranced by his faux sentiments, Gail smiled and gave Sam his medication. He palmed it and noisily slurped some water in an enthusiastic swallow. The moment Gail turned to leave he tucked the pill into his pajama pocket.

***

The quiet of the late evening enticed Sam to begin his nighttime activity. He enjoyed the Tai Chi sessions becoming oblivious to the troubles around him.

Assuming a meditation posture cleansed his mind allowing him to focus on the issues. Sam accepted the fact that every resident in his immediate area were in trouble and they were feeding him drugs for the sole purpose of making him a vegetable. His mind now churning forced him to break his stance.

With stealthy motions, Sam stepped out into the hallway towards and then into Mary Archer's room.

"Thank you. I prayed that you would come."

"I heard them talking."

"Sam, I need to talk to you about justification."

"Justification?"

"Sam, please — just listen."

"Okay."

"Do you believe we've been abandoned?" He started to answer. She stopped him. "Do you believe we have the right to protect ourselves? We talked about this before. Sam, I have to be certain you understand."

Sam taken back by the schoolteacher's low, albeit piercing voice, hesitated and then answered, "Yeah, we're alone and we're hurting."

"Sam you didn't answer. Do we have the right to protect ourselves?"

"Everybody does."

"That's the issue. We have God given rights. Sam you came here as a very sick man. Now I feel I can ask you. Do you want to help?"

"Miss Archer you know I do."

"Sam, are you a good moral man?"

Sam replied sheepishly, "Kind of. I didn't go to church too often. I believe in the commandments and the golden rule."

"Do you believe executing an individual is a sin?"

"Yes! I guess I mean no. " Then trying to clarify his answer, "No it's not a sin to execute someone! Yes it's okay if that person is convicted of a serious crime and sentenced to die."

"In our country, each and every state has its own statues. Since we are an island of people, abandoned by the world around us, we also have that right to make our own rules."

"What are you trying to tell me?"

"Sam we established our own court. Then we tried, convicted, and sentenced Jack and Gail."

"And what does that mean?"

"Jack Tridon and Gail Summun have to be punished."

"You can't say it, Miss Archer, can you?"

"Yes Sam I can. The important question is: can you accept it?"

"I don't know."

They both remained silent waiting for each to take the next step in the process that started slowly and was now avalanching them into a world of new unknowns.

"Let's assume we can do something. Aren't you afraid?"

"We've reached a point where our questions don't have answers. The moment we started to welcome our own death any sense of fear lost its meaning."

Sam reached over and gently covered Mary when the sheet fell away and exposed her nakedness. He shook his head in the frustration of their circumstance. "I can't stand the thought of you being in this bed. They have you ready for their pleasure. It fills me with embarrassment and unbelievable anger." He stopped took a deep breath. "I've been sucked into this sinkhole. You're here and now I'm here and I don't know why."

"Sam, we need you. Working together maybe we can stop them. How do you think you can help?"

"I don't know. When I came in here I thought you would tell me. Since you're asking, I guess it's up to me. This is something so different — you know we're not talking about a polite 'please stop', this is about killing someone. That makes me shiver. I never, ever thought, I would or could do that. Is there any other way to stop these animals?" Sam and Mary remained silent. "I'm so confused," Sam said, "talking to people was not the answer. I guess the only way is — I guess it has to be done — am I right? Please tell me." Mary continued her silence. "That's okay Miss Archer, you don't have to say it. I know what has to be done. It's me. Oh God, I'm your executioner."

"Sam, I will make you a sacred promise. If you are challenged by anyone, in anything you do, we are with you. You will never ever be alone."

"And I make you a promise. I promise you, with all my heart, you will not suffer more than one more day. Oh Miss Archer, please try to hold on. I know tomorrow will be another bad day. I will not be able to help you. I need some time."

"Do not take foolish chances. Knowing you're with us gives me all the strength I need to suffer through anything that they do."

"Miss Archer, I am not a violent man. In fact, I'm an old coward. That means doing things with caution. Just thinking about this makes my knees weak. My heart is pounding."

"Sam . . ." Mary Archer started to say.

"Please don't say anything more. I know you're a gentle person. This is against your nature."

"If tears and wishes could cure our circumstance it would have been over a long time ago. We're in a desperate way, and you're an answer from heaven. Don't say you'll fix things in one day. We can hold on for a lot longer knowing you're helping us."

"No, waiting will only steal what little courage I have. One more day is all I need. Please keep praying," Sam said. "If I'm lucky, within two days, one of them will be gone. I may fail and . . .," His voice trailed off as he envisioned his own death. Then breaking the spell said, "If I fail the scandal should give some relief."

"Bless you Sam. My prayers will be for your safety."

"I'm sorry for what you'll have to live through. It's making me sick to know you'll be — and I can't help you."

Sam reached in, squeezed Mary's hand and walked out of the room.

***

Sam climbed into his bed trying to find answers to his promise. With his mind racing, he could feel his heart beating and then his head searing with pain. He threw his hands up to his head and tried to work out the torment. Small sobs of frustration came out from deep within his chest. Tears rolled down his face and he tasted them when he bit his lips. The taste of the moisture made him realize he was in a rapid spiral and sinking into a serious depression. He wiped the tears from his eyes and said aloud, "I'm a coward." He pulled in a breath and sputtered, "I'm a coward, a coward crying out of fear and frustration. Here I sit in the dark and tremble because of what? I'm scared that's what. Oh God please I beg you help me!" He remained quiet for a while then his mind flooded again with thoughts, *"Am I doing right by taking someone's life? Then — maybe it's not me, instead it is through me."* The idea perked his spirits. It gave him a little relief.

Sam's head ached. He got out of bed and tried to assume a meditation stance. Failing to clear his mind, he dropped his arms and all thoughts channeled into a renewed determination. He had to keep his promise to Mary Archer. The promise meant he had to find a way to kill Jack.

Choosing Jack as his first prey had major advantages. If he found a way to eliminate him, he thought Gail would freeze in anticipation. Plus Jack's death would have police running all over the Belvedere. Everyone would be safe — for a while.

Sam knew the man, if challenged would fight with a brutal vengeance. In comparison, he was a Mister Nothing. Sam would never succeed during a toe-to-toe confrontation. When he watched Jack attacking Emma, Jack was totally engrossed and that made him extremely vulnerable.

Sam had one major element in his favor: total surprise. The advantage of surprise was of little value, unless he had help, or a significant weapon

A pistol would do the job, if he could locate one. In the short time he resided in Belvedere he never saw anyone carrying. He doubted that any of the managers would have a reason to keep a gun in their desk or office. Thoughts of an assault, at a distance, dissipated.

He looked around his room and shook his head. Nothing appeared to satisfy his need. Gazing up at the clock, Sam had very little time left to search the area. His gut rumbled. He began to think about the energy bars that Mary gave him - bars she got from a woman who has a daughter - a daughter who visits. Not remembering the woman or the daughter's names did not matter. He had an outside connection.

TWENTY THREE

The usual din of chirping sounds made by the constant squish of rubber soled shoes on polished floors signaled the arrival of the early morning crew. Since most carpooled they came and moved as a group; their resonance flowed in a melodic wave as they chatted away in their native patois. For Sam, he didn't hear them come in nor did he hear them begin their rounds. He focused his thoughts on trying to find a possible solution to his seemingly impossible dilemma.

"Good morning," Lani said while fussing with his covers.

"Morning," Sam said while reaching for and holding her hands. "Thank you."

"And why are you thanking me?"

"For everything you did for me."

"You don't have to thank me. You needed help, and I am doing my job."

"Again, thank you."

"It's obvious you're working very hard. Are you ready to go home?"

"My body is probably ready; my conscience isn't."

"You can talk to me. I can. . ."

"Lani, I am a healthier guy — because of you."

"And now let's talk about your problem."

"No -- no Lani, I can't put that burden onto your back."

"Do I have to remind you that I warned you about this place? I know what troubles you. These are very dangerous people. They will kill if they have to; they can hide anything they do. You my dear Sam, you are still a very frail man. Heal and get out of here. Go home and don't even think you can fight them."

"Lani I have to tell you something. All my life I wished — I wanted to have a lot of people to love. That didn't happen. I guess — I know it's my fault that I don't have a family. My so-called friends are just casual acquaintances. I don't believe anyone came to visit me while I was in the hospital. And if you noticed, even though I haven't been here very long, no one comes to visit. In just a few weeks I found I have very deep feelings for some of the people here, folks who showed concern for me. They cared for me; and helped me; and because of this place, as bad as it is, I found a family. Now this family, my family needs help; and I mean big time help."

"Sam, I know you're getting well. You're thinking about others instead of yourself"

"You said I'm frail. I hope I'm well enough to use what little strength I have to aid my friends; friends who are in pain, a never ending pain." He drew in a deep breath and continued, "And worse of all, that brutal physical hurt sears directly into their souls. Oh Lani, It's driving me insane. Where's the justice in this ugly world?" He stopped and sighed and continued, "Everyone says justice isn't blind. Oh yeah, it sees. It doesn't care. That means we have to take care of our own."

"Sam, please . . ."

"Lani, before you go, there's one thing you can do for me. Do you remember who gave me those energy bars?"

"Mary."

"No, who gave them to Mary?"

"A woman in C -- Florence Danzell."

"Oh yeah, that's her. Do you know her daughter?"

"No."

"I'd like to talk to her daughter -- if she visits today."

"My people will keep watch. If she comes in, I will give her your message."

***

"I have to find a way," Sam mumbled with closed eyes. *"I have to find a way. Today and tonight – that's all I have -- and maybe Danzell's daughter."*

***

Sensing someone entered his room, Sam, opened his eyes, turned and saw Lani. She withdrew a wad of latex gloves from her pocket, put them into his table drawer and whispered, "Please remember. If someone asks, tell them I always keep some of these here." When he didn't answer she asked, "Do you understand?" He nodded, and she walked out of the room.

Lani just showed her approval — and conspiracy.

***

Sam sat up in bed trying to formulate his options. He kept returning to the same conclusion: he didn't have any options. Getting help from the outside world was a waiting game. Finding a weapon became his prime focus.

***

Gail strode in without speaking a word, handed Sam a cup of water and some medication. He, without questioning why, took the offering and went through the ritual of popping a pill and swallowing a gulp of air. Downing the water completed his act. Sam had palmed the pill. He offered Gail the empty cup. She left as quickly as she came.

Sam deposited the clandestine dose into his pajama pocket. Now he had a tiny collection, and a potential weapon.

It was too early in the day for a word about a visitor. He felt alone. The stress tortured his mind and body. The coming evening would be even more stressful. He tried to get some rest.

Sam could not relax. His promise to Mary Archer flooded back: he said this would be the last day of torment. It could be an impossible promise to keep.

He needed his rest. Sleep would not come.

***

Sam kept his eyes closed. He willed himself into a trance; it shattered when he heard Jack enter Emma's room. Emma's very weak cry for help spiked his anxiety. It forced a surge of anger. Clamping that emotion proved difficult; he could do nothing; her pleas would go unanswered. Sam buried his head into his covers. He tried to sob away his torment while hating his frailty. While attempting to block out the ungodly noises from Emma's room he thought he heard sobs of distress coming from Mary's room.

It wasn't his imagination it was real. He didn't hear Gail entering Mary's room nor did he hear the beginning of her preparatory ritual. What he did hear were the sounds of Gail's sexual frenzy. She had no concern for the world around her. Her loud groans and moans of ecstasy were not stifled by the walls or the door of Mary's room. Sam wanted to rush in and rescue his friend — the timing was wrong. Interrupting the ravaging would be for the moment — and completely ineffective.

"Hold on Mary Archer, please be strong," he said in silence. He prayed she could receive his message.

***

Jack left Emma's room long before Gail walked past Sam's doorway. She hummed a tune as she walked and indicated she was happy with her mid morning's activity. The brief glimpse of Gail walking by gave Sam a flow of hatred he never imagined he could feel. He flung his head back releasing a deep groan, coughing a sob.

***

Overwhelmed by his hatred, sleep would not come. He rested for a while, stirred when lunch came, eating it with mechanical motions. The food, a necessity, gave him no joy. Slumping down again he fell into a dull stupor. Half awake and yet dreamy eyed he begged his body to yield to the required slumber. The afternoon slowly rolled into the evening. Sam consumed his meal because he had too. Acting the part of a good patient meant calling for the bedpan and utilizing the portable urinal.

"These needless humiliations will soon come to an end. I know I have to play the game by your rules — for now. Control yourself Sam, control yourself," he murmured while returning the urinal to the bed rail.

***

Though Sam finally fell into a deep troubled sleep, he woke from this escape from reality by an insistent taping noise, of metal-on-metal. He lurched up, looked around and quickly found his roommate alerting him to the late hour. The clock showed one in the morning. *"How could I?"* he reprimanded himself. Sam's two hands came together in prayerful pose and stretched out to Mr. Whitson as he mouthed the words, *"Thank you."*

A slight wave acknowledged the message.

Sam slid out of his bed, skipped his stretching and Tai Chi and immediately began to examine his closet. He didn't hear anything about a visitor. And yet he had to hope that help from the outside remained a distinct possibility. Without that outside assistance, he needed a significant weapon. Anxiety took control of his body. It drove him to work with snappy motions. He moved things quickly and searched with darting eyes. Nothing rested on the floor that he perceived as usable. The clothes hangers, made of skimpy wire and bendable with little effort were useless. The shelf seemed substantial. He found it permanently attached; it couldn't be removed. Sam tugged at the clothes bar, and it too would not come free. The bar, held in place with solid metal hardware required a screwdriver to remove it. His closet yielded nothing.

Sam examined his bed and looked for removable parts. The bed, built to last could not be taken apart without some sturdy tools. He looked around the room and then in the toilet. So far, nothing was usable. Mr. Whitson's and his chest of drawers, stuffed with soft clothing, didn't contain anything that would solve his problem.

The furnishings in the entire room were useless. This failure to find a weapon gave him a surge of uncertainty; it squashed his confidence. Sam's anxiety soared. His breathing became shallow and rapid; his mouth tasted the dryness of fear; he remained motionless.

Mr. Whitson had watched Sam searching the room and then witnessed the collapse of the man. Fear stole Sam's energy. And that fear could control his destiny. Anger flooded Mr. Whitson's body; he couldn't, he wouldn't allow this. Taking up a small tissue box, he utilized every bit of strength remaining in his arm and flung the box towards Sam. It landed half way between them making a distinct muted sound as it hit the floor. This mini-violence by the bedridden man stung Sam. He walked over, picked up the box and gently placed it back into Mr. Whitson's bed.

"It was that bad, huh. I owe you big time."

Mr. Whitson gave a thumbs-up acknowledgement.

Sam stretched for a few minutes. He tried to meditate. Concentration still failed him. Stopping the exercise and merely sucking in some deep breaths gave him some succor.

He fluffed up the bedding to simulate his body. When it appeared to be presentable, he moved towards the door. Then he remembered the latex gloves. Tugging them on with fast motions warmed his cold hands; he soon felt the perspiration welling on his skin.

No one was in sight. Sam moved into the hallway, past Mary's room and towards the service corridor. All rooms, on both sides of the hallway, had their doors open in compliance with the standard practice. All were open except for Mary Archer's room and A130. This last room had to be vacant or perhaps had something usable.

The door to A130 opened with the typical squeal of oil starved hinges; he grimaced at their high pitched screech. Darkness within, necessitated leaving the door slightly ajar, using the ambient light of the hallway. The disarray of a renovation greeted him. A large plastic drop-cloth protected the bed from potential debris. A couple of adjustable tables and two dressers were pushed into a corner. They too were covered with a tarp. Sam assumed workers had to move the furniture into a corner allowing for working space. He entered and immediately noticed the uneven floor. Floor tiles were missing. A quick check showed an opened box of new flooring and a large tool chest.

Sam walked back to the door, checked the hallway. The quiet prevailed. He returned to continuing his search, especially the toolbox. The owner secured it with a small pad lock on the hasp. The lock proved effective. There had to be other possibilities within. Sam froze when he heard someone walking in the hallway; they were approaching the room.

Sam dropped to the floor crawling towards the bed. He slid beneath the draping cloth wiggling to the far side. The bottom of the bed with its plastic shroud made him feel a little claustrophobic. He drew in silent breaths and exhaled through his mouth trying to settle his anxiety. Perspiration developed on his face while the exhalation dried his mouth. He shook with fear unable to control the trembling. The steady paced noise stopped at room A130. Sam worried about leaving the door partially open. Now that act may have precipitated a need to investigate. Subdued hallway light swept into the room in concert with the door swinging open. Someone walked in, hesitated then energized the overhead lights. He held his breath when the blast of the light made the plastic sheet seem to be transparent. He could hear and see the person walking all around the room and then towards him. The walking feet came close, went past and into the toilet. Sam remained motionless. Moments later he heard the splash of water as the man urinated noisily into the bowl. Without flushing, he reentered the room, snapped off the room lights closing the door with a squeal and solid thump. Sam and the room now coexisted in darkness.

The near miss experience zapped Sam's energy; he remained motionless.

Moonlight came through the window in dull gray shafts; a trace of it touched the bottom of the bed sheet. Although the slivers of moonlight invited Sam, he waited a long time before venturing from his hiding place. That long wait allowed his eyes to acquire a degree of night vision. He peeked out unable to recognize the configuration of the room other than the location of the toilet. Sam crawled from beneath the bed moving slowly while using his hands to guide his way. He felt the edge of the existing floor covering, then the loose tiles; each piece moved with his gentle touch. Groping around Sam found other tiles scattered about including an entire stack of new material. Still wary of another intruder, Sam, with very limited visibility, crept forward on his hands and knees. Though his motions were slow and deliberate, his hand hit an object. It skittered noisily away from him. Sam cringed hoping no one else heard the clatter.

Unable to see, Sam fanned his hand out in a circular manner. Dust accumulated on his hand as he made contact with the surface of the floor. He moved a bit while continuing the slow circular searching motion; then moved again. Finally, his hand touched something and carefully pulled the item towards him. He felt its form and its sting as it pierced his glove. The minor pain did not stop him from feeling the form, although now he examined it very carefully. The handle and blade felt familiar; he recognized its design. The six inch long blade, mounted in a sturdy wooden handle had a sharp hooked point. He knew the knife's keen edge turned ninety degrees allowed a technician to insert the blade into a tile and make an accurate cut. The handle felt clean, as clean as anything he could feel through his latex gloves. Whatever its condition, he had a primary weapon.

Sam felt his way into the toilet and hoped some toilet paper remained on the roll. The configuration of the bathroom seemed familiar. The toilet bowl emitted a pungent odor of urine; it repelled him. He held his breath and reached around until he located the mounted roll of paper. He dressed the knife in a number of layers of paper then moistened the last layer to sort-of glue it in place. Sam placed the paper-sheathed knife into his briefs. He wondered if he used enough paper.

He found his weapon and yet believing there could be something better made him want to continue his search beyond this room.

The door gave a short "eek" and opened about eight inches. He waited a few seconds hoping he wouldn't hear those shoes running down the hallway. Peeking out, he released a sigh of relief. There wasn't a soul in sight.

Sam decided to try the service corridor. He walked close to the wall towards the double door.

The unknown beyond the swinging doors made him stop and take a deep breath. One of the doors responded quietly; he pushed it just enough to see into the corridor. The area, quiet and lit with tiny nightlights, seemed eerie as he moved forward. A new set of doors, on the left, were marked 'MAINTENANCE SHOP'. Both were locked.

Sam didn't have to check to see if he still had the sturdy knife. Its bulky mass pressed against him creating a constant reminder.

Another set of doors halfway down the corridor beckoned. Sam shook his head, stopped and turned. He couldn't take the risk to go deeper into the facility.

Sam had a weapon. It was small; it felt good in his hands.

He reentered his hallway and ran past all the rooms and directly into his own. The excursion drained him. Sam withdrew the knife, very gently, from his underwear and tucked it beneath the mattress of his bed. The gloves still showed a tiny bit of blood mixing with his perspiration. After wiping the sweat on his pajamas he rolled the gloves into a ball and stowed them under his pillow.

Sam removed and draped his damp nightclothes and shorts on the bed railing.

He tried to settle in while his heart pumped a hard steadying rhythm. Feeling smug finding a weapon suddenly turned into dismay. Sam's mind searched looking for answers; answers that would not come.

TWENTY FOUR

Although exhausted from his nighttime excursion Sam awoke with the first signs of the morning activity. Lani was again at his side removing the spent clothing from his bedrail. He grabbed her hand, retrieved his pajama top and frantically searched for the pocket. Thrusting his fingers into the damp clothing he found his precious pills. The medications appeared to be okay. They survived his perspiration. Lani, realizing his dilemma pulled a tissue from its box.

Worry lines pulled Lani's pretty face into a look of concern; she held the damp clothing, evidence that showed Sam's resolve. Lani noticed the tiny stains on the pajamas as she stuffed them into her laundry bag. Sam handed her the ball of latex gloves and asked, "Please throw these away?" Lani's eyes started to tear as she shoved them into her pocket.

"We didn't see any visitors yesterday. She could have been here. We didn't see her. I'm sorry."

"Thank you Lani. I don't need her now."

Sam refusing the usual sponge bath asked for a clean set of nightclothes. Lani acknowledged by a nod and retrieved some fresh pajamas. She noticing his nakedness, reached for clean shorts. Sam said sternly, "No underwear!"

Before he tugged on the top Sam tucked his package of pills into the shirt pocket. It made a small bulge that he patted into a reasonable flatness. Lani stood by in silence.

Sam, now reasonably refreshed, looked up at her and smiled. "Lani your friendship is something I cherish. I'm a very lucky guy. You made my mind clear. And while they waited for me to wither into a helpless mess, you made me well. Thank you." Lani lowered her eyes and gracefully listened to him. "You dear lady took care of me. Now it's my turn. It is extremely important that you listen and understand what I'm going to tell you. When you leave this room, go and do the rest of your rounds very quickly. When you are finished do not, and I mean it, do not come back here." Lani started to say something. Sam held up his hand and continued, "Please Lani, don't ask any questions. I want you to promise me you will do this one simple thing. Will you promise?"

"How can I answer when I don't know what you are talking about?"

"Oh Lani, I'm so sorry I'm babbling. I'm very nervous and excited. I want to do the right thing."

"You're not helping yourself. Calm down. What do you want of me?"

"Finish your rounds quickly and then get away from this hallway. And make sure you're always in the company

of someone who works here full time. It has to be one of
the cooks, or a person in charge of laundry, or any other
supervisor. Please be with someone one hundred percent
of your time. Don't even go to the lady's room. It will not
be very long. Do you understand?"

"You're breaking my heart, and yet I know . . ."

"Lani, please remember, you know nothing. I want
you away from here. Do you promise?"

"Yes, I promise. Your — your trust in me is too
great," Lani said with tears welling in her eyes.

"It's not simple trust; it's a special love. Lani,
because of you, I'm reclaiming my health. I can't and I
won't jeopardize your safety. Now please go and make
certain you're heard and seen by many people; anywhere
except here." They both remained quiet for a moment and
then Sam pointed to the door. Lani turned towards his
roommate. She thought Mr. Whitson nodded his
concurrence.

***

Danielle Turner came early and just waited in the
parking lot watching for Doctor Juliano's arrival. A few
delivery trucks drove in and disappeared as they aimed for
the back entry. Finally, a large white luxury sedan pulled
into the lot. The man parked in a place reserved for the
handicapped.

Danielle exited her car, quickly covered the distance
between them and yelled: "Good morning Doctor Juliano. I
waited for you. Thanks for coming."

"Come along this should take just a few minutes."

They both whisked right in and without announcing
their arrival continued on to Florence Danzell's room. The
receptionist spotted their arrival and alerted Sal. He in turn

called Milo, "Go to Danzell's room and see why Juliano's here. He never comes in like a comet; and call Jack or Gail."

Milo didn't want to waste time with a telephone run-around. He keyed in the public address system and paged Gail. She recognized the stress in Milo's voice and instantly responded to the page.

"I need you or Jack in C. Juliano just came in. He's going to ask some tough questions. One of you has to get over there, right now." Milo didn't wait for a reply, cradled the phone, and darted out to catch up to the visitors.

Gail slammed the phone in frustration and said, "Stay good and loose. I'll be right back. If we can't have fun this morning you can count on a wonderful afternoon of frolicking." Gail slipped into her white shoes and left Mary Archer's room. In her haste to respond she forgot to close the door. An open door was an unwritten rule that the aides understood. It made them responsible for the sanitary care of the room's occupant.

***

Lani thought her tasks were finished, started to walk towards the kitchen then looked back and saw a room within her responsibilities had its door open. She returned saw a resident in the private room.

Mary, with her back towards Lani turned to her and said, "I could use some ice water."

"Let's get you clean first. Pulling back the single sheet she noticed Mary's nakedness. Lani covered the woman, strode quickly to the dresser retrieving a fit-all institutional night garment.

"A fresh set of clothes next to my skin? Yes, that is a nice thought. Please don't. Gail will -- go now — you shouldn't be in here. Please leave. Leave me the way I am.

Make certain the door is closed. Thank you for your
kindness. Please go!" Lani remained silent. "Please for both
of our sake — just leave. Don't try to understand all of this
– just go."

Lani tried to think of some way to extend some
sympathy to the tortured woman. Knowing she had no
resources to help merely shook her head in exasperation,
and left. Small tears came into her eyes. She smeared them
away with the palm of her hand.

***

Lani obediently followed Sam's request to be visible.
She gave up her normal break from the tedium continued
through the corridor door towards the kitchen. Being a
half-hour early proved convenient for the chef. She
welcomed Lani's assistance preparing the noon meal.
While both toiled, Lani stimulated the chatter. She
understood Sam's edict allowed her fluency in English to
solidify this contact. Lani, looking for topics to energize
their conversation, offered her knowledge about native
foods. She regaled in defining the complex methods used
in preparation while touting all the wonders of Jamaican
cooking.

***

Gail caught up to Milo by taking the short cut across
the middle corridor. Without speaking both went directly
to Florence Danzell's room. Upon arrival, they saw Doctor
Juliano attempting to communicate with a very drowsy
woman. Juliano frustrated by her lack of response looked
at Milo, pointed repeatedly at Florence and demanded,
"What sort of medication did you give this woman? She's
totally out of it." Doctor Juliano then turned and shouted at
Gail, "What do you know about this?"

"I did not give her any medication -- I think it's — please wait a moment I'll check her. . ."

"Stop babbling and go get the records. And find the person who administered whatever they gave her."

Gail ran from the room, grabbed the portable computer station, commanded a display of the woman's charts and smiled. She pushed the trolley back to Florence's room, turned it towards the doctor and said, "Here's her entire file. If you look right here you can see we administered the medication that you prescribed for her condition. And we followed your directions: to be dispensed as needed." Gail recognizing the doctor's dilemma said, "Mrs. Danzell received what you prescribed — and in the dose you stipulated."

"Good Lord woman. I ordered this medication because your staff physician asked for . . ." he trailed off his answer. His face flushed a deep red of embarrassment. His fluster acknowledged that her condition was his fault. He never allowed others to usurp his control. "I am rescinding this drug order," he said as he scribbled something on a prescription pad. "Now I want this woman out of bed. Get someone in here to take her to the shower room. I want her cleaned up, and I mean now."

Milo left the room with a simple smile of quiet satisfaction.

"Doctor Juliano is Mom in trouble? What did you prescribe?"

"No your mother is not in trouble. She'll be fine. I gave the order for a strong tranquilizer, just in case she exhibited some symptoms of depression. I hate to say it — I can see now that I gave them too much control. I assure you it will never ever happen again. They should have called me. They always call, even for the simplest of things. Why at this time? I just don't know."

"Doctor Juliano, would you mind taking a quickie look at Mom's friend, Mary Archer. If you remember I told you she was my teacher."

"Yes I know Mary Archer."

"She's a resident on the other side of the building," Danielle knew she was pushing the Doctor into giving some free service; she didn't care. The Doctor screwed-up and she knew it. He owed her, and she was going to collect.

"Not at all," he fibbed. I'll do that — first I want to talk to Mr. Manfassi. Do you know Archer's room number?"

"She's in A123. Half way down A Wing."

"I'll meet you there as soon as I'm finished with Manfassi."

***

Milo returned to his office just about the same time Tina Morris entered the building. She waved happily to the Belvedere staff as she passed and made her way to his office. Her mini-dress flattered her slim figure. She presented herself with a smile and said, "Hi Milo. Are you still mad at me?"

"Tina how can you say that. Me? Mad at you? No way. Maybe a little confused by some of your actions but you're my favorite person of the female persuasion." Milo grinned at his clumsy attempt to sound funny. "I'm happy you called and doubly happy you wanted to visit. Please, please sit down. How are things going?"

"Work is a drag. They just load me up with a ton of things to do. I'm very busy; and I could use some help. They're too cheap to hire anyone." Milo didn't respond. "I guess the biggest thing in my life is my waking up and accepting the fact that I was getting to be a very greedy person."

"You're a fun person when you wake up."

"Yeah we did have fun -- as I was saying, that one time — that was not Tina. And you know what? I didn't like that person. I didn't like what she was doing to you and to me. I'm a fun person, happy with my life. Milo, I don't know what happened? I do know I want things to go back the way they were. Is that too much to ask?"

"That's all in the past, Tina. I'm happy you're back to your old self. I mean young self. You are a beautiful young woman and . . ."

"You think so?"

"I know so. Tina let's talk about business for a second. I want you to know we don't make a ton of money on these free loading characters you dump in here. Sure we get a dollar here and a dollar there. The government is kind-of cheap and limits what we can earn. So we take in a little — when the expenses are subtracted, for us, it becomes peanuts."

"Yeah, that's some of the stuff I didn't see. Do you still want me for your special friend?"

"Tina, I really missed you. What happened was ugly and pretty sad for both of us. I want things to be the way they were."

"It can be — if we work on it." Tina winked and smiled as she answered.

"We're going to have a ball making up the lost time," Milo said as he got up and closed the office door. He extended his arms welcoming her to come to him.

"Milo, please close your eyes, for just a minute. Close them hard and let me give you a wonderful surprise." He looked at the smiling seductress then obediently yielded to her demands. Tina saw his body responding in the anticipation of an unknown delight.

Tina withdrew a hefty steel rod from her bag. At two and a half pounds, the ten inch long one-inch round shaft felt heavy in her hand. She lowered her hand, swung her arm back in a bowling motion, paused for just a moment and then whipped it forward in a vicious arc. The rod gained speed as she accelerated it with all of her energy. The solid mass of steel plunged into Milo's groin. The violent blow knocked the breath out of his body. For a fleeting moment, his feet left the floor. For him, it seemed like an eternity as the pain shot throughout his system. He sank to the floor gasping for a breath of air. His hands reached down — he couldn't touch his severely damaged organs. Milo moaned in agony. Tina smiled, looked down towards him then kicked with a pointed shoe hoping to inflict more pain.

Sal, hearing the commotion, ran to Milo's office, pushed on the partially closed door and entered. He saw Milo, lying on the floor, writhing with pain, gasping for breath.

With some of her clothing in self-inflicted disarray, Tina said, "He tried to rape me — I defended myself. You can call the police, if you want to. I really don't care. He got what he deserved." Tina while rearranging her clothing said, "I think Milo needs a little help. Are there any real medical people in this place?" then added, "You don't need me. Do you?"

When Tina turned to leave, Sal pushed her aside and bellowed towards the receptionist, "Get Jack down here — fast. See if you can find Lunkens."

***

Gail hearing the page grumbled knowing Jack was busy with Emma. She picked up a phone and punched in a number.

***

Sam didn't have to wait very long before he heard Jack entering Emma's room. His heart pounded accepting the fact that he had to prepare for action. Sam lowered the rail, slid out of bed and moved towards his closet. While out of sight of his open door, Sam stripped off his meager clothing grabbed a pair of socks, and the last pair of latex gloves. Sam, sans clothing, except for the socks and latex gloved hands, arranged the bed for a quick reentry. He prayed no one would see his nakedness lifted his mattress and withdrew the tissue covered knife. He ran towards the shared toilet entering as quietly as possible.

Sam fondled the knife while removing the toilet tissue from the blade. It appeared to be relatively new. Testing its cutting edge showed it to be super sharp. The menacing point gleamed and reflected the light off of its polished surface.

The knife felt good in his gloved hand. Extending his arm, Sam practiced potential strike motions -- he incorporated the balance of some Tai Chi moves. Adjusting the knife's position in his hand a few times he danced the thrust of lethal violence. In an attempt to remove any evidence, he polished the blade with the tissue then tossed the paper into the toilet bowl. For a short time it floated on the water, and slowly became translucent.

Sam's body sparkled with drops of perspiration. He pushed on the door to Emma's room, very gently.

***

Jack knew a downer would temper his ardor opened a vial and selected a couple of pills. He didn't need any

water, just swallowed. Smiling at the thought of a long
enjoyable romp, Jack prepared Emma with care. "No need
to rush things today. What say young lady we go for an
endurance record."

Jack set the stage with billowy pillows propping up
his victim. Emma lay there in sheer horror knowing she did
not have the power stop him. Her sobs were of no value
and did not aid in her physical or mental escape. Jack
began his assault with a brutal vigor. His lust demanded an
urgency of action.

The drug did its job. It clouded his mind; he ignored
the world around him.

Sam, making certain no part of his body touched the
door, pushed it open just enough to allow a clear view of
the assault. He remained hidden in the shadows while
witnessing the brutalization of Emma.

Containing his roiling anger Sam remained frozen in
place yet poised awaiting his moment to attack. Jack,
oblivious to any impending danger, seemed inexhaustible
as he maintained a fast tempo. Sam knew he had to wait.
Hearing Emma's pleas for mercy instilled an urgency to
lunge out. Sam grimaced knowing he still had to wait.

Then the moment arrived. Jack began to slow his
rhythm. With the change in pace, Jack started a slow
turning of his head from one side to the other. If Sam
guessed right, the lolling motions would give him the
advantage he needed.

Jack was facing him -- Sam waited. Then Jack raised
his head turned away very slowly towards the window.
Sam pushed on the door. With its squeaky hinge groaning
in rebellion, the door bounced off the stop concurrent with
Sam lunging towards the bed. Before the sluggish Jack
could respond to this noisy entrance, Sam grasped Jack's

hair with his left hand, pulled his head back and simultaneously plunged the shiny hooked point deep into the front of Jack's throat. With a lightning fast and violent motion Sam pulled the knife through instantly severing Jack's carotid artery and jugular vein.

Jack, with eyes wide-open in panic and disbelief, twisted out of Sam's hold. His arms reacting to the torturous assault flailed for a few moments before he yielded to the sudden hemorrhage. With his head hanging over the rail, the blood continued to drain from his body.

Momentarily mesmerized by the carnage, Sam turned towards the wall and plunged the knifepoint into the plasterboard. He returned to Emma, leaned in and whispered in her ear, "You are now free of the devil . . ." Sam heard the room door open. He paled, stood still, waiting for his imminent capture.

Gail had opened the door a crack and without looking into the room merely yelled, "Jack hurry up. Sal's looking for you." Gail satisfied that she delivered Sal's message, re-closed the door with a slam.

Sam stunned by that interruption regained his senses and retreated to the toilet. Removing the gloves, he flattened and knotted them to seal out any air. Now holding a small compressed mass, he plunged his naked hand down into the cold water and pushed the gloves up and hopefully into the trap. It should move with a flushing of the bowl.

Sam held his hand and arms under some running water; he splashed a little on his face washing away any evidence of Jack's blood. He didn't have any time to be certain he cleaned off any that may have spurted onto him. He had to flush the toilet. Cringing with the noise announcing his presence, he couldn't wait to see if the water drained properly.

Sam still slightly wet as he reentered his room pulled off his socks and quickly redressed. The pajamas soaked up the moisture as he got into bed. He examined the socks. They were dirty; they felt dry; there was no evidence of blood. He pushed the socks under the covers and all the way to the bottom of the bed. Sam reached for his cup of water swallowed two of the pills he saved. There were others plus the one he received this morning. He threw them towards his open closet.

Sam glanced towards his sleeping roommate then pulled up the covers. While his heart hammered from the horror he created, the area remained quiet. By that silence, Sam knew no one, as yet, discovered the gore next door. Emma also remained quiet; he then worried about her condition.

"God what that poor woman lived through — and now murder, I pray someone comes and relieves her from this trauma," Sam murmured. The double dose of medication began to kick in. His worries disappeared as he fell into a drugged sleep.

TWENTY FIVE

"Family only in this wing," Gail shouted.

Unfazed by the gruff greeting Danielle answered back, "I am family. I'm family, and I'm going to see Mary Archer. Isn't that her room?"

Gail stunned by the woman's aggression, lost her bravado and stammered a reply: "Ah — no — she's in A126." Realizing she just violated the Manor's privacy policy, Gail recovered some of her courage and said: "I cannot allow visitors to disturb our residents."

Gail turned toward the noise: she heard the thump of Sam impaling his knife into the wall. Since falls were common, any unusual sound always required an immediate investigation. Knowing Jack was in that room presented a conundrum. Gail turned towards Danielle and said, "Come on. I'll show you the . . ."

"Just stop your babbling," Danielle said in anger. "Doctor Juliano is here and we're going to see Mary Archer. If you have a problem with that I suggest you call Mr. Manfassi."

Gail grimaced. Thoughts poured through her head and fear hit her as she pictured Mary Archer complaining about her ill treatment. A brushing wave of her hand showed her total disdain as they arrived at Mary's room.

No one responded to Danielle's not-to-gentle tapping on the door. She pushed it open, peered in and heard: "Please, whoever you are, just go away."

"Hi, it's me, Danielle Turner." She continued to walk towards Mary's bed. "We came to see my Mom. How are you this morning?" Mary Archer did not respond to her light banter. Danielle leaned on the rail and then noticed Mary had pulled the cover up to her chin. "Are you cold? Can I get you an extra blanket?"

Mary ignoring her questions asked, "How's your mother?"

"I'm concerned about Mom. She's awful sleepy. They have her bedded down, and that's not her. She was always feisty and alive."

"Danielle, do your mother a big favor and get her out of this place. There's some horrible trouble here and . . ." Mary stopped talking when she heard the loud scream.

Danielle ran to the doorway. She saw Gail gesturing frantically while shouting out obscenities then slumped against the wall and slowly slipped down to the floor. She sat with head hanging to her chest. Gail no longer shrieking held her mouth agape in horror. Her white uniform, streaked with smears of blood, offered some evidence of the woman's despair.

Danielle ran towards Gail, saw her face twisted in anguish and babbling something unintelligible while pointing to Emma's room.

With the door now opened wide, Danielle peered in. She gasped at the horror, backed out of the doorway and ran down towards the nurse's station. At the same time, she saw Manfassi and Juliano running towards her. Within moments they converged.

"Something — really bad happened in that room." Danielle turned. They ran where she was pointing.

Sal immediately assessed the tragedy, ignored the gore, raced into the room and picked up the phone. He hit the keypad with lightning strokes accessing the page system. "Stat, Room A122," he said as he issued a call for a major medical assistance. He broke the connection, retrieved an outside line and reached 911. "I need an ambulance and send the police to Belvedere Manor." Name's Manfassi. Just hurry." Sal wanted to get off the phone. The 911 dispatcher kept asking questions. Sal turned to Danielle Turner and said, "Here, maybe you can supply some answers."

Two nurses from the other wings responding to Sal's call for help stopped when they reached the doorway. They saw a naked blood-drained body with head draped over the bed rail. Non-seeing eyes were wide-open. The neck wound gaped; it seemed to ooze a trickle of blood.

Emma stirred. She tried to move; Jack held her captive this time with his dead body. Sal seeing the woman struggle, realized he had to remediate her agony. He pulled on the bed, exposing the pool of blood. Summoning the traumatized nurses into the room, they as a team pulled on the naked Jack until it allowed them to free the equally nude Emma. He lifted Emma away from the gore. "Leave him just the way he is. Throw that blanket on this woman," he said to the nurse. Turning to Danielle, he added, "You stand guard and don't let anyone into this room."

Sal knew A130 was under renovation and ran with the traumatized woman. Nurses automatically followed him. "Get that bed opened and I want this woman cleaned up. Don't leave her alone," he said pointing to the one closest to him.

Doctor Juliano had raced alongside of Sal when they reacted to the screams. He too saw the horror and though tempted to intervene, believed the man to be dead. He hesitated to approach the bloody mess and watched as Sal took control. He also retreated when they moved Emma from the death grip of Jack.

Now alone, albeit with Danielle still standing guard, he did not want to examine the corpse. The man was beyond medical help. Juliano walked over to Emma's stoic roommate. When she didn't respond to his questions and he rolled her onto her side. Juliano, staying clear of the bloodied bed asked Danielle. "Where did they take the woman?"

Danielle pointed to a room down the hallway and said, "Right there."

Juliano strode into A130 and walked up to Emma. Sal saw the doctor enter the room. He lowered his head, started to leave then stopped, turned towards Doctor Juliano and said, "We've got bad trouble."

"I didn't even have to examine him. That man is dead. However, what he was doing is beyond human reasoning. Right now, I want to see to this woman." Doctor Juliano felt the rush of anger, as he looked at her. "Get out of my way," Juliano barked.

Sal yielded to the Doctor's demanding command. As he moved away from the bed the doctor's words sank in; he had to think about the repercussions. When Tina attacked Milo their controlled world started to unravel, and now this. Feeling faint with his gut churning he saw the police were already in the hallway.

***

The Police quickly secured the crime area. Although a gaudy yellow police tape strung across the doorway demanded all to keep out, Sal walked up to the officer and said, "We've got a resident in that room. She should be moved."

"Yeah we know. We tried to talk to her. She didn't respond. Is she alert enough to know what went down?" the young police officer inquired.

"No! She's not competent. Look I'm going in there to carry her out. You can either help or get out of my way."

"Hold on Mister. We'll get her out without hurting her."

"She's not fragile. One of you can scoop her up and carry her without concern."

The officer acknowledged by a nod then asked: "Where do you want her?"

That was a good question. With one room out of service, and moving Emma into A130, there wasn't an empty bed in the facility. Sal, unable to find an adequate solution told him to put her on a couch in the recreation room.

***

An ambulance arrived almost simultaneously with the police. Although called to attend to Jack, Milo needed immediate medical attention. They loaded him on a gurney and sped off to the hospital. Since it sounded plausible, everyone accepted the story that Milo lost his balance and fell onto a chair. Since the accident occurred in the front office area, and his office is a substantial distance from the crime scene the two incidents were judged to be unrelated.

***

Jack didn't need an ambulance he needed a body bag — and a hearse. The chief of police accepted the first responder's assessment and immediately placed a call for assistance. The State Major Crime unit reviewed the roster of available detectives and assigned Jules Cornier to the case.

Cornier and a small team of professionals were at Belvedere Manor within a half-hour. A photographer took pictures from every possible angle and thoroughly documented the assault. Cornier personally analyzed the scene. Assured that the forensic squad and the coroner had adequate time to perform he released Jack's body for a detailed autopsy.

Blazing yellow Keep-Out tape stretched across the door that gave access to the main hallway, and they taped the door leading to the shared toilet. To complete the sealing of all access portals, the toilet door from Sam's room exhibited a large X of the isolation banner.

"Those two guys in A124 can't walk and don't need a toilet," Sal said showing his cooperative spirit to the police.

***

Doctor Juliano, one of the first on the scene and considered a witness, ignored the legal ramifications. He boldly took charge of caring for Emma. While still showing signs of his anger, ordered an ambulance. Cornier hearing the rants of the man as he took charge medically, allowed him freedom to perform, ordering an officer to stay with

Emma. The second ambulance arrived quickly. Emma, wide-eyed and frightened, left Belvedere Manor and entered a caring world.

***

Emma's roommate, sans emotion on the abrupt movement, rested on the recreation room couch. The Manor's receptionist, pulled from her normal task sat by her side holding her hand.

"Thanks for helping out." Sal said. "I have it now. Can you remain in the office during your lunch hour? We'll be inundated with calls."

"Sure thing, what do I tell people?"

"Tell them — tell them — Oh hell what do we say? Just say we can't have visitors today. Inform everybody, whether they're calling or walking in there's no visiting — because — a — medical emergency with a member of the staff."

"Sal, if we . . ."

"Ah, that's not — maybe we should tell them someone died. A member of our staff died. That's it. Tell them a member of our staff died."

***

Jack was dead. Gail knew whoever did it, killed him at his most defenseless time; alone and in a sexual reverie. A chill raced down her body. Gail realized the killer or killers watched and waited for this moment. Gail nervously scanned the area checking for anyone observing her. Not seeing a threat did not ease her mind. With many people dashing about she felt safe -- and yet vulnerable.

Gail tried to visualize who murdered Jack. It had to be a powerful man. Only a guy could inflict, in such a violent manner, some much damage against a macho guy like Jack. She shuddered knowing she could be next.

Gail rushed to the nurse's lounge, pulled open Jack's locker and rummaged through his street clothes. She found his wallet. It contained a little over three hundred dollars in cash. She pocketed it while looking around for a witness to her theft — or a possible murderer. Reconsidering her theft to be too obvious, she returned a few of the smaller bills back into the wallet. Leaving the lounge unnoticed, Gail proceeded towards the general office area. She, not knowing the passwords couldn't access the computer file, yet knew the location of the hardcopy records. Gail, with streaks of drying blood on her usually pristine white uniform, worked with a survival mode determination pulled four folders, jotted down the information she sought then returned each to its proper place. Even in her extreme haste she took time to pat the folders down to their original neatness.

***

Striding like a woman on an important mission, Gail entered the A wing's nurse's station, opened the desk and removed a set of keys. After unlocking the pharmaceutical cabinet, she ignored the neatly stacked and labeled basic prescription drugs and spun the dial of the small safe; a safe that protected controlled substances. It opened with a simple tug. Within moments, the narcotics went into her large handbag. Returning to the nurse's lounge she placed the handbag near her coat and sat down to calculate her next move.

Not knowing who killed Jack meant getting away from Belvedere. She would need money, a different car or new plates on her car.

Gail decided to rummage through some of her associates' lockers. That search didn't yield anything.

***

Gail walked to Sal's office, realizing others were with Detective Cornier. She waited impatiently in the hallway. With every extra moment she felt her anxiety growing. When the door opened Gail said, "Detective, Sir, please, may I speak with you?"

"I'm very busy."

"Look at me. I'm a mess. My clothes are covered with Jack's blood, and I can't do anything looking like this. We shouldn't work with blood on our clothes. Even if I could, it upsets me knowing it's his blood. I don't know what it would do to the residents," she said and held out the skirt for him to see. "May I please change my clothes?"

"Absolutely, I'm sorry. I should have asked you to take those clothes off and put all of them into an evidence bag. Do you have any other clothing?"

"No sir, I'll have to go home," she lied.

"Can't you borrow some? How about wearing a set of scrubs?"

"Sorry Sir, this is not a hospital. We don't use scrubs. And a gal doesn't like to wear other people's stuff. I live a very short distance away. I can be back within the hour."

"I can't have you sitting around in those -- Officer Heidi Willet will accompany you for a fast trip home."

"Thank you, I appreciate your kindness." Cornier gave a wave of acknowledgement and walked away. Gail waited by the office and within minutes, Officer Willet appeared.

"Ms. Summun?" Willet asked. "If you're ready just lead the way."

"Have to get my coat and things. Be right back."

Officer Willet watched the woman walk quickly down the hall and into a doorway. It seemed as soon as she went in she was on the way back. "Got everything you need?"

"Yes, I do, thank you. Why don't you let me drive? It'll be easier that way. And to tell you the truth, I'd rather not be seen coming home in a police car. Okay? Do you mind?"

"Well I should be the one taking you to your home. You're right. You are a mess. I wouldn't enjoy getting some of that blood on my car." The officer gave a little laugh and said, "You're not going to run away on me are you?"

Gail returned the laughter saying, "Run away and miss all of this fun, no way."

"No fun for me. It's all work. Let's go."

Gail drove cautiously. She proceeded controlling her speed to preclude a comment from her official passenger. They chatted about police work, and Gail showed great interest in the woman's job. The officer relaxed and seemed to enjoy the break from the horror at Belvedere. Ten minutes later, Gail announced their arrival, "Well here's home sweet home."

The parking area, with most of the condo owners, or renters, working during the daytime, appeared empty. Gail wheeled her car with authority and parked close to the entrance of the condominium.

"Come on, I'll show you the place."

Gail jumped out of her car; Officer Willet moved quickly behind her. They both walked briskly entering the building.

"I'm upstairs. Some people jog up. I take the elevator," she laughed.

"What floor?"

"Fourth."

"Where's that elevator?"

"If you're a coffee drinker, I can put on a pot."

"No thanks. You're supposed to change clothes and get right back. They'll be looking for us."

"Oh, not for a while, I told your Detective I would return within the hour. He said that would be okay. Since it took just a few minutes to get here, there's loads of time. We deserve a good cup of coffee. If you want confirmation, give him a call."

"Not necessary, you're right. We have a moment for a little break; coffee sounds great." The officer smiled at her newly found friend and asked, "Have you lived here very long?"

"Only ten months, and I love it. We have a swimming pool. It's outdoors. I enjoy it especially on those hot summer days. Also have two tennis courts in the back. I get to use them, occasionally, when I'm lucky, if you get the picture?"

"I think I do."

Office Willet trailed behind Gail as they walked the short distance from the elevator and entered Gail's home.

"Oh my, this condo is beautiful. I like it. I really like it." She hesitated for a moment and asked, "Can I take a tour?"

"Of course you can. In fact, I insist you see it all. You just go on and explore. You're welcome to open every doorway you find. Go on, don't be shy. Check it out. Maybe you'll like what you see, and we'll be neighbors."

Gail waited for a moment then entered her kitchen. She filled the reservoir of a six-cup coffeemaker with water and placed some of her extra strong dark coffee into the basket. Gail flipped open her handbag, searched through until she found what she wanted. Pulling the capsules apart she tapped the enclosed powder into the empty glass coffee server. Water, steamy hot, began to drip. Within moments the powder disappeared as it blended with the stream of dark aromatic coffee.

Gail broke open a package of chocolate-covered mini-donuts arranging them in an inviting circle right next to the brewing coffee.

Gail left the kitchen and found Heidi Willet looking out of her bedroom window. "Like what you see?"

"It's beautiful. I didn't get very far and I want to see it all."

"And I need a quickie shower," Gail said believing the woman would understand. "Coffee should be ready. It's my extra special Madagascar brown. It has a wonderful aroma and unique flavor. Look around and you'll find the cups in the upper cabinets. Cream is in the fridge; sugar on the counter and feel free to pig out on the minis."

"Don't get your clothes wet. Pile 'em all together and put them into this evidence bag." The officer handed Gail a folded plastic sack and said, "Neatness does not count, just push 'em in."

"Will I get them back?"

"You really want those back?"

"No. Burn them for all I care." Gail began to strip off her clothing as she watched the woman walk away. After toeing the bathroom door partially closed Gail turned on the shower full force. The stream of water beating a constant vibrato gave her the background noise she sought. Sticking her hands into the flow purged the blood from her hands.

Gail pushed the bathroom door just enough allowing her a peek. She guessed the aroma of the coffee did its job; it tempted Officer Willet to go into her kitchen. Gail, barefooted, ran to her bedroom.

As Gail surmised, Officer Willet followed the scent of the brewing coffee. Pulling open the many cabinet doors appeared to entertain her; she continued to scrutinize everything long after locating the cups.

The coffee, dark and alluring, tempted Heidi to pour a cup and sniff the aromatic brew. Cautious of its heat she sampled a taste. The bite of bitter hit her tongue. Its fascination proved irresistible. She toyed with a mini-donut for a minute before ramming it into her mouth. Then grabbed another and chewed it, albeit this time very slowly. With portions of the chocolate donut still in her mouth, she sipped the hot beverage and savored the combined flavors.

Officer Willet enjoyed her coffee very hot. After consuming two donuts and downing the first cup, she poured a refill and reached for her third donut. Remembering the reason why they were here, she walked towards the bathroom heard the water running, checked the time, and returned to the kitchen.

Even after three mini-donuts and two cups of coffee Officer Willet felt the need of a refill just to alleviate the dryness within her mouth.

The narcotic started to kick in. She shook her head in an attempt to clear it. Her eyes started to lose focus. Willet stopped pouring the coffee. With the cup partially filled she walked into the living room and placed the coffee mug on the side table. Feeling like everything was moving in slow motion she sat down very cautiously. Trying to relax Officer Willet closed her eyes. The muted sound of water pouring down in the shower started to lose its intensity. Soon that noise disappeared; Officer Heidi Willet fell into a drugged sleep.

Although her escort would remain sedated, Gail decided to carry everything she needed, in one trip. A careful selection of clothing, for southern living, received gentle care when packed into the large suitcase. An overflow of items, including a small caliber pistol went into a smaller matching case. Comb, toothbrush, and cosmetics received rougher treatment as they were thrown into a shoulder bag. A small adjustable wrench plus two different screwdrivers were essential for today's work. She stuffed those on top of all the material in the shoulder bag.

Officer Willet remained in her stupor. Gail searched the woman and found a twenty-dollar bill tucked in a small pocket. She placed it in her wallet. With the shower water off, the coffee maker shut down Gail dashed around the apartment extinguishing all the lights. Now ready, Gail lugged her fully loaded bags and trudged out the door. The hallways, as common during these hours, were very quiet.

She arrived at her car without seeing anyone. Stowing her bags in the trunk Gail drove into the secured parking garage stopping next to her neighbor's car.

Gail struggled in an attempt to remove her own license plate screws. It took much longer than she anticipated. One screw came out easy, the other refused to yield. Gail wiggled and bent the plate in all directions until the metal fatigued and broke. The corroded screw remained in place. Removing the plate from her neighbor's car and mounting it on hers proved to be an easier job. She had to hope that the stolen plate, with only one screw holding it, would remain in place.

Gail drove out of the condominium garage. Her next stop: the nearest ATM. She had a little over seven hundred dollars in her account. Withdrawing two hundred at a time should work. Gail began the day with eighty-two dollars in her wallet. Adding Jack's money, three hundred and seventeen, and now an additional two hundred gave her a five hundred and ninety nine dollar kitty. Gail tried ATM's in two different locations. Both yielded two hundred more. The fourth ATM retained her card protecting Gail from a potential scammer. She drove slowly and hopefully away from her problems.

TWENTY SIX

Everyone heard the words: "You will stay in the building until we complete our preliminary investigation." Doctor Juliano protested and insisted his patients needed his care. It appeared that everyone, whether visitor or staff, had a good reason to leave the premises. The doors were locked. Detective Cornier assigned a calmed voiced officer the difficult task of listening to the woes and then firmly rejecting every plea. On the other side of the door, visitors were refused admittance.

**

All work within Belvedere stopped with small groups of employees gathering to share their knowledge about the crime. Cornier couldn't clamp the wildfire spread of misinformation. He had to interrogate people before he lost valuable bits of valid facts. Analyzing the murder room would wait until he interviewed all witnesses. He started with the residents of A wing. They were closest to the scene and potentially the best source of information.

He began at one end of the hallway and worked his way down; he knew room A130 was empty at the time of the murder. A bedridden woman lived in A128. He had to shout his questions and quickly recognized talking to a woman with extremely poor hearing wouldn't yield anything. He had to move on.

Cornier entered Mary Archer's room made note of her nametag and said, "Hi, my name's Jules Cornier." She looked at him stoically, and he added, "May I ask you some questions?"

Mary pulled up the covers leaving just the tips of her fingers exposed. She looked directly at the stranger. "Are you a nurse or a physician? Cornier didn't answer promptly enough, and she demanded, "Please tell me why you're here?"

"I'm Detective Jules Cornier," he said then turned and scanned the stark room. A room devoid of little elements of personalization yet it seemed clean and well maintained. It did appear to be institutional, felt cold and lacked the touches of home. Cornier returned his attention to the woman. "We're investigating a serious problem," he said as he pulled out a badge and allowed it to hang from his pocket. "Am I correct in assuming you're Ms. Mary Archer?

"Yes, I'm Mary Archer," she said. The detective waited to see if she would volunteer any information. Instead, she retorted, "And it's Miss Archer."

"Sorry about that Miss Archer. May I ask you some questions?"

"Of course you may ask some questions. Are you going to tell me what happened?"

"Answer my questions first, okay?" Mary offered a barely perceptible nod, and he continued, "Did you see or hear anything unusual this morning?"

"Are you asking did I hear the yelling, that noise of someone shouting out in sheer terror. Of course I heard it. What happened out there? Who screamed?"

"Did you hear anything, or see anything, unusual before the scream?"

"They've got me pretty doped up, and I sleep a lot. What did I miss?"

"You seem to be a with-it person Miss Archer and . . ."

"Don't you talk to me in that tone of voice," She chided. "If you think I'm mentally alert and competent, then say so." She glared at her visitor as she tugged the covers up even tighter. "I answered your question. And I'll tell you again. I did not hear anything before the screaming." She stopped for a moment and said, "I would appreciate it if you could tell me what happened." Her pleading voice didn't move him. She glared at the man and demanded, "What caused the commotion?"

The detective smiled at her determination and enjoyed the air of authority emanating from the woman. He finally answered, "Jack Tridon; the floor nurse died. He died a violent death. He's dead. Now it's my job to find out how it happened."

"May the Lord have mercy on his soul," Mary said with a touch of real sincerity. She closed her eyes and silently prayed, *"Dear Lord. I pray that you will forgive our actions. We knew no other way. Forgive us dear Lord. Please forgive us."* She opened her teary eyes, wiped them on the bed sheet, and then looked at Cornier while saying, "He was such a young man. How did he die?"

"Let's stick to my questions. Okay? Do you know anything about his demise?"

"Detective, look at me, I'm in bed. I can't get out of this bed for two reasons. I can't do it myself, and because they have me naked as a new-born babe. They took my clothes and kept that door closed. And here you are asking did I see or know about a man's death."

"Sometimes a dumb question gets a not so dumb answer."

"Are there any other questions, questions that I can answer?"

"Did you like him?"

Mary sneered, as she answered, "No." Then she added with a sharp demand, "How did he die?"

He parried her question and answered, "We have to wait for the coroner's examination to determine the exact cause of his death."

"Mister Detective. Half of this place probably saw Jack before you got here. And, based upon the amount of yelling and screaming that went on they all know something. You know the nurses will tell me; they'll tell me as soon as you leave. Why don't you be a nice boy and give me an honest answer?"

The old school teacher had him beat, and he offered, "He bled to death. It was kind of nasty; someone cut his throat. It was cut while the man . . ." Cornier stopped, recognizing he was saying too much.

"Oh my dear Lord! That is a horrible way to die." And Mary quickly added, "Were any other people hurt? Was there a big fight, a struggle?"

"You ask great questions, Miss Archer. Who do you think would fight with Mr. Tridon?"

"I don't know of anyone foolish enough to challenge Jack Tridon's strength." Mary sensed her question gave the detective too much information. She had to stop the debate and said, "Please send an aide in. I want to get out of this bed."

"I have a feeling I should ask one more question. Let me start again. Mr. Tridon was in the act of committing a felony when he was killed. Have any ideas on what it could be."

"I wondered when you would get around to that subject. I think I can if you tell me the time and where he died."

"Room 122 and about ten this morning."

"That's Emma's room. In that room, and at that time of the day, he would be forcing himself on Emma. Use your detective skills to fill in the rest."

Cornier stared at Mary Archer and absorbed the crisp answer before saying, "That was a fast answer. I thought you didn't know about the details of the murder."

"I didn't tell you anything about a murder. I know what Jack does to the women in this place."

"How do you know?"

"Take a guess Mister Detective."

"You're telling me this incident is not the first time?"

"Does the word rape stick in your throat? And it's not an incident; it's part of a continual horror."

"You?"

"Yes me, and just about every female in this wing. Please I've had enough. Go now and find an aide to help me."

Detective Cornier knew a dismissal when he heard one. He jotted a few notes into his little book. "Thank you, Miss Archer. Please call me if you want to tell me anything else." Cornier gave a weak smile and waited for a moment and said, "I think you know what I want." She remained mute and he slowly retreated out of the room.

***

Cornier felt prepared to interview the rest of the residents now armed with vital information. He left Mary Archer's room remained on the same side of the hall and entered Sam Termine's room. He stared at Sam Termine while walking towards his roommate. Cornier tried talking to Mr. Whitson — he knew the words were deliberately floating past him. The man ignored the Detective. He did not look at Cornier nor respond to his friendly greeting. Frustrated by the snub, he looked upon him with suspicion then realizing he wouldn't gain any information, scribbled another note into the little black notebook.

Cornier approached Sam's bedside, reached in and shook him gently. Sam, in a deep stupor, did not react to any amount of oral or physical urging. Cornier knew this room, somewhat connected to the murder scene, had to yield some important clues or perhaps these men were witnesses. He picked up the room telephone, identified himself and said. "Please retrieve the medical records for two residents, a Mr. Termine and Mr. Whitson. And ask Doctor Juliano to come as well."

Within minutes, a nurse entered the room with the computerized cart of records. Doctor Juliano followed right behind her.

"Doctor Juliano, this is going to be outside of your responsibility. It's very presumptuous of me. However, could you give me a professional opinion of the two residents in this room?"

Juliano growled, yet puffed up by the quasi-official request, reviewed Mr. Whitson's medical history then asked the nurse to recall Mr. Termine's record.

"The man next to the window, Charles Whitson, is non-ambulatory and mostly non-communicative. He can't get out of that bed. According to a special notation, although he can, he does not usually respond to normal conversational interaction. This again is according to the record." Juliano then added, "You would have to run tests to determine the accuracy of the notation. As to Mr. Termine, he is on some powerful medication; and based upon these records it's been administered for a long time. He's probably drugged out of any sense of reality. Can you wake him up?"

"That's the problem and the reason I called you. I can't wake him up. I want to talk to him."

"I don't doubt you can't stir him. His treatment is unreasonable. It needs to be reviewed by a medical and pharmaceutical board. We better get a hold of Doctor Lunkens and begin a . . ."

"You're telling me this man would not know if someone was committing a murder right next door."

"I'm telling you this man doesn't know we're standing next to him. I recommend we draw some blood and do a complete analysis."

"That's another problem and not my immediate concern. I have to find a murderer. Thank you Doctor Juliano and you too Miss. I appreciate your help," he said in a form of dismissal.

***

Detective Cornier withdrew his little black book and looked over his notes. He interviewed all the residents, all that he felt could give him clues on what happened in room A122. He flipped back a few pages. It showed Gail was a mess, and he sent her home so she could clean up and change her clothes. He grimaced recalling he sent a female officer to go home with Gail, pondered for a moment followed by jotting an additional note: Gail Summun agreed to release her bloody clothes for analysis. On another page, he scribbled: Danielle Turner has permission to stay with her mother. He underlined a note quoting Turner: "It didn't matter whether you granted permission or not. Under these circumstances, I will not leave my mother alone in this building." His notes also showed: hold Danielle Turner for further questioning. On the next page he wrote in bold: SEXUAL ABUSE.

TWENTY SEVEN

Cornier's notebook, full of interview information, could not point towards a perpetrator. The investigation needed more energy. He called his attending officers to a meeting gathering them near the murder room. The three policemen stood near the door waiting anxiously for the detective.

"You all know there was a vicious murder committed right here, in this room," Cornier said while pointing. "We were on this scene within minutes of the crime. That means the murderer could have been very close when you arrived. The initial interviews with some of the residents and visitors are not getting what we need. I need your help. Sergeant, I want you to organize and interview all the Belvedere workers, not just the managers, all the employees. Generate a list of everyone who was here within an hour or so of the murder. When you can, crosscheck their stories between the residents and with other workers. The information you pull out of these people will be important so please keep detailed notes on everything. Okay?"

"More than okay, we appreciate your confidence. We know we can help."

"That's good. Right now, there are only three of you. One should be free to keep an eye on this place; and two of you do a team interview. Rotate every couple of hours so you all get a chance to crack this case. Some probably finished their normal workday and are getting antsy just sitting around. Talk to them first. I trust your instincts. If you're satisfied with their answers, then let them go home."

***

Although he didn't need it, Cornier received official telephone confirmation on the sexual abuse of Emma. Now there were good reasons for a justified killing.

Not ferreting out a bunch of viable suspects taunted him. Mary Archer gave him the only viable lead he had. She had to know more than she offered.

***

Cornier returned to the crime scene. He tried to envision the murderer coming into the room — using either of two doors because the windows had screens and were secured on the inside. Cornier stood on a chair while pounding on the ceiling. The effort proved, with its muted sound, the ceiling was solid. The area did not have any ductwork. Baseboard radiators supplied heat. The individual room air conditioners were large, heavy and installed with substantial hardware.

Cornier entered the hallway and returned to the room murmuring, "Who ever committed the crime had to be known by the staff, or was staff. Therefore, he, or she, could enter the room without being challenged."

Cornier decided to try the second path through the toilet. Starting from the hallway, he entered room A124. Sam Termine was still curled up and in a deep sleep. He walked into the shared toilet. He opened the opposite entry.

The room began to feel familiar. He sensed the rage that exploded within its confines. The violence and accompanying sounds seemed to continue reverberating off of the walls and ceiling. Visualizing the horror as it occurred earlier in the day, Cornier grumbled with frustration. He broke the spell by concentrating on the scene and creating a possible murder scenario.

The man's body was found on top of the woman. That's according to the witnesses. A phone call confirmed he sexually attacked her. Picturing the two coupled in a gruesome tryst Cornier frowned at the thought of the series of felonies. Looking at the vacant bed, he couldn't fault anyone for moving the woman. They had to help her. Or did they have a motive to tamper with evidence. His mind swirled with the potential of duplicity. Gail Summun bloody uniform shows she was intimate with the crime scene. Cornier paced a bit and continued his guesses. His thoughts came out with him mumbling a little too loud: "Also — also Manfassi. Could Sal Manfassi be involved? Turner — what about Danielle Turner? She was here. Right here — she doesn't seem to fit — and yet." He walked around the bed and then tried to relive his concept of the killing. This time he retreated and pretended to ram the knife into the wall.

Cornier stared at the damaged wall. The knife left an elongated piercing hole, indicating the blade's profile: thin and triangular. A bloodstain at the site of the knife's penetration gave a smeared image of a retreating hand.

Even though the technicians photographed the entire scene, he felt the need to use his phone and took his own picture. This was one of the few solid bits of information the killer left behind. Cornier approved removing the knife from the wall sending it to the forensic laboratory for analysis. He didn't need it to dramatize the violence as he reached up and simulated various methods of someone plunging the knife into the wall. The angle of the weapon entering the wall indicated an approximate height of the perpetrator. Cornier stared at the wall turned and realized he was very close to the toilet door.

Moving in slow motion, he simulated the thrust of the knife and then rotated towards the toilet. It was a simple and a practical egress from the room. The moves were very natural and convenient; he concluded it to be the probable retreat path.

Upon opening, the door hinges protested with a squeal. Proceeding with gloved hands, Cornier flicked on the light taking care not to touch anything else. He looked about the tiny room. The forensic team would make a thorough examination for fingerprints or for other possible bits of evidence. Lifting and analyzing the multitude of prints and whatever other elements of importance they find, takes time. He needed some answers now.

His thoughts returned to that noisy door hinge. It emitted a slightly different tone when he changed the degree of opening. Moving it faster gave off another diverse sound. Any normal person had to hear the opening and closing of that door. Any normal person had to hear the noise of the atrocities occurring in room A122 that morning.

"Are you a normal person Mr. Sam Termine?" Cornier said aloud while he continued to play with the door. Again, he swung it open and this time pulled to close it. The hinges squeaked; the door resisted closing. It took a substantial tug to latch the door. When released, the door sprung open a few inches. A fast examination of the frame showed some debris in the doorjamb.

***

After the forensic team took a series of pictures, they nudged free the foreign substance in the doorjamb. It yielded upon touch. However, almost instantly fell apart into a few pieces. They scooped up the particles, guessed they were pieces of a pencil and placed them into a small evidence bag.

Everyone surmised that putting a portion of a pencil in the doorframe was a deliberate act to preclude its closing. The big questions of why and who did it remained part of the puzzle.

***

Cornier decided to reenter Sam's room. Upon opening their door neither Sam nor his roommate stirred. These two guys didn't even grunt, and it was already midday.

Charles Whitson's shallow breathing needed dedicated scrutiny for confirmation. Mr. Whitson sensing his presence remained motionless enjoying adding to the detective's dilemma.

Cornier shuffled about their room while continually looking for anything of significance then walked out into the hallway. His instinct kicked in. Retreating back into Sam's room, he grabbed the telephone and called Sal Manfassi.

"I want to review Sam Termine's records. I'll be in your office in a few minutes." Looking at Sam and then towards Mr. Whitson Cornier said, "Have a good rest — a good rest for now gentlemen. You know I'll be back."

***

Sal stood up greeting the detective, offered a chair and said, "I pulled up Termine's charts." Spinning his monitor around asked, "What are your concerns?"

"Why's he in bed?"

"He had complicated surgery. The hospital sent him to us for recovery. The man's non-ambulatory. He doesn't respond to therapy. As for his stamina: it's very low and as you witnessed, simple medication knocks him out."

"What therapy?"

"Physical therapy for one, it's performed by our consultant George Faulkins. Here, let me show you his entries. Faulkins works with Mr. Termine almost every day. That is, the days he's here. 'Been doing it for a while — we're not making any progress."

"This log indicates he worked for half an hour on Friday. How could he work with a guy who is as zapped as the one I just left?"

"That's part of the problem. He won't cooperate and try."

"Why does he need to be so heavily medicated?"

"Oh! His pain has to be suppressed. Doctor Lunkens always makes certain his patients are very comfortable."

"Do you really believe that?"

"What are you inferring Detective? We here at . . ."

"Okay! Okay, let's not visit that issue. Let's just try solving the crime. Where's this George Faulkins?"

"We can have him here tomorrow at nine, nine in the morning."

***

The police officers, enjoying the assignment to interview the staff, pursued it with vigor. And it didn't take very long to find some vital information that another person was in the building. Tina Morris of Memorial Hospital visited Milo Drew and she was with him during the time of his accident. Learning the accident occurred approximately the same time as the murder, they rushed the information to Cornier. He fumed believing the administrators hid important information.

"Go to the hospital and visit this Milo Drew. Get the straight facts," Cornier ordered. He stormed down the hallway went directly to Sal's office and walked in without knocking. "Tell me about Tina Morris," he demanded.

Sal reddened at the words and realized he made a serious error. "She's from the hospital and works with Milo on new resident admittances. She wasn't here very long since . . ."

"Since what — I have a very suspicious mind, especially when people deliberately hide essentials from me. He didn't fall on any chair, or table. That was a big lie. You knew he didn't lose his balance." Cornier stared at Manfassi and said, "Let me give you a big warning."

Sal quickly answered, "That's not necessary Detective. I'm sorry for not telling you before. The truth is Tina Morris either hit him or kicked him. I don't know which. No one saw what happened. They were lovers and had a serious falling out."

"Is that the only reason she hurt him?" Cornier stared at Sal waiting for the complete story.

"That's the only one I know," Sal lied. He waited for Cornier's reaction. When none came he offered, "We didn't report the assault because — as I said, no one witnessed it.

And the guy's married — we need the woman for future clients."

"You withheld vital information. And for what -- because you need this witness, or murderer, for new business? That makes me question your spirit of cooperation. You held back and now I wonder what else you're not telling me."

"Again I apologize. Please tell me. How I can help you."

"In this incident, you gave inaccurate information to an officer, and it's probably part of his report. Somehow we'll have to correct that report. You're going to have a little problem with this issue Mr. Manfassi. There's something about obstruction of justice that makes me very unhappy." Sal, displaying obvious discomfort, squirmed in his chair. Cornier observing his reaction continued his inquisition. "Tell me Mr. Manfassi. Did the State ever come in here for an audit of your operation?"

"Yes they did. They were here last week and stayed for three whole days. We received an excellent rating." Before he could continue the telephone rang. Sal quickly answered, listened for a moment and handed the handset to Cornier. "It's for you."

He listened, thanked the caller, and returned the phone back to Sal. "That was one of my guys. He decided to check up on Mister Drew. Well, your manager's in bad shape. They may have to remove one or both of his testicles. He's sedated, and we can't interview him. Let's get back to you. Are you sure I've got the entire story?"

"To the best of my knowledge," he said emphasizing the word my.

"Who's the State auditor?"

"There were four of them. Paul Tolski was the lead auditor."

"He's been here before?"

"The three women were; this was his first visit."

"I want his phone number."

Sal dug around his desktop and located Tolski's business card. "I'll make a copy for you," he said.

"Just want his name and number." A few fast scratches of his pen and the information became part of the little notebook.

"Anything you want to tell me before I contact this Mister Tolski? I won't tolerate any more surprises."

"We had an excellent audit. Mister Tolski will tell you the same."

"Mind if I use Mister Drew's office for a telephone call?"

"Not at all, just dial nine for an outside line."

"Don't need the phone just the office."

***

"Mister Tolski please, I'm Detective Cornier." He waited more than a few seconds for the man to get on the line.

"Paul Tolski speaking! Do I understand correctly that you're with the police department?"

"Mister Tolski. I'm investigating a murder at the Belvedere Manor."

"A murder at Belvedere; I was just there last week. Who was killed?"

"A male nurse: Jack Tridon."

"I met Jack. How did it happen?"

"Mister Tolski, I don't want to discuss any of the details. Can you answer a few questions about your audit?"

"Of course — if I can. Some information is privileged and needs proper approval for release."

"I'm not interested in that kind of stuff. I'm looking for the unusual, things out of place. Do you recall anything like that?"

"We had a very clean audit. Their records are very crisp."

"Yeah, I believe that would be the case. You walked around. Did you see or hear things that got your attention?"

Paul hesitated and pondered the question. There was a murder, and the police were looking for information. His gut said to tell all he knew and do it now. He took a breath and answered, "Not really. Well, there was one thing that bothered me."

"Tell me about it?"

"I interviewed some residents and got strange inputs from two people. A Mister Termine did not want to talk to me at first and then when we were one on one he said the residents were treated badly. If I recall his words, he said tortured. I discounted his input as a fantasy of his imagination. That was confirmed when I came back to my office. Mister Manfassi called my supervisor and explained Mister Termine was on medication. He has a tendency to tell stories. I put the information in my files. It's not in my report." He knew he threw away the notes. His conscience urged him to relate the facts. The file was fixable.

"Mister Termine was awake and lucid?"

"Well kind of normal and definitely awake. He could hold a reasonable conversation. I didn't have any trouble speaking to him. It was his story that was troubling."

"And who was the other?"

"Mrs. Danzell. Initially, she was very nice and friendly. The interview went well. It ended abruptly after she asked me a question. As I said at first she was friendly then became belligerent. She asked if I believed what people told me or did I consider them a bunch of loonies. Her tone and demeanor were very direct. She told me not to answer if I was going to lie."

"Did you?"

"Did I what?"

"Answer her, or lie, or whatever?"

"I couldn't do either. That was the end of it. She dismissed me and told me to leave."

"Is that it?"

"Yes, that's all. What do you think?"

"I think you better plan on getting your rear end back to Belvedere. Thanks for your time." Cornier terminated the call before the man could respond.

***

Cornier left Milo's office and went directly into Sal Manfassi's and said in a demanding voice, "You have a resident by the name of Danzell. What room's she in?"

Sal pulled up the listing and said, "325 in the C. It's a private room. Come I'll show you the way."

"That's not necessary. I'll find it." He walked swiftly down the corridor, up the C wing towards the entrance of Danzell's room.

"May I help you?"

"I'm looking for Mrs. Danzell."

"She's in the recreation room — with a visitor. I believe it's her daughter," the nurse said as she pointed in the proper direction.

"Ah, there you are Mrs. Turner. I trust this charming lady is your mother. I'm Jules Cornier of the Police." He said as he extended his hand to greet the woman.

Florence Danzell looked up refused to accept his hand and asked, "Why are you here?"

"I assume you know there's been a death in the facility." She didn't respond. "We're conducting an investigation into Mr. Jack Tridon's demise. If I may, I would like to ask you some questions."

"Is that all you're investigating, the death of a slime ball? Where were you when he was raging his filth on the women in this place? Go away, I have nothing to say to you."

"I appreciate how you feel. I have a job to do."

"You know nothing of my feelings. Go and do your job elsewhere."

"Mrs. Turner we can get your mother to cooperate. It is a simple . . ."

"Detective Cornier, I strongly suggest before you do something very stupid that you exhaust all other means of getting your information. My mother is a new resident and as you already know was heavily sedated. Go ask Doctor Juliano. She's not your killer, and you know it," Danielle said angrily.

"That may be true. My intuition says she may know something that will lead to the killer." Cornier looked at each woman in turn and then asked, "How about you Mrs. Turner? You're showing exceptional signs of anger right now. Are you involved? We know you were right there." Turner didn't answer and Cornier continued, "I think it's time we had our talk. Let's go somewhere a little private." He took Danielle's arm and started to lead her out of the room. "Say good-bye to your mother. Sorry to take your visitor Ma'am, we'll be just a short while."

***

Detective Cornier released Danielle's arm; they walked silently towards Milo's office. "Please sit down. We might as well be comfortable." Cornier sat in Milo's chair and put his feet up on the corner of his desk. "Tell me again. Why did you come in this morning? Visiting hours begin in the early afternoon."

Danielle puffed out a breath of frustration and said, "As I told you before. I came in with Doctor Juliano to check on my mother. I had a deep concern about her wellbeing." She relaxed a bit. Showing concern in her voice added, "Mom was always an alert woman."

Cornier ignored the emotions and asked, "Did you have any contact with people in the wing? I mean where the murder occurred."

"Just a little, there's only one person I know: Mary Archer. I've known her since the eighth grade. She taught the class. I found out she was here just before I brought Mom. I thought it a Godsend knowing someone. I didn't want my mother to be alone. She and Mom were getting reacquainted."

"Tell me about the last time you talked to Mary Archer."

"I talked to her a few days ago."

"So what happened?"

"I thought we were going to have a nice relaxed visit. There was an undefined urgency with both talking about bringing in special food and making certain I brought some every day. It sounded weird."

"Talking about food isn't unusual."

"You should have heard them. As I said the conversation had an urgency — and mystery. It wasn't normal. I went to see Mr. Manfassi. I felt I had to share the experience with him." Danielle stopped and pondered what she just said and added, "She's been out of it ever since."

"What did Mr. Manfassi say to you?"

"He said prescriptions were on file; medications to help my mother for this kind of sickness."

"He said she was sick?"

"No, not sick. I can't remember his exact words. He told me most new residents suffered through a mild depression."

"Including Mary Archer," he said interrupting her.

"I don't know that."

"Did you kill Jack Tridon?"

"My God what are you saying? No! No, I did not."

"Did you know him?"

"I met him once — I don't know much about him."

"Why were you in the wing?"

"Doctor Juliano's reaction to Mom's condition made me want to check on Mary Archer. When an aide took Mom for a shower, Juliano wanted to talk to Manfassi, so I decided to find Miss Archer." Danielle shook her head at the thought of the day's events then suddenly asked: "I heard something else happened. What's with Mr. Drew?"

Cornier didn't like the change of subject, let out a sigh and said, "Mr. Drew was assaulted — on his private parts. Whoever did it made him a eunuch." Cornier wiped his mouth with his hand and then stood up and challenged, "Mrs. Turner, your Mom knows something. You've got to help us. See if you can get something out of her." He sat down and whispered, "And off the record, I don't think you killed anyone," then dismissed her with a wave of his hand.

Danielle didn't challenge Cornier's crude non-oral signal to go, simply turned and walked away. Striding with anger-charged determination she aimed towards her mother's room stopping short after seeing her sitting in the recreation room.

The residual power of the medication held Mrs. Danzell in a drowsy mode. She stirred almost immediately when Danielle touched her.

"Mom, do you want to go back to your room?"

"Not now sweetheart. Can we see Mary?   I'm concerned about her.

"Doctor Juliano said she's okay. I suspect we will be able to go over later in the day."

"I know about Jack. Are you involved?"

"Only by being here when Gail found him." Danielle pulled up a chair and said, "Mom please tell me what's going on."

Florence looked around and said, "Jack Tridon and Gail Summun were abusing the women in the wing. When it started the women talked to the administrator. He did nothing. When those two found out, they came back inflicting additional punishment. Oh Danielle, bed confinement became a prison; unable to move equated to be pure torture."

"And no one complained to outsiders?"

"Some ministers listened then apparently carried that story to somebody because the complainer got another dose of punishment. No one believes the tale of torment. And do you know why? I'll tell you why. The residents are viewed as mentally incompetent. Don't look at me that way. You didn't do as I asked. No! You probably went to the office and told them I was acting strange, right?" She did not wait for an answer. "And you know they punished me with drugs."

"I'm sorry Mom. I only wanted what was the best for you."

"If you had doubts we could have called Doctor Juliano, then I would not be drunk with these horrid drugs."

"We'll get you out of here and into another . . ."

"No, you will not," she said firmly. "This place will be going through a purge. The garbage will be thrown out. People will be all over Belvedere Manor. The oversight will be overwhelming. Every agency in the state will want to do the right thing. Probably have some federal people needing a piece of notoriety. No, for a while this will be a fine place. It will be because a lot of people, including you, will make certain it is."

"What shall I tell Detective Cornier?"

"Tell him to bring in counselors. I mean real professionals, meaningful people who have years of experience. Cornier, if he wants to know what's going on, he should make certain they listen and put the entire story together. Killing anyone is a terrible tragedy — in this case it is an absolute blessing. This detective may want to solve his murder. There are other important issues needing attention." She stopped and took a deep breath and said, "Enough. Let's go see Mary."

"We will. Not today Mom. Not today, okay?"

***

The police officers continued working on their chart showing who and where people were during the morning. It was a larger job than they originally imagined and now understood why Cornier needed help. Interviews with the office staff yielded the important information about the woman who assaulted Milo. That success gave them a renewed energy to dig up additional clues, clues that hopefully will solve the murder.

Cornier thanked them for deriving good information. He applauded their success in finding Tina Morris and urged them to continue interrogating the people who had access to the wing.

Interviewing the aides proved a challenge. Since most were recent immigrants, they maintained the pretense that they spoke little English. Working from an employee list of those present, the first one called responded to their name, then merely offered a puzzled look to any questions. Lani, knowing their conundrum, offered to intercede as an interpreter. Lani said she was fluent in both Jamaican Patois and English.

"Please tell us where you were when the murder occurred."

Lani looked at the young officer and smiled while answering. "Please tell me the time you want me to cover."

"Sorry about that. Where were you between 9:30 and 10:30 this morning?"

"I finished my morning clean-up duties just before nine. Then, as I am required to do, I went to the kitchen to help with the noon meal."

"Can anyone verify that?"

"Of course; I suggest you talk to the chef. We worked all morning."

The officers scanned their listing, located the name of the chef and made appropriate notes to check on her story. They continued,

"What do you know about Jack Tridon?"

"He was the head nurse of the wing."

"You said was."

"Mr. Tridon is dead," she said without hesitation.

"Do you know who killed Mr. Tridon?"

"I'm sorry I cannot say. Mr. Officer, they keep us very busy; we work hard all day"

The policeman didn't understand the subtlety of her immediate response. He continued with the interview. "Do you know anyone who wanted to kill him?"

"From what he was doing he was an evil man. I am sorry. I did not see anyone trying to kill him."

"Are you telling me he assaulted other women?"

"No, no, I do not know. What I do know: he did not bother the workers."

"Were you a witness to any assaults?"

"No."

"What more can you tell us about rooms with closed doors?"

"I tried to answer your questions. Are you finished with me?"

"Not yet. If there were other sexual crimes why didn't the victims come to us?"

"I'm sorry I cannot answer for other people."

The interrogators made their notes, looked towards the woman wanting to ask more questions, relented and merely offered, "Thank you for your cooperation." Lani began to rise and heard, "Please stay."

"I thought we were finished."

"Didn't you offer to help us with your associates?" Lani merely nodded her assent.

***

"Where's Willet?" Detective Cornier asked.

"They're not back yet. We've tried calling her even called the woman's home and, no answer. They probably went shopping and lost track of the time."

"You know that's not Willet. She's all business. If they're not back within the hour, go find them. Got it?"

***

Locating the long delayed Officer Willet and the first-on-the-scene witness, Gail Summun, became top priority. Finding Willet's cruiser in the Manor's parking lot created a new set of consternation. Did they return and were sequestered somewhere in the building? Or did they go in Summun's car, if she had one?

***

The superintendent of Gail Summun's building, a retired police officer, enjoyed the interchange with the young officers. He knew his business and was not going to allow access to anyone's apartment, without a search warrant. That standoff continued until the two of them understood his terms. All he wanted was some courtesy and a nice 'May I'. When the two showed him proper respect they were quickly escorted up to Gail Summun's unit.

The super knocked on Gail's door and when no one replied, knocked again. He looked at the officers, shrugged his shoulders and placed his key into the door's lock. "Look guys, if she happens to be sleeping, I've got to give the tenant a chance to get decent. No rushing in, okay?" They nodded their agreement. When the door opened a tiny amount, the superintendent called, "Ms. Summun, hello, are you home?" Receiving no answer, he pushed on the door, walked into the room and repeated his call. The policemen strode in behind him, ignored his gentle approach, quickly passed him and dashed into the apartment.

They found Officer Willet, seemingly unconscious, in an easy chair. She responded to their prodding in a manner they've seen before. She had all indications of an overdose. Knowing Willet was a staunch enemy of drug and alcohol use, this woman would not consume any, willingly, and needed medical attention.

"We've got to get this gal to a doctor."

***

As the cruiser raced toward the hospital, they informed Cornier about the poor condition of Officer Willet.

Locating Gail Summun shifted back to Cornier and elevated in priority.

***

Detective Cornier felt the strain of a long day, and yet he needed more time to analyze all the details gathered. The newest twist, Gail Summun's flight, had very deep implications.

***

Belvedere, now functioning with temporary personnel filling in the void, made Harry Benas appear competent and professional. With Sal immersed in legal maneuvering, Harry grasped control of the operation of the facility.

Cornier thought some of the residents still lived in fear. He requested help from the State Police, believing a strong presence of uniformed officers would instill a new level of assurance. A team of four troopers arrived assuming the duty of around the clock visibility.

Cornier left Belvedere deeply fatigued albeit satisfied he did all possible during this difficult day.

TWENTY EIGHT

Knowing the circumstance of her assault, the medical team took special care to treat Emma with compassion. Performing a thorough physical examination required invasive procedures making Emma tremble with every touch. She did not respond to any question. Remaining mute, her blank stares and tensed body showed the mental effects were more severe than any physical damage caused by the trauma. Various members of the psychiatric staff and social workers visited. Each failed to penetrate her protective shield. However, all were confident with medication and counseling she would again be mentally viable.

Upon completion of the exam, they concluded that Emma didn't need the services of a hospital. She did need continuing care at an appropriate level available elsewhere. They decided to send her back to Belvedere Manor.

"Ms. Joslin. Hello. Is it all right if I call you Emma?" The floor nurse said as she held her hand. "Sorry you had to experience all those nasty procedures. The good news is the doctors believe you're okay. They can't find any serious problems. Everyone believes it's best for you to go back, back to your home in Belvedere Manor." The moment the nurse indicated she would return to Belvedere, Emma squeezed the woman's hand; her eyes opened wide in terror; she didn't utter a word. "Please don't be frightened. They told me the police are now in charge of Belvedere; there's a quite a few of them patrolling the facility. You'll have nothing to fear. I believe everyone will be watching over you."

Tears welled and then rolled from Emma's eyes as her hand relaxed. Emma closed her watery eyes, shook her head violently in disbelief.

***

The Belvedere maintenance staff received word: Emma Joslin will be returning. Harry Benas decided to convert a private room in A Wing into a double accommodation. Although there were two usable beds in room 122, they could not convince the police removing one bed wouldn't disturb the scene.

"Harry, they won't let us use the good bed in 122. I got'ta buy a new one. Sal and Milo ain't here, so how we gun'na get the purchase order? We know we can pick up whatever we need at the warehouse. We just need the paper."

"Hey guys, no problem. Just go, pick out what's needed, and you'll have the approval by the time you get there," Harry said with great authority.

The man looked at Harry, and then at his partner and gave a shrug with his shoulders and said, "Okay, you're the boss. If we have any luck, should be back in a couple of hours."

Harry Benas, dressed in a dark suit with a white shirt and patterned red power tie, walked into the general office area. "Can I have your attention please?" The office staff looked up and waited in silence. "You've all been great. Thanks for the effort. We have to keep this place going and for now I'll be the heavy. I don't have to tell you that Sal and Milo are very busy with a ton of problems. So, I'll take responsibility for all managerial issues." They looked at him without comment, and he said, "As you know, I brought in contract people to help us. They will stay as long as we need them; they'll be here until we can hire full time replacements. Sometime during the day I want to talk to each of you, one on one, to answer any questions you may have about what happened. And as to our future, it is very simple. I need each and every one of you. Of course, it'll be tough for a while. I know we can do it. So, please, no questions right now, just go out there and let's do our job. If you can, please accept any calls from concerned family members. Some may be a little difficult, if so, just forward them to me. Okay?"

No one answered merely nodded in muted understanding. "Oh, one thing, I need an open-ended purchase order for the Medical Supply Warehouse. We need to pick up a new bed, accessories and probably a lot more." He received a thumbs-up response from the woman handling purchasing. Harry turned away smiling and wondered how he could use this newly found authority to his advantage.

***

The maintenance crew walked into Mary's room and said,

"You're getting company." They began rearranging the furniture.

"No one told me."

"Well then, I guess you didn't hear. Emma's coming home. You two are going to be roomies."

"Emma? Is she all right?"

"Sorry, don't know anything, other than she's coming back — sometime soon."

Minutes after the crew left an aide expertly dressed the bed with clean linens.

The sometime soon prediction occurred within a half hour. Transportation attendants wheeled Emma into the room. A man, slight in build, along with brawny woman gently lifted Emma from the gurney. Experienced hands maneuvered her into the freshly made bed. An LPN, recently hired through an agency, performed as the floor nurse. She monitored Emma's arrival fully aware of the horror the woman experienced, welcomed Emma with a loving hand.

"Hi Emma, it's me, Mary." Emma remained mute. "It's all over Emma. They're gone from our lives. They're gone forever." Emma still did not reply presenting a state of frozen rigidity.

Emma, heard Mary's message, tried to ferret out some sense of reality. The medication, prescribed by meaningful experts, not only secured the cloud over Emma's mind it made her sink deeper into a denser fog.

***

After a peaceful night's sleep, Mary woke up alert. With Emma back, everything began to look normal. She did not want to be in bed, reached for the call buzzer and summoned the floor nurse.

"Yes, what's the problem?" The voice said over the intercom.

"I want to get out of this bed. Can you get in here and help me?"

"Sorry Miss Archer no can do. We have our hands full. We're spread very thin. I can only perform vitally necessary functions. We'll get to you as soon as possible." The intercom clicked off, and Mary puffed in frustration.

***

"Hi Mom, did you have your breakfast?"

"What's with the idle chatter about breakfast? No kiss for your mother this morning?"

Danielle fell back into the obedient daughter mode. Gently kissed her mother and said, "Anyone give you any medication this morning?"

"No way! I'm done taking that garbage. Now that you're here, let's do something productive. I want to see Mary."

"Mom, why don't we just stay away from that wing for a while? The authorities have to do their thing. Miss Archer will be fine. I'm quite sure there're good people all over the place by now."

"What kind of a daughter did I bring into this world? Are you going to push me over there or do I do it myself?" She looked at her daughter who shook her head in defeat. Without answering she merely took hold of the chair and started walking out of the room.

Neither said a word until Danielle and Florence Danzell came to Mary's door. Florence announced their arrival, "Hi. You want company?"

"I always want company. Come in. Did you hear Emma's my roommate?" Mary turned towards Danielle and said, "I guess I have you to thank for my last few days of discomfort?"

"I — Miss Archer I..."

"Ah, see I was right. Your stammering is — don't say anything more. Everything is going to be okay," Mary said.

"I wished I knew what was going on. I could have helped. Mom came here to be cared for, and it's been a horror."

"Danielle, I want you to take a little walk. Mary and I need to chat. We don't want to bore you with old woman's talk." It was more than a suggestion.

"The last time you two . . ."

"Please," she said interrupting. "It's not like the last time. Things are different. We need to be alone. Just for a little while. Please?"

"Okay Mom, right now I have a very bad case of the guilt's. I'll be back in five minutes," she said while quickly departing.

"How's Emma doing?" Florence asked.

"Poor thing lived through hell. Do you know his blood was all over her? They found him on top of her — dead."

"Jack's gone. What about Gail?" Florence asked.

"She's not around. No one's saying anything."

"Do you — do you know who?" Florence asked

"Now Florence, how would I know such a thing," she said with a frown.

The two women sat next to each other and became lost in their thoughts. They appeared to lose a desire to talk. The ugliness of the past week and the trauma of yesterday lay heavy on their hearts. It was a comfort for each to see the other safe, and in good spirits.

"Let's get together often, no make it tomorrow. We'll have a good chat," Mary said breaking the silence.

"I'm happy you're showing signs of being the Mary Archer of the good old days. Yes, let's do that. Let's get together tomorrow. I'll come over here. I need the exercise."

***

The two doorways leading into the murder room remained taped shut. That meant, with the toilet being unavailable, Sam would have to continue using the bedpan and a portable urinal.

Although the drugs mostly stifled his senses, Sam knew he rescued a frail woman from a torturous attack. He began to mumble: "Did I have to kill him?" Surprised to hear his voice, Sam looked about. Other than the noise of his musing, the room was quiet. Sam knew the answer: he had to do it. It didn't matter what other people said or asked of him. Witnessing Jack in the act drove him to help Emma. Now, Sam feared killing that man, would torture him forever.

***

The moment Lani came into Sam's room, she opened the drawer and not finding any latex gloves asked, "Is there anything else?"

Sam reached into the foot of his bed and withdrew the damp socks and said, "I don't need these."

Lani thrust the socks into her pocket. "That's everything?"

Sam started to nod his head, suddenly remembered and whispered, "A wad of tissue and some pills are over there."

Lani rooted within the bottom of the closet, retrieved the drugs and pocketed them. She turned to Sam, acknowledged finding both by patting her smock. Lani inquired, "Are you sure there is nothing else?"

"That's it, thank you — I could use a wheelchair."

Lani sent her eyes upward symbolizing her assessment of his need to flaunt his independence spun around and returned with a chair. Lani feigned struggling motions, whisked him out of bed. "Don't let anyone see how strong you are."

"I'm still feeling very loopy. How about a change of scenery and shove me into the hallway."

TWENTY NINE

Detective Cornier was in the process of arranging his mini-notes into a chronology of events when a knocking on the door broke his deep concentration.

"Hi – I'm George Faulkins."

"Mister Faulkins, come on in." Cornier eyed the man and after perceiving a nervous tension in his voice said, "You're responsible for all the physical therapy, right?"

"Yes I am, sometimes I have an assistant. I usually work alone."

"Do you have any idea why I wanted to talk to you?"

"Sal called last night. He told me about Jack." His words sputtered out in a rapid flat monotone.

Cornier decided to validate his authority and flipped the impressive detective badge out of his pocket. "I'm the lead detective for a murder investigation. You do realize you didn't answer my question." He delayed a moment allowing Faulkins time to absorb his potential dilemma, and then added in a slow demanding voice, "Alright – you're here and I expect your full cooperation."

Faulkins paled with the stern admonition. He stared at the aggressive detective while trying to say something. It didn't work. He lost his voice; his mouth merely gaped open.

Cornier did nothing to aid the man as he froze before him, totally paralyzed. These symptoms spoke louder than any oral answer. "Where's your office?"

Faulkins found a little courage and said, "It's down the hall."

Cornier indicated he should lead the way. They walked a few steps down the corridor, and Faulkins pointed. "It's right in here." Flipping on the light switch showed some exercise equipment plus a tiny desk located in one corner of the room.

"Mr. Faulkins, you're a registered professional; an expert in all aspects of physical therapy. I need an opinion on the physical abilities of some Belvedere residents."

Faulkins drew in a deep breath, tried to settle his nerves, and responded in a fairly normal voice, "Of course, however, my knowledge is limited to those who are referred to me for treatment. Only a physician can prescribe the type of therapy that's required." He waited for a comment then quickly added, "I do it right here at this facility."

"Mr. Faulkins, all I want is some information. Let's get right to the point. You said you know about Jack Tridon. The man's dead. Who, and let's stick with the A corridor, who is ambulatory? Who has the strength to kill a man? Even of more interest, who has the strength to kill a big guy? Kill a macho man like Mr. Tridon – in such a violent manner?"

"You're interested in who has the strength. Okay, rather than use a shotgun approach. Sorry about that. What I mean, I want to be accurate. I'd like to review all the residents, starting with the ones who are in active therapy." He keyed-in and then pointed to his computer screen and said, "We have Mary, Jessie, Betty, Sara, Karen, Jane and Sam; six women and one man. They're all non-ambulatory. None are responding to treatment. A few can stand and move about with a little shuffle. That would be Mary, Jessie, and Betty. All the rest can't do a thing requiring any strength or balance."

"So, you're telling me, none of these seven people can move about to kill and then quickly disappear."

"They can't walk. Maybe some could crawl. I don't encourage that form of propulsion. None of them can walk. None has the ability to challenge anyone – and that's my professional opinion," he said with pride.

"I'd like to talk about Sam Termine. Tell me what happened the last time you worked with Sam Termine?"

"Faulkins called up another file and said, "My records show we had a half hour session on Tuesday morning."

"Mr. Faulkins the medical record on the floor indicates Termine was heavily medicated from Monday through Wednesday. It also shows he's on mandatory bed rest. And for your information, I saw him on Wednesday. He was in bed and apparently in a drugged induced sleep. So back to the question, when and where did you perform this therapy?"

The beads of perspiration flowed and sparkled on his face. "I bring all clients to this room and use the equipment that you see . . ."

Cornier held up his hand and demanded, "Mr. Faulkins. I will inform you once more, and you better listen. This is a murder investigation. We're in an information gathering stage. I'm trying, trying very hard to be nice to you. Your answers stink. And you know how odiferous they are." He allowed a little time for the challenge to register with Faulkins. "This is where we are: you're playing a dangerous game, and I don't like it. Lying to me is an obstruction of justice, a felony. Up to now you've wasted my time, and it's going to end right now. If you persist, I will have you brought in. Then you will be questioned by other people. They're very intelligent and will know why I had you brought in. Being treated as an uncooperative witness, a hostile witness is going to be extremely uncomfortable. The query will be formal, intense, fully documented and recorded for any future action against you. So, I will begin again – and it's your choice. Either you give me crisp accurate answers, information you believe is the truth – or you can make a trip downtown." Cornier glared at the man and asked, "What's it going to be?"

"I'm very nervous."

"You should be. Now don't waste any more of my time. Let's ignore these purported records. Tell me the exact time and date of Mr. Termine's last session of physical therapy?"

Faulkins knew his answer could be the start of his legal problems. He flushed a deep red and answered, "I never gave him a treatment. He wasn't ready for therapy." Cornier grimaced and stared at him. Faulkins immediately offered, "I know it wasn't the right thing to do. I will make it right. When he gets a little more stamina, I will give him the best. I promise."

"Fraud is a different issue. At this moment, it does not concern me. Who determines when a resident is ready for therapy?"

"Jack."

"The Jack who's dead, the guy who can't verify you're a truthful man."

"Please believe me. You're getting the absolute truth."

"Alright, tell me about the women?"

"It's the same thing with the women; I'm waiting for Jack."

"So if I understand what you're telling me. By an order from a physician, all of them are your clients. And because of Jack – you're not working with any of them. Did you submit a bill for your services? Don't bother answering. Go out and get yourself a good lawyer. And remember Mr. Faulkins, we have a killer loose. I've got a pretty good idea who it is. Don't you?"

"No, no I don't. God I hope you don't think it's me."

"Where were you yesterday morning from about nine to eleven?"

"That's an easy one. I service the Jancin's Health Center every Wednesday morning, from nine until twelve thirty. Six patients received therapy yesterday morning. In the afternoon I . . ."

"Don't care about the afternoon. If I talk with the patients at Jancin's are they going to know who you are?"

"Absolutely. They like me over there, and I have a good success rate with their therapy."

"Draw up a list of names. We'll want to check on your story. Right now, you don't have much credibility. Especially with what you did or didn't do here. Here's an interesting point, if you go to Jancin's on Wednesday how could you treat people here, at Belvedere, on Wednesday? Forget I asked. That's another guy's problem. I need those names – right now. I'll wait."

George Faulkins composed the list from memory. His stomach rebelled; he started shaking. His facial skin developed a gray pallor while passing the details to the detective.

Cornier accepted the tabulation without scrutiny. Faulkins ran out of the building.

***

The Detective, in deep thought, sauntered back to Sal's office. Harry Benas looked up when Cornier walked in.

"I had a nice talk with your physical therapist. He didn't look very well. Sure was a talkative one. I learned a few interesting things. He informed me of what you people do around here. I really mean, don't do. I'm going to use Mister Drew's office for a telephone call or two." He wasn't seeking permission. He just felt like tweaking the guy into a little discomfort.

Harry reddened, envisioned Faulkins caving in and confessing. "He dumped and left without a warning," Harry muttered.

***

"Lieutenant, I need some help. This place is rotten and needs a good sweep. Can we get the fraud squad in here? While working the issues I dug up a few stories about possible insurance scams. Just a feeling this could be kind of deep. Maybe the FBI will want to be involved." He then added, "Yeah we've got solid motives for a murder. Just have to work a little more to lock down some good suspects."

***

Sam rolled down the hallway and stopped at the nurse's station. "Where's Gail?" He asked.

"Sorry Sir, I can't tell you. Harry told us not to talk about any of the personnel. Do you need help?"

"No thank you. I can make it on my own." As he went by he gave her a wink of confidence. Sam smiled and continued on into the recreation room. He spotted Mary Archer in the far corner. She sat stoically looking out the window onto the courtyard. "Good morning Miss Archer. Hope you're feeling well today."

"Good morning Sam. Isn't it a wonderful day? It's a pleasure to see you up and in such fine health." Sam came closer and she lowered her voice and whispered, "When you were in my class, I wondered how you would develop. Now I know. The guessing game is over. I know you're the best young man who ever passed through my room. You have the mental alertness and fortitude to accomplish any impossible task. Everything you do just put you right on top."

"I question that."

Mary pulled very close and lowered her whisper, "Sam I'm so proud of you. I can't even picture how it happened. You've rescued all of us from some terrible people."

Sam looked about to make certain no one could hear, and he too whispered, "Miss Archer I'm still in a fog." He took a shuddering breath and continued, "It's like a dream, more like a nightmare, a nightmare and there were no heroics. Emma suffered and I hated using her."

"Don't find fault. There was absolutely nothing wrong with what you did. You accomplished what no one else could do. Sam, you have our eternal gratitude."

"There was one failure. Everything happened so fast. I didn't tell him. He didn't know why. Jack died in an absolute panic."

Mary sat stunned listening to the few vivid details. Sam waited for her and she relaxed and said, "It wasn't your failure. I was wrong, all wrong asking you to do an impossible task. It wasn't you, it was me. I got lost in my thoughts of trying to do everything right. Sam, you didn't fail. No one had to tell him. When you struck, Jack knew. Believe me no one had to tell him." Mary took his hands and held them while he slumped down into his chair. She tried comforting him while he fought for his own sanity. "Sam, stop thinking about it. The women in Belvedere Manor can smile again. It will take time Sam. I promise you, Jack's agony will disappear from your memory."

"I hope you're right." Sam sat for a while and then leaned into Mary and whispered, "You know they might just figure it out. They may look at me and say he's the only one, the only one in a position to do it."

"I don't think so. All of us know you were in bed or on occasion in a chair. It took a superman to kill the loathsome Jack Tridon. Put your mind to rest. They have to convict a person beyond a reasonable doubt. There's not a chance a prosecutor would take on this complete wing of witnesses. Can you imagine all of us in front of a jury?" Mary saw Cornier in the doorway.

"It's nice to see both of you up and looking fit. You folks were pretty much under the influence yesterday," Cornier said as he approached them.

"Drugs and I don't get along." Mary said and added, "Thanks for your concern."

"Everywhere I turn a certain name crops up. I keep hearing: Mary Archer. Why are you so popular around here?"

Mary frowned. "I don't understand your question."

"Let's change the subject. Mr. Termine, I talked to Mr. George Faulkins, the physical therapist. Do you know him?"

"No – did he say I received some therapy?"

"Yes and then no. At first, he did and then he recanted and said he never did. I called the Fraud Division, and they'll want a statement from you and from you too Miss Archer. His records show you received his skilled services."

"Oh my, we have such lovely people in this world."

"The fraud group will be looking into everything so get ready for a lot of interviews. Mr. Termine may I talk to you? Alone, if you don't mind Miss Archer." Mary Archer looked at the detective and then at Sam. She shook her head and slowly turned her chair pulling herself into the hallway.

"Can I call you Sam?" When Sam nodded approval he continued, "I was in your room yesterday, and you were in a deep sleep. I'm happy to see you're able to get around."

"That makes two of us. Believe me; I'm happy to be up. I've been in bed for a long time."

"That's interesting, very interesting. Is it the truth?"

"That's a strange question. Why don't you check the records? Determine it for yourself."

"I've looked, and TA DA, like magic, they support your story." Cornier stared down at Sam. "I'd like to talk about the murder. You do know a murder occurred yesterday?"

"Of course I do."

"So we can talk about it. Okay with you?"

"It is the topic of the day around here. I don't know how I can help you."

"Well let me tell you my story. I've talked to a lot of people and examined a lot of evidence. I constructed a nice timeline and put people here and there, and things started to firm up. Sound interesting so far?"

"I'm a fan of mysteries. I'm all ears."

"Great! Here's my tale of adventure. The motive behind the killing was simple. Jack was brutalizing the women, and he had to be stopped. We know the administrators should have stopped him. They didn't. Any number of people could have done what was needed. All the wonderful people who came in to perform a community service did not believe nice Ole Jack was capable of such behavior. He had them all in his hands. Jack recited his professional opinion, and everybody believed the women in Belvedere had to be fantasizing. He was such a handsome stud. We do have some facts: he lived a horrible lie, and many women suffered at his hands. We know the authorities outside of Belvedere wouldn't investigate this terrible problem therefore the assassin had to be someone on the inside. A person who believed, or somehow knew, the atrocities occurred – or could have been a victim – or maybe someone who actually witnessed the assaults."

"Why are you telling me all of this?" Sam inquired.

"Just go along with me. Listen to this yarn. You said you liked mysteries, and this is quite a story. For a start let's say that Jack was a very malevolent person. He was pure bad – and he had to be stopped. Now I do not believe Jack's killer had to be a giant. He or she could be limited in ability -- why – because he, or she, attacked swiftly. The killer came in fast, did it quickly and since no one witnessed this action, exited without adding any commotion. Now how did he enter? We know, he, or again, perhaps she, had no other choice other than entering the room from the hallway or through the shared toilet. This same toilet has direct access to your room. Are you staying with me?"

"I hear what you're saying. I still don't get it."

"Oh Sam, I think you do. I think you understand. Allow me to continue. No one heard or saw this killer. Keep in mind it was ten in the morning. People were coming and people were going up and down the hallway, and they didn't see anything. They didn't hear anything. Let's talk about the people coming and going. Nice folks and they all had a great alibi. They said they had witnesses proving they were not in the A wing at the precise time the murder occurred. And they indeed had reliable witnesses who could verify where they were. Isn't this a great story?" Sam shrugged his shoulders. "We know the time of the assault. We also know some very key people were in the area. We have the nurse, Gail Summun, running around trying to find help for Mister Milo Drew. Did you know about the Drew attack?"

"I heard he fell or was hit, and he's hurting somewhere in the groin. What really happened?"

"We'll get back to Mr. Drew. Let's stay with Jack. The kitchen had a lot of people working on the preparation of the noon meal, and no one left the area. The laundry had all their people working, and no one left the area. Now we do have some of the key roamers. Mrs. Turner, a visitor, was in the hallway and bumped into Gail. They both were near the murder room. Some others were further down the building. I believe we've accounted for everyone. And you know what? Everybody has a terrific alibi."

"Is that the end of your story? If it is, I still don't know why you're telling me all of this."

"Sure you do. I've covered everyone in the hallway. Now how about the two of you in room A124?"

"Mr. Detective, my roommate, Mr. Whitson, is bedridden. I've never seen him up and around. He doesn't talk very much."

"Oh I agree with you. I don't think Mr. Whitson is guilty of any murder – how about you?" Cornier moved closer and pointed his finger at Sam.

"And as you already know, I was under the control of drugs. I didn't see or hear anything," Sam added.

"Yeah you're right. You were drugged. I can verify that. I saw you, after the murder, and Doctor Juliano was with me. Man, you were really out of it. Now here's a good question needing a good answer. When were you drugged? Tell me Sam. Were you drugged before the killing or perhaps right after the killing?"

"Are you saying I murdered Jack Tridon?"

"Yes I am. We both know you killed Jack Tridon."

Sam paled at the words and closed his eyes waiting for his arrest.

Cornier also waited a moment before he said, "Yeah Sam, we both know -- we know, and yet I have one big problem. And it's a whopper of a problem. You did a great job covering up. The best I've ever seen. Tell me, are you going to confess? Before you say anything, let me continue. I've got to tell you about a very important issue. I don't have very much physical evidence proving you did it. By that, I mean really hard evidence to present to a jury. In fact, the evidence I do have has serious doubt written all over it. Then there's the defense's evidence. You were drugged. We all saw that. You can't walk or so the records show. Can you walk? You see my problem? Unless you confess to this crime, I can't see anyway of convicting you. So I'll ask again. Are you going to confess Mr. Termine?"

Sam relaxed and finally laughed, "No Detective Cornier. No, I can't do that."

Cornier looked at Sam and smiled and said, "How difficult was it to get that piece of pencil to stay in the door jamb." He waited for Sam's reaction and when none came he said, "I think we can prove you handled that little piece of a pencil. Your DNA is probably all over the thing. Was it big enough to do the job? I think it was. It held the door open just this much." Cornier showed a small distance using his thumb and index finger.

Sam showed no sign of acknowledgment, merely waited for more comments from his visitor. Cornier also waited, and both sat in silence. Cornier finally broke the quiet and said, "Sam I thank you for your time. I want you to know as far as I am concerned this case is going into the inactive file. This case is similar to the OJ murders. I believe I know who the killer is, or maybe I should say executioner. Is that a better word? Well, whatever, and I know I can't get a prosecutor to take what I have. This case also has all the aspects of being a justifiable homicide. A jury will never get to hear the meager evidence I've got. Unless you confess, for now, Sam you got away with it."

Cornier started to walk away and then returned and said, "I wish I had the courage to do what you did." Cornier leaned closer and whispered, "I want one promise from you."

"What's that?"

"There's ugliness all around this place, and I know a lot of stuff needs fixing. Don't take the law into your hands again. Call me if it gets to a point where you need help. Okay?"

Sam looked at the Detective and smiled and stretched out his hand. "You're a great story teller. Ever think of writing a book?"

THIRTY

The attendees sat around the small conference table and waited impatiently for the dynamic prosecutor. He entered the office with flair and ingrained authority, plopped down into his chair and said, "Let's go. What do we have so far?"

All looked towards Detective Cornier assuming he would be the one reporting upon the murder of Jack Tridon. Instead Lieutenant Gabriel broke the silence and said, "We've got a very complicated crime scene and other circumstances. There's the murder of Jack Tridon; Gail Summun, a possible perpetrator running away; the assault of Emilo Drew; numerous accounts of rape and sodomy; and the very high probability of fraud in many areas of the business. I have three teams investigating the problems. We expect some arrests by early next week."

"So you've solved the murder, and you wait until this meeting to tell me," the District Attorney admonished.

"No, sorry to say that's not the case. The murder's still a big problem for us. Detective Cornier can tell you what progress he's made." The lieutenant looked down on his pile of papers as he passed the hot issue to his subordinate.

Cornier smiled at the political fast shuffle and began, "I believe I know who murdered Jack Tridon. However, there are major concerns. What I have is mostly a theory with extremely limited evidence pointing towards a perpetrator. As to getting a conviction, we have a big problem. The guy I believe did it is protected by many legitimate medical documents indicating he could not have committed any crime. I am referring to Samuel Termine, a resident in the room next to the crime scene. I believe he entered room A122, better known as the crime scene, from room A124, his room. For him, it was easy to go through the shared toilet and kill Jack Tridon. Mister Termine was then, and is now, a resident in room A124. We have the murder weapon; he used it and plunged it into the wall before leaving. The hooked knife doesn't have any useable fingerprints. Other than the weapon, we have a little piece of a pencil used to keep the toilet door, leading to room A122, open. Our forensic people will probably find Mr. Termine's DNA on that piece of evidence."

"Any eye witnesses?"

"No viable witnesses. There were workers in the building. We know people were near that specific room, prior to the occurrence. The problem we have: no one saw anyone going into or leaving the room."

"Then all you have is your guess and a little piece of pencil hoping it holds some human's tissue for a DNA test?"

"We do have the murder weapon. As I said, it is a hooked knife, an industrial tool used to install flooring. The decedent's blood appears to be all over the thing. A hand image is sort of evident on the handle. The thing is smeared with no fingerprints."

"You said there were no viable witnesses. Tell me about your non-viable witnesses?"

"The decedent died while on top of a woman. We don't know if this was a consensual circumstance or – the woman is in shock and non-communicative; so far, we can't reach her. Perhaps in time she will tell us her story – I wouldn't count on it. Her roommate cannot or will not talk to us."

"So all you have is a little piece of a pencil and a wonderful theory of how the murder – if it is a murder occurred."

"That's a very good summary. The conditions get a little worse when you take into account the pertinent records. There are documents showing Mr. Termine was heavily drugged. Doctor Juliano witnessed his state-of-stupor within a very short time after the murder." Cornier looked through his notes and paused to allow comments on his statement.

"You're saying this Termine guy could be faking or took the stuff after he did the hit. Is there anything else protecting him?"

"The records at Belvedere, and at the hospital, indicates he is non-ambulatory. The physical therapist at Belvedere confirmed Mister Termine could not walk. A good defense position would show a perpetrator had to be agile pouncing on a big guy like Tridon. Judging from the scene, a scene without a combative struggle, the killer hit him fast with a fatal strike. Then he plunged the knife high into the wall and left the scene. Records exist that show Mr. Termine can't do that."

"Can he walk?"

"My guess he probably can get around, good enough to do it. We haven't challenged him."

"So let's forget about him - any other suspects? How about the woman who ran away? Wasn't she the first one on the scene?"

"She ran away before we had a chance to talk to her. I don't believe she killed Tridon."

"Then why is she running?"

"She's involved with the molestation of residents. This wasn't simple stuff, big time orgies; she knew within the day we would find out. As for the murder, I don't think she killed Tridon."

"Who else was close enough, close at the moment of death?" The District Attorney asked with his frustration evident in his speech.

"Danielle Turner, a visitor, and Doctor Juliano were right there when Gail Summun screamed her alarm. Turner's mother, Florence Danzell, is a Belvedere resident and Doctor Juliano is her physician. They both were there. Neither showed any indication of being part of the problem. They actually helped to stabilize the scene."

"Okay gentlemen, you're the law enforcement. What are you going to present to me? And I'm not talking about the fraud and assault crap." The prosecutor threw down his pen and pushed away from the table.

Lieutenant Gabriel saw his opportunity to take charge and said, "Detective Cornier will continue to work the issues and see what he can develop. I'm certain that by . . ."

Cornier interrupted his superior. "You're trying to squeeze a dehydrated apple and make cider. There's nothing of substance here Lieutenant. We can work for another month, or you can assign another team. Believe me there's little more to be found. There is one way, and that's to get Termine to confess; I tried that. Mr. Termine doesn't admit nor deny killing Jack Tridon. He knows there's reasonable doubt all over the place. He just won't talk about it; he doesn't talk because he knows he doesn't need to say anything."

"Cornier are you telling me you can't solve this murder?" Lieutenant Gabriel challenged.

"It is solved. I just can't prove it to you or to a jury. And do me a favor and accept that fact. Assigning another guy isn't going to work and will merely waste his time." Cornier leaned back into his chair and looked about for any comments. The room remained silent.

"So Lieutenant Gabriel, tell me how a new detective on the job is going to establish that Gail Summun killed Jack Tridon. Killed him, violently, with blood pumping all over the place and then ran away. Ran away because she's guilty and knew we could prove it. Lieutenant, that kind of a solution will satisfy me. That would also satisfy the public." The District Attorney smiled at the Lieutenant indicating it was time for him to answer.

"Sounds like a perfect approach. If you approve, I'll make arrangements for a press conference on, oh, let's say Monday afternoon. I'll do the presentation, directly to the press, and you can trust me on this. I'll lead them into a reasonable conclusion. Will your office participate?"

"Of course not – just keep in mind, I didn't approve anything. This is your show. Of course, we'll be involved if or when you arrest anyone for any of the crimes you listed.

This press conference is your baby. If you do it right, it will give you a time to shine."

***

The noon meal witnessed the gathering of those who were mobile. Sam rolled into the dining room joining Mary at one of the tables. Food trays reached the intended resident and they began the meal, as usual, in complete silence; the silence demanded by the staff. Sam looked around. The women noticed his motions, lowered their heads trying to ignore his intrusion.

When Sam spotted the floor nurse entering the dining room, he slapped the table with his hand while bellowing with a colorful voice: "Miss Archer if you please, may I have the JELL-LAY."

He said the words in mock imitation of a very old popular commercial. His perfect rendition triggered Mary Archer into a roar of laughter.

The nurse within the room, with an accusatory finger pointing towards Sam said, "Mr. Termine . . ."

Sam immediately interrupted her aggression. "You got a problem with a little laughter in this dining room?"

The instant rebuke instilled a new silence. All present stared at the wilting woman. She realized a new paradigm with a sense of civility now existed within Belvedere. The old rules died with Jack.

With a wave of her hand, as a survey of the dining room, she said, "No problem with laughter. How can she pass the jelly when there's none on any table? I'll try to find some."

Mary took the cue and asked, "Sara, have you got the man's JELL-LAY? By the way Sam, did you notice the nurse? She's been here before. She thought she knew the drill and practically peed in her jeans. Please pardon my language."

Sam laughed and enjoyed seeing her happy and carefree.

Sara in turn caught the mood and repeated the inane question and each in turn laughed and queried the next one. Before long, the room roiled with a noise not heard for a long time. The residents alive with the silliness of the moment relished the newly found freedom.

Sam pretended to start a food fight by loading his spoon with mashed potatoes and stopped when Mary said, "Sam Termine – don't you dare!"

The lunch party lasted more than an hour. The women, mute for ages, started chatting feeling the élan of living. They enjoyed the new found sense of conversation snickering over nonsense items, and regaling in stories of the past. Everyone participated. It gave Mary a reason to be proud of her community.

Sam marveled how quickly these women could get past the horrors of Jack and Gail. They were an example, to him, on how to begin his healing. His hand released these fine people, and now his hand must find his own peace.

***

The women, exhausted from the hour of socializing, retreated, a few at a time to their rooms. Sam and Mary remained behind. They were quiet while the aides cleared the tables and waited until they knew no one else would bother them. Sam moved closer to Mary. "Miss Archer I have a problem. I made a promise to you about two individuals. I took care of one. I don't know what to do about the other. Cornier knows, or thinks he knows I killed Jack. He warned me not to try anything else."

"Sam, as I said before, we were less than novices when we conducted our trial. We talked a great plan not understanding how difficult it would be to implement. I should have known better than getting caught up in the moment. It was wrong to put such an unattainable task on your shoulders."

"They were wicked people and I think what we did was right. She's out there. I don't think they'll find her."

"Sam, when we sentenced Gail, we believed the ultimate punishment was death by execution. It seemed right at the time. Now I don't know. All hell broke loose when we – when you punished Jack. I should have realized the impracticality of two executions. It doesn't matter. We have something far more effective. Think of it this way. Gail received a stiffer punishment. She left behind a life of comfort and now is on the run. Gail's in a state of panic and believes some day she'll be found. She's inflicting her own punishment and will suffer every day for the rest of her life. That young body will age quickly, and hopefully she'll die in torment. Sam, the two devils are gone from here, and we're indebted to you my friend. Get Gail out of your mind. She's gone and will never be back. Forget her."

"I'll try – for now." Sam lowered his head, ran his hands through his hair and then looked at her. He told her in a solemn voice, "Miss Archer that's not all. I need strength, your strength to help me. Jack's death is taking a terrible toll on my conscience. I relive it over and over."

"Time will help to soothe those feelings."

"I still can't believe I did it. I'll never be the same man. I know I'll be haunted for the rest of my life."

"You are not alone, my dear Sam."

"I believe you. I also believe that my burden, concerning Gail, still exists. It's not over until Gail Summun is punished."

"Oh, Sam let it be. Let it be. We're free."

"I prayed. Oh I prayed so hard. I prayed that it was all finished. Miss Archer, it's not. There's a terrible feeling inside of me. It just doesn't go away. I have to find a way to feel free," Sam said as he rolled away.

***

Sam left Mary and went directly to Emma's room. He approached the door, wanted to enter, hesitated for a moment and then decided to go to his room. Again with uncertainty he moved out and returned to Emma. He went past Mary's empty bed and went directly to where Emma lay. Her eyes appeared blank and staring into space. He moved very close to her and said in a barely audible voice, "Dear Emma, I don't know if you can hear me. I wished it could've been different. Seeing what he was doing made my heart cry for you. Witnessing your torment drove me crazy. I couldn't help you. The only way to stop that demon was to . . ." Sam sobbed and backed away, regaining his courage, he returned and continued, "I had very little time to prepare; I needed someone to help me. That someone turned out to be you. You were the only one. Jack was such big a man – he was so strong and I'm just able to get around. Using you gave me an advantage and for that I am thankful – and yet so deeply sorry. I will regret it for the rest of my life. Only a coward would leave you while he bled his life away. How can you ever forgive me?"

Sam sank into his chair feeling his torment. He rested his head on the bed rail trying to contain his grief. After a few moments Sam sat up and turned to leave.

Hearing a weak voice made him stop; he spun back. Emma beckoned him to come closer to her. Her frail hand reached out; he returned to her bedside. Emma's hand felt cold; she presented an almost Mona Lisa smile saying something. Sam not comprehending leaned in closer. Then heard: "Thank you my wonderful guardian angel."

THIRTY ONE

During his press conference, Lieutenant Gabriel never accused Gail Summun of murder; he merely skewed the circumstances making certain that his rapt audience would draw a proper conclusion. He made the conditions fit a detailed time line presenting the impracticality of any Belvedere resident doing the deed while constantly reflecting back to Gail's sudden disappearance. He ended his presentation with arms flailing while asking: "Why would a woman, a woman in blood soaked clothing, assault a police officer – and then run away?" After positing his question, the Lieutenant scanned the audience, and slowly backed away from the podium. The reporters, rapt and tense, wanted to hear an official condemnation. The best they would receive was a silent nod of affirmation. Lieutenant Gabriel turned and left the podium.

Interpreting the nod supplanted receiving an official answer to his closing question. It gave those in attendance an opportunity to spin the presentation. Reporters from the various media eagerly bought the basic story knowing an absence of pertinent details allowed for more than a little twisting of the facts. They had a great lead story: A local tragedy; a murder committed by a known killer – and a terrific potential for additional news.

The newspapers, television and radio stations, guided by the manipulative Lieutenant offered the public the latest news. Meager facts exploded into a plethora of words. As he predicted, experienced reporters embellished Lieutenant Gabriel's presentation. The intimated circumstances suddenly became a firm conclusion based on extremely strong evidence. The printed and spoken words pointed towards Gail Summun, a horrid woman, a woman on the run, a woman who killed Jack Tridon.

***

Blazing headlines and prime-time news reports disappeared after one evening and a day of intensive coverage. Then the newscasts stopped. Mundane follow-up stories with pseudo facts were relegated to the back pages of printed media. Along with the absence of fresh news, the public's interest waned.

***

Other than finding Gail Summun, new leads didn't exist. Everyone knew Cornier made a mistake. Allowing the woman a little slack gave her an opportunity to slip out of his control and that exhibited poor judgment. Detective Cornier, though he asked to be relieved, remained assigned to the case.

Frustrated by his commander's decision plus his inability to locate Gail, affected his normally laissez faire attitude. His associates learned quickly to avoid his grousing and sharp words.

Although Cornier's full time assignment remained solid, no one else wanted to find Gail Summun. After four weeks on the run, Gail's trail remained nonexistent. The woman just disappeared. Detective Cornier couldn't find her, and the politicians didn't care.

***

Sal Manfassi, envisioning his problems as huge, hired a brilliant attorney. After researching and understanding the complexity of the circumstances his lawyer expertly reworked all the potentially damaging events. He massaged the details, making them a set of positive occurrences, all to Sal's benefit. Sal assuming he would see jail time learned very quickly his lawyer knew how to use the judicial system. The law says he was innocent until proven guilty; his attorney turned the accusations into glory. Simple digging into Belvedere files showed their Operations Manager Milo Drew did a wonderful job maintaining files totally compliant to regulations. The police had accused the company of false billings. Yet the supposedly fraudulent billings were based upon services prescribed by authoritative individuals. He showed every single action was accurately documented in a normal and exacting manner. Auditors could not critique the billings. Nor could they determine these billings were fraudulent. If anything, the lawyer contended, it shows the entire operation appeared to have an overzealous concern for their residents. It utilized available funds for their health and welfare. A complex trail of paper supported his conclusion. An occasional missing document gave the filing system a feel of human frailty and not viewed as a deliberate act of hiding something. Also of no concern was the lack of x-ray film in personal files. The lawyer deemed these to be irrelevant; he made a plausible assumption they were probably destroyed in an effort to save computer space. The records for prescription drugs and every other service or material were in place, fully authorized and skillfully documented by paper or efile. The investigators and auditors did not find anything of substance. He postulated the police did not find anything implicating the Belvedere management in any crime.

Since fraudulent activity could not be verified, the case against Sal Manfassi began to evaporate. Prosecutors retreated knowing it would be impossible to press fraud charges; they did not have any prosecutable evidence.

***

Doctor Carl Lunkens recognizing his culpability resigned as medical director of Belvedere Manor. In response to pressure from the medical board, he relinquished his right to perform any services as a physician; he surrendered his medical license. The professional associations and health agencies accepted his resignation without comment. His mental outlook changed. Doctor Lunkens carried a heavy guilt due to his actions and more so for his lack of action. Although knowing he failed in his performance, he could not understand how his business associates could return to Belvedere Manor behaving as if nothing happened.

***

If Sal's attorney hadn't envisioned a potential escape, George Faulkins' capitulation could have been a big problem for all of them. He postulated that George Faulkins, an honest professional, traveled to Belvedere, on a fixed schedule and for the sole purpose of offering his specialized services. As for written and eprescriptions for the physical therapy services, they were on file. The lack of performing any therapy became the burden of the deceased, Jack Tridon. Jack Tridon failed to prepare a resident for physical therapy. It was his responsibility to interface with the client and therapist and to report progress or lack of progress to the prescribing physician. The entire circumstances of fraudulent charges revolved around Jack Tridon. Jack was the problem, and Jack was dead.

Sal's attorney again performed his magic. Charges against Mr. Faulkins never materialized.

***

The horror and fraud at Belvedere, at first, appeared to be a prosecutor's opportunity to shine. They learned very quickly the perpetrators at Belvedere had a powerful attorney; an attorney who knew how to play the game. Fumbling the potential cases at Belvedere Manor could become a political nightmare. It became very convenient to abandon all fraudulent charges by simply pointing an accusatory finger towards Jack Tridon.

***

Within a day of Belvedere's tragedy, state social workers and psychologists arrived to counsel the residents. Some of the professionals believed the terrible stories and others, just like people before them, absorbed the information and classified it as fantasy. A few believed that Jack provided consensual carnal release. Recognizing the outsiders still looked upon them with suspicion the A wing residents refused further contact with the counselors.

***

Lani and Sam developed a stronger friendship than either thought possible. They talked, laughed and felt a wonderful kinship while loving each other, not as a male to female relationship, just good friends. Lani helped Sam's return to health by her encouragement and care, plus she supplied mysterious homeopathic herbs. He consumed them without questioning their worth, or their potential side effects. What they were or why he took them was a mystery; a mystery he knew would be unsolvable. Lani tried to hype the benefits of some of the material. He listened to her melodic words, smiled at her sincerity and consumed the potions. For all he knew he was consuming a bunch of placebos. It didn't matter, because he felt stronger with each day.

***

The nightly police patrol ended two days after Jack Tridon's murder. Sam recognized the silence and with it came freedom to practice his late night Tai Chi. He stretched, performed the routines and always ended with a period of meditation. The nightly sessions became his standard way of life. However, while his body continued to develop his mind remained mired in the sinkhole of past horrors. The mental anguish drove him from his bed into a consuming physical activity.

***

George Faulkins may have dodged serious fraud charges, he didn't escape from a personal shame and damaged ego. He knew he almost lost his freedom and possibly his license to practice. Seeking some solace, George felt he had to atone for his past sins. As a self-imposed penance, he determined he would dedicate some of his own time to improve the life of a resident. He owed Sam Termine many hours of prepaid services. George decided to make this man a personal challenge. He would help Sam Termine walk again.

Amazed by the suggestion of no-charge therapy, Sam happily accepted Faulkins' offer. George Faulkins worked hard and took all the precautions necessary to prepare his patient for a normal life of upright activity. Sam's muscle tone was a surprise; his limber joints added to Faulkins' befuddlement.

"Do you do any kind of exercise?" The therapist asked.

"Yeah! I jog around the building every morning before breakfast and get on Nautilus equipment in the afternoon. Care to join me?" Sam answered in jest hoping the man would drop the question.

"Seriously, your conditioning is much better than I expected," he continued.

"The only exercise that's possible, is the tossing and turning in bed. I can't sleep, and I flip and flop all night. Come the morning, the covers are a mess. Is that sort of an exercise routine?"

"That makes sense. I think I'm going to have you on your feet very quickly. Remember, we have to be careful. I don't want to hurt you."

Sam enjoyed the thought of working with the man yet stifled an urge to laugh. "Please, I don't want to break any bones."

"We have time and we'll go very slowly."

They did go slow and Sam played the game to perfection. He showed fear. They worked on that issue and overcame his feigned hesitation to try. He showed an inability to stand and held onto his therapist with a deathly grasp. Eventually, Sam yielded and George Faulkins proudly applauded all of their small accomplishments. It was a game that gave Sam and the women of the wing some entertainment. Everyone enjoyed the physical therapy sessions of Sam Termine.

***

Detective Cornier visited often and at times witnessed Sam and George at work. Unable to see his body condition, due to the floppy institutional garb, Cornier did not recognize Sam's strength. He smiled watching their strange dance.

When the physical therapy session ended, Cornier commented, "Man, you're a wonderful actor; you should seriously consider a career on the stage." They both laughed each understanding the message. George not fathoming the humor still offered a simple guffaw.

***

When Sam took his first official steps, his coach, George Faulkins, watched with pride as his ability to walk returned. George Faulkins paid off one of his debts to society, or so he thought.

***

Mary Archer remained the roommate of Emma Joslin. It was a relationship of bonded sisterhood between two women who suffered a common pain; a bond without oral communications. If Mary thought Emma heard her, she told her the news of the day making certain she learned about the events of the outside world.

Emma had a few visitors; some were professional, and each received the same stoic and muted reception. She remained frozen to all approaching her, with one exception. When Sam Termine came into the room, that subtle smile always developed. He could see the gratitude in her eyes.

***

"Hi Miss Archer, Hello Miss Joslin, how are you this beautiful day?" Sam said in his often-repeated greeting.

"Thank you Sam, we're just fine. Emma and I've been discussing the world events. You have any news for us?"

"Yep, sure do. I took my first step today. Mr. Faulkins said I'm making a remarkable recovery," Sam said as he gave Mary Archer a wink.

"What's his prediction?" Mary said sadly.

"As far as walking and doing things for myself, I should be okay, within two weeks. My operation healed. Apparently, it doesn't need any nursing skills. Now for my biggest news . . ." He waited a moment, trying to achieve a dramatic effect, and then added, "I asked for an interview with the big boss, you know, Mr. Manfassi."

"That SOB, why?"

"You know Detective Cornier's been visiting. We're buddies now, and I told him I'm getting ready to leave. I asked him about my things and where I believe they're located. He was great and promised I would get everything back. All I had to do was ask for it. If they didn't come up with the stuff, he'll ask for me."

"They're still slippery people Sam, beware of what you're getting into," Mary offered.

"No. No more watching out for the boogie man. They got away with stealing a lot of things. I want what's mine. I want it all back, plus."

"What do you mean, plus?" Mary asked with concern.

"I think I can play their silly game, and it's going to cost them for my agony. My list isn't too long. I'm a reasonable guy. If they've lost any of my stuff, I'll settle for actual value. And then, what's my nightly torture worth in dollars? You know I can't sleep, and I constantly walk these halls at night. I relive the trauma of that day, over and over, every single night. What's that worth in dollars?" Sam asked with apparent anger in his voice.

"No one can put a value on those things. Not you, not me, not anyone."

"Do I have your blessing O'great leader of our community?" Sam asked with a snicker.

"Dear Sam, you have my blessing for your health and well-being. You have my permission to get everything that you believe you can. You have my love and admiration for your strength and dedication to all of these people."

"A little blessing here, a little permission and love plus admiration, what else can a guy want from life?"

"What are your plans? And you know what I mean."

"As much as I want to stay in this area and be able to visit with all of you, I want to travel," Sam said as he lowered his eyes to the floor.

"Travel? You want to travel? Sam what are you up to? You're going after her, aren't you?" Mary wheeled up close to him and looked directly at him awaiting an answer.

"Going after her?" Sam retorted. "Who's her?"

"Don't get cute, Sam Termine. Look at me and tell me what you're up to."

"Miss Archer, we have brilliant detectives looking for her. They're not having any luck. How do you think I can possibly find that witch?" Sam looked at Mary, smiled as he turned and said, "Bye. See you later."

"Sam, you come back here. We need to talk. Sam!"

***

Sam Termine quickly wheeled down to Sal Manfassi's office and arrived ten minutes before his midmorning appointment. He knocked on the frame of the open door and said, "Good morning, am I too early?"

"Come in. Your timing's just fine. You're looking great. How are you feeling?"

"That's why I'm here. I feel wonderful and believe I can leave and be on my own within a few weeks."

"That's news to me. The staff hasn't reported that kind of progress to me. What's the Doctor say?" Sal asked as he looked down at the man's legs.

"He says I can leave when I can walk out the door."

"Now Mr. Termine, let's make certain you understand your physical condition. Realize what you've been through and the very small possibility you're ever going to be on your own. You came in here a very sick man. Everyone involved in your care acknowledged the fact you would be with us for a long time. Please don't set your hopes and goals beyond what we can accomplish."

"I've set my own goal. I will walk out of here within two weeks. That's why we have to talk." Sam pulled up close to Sal's desk and said loudly, "I'm getting ready to leave, and I want all of my possessions returned to me: my truck, my computer, camera, and clothing. Here's a list for your convenience. I placed a value on some of the items. If you don't have the stuff, I'll take cash." Sam leaned forward and passed the hand written list to Sal.

Sal looked over the paper and exclaimed, "This is ridiculous. You never had this stuff, if you did, we never received it. What are you trying to pull? We treated you with the finest care available, and now you want to cause trouble. Get out of my office," Sal said in deep anger.

Sam stayed where he was and said, "Mr. Manfassi! Detective Cornier has a copy of this list. He reviewed it and believes my demands are very reasonable. He said he wants to help me. He thought he should be here today. I told him you were an honest man, and it wasn't necessary. Now you can expect a call from Detective Cornier." Sam Termine turned to leave the office and heard Sal's voice.

"You understand many people handled your possessions. They may not be in good condition. You can have whatever we find. I don't guarantee the condition of any of it," Sal said with a smirk on his face and with a challenge in his voice.

"Apparently you don't understand. When you took my possessions, you also accepted the obligation to protect my things. Cornier used some fancy words like 'fiduciary or fiduciary responsibility', whatever that means. It sounds awfully technical. I guess he knows what he's talking about. Mr. Manfassi, I'm a reasonable man, and I like to do things simply. Keep the stuff and I'll take the value of my property in cash. As you can see the bottom line is a small number, only eighteen thousand four hundred dollars."

"You're crazy," Sal said in frustration.

Sam looked at Manfassi and spoke in a harsh tone; "I'm finished talking to you. This conversation is getting me angry."

"Wait - wait, I apologize. I didn't mean to be - it's just so unusual for someone to . . ."

Sam Termine jumped in and added with a laugh, "To leave Belvedere. You are a real joker."

"Enough of this, I'll get back to you in a couple of weeks and let you know what I find."

"Oh no, that's not good enough. You don't seem to get it. Now I'll. . ."

"Get out of my office."

"Cornier said he'll call your lawyer." Sam turned his chair and wheeled out of Sal's office.

***

Sal's lawyer graciously accepted the detective's call. Within a couple of hours, Sal got the word, "Pay the man. It's cheap compared to the cost of trying to evade the demand." He listened to Sal and said, "No. It was not extortion. The man's merely demanding the return of his property. It's normal and reasonable."

"I'll give him the big stuff, like the truck, computer, camera, and . . ."

"And he'll tell you the items have been abused and not in the same condition when you received it. It'll go on and on, and your name will be in the newspapers again. The reporters will love it and drag you through a pile of crap. Let's face facts, he's got you. You want my professional advice? Pay the man! Pay him and add an extra thousand as a good will showing."

"That's nineteen thousand. I'm not going to do it," Sal exploded.

"I just gave you some good advice. Of course you can refuse to follow it. If that's the case, you can get yourself another lawyer. Good bye Mr. Manfassi."

"Wait, wait, I'm sorry. It's been a rough couple of months, and I'm not thinking right. Okay, I'll do it -- it's still extortion."

"As you know all of our conversations are recorded. I called you to offer some free advice. Got that, it was free advice. Now you've persisted in a very obstinate way and continually challenged me. We have been on the phone much longer than my free one-minute rule. You will be billed for this extra time. Do you understand?"

Sal sat quietly with the phone next to his ear and said in exasperation, "No, no objection, no I mean yes I understand. Sorry, I'm kind of upset. Thanks for your concern. Please be there for me, although I hope I don't need your services again." Sal stopped talking when he heard the constant dial tone.

***

Sal left his office and walked down the hallway and as he was ready to turn into A wing, he stopped and returned to his office. He sat down and withdrew his personal checking account register. The balance indicated four hundred and twenty nine dollars and forty-four cents. Nineteen thousand dollars was a lot of cash, and he didn't have it. He felt the company should be liable for these kinds of dollars, albeit knowing the auditors would pick it up as an unauthorized business expense. He was debt free and now this demand put him in a financial squeeze and probably put him back into debt. Sal twisted his pencil, poked a hole in a piece of paper and pondered the dilemma. He threw the pencil down onto the desk with determination and decided he would try to negotiate with Sam; use his skills and work for a better deal. He left his office and boldly walked to A wing.

***

Sam was in the recreation lounge participating in a heated discussion between a few women. Sal walked up to the group and said, "I need to talk to you for a moment – alone?"

"Whatever you have to say, right here's fine. These wonderful people are my friends, and they know all about my business. Please feel free and tell us what you want," Sam responded.

"This is very unusual Mr. Termine," Sal huffed. He looked down at Sam and bellowed, "I demand to see you alone and in my office. And I mean, right now."

Sam pointed his finger at Sal and yelled, "Mr. Manfassi spit out what you want – or leave us alone. We don't have to put up with any of your nonsense." Sam glared at Manfassi and challenged his authority.

Manfassi paled hearing the immediate retort. He sputtered his response, "I – I – didn't mean to sound pompous. We need to talk. The list it's kind of – the amount is very large – I've got lots of problems."

"I'm leaving this place, and that's a certainty. Two weeks from today I will walk away. When I do, I want my possessions waiting for me. Waiting for me or receive a certified check for their value. What more is there to talk about? You won't have to worry about me when I walk out of the front door. I'll give you another tidbit of information. Detective Cornier promised to be here and drive me home." Sam waited for a response. Sal stunned by the oral attack remained mute. "Tell me, Mr. Manfassi, can you deal with another fraud investigation? Can you imagine the uproar over a fraud, involving the disappearance of personal assets of a Belvedere resident?"

The women listening with great interest could hear everything because Sam shouted his words. First they looked at Sal, then at Sam, back to Sal and enjoyed the distress forced into Sal. He felt defeated and showed his defeat in front of the residents of A wing. Sal drew in a deep breath and lost control; he shook his fist violently and then pointed at Sam and exploded, "I'll get you – we should have gotten rid of you when we had the chance. We

. . ." He stopped realizing he'd lost control by threatening Sam and a group of residents witnessed his outburst. Sal grimaced, turned and left the room.

"You pushed him too hard. He's a very dangerous person. You're still in his place and – just watch out," Mary said and then shook her head in despair.

"Miss Archer – everyone – please listen to me, this is not the time to back down. Don't be frightened. Right now we have the upper hand, and they must never feel they can do it again. We will not – and I mean not ever again be subjected to their cruelty. Mr. Manfassi has to be crushed. He may be vindicated of a big time fraud. If so, I promise you, they're watching him. He knows it, and he's not used to oversight; it makes him very uncomfortable. Keep remembering his discomfort is our protection."

"I hope you're right. What happens to us when you leave?" Karen asked.

"You have Detective Cornier's business card."

"We'll miss you Sam," Mary Archer said with sadness.

"You're my family and you'll never know how much I'll miss all of you."

"Are you going to stay out of trouble?" Mary asked showing her anxiety.

"I have to get rid of my torment. If that means more trouble for me, then so be it. I have to put my mind to rest."

"Sam, you can get hurt; maybe end up dead pursuing the impossible."

"Miss Archer, you're not afraid of dying; neither am I. I'll be very honest with you. I don't know where I'm going or even how to achieve my goal. I guess I'll be like that guy with a lantern looking for whatever he was looking for."

"An honest man, Sam – an honest man."

"Wow that's a laugh. An honest man, huh, I guess I am on a mission impossible."

THIRTY TWO

Gail drove south on US95 stopping only when the gauge indicated she was dangerously low on fuel. Her high level of anxiety stimulated a continual need to empty her bladder. Discharging a minimal quantity during each stop did little to suppress the feeling of urgency. Ever tense, Gail determined to maintain the posted speed limit yet acquiesced to a faster rate drifting along within the flow of traffic. She suppressed a compulsion to stomp on the accelerator and challenge cars passing and cutting through her lane.

With the stolen license plates firmly attached, Gail believed she was transparent. She was just an ordinary citizen trying to drive carefully and avoiding traffic problems. Frequent, repetitive, mesmerizing lane markers commanded her attention; she fought to stay awake during the long and tedious drive.

***

After almost eighteen hours, Gail decided to change her traveling mode. She exited the highway onto a two-lane road leading into the city. She located a convenience-store-gas station, parked close to the building, used the restroom then searched for a pre-made sandwich. Selecting one that looked like the best, it felt cold and stiff. After paying for the food, and a bottle of water, Gail shuffled out the door. Holding the sandwich in one hand, her phone in the other, she thumbed in a search for used-car dealers.

***

Twenty minutes from the highway she found the promised row of car lots. Each dealer appeared to be a clone of the other with their simple signs offering to buy and sell. Friendly Fred's Fine Cars appeared to be smaller than most and most likely, less busy. She memorized its location continuing towards the business center and hopefully a bus station.

After a few attempts, parking close to the Bus Terminal proved impossible. However, 'P' signs with nice white arrows pointed the way. Gail grimaced as she drove further away from the depot towards the town's parking area.

Gail gathered her luggage, a large wheeled bag and two smaller ones with shoulder straps. Stacking one on the large bag and toting the other allowed her to push her possessions in front of her while trudging back to the bus terminal.

Gail thought the people within the station watched as she approached the ticket window. Turning around, after she passed them, gave her the assurance she needed: they had zero interests in her as their eyes roamed to other curiosities

The ticket agent looked up. He gestured with a nod of his head implying that she had his attention.

"What's the schedule for buses going to Miami?" Gail asked.

Without uttering a word, he handed her a fan-folded brochure. She pushed it back asking: "How about a recommendation?"

"Wait for the express, takes about five hours with a couple of stops. Only problem is, it ain't here yet and you've got to wait a couple of hours before it leaves."

Gail, using cash, purchased a one-way ticket. Since her bags were already safely stowed in a rental locker, she walked out of the terminal.

***

Trying to recall the simple way back to the used-car lot and after making a couple of miscues, Gail pulled into her chosen dealer. Concurrent with exiting her car, she heard: "Hi, what can I do for you today?"

"Well we can help each other. I'm selling, and I'm guessing you're buying. Starting a new job here in your beautiful town is wonderful. Only problem is, I need some cash." The man smiled and allowed her some time to tell him more.

"I need money a lot more than I need this car. So are you buying today?"

Hearing the right words the man's eyes sparkled in anticipation. He blew out a deep breath as he said, "Got a lot of wheels as you can see. They ain't moving. No one's buying." He paused and waited for her reaction. She remained stoic. "Now if your price is right – what are you asking for this old vehicle?"

"Why don't you just give me a nice number? Make it fair and make it final. I don't like to haggle. If you want to buy okay, if not I'll go on down the street," Gail said in a firm confident manner.

"You want a trade in. You know like, get a couple of bucks and some good transportation?"

Gail placing her hands on her hips as a show of anger said, "I guess we don't speak the same language. I need cash not another car. Thanks for your time." Gail feigned a reentry to her car.

"Now don't get the wrong idea. I'm a good guy just trying to help you. If you don't want a nice little car for driving around town, that's okay by me." Strolling around her car, he noted the out-of-state plates and the car's fine condition. "What's the mileage? How's she run?"

"I don't know the mileage. Take a look, start the engine, run it around the block, do what you have to do, just tell me what you're offering?"

The man pondered the deal, looked at the woman and tried to size up her needs. "Tell you what. I'll give you two grand and that little red car over there. How's that for a great deal?"

"Goodbye," Gail said as she entered her car and closed the door.

He tapped on the window. Gail believing he got her message lowered her window to hear his proposal. "I can tell you're a northerner. Don't be in such a hurry." The dealer tried to indicate he was determining his number by again walking around her car.

"Best I can do is three thousand."

"This car's worth two times that amount and you know it."

"Maybe it is. You might get a little more than three if you got the time to advertise in the newspaper. Then sell to someone who wants your car. Buying and selling takes time and a lot of work. I buy wholesale. Then I have to put money into a car before I can sell it. See this place. To you it may look like a dump. Even this lot sucks up expenses; plus I need to make a little so I can live. Believe me, this is the best offer you'll get from anyone."

"That's three thousand cash."

"Don't usually have that much on hand. If it's strictly cash, give me a second." He entered his rickety office via the slamming creaking door only to reappear a few minutes later. "I got twenty seven hundred and eighty-six dollars, and you can look in my wallet. That's the cash deal. Or you can have a personal check for three thousand."

"Will you take me to a bank and cash the check?"

"Nope. As you can see I'm the only one here. So the deal is a nice amount of folding money or a check, it's up to you lady."

"If I take the cash will you drive me into the center of town?"

"Sure we'll use your car and . . ."

"Oh, no, I need my license plate. Take it off and let's make the deal."

"You are a strange one. I hope you have the title."

"I do, yes."

"I'll get some tools – and your money."

After signing the required papers, he pushed a small stack of bills towards Gail. He didn't count it nor did she. Grinning in satisfaction, Gail knew she picked the right lot to sell her car. She shoved the small bundle into her purse.

Noticing the frozen mounting screw, he grumbled while backing out the single working fastener then gave Gail her license plate.

"You wanted to get to the center. Right?"

"That's right."

"Hop in that Caddy over there and we'll go in style."

***

Two blocks before the bus depot, she indicated to stop. "Are you sure?" he asked.

"Of course, this is perfect, thanks," Gail said as she got out.

Walking a couple of blocks seemed like a good idea until she realized the long drive exhausted her stamina. Gail, plodding along wearily retrieved her bags, found a seat within the terminal – far away from the crowd.

***

Gail fought the urge to sleep. Knowing she could not afford to miss that bus, shook her head, pulled in deep gulps of air, rubbed her hands, and jiggled her legs. With eyes locked into a stare, Gail felt her body falling into a deeper exhaustion. The announcement that they were ready to board gave her some respite; she fell asleep before they pulled away from the terminal.

***

The gentle rocking of the bus kept Gail in a deep slumber. She was oblivious to the beauty of the landscape. The bus continually emitted its steady drone and rapidly moved closer to Miami. Her exhaustion kept her in a deep comatose like sleep. She did not stir during the occasional stops.

Gail stirred as the bus rocked into the last stop before Miami. Feeling a pressing urge to urinate Gail looked towards the back and decided to use the bus's lavatory. The small cramped toilet smelled with the various odors of casual users. Believing shallow breathing would get her past this moment, Gail tried to satisfy her need.

Tepid water trickled out of the tiny facet. She attempted to wash her hands then rubbed some of the liquid onto her face. A pale drawn woman stared back as she peered into the small mirror. Rubbing with the rough paper towels made her pale skin slightly pink. Gail seemed to come to life.

***

At the final destination, people shuffled down the aisle stepping out of the sleek vehicle. Gail gathered her luggage and looked at the dark bus terminal. It appeared ominous and uninviting. Although she felt the hunger, she quickly discounted any thought of buying food. Her immediate needs were not food.

Gail entered the building, glanced around then placed her bags next to a vacant bench, withdrew a paper from her purse, unfolded it and started to examine its contents. She pondered for a while then with determination placed the point of the pencil on the paper. A circle formed around the name Emma Joslin.

"I liked that woman. She was a doll, and I enjoyed her. Yeah, I am Emma Joslin and let's see – my Social Security number is . . ." Gail flipped the paper over and continued to murmur, "That's an easy number to remember. Goodbye Gail, hello Emma."

THIRTY THREE

Now caring to his own personal needs Sam showered, dressed and tidied up his Belvedere room. Since Lani's workload, in Sam's area, became minimal, they could and did talk about anything and everything.

"Sam, when you leave here, where are you going?"

"My dear Lani, right to the point, as usual – that's one of the things I love about you. Well, I'm going south."

"Do you think that's where she is?"

Sam, recognizing her intuition, smiled and said, "Best guess. She could have gone west or east. And I doubt she went north."

"Sam, you know my friends listen to everything. We think we know, well, sort of know where. She and Jack talked a lot. At times, they spoke about their favorite places and future dreams. Jack liked the mountains."

"And?" Sam asked in exasperation.

"Florida, she always talked about going to Florida. Gail liked the warm weather with the bright sun and the skimpy clothes, and . . ."

"Where in Florida? It's a very big state," Sam said as he urged her for more details.

"We don't know," Lani said and seemed personally depressed that she didn't know the answer.

"That's still great information Lani. Thank you for sharing. Tell me did anyone tell the police?"

"The police didn't ask. I am sorry to say they didn't treat us with very much respect. They were loud, crude and frightened my people. We know, from experience, in our country it's best to answer any question very quickly. And use very few words. That's what we did. People in uniforms, even in this country, frighten us."

"I can understand that."

"The police treated us like we were guilty. My friends were numb with fear. They made one big mistake asking me to act as an interpreter. It didn't matter what was said. I gave answers I thought they wanted to hear. All of us were very nervous. I wanted the inquisition to stop." Lani smiled and put her head down in make-believe modesty. She started to move away and said, "Before you go tell me how I can help you."

"What do you know about Florida? Do you have any relatives or friends down there?"

"Our people are in Florida, in many different places. How do you think they can help?"

"I don't know. The thought just jumped into my head. If I think of a way, will you ask them to help me?"

"Tell me how and I will try."

***

Every week Detective Cornier visited Belvedere. He still had the burden to locate Gail Summun and felt the answer, if there was one, would come from someone at this facility. These visit always included a few minutes with Sam.

"Good morning Sam. Are you ready to run out of this place?"

"Don't know about running; I'm feeling pretty good."

"Is there anything new on a settlement for your possessions?

"Not yet. Thanks for trying to get my stuff back."

"Happy to help. Just remember most of the material items are gone."

"Except for my truck," Sam added quickly.

"Except for the truck," Cornier acknowledged just as quickly.

"What's the latest on your search for the wicked witch of Belvedere?" Sam asked.

"You think I'm going to share my clues with you? You're a slick and slippery guy. I think you're ready to become the second Sherlock Holmes and show me up."

"I'm not the guy you think I am."

"Be careful."

"If you find her, will you bring her back? And if you do bring her here, what are the chances of prosecution and conviction?"

"Those are tough questions. Let's make a guess. Assume we go to trial. Will there be a murder conviction? No way, that's impossible and you know it. I don't mean to rehash an issue – she didn't do it – and we both know it. A good lawyer would turn a prosecutor's case into a verdict of not guilty. A good judge would throw the case out and not even try it." Cornier said emphasizing the word, judge.

"So, why do you want to find her?"

"It's my job. That's my punishment for giving Gail the opportunity to run away."

"Will they charge her with sexually abusing her patients? Notice I didn't say convict. What's the strength of an abuse case?" Sam looked directly at the man speaking with a challenge in his voice.

"If we charge her there's no hard evidence. Records show psychological issues. We do have Mary Archer. Then again, even with Mary, there's the issue of defining time and place. As for the others concurring with Mary, I think they would stammer and hesitate, leading a jury into believing in the beautiful Miss Nightingale."

"Would a prosecutor take the case?"

"I doubt it. When I think about it, Gail made a huge mistake by running away. She could've beaten the rap. Look at the scoundrels up front. They're walking around, with their heads up high, acting like they are first class citizens."

"What about the assault on the female officer? Didn't she harm that woman?"

"Physically, Gail did not touch her. I truly believe she drugged her and ran. Without a witness, Gail could claim they tried to be buddies. They both popped a few pills and our officer, taking advantage of a free ride, downed more than she could handle. A lot of stories are possible, especially with the imagination of legal advice."

"So why are you looking for her?" Sam blurted.

"I told you before. It's my job." He glared at Sam. Pointing a finger at him, he said, "Don't let it become your job." Cornier lowered his voice. "Sam -- it is not your job."

"Hey, the only way I ever want to see Gail again is when she's dead."

"That's what I'm afraid of Sam. That's what I'm afraid of," he said seriously. "When you get out of here, I want you to enjoy life, have fun and forget the garbage of the past few months. Understand?"

"I don't need any more trouble for the rest of my life," Sam lied.

"Look at these gladiators ready to rumble. What's going on guys?" Danielle Turner said as she walked into the room.

Both looked up at the woman, understood her message, and Sam said, "Welcome to the arena. I'm exhausted and could use a substitute. This man's wearing me out."

Detective Cornier spoke up immediately, "You can sub for me. I'm going to see Manfassi. Got to check on what progress he's made on locating your possessions. Nice seeing you Mrs. Turner. How's your Mom?" Without waiting for an answer he added, "Enjoy your visit."

Turner waved at the departing detective, turned towards Termine and said, "So I hear you're still on the mend and keeping to your schedule. That's good news. Is everything else in place for your parole?"

"Parole, that's an interesting word. I guess this place is like a jail."

"So, where are you heading? All I heard is you're traveling."

"I want the warm weather. Yes I'm traveling, making a straight shot down to Florida." Sam said as he tried to sound happy.

"You're going to see Mickey?"

"No. I'm more interested in the simple things in life. You know, the ocean, the gulf; I hear the beaches on the panhandle are spectacular. Maybe I'll tour some big cities, and of course the little communities."

"Sounds like a wonderful plan. I wish I could do the same. How are your resources? Can you afford to do this kind of travel?"

"Yes – and I don't know. My pension will help; Social Security will be my major income. I could put a camping cap on my pickup and sort of live out of the thing."

"Become a nomad and live off of the land?"

"Campgrounds have showers and rest facilities. I think it'll work."

"You're going to live a dream of every guy. Get into your truck and go. Leave all the troubles and responsibilities behind. Good luck to you Sam. Is there anything I can do for you?"

"I hoped you would ask. There's one thing if you will. Could you look in on Miss Archer? See needs a friend, someone from the outside. Someone she trusts and will believe her. She doesn't need things like presents and that sort of stuff. What she needs is to talk to folks who can think. She enjoys a normal conversation about the action of everyday living as well as the wonders of the world. Will you do that?"

"I planned on it. Now that you asked, I will commit to doing just that."

"Thanks Danielle. It means a lot to me knowing Miss Archer will have a friend."

"Will you stay in touch?"

"I'll try."

***

Detective Cornier walked briskly through the hallway, arrived at Manfassi's office, poked his head in and asked, "Got a minute?"

Sal Manfassi knew what his visitor wanted, and he expressed his frustration by answering, "If I had a minute you would try to extort it away from me. Come on in."

"Those are very bad words Mr. Manfassi. I'm here to help you avoid a serious problem. You want to cut right down to the issues or . . ."

"Please, I'm sorry. I'm not used to – look can we get a little reasonable about what you're asking? How about a couple of thousand and we all go away happy? Mr. Termine will probably be pleased with big pocket money. Let's . . ."

"See you in court Mr. Manfassi. I don't have time to play these games," Detective Cornier turned and started towards the door.

"Wait, please wait and please listen." Cornier stopped at the doorway, leaving his back to him. "Okay – okay, you win, I'm sorry – please don't leave."

Cornier turned, looked at Sal and challenged him: "First thing you need to do is get your pen and check book and start writing."

Sal opened the middle drawer and withdrew a large spiral book. "You going to give me some paper showing I'm clear of all further demands?"

"You will get a receipt that shows you purchased personal items from Mr.Termine. And to show we're sympathetic to your misery, just make the check out for fifteen thousand." Sal smiled until he heard, "And Sam Termine will get his truck. Sounds real fair to you, right?"

"But – but, most of the value is in his truck. The rest is . . ."

"The rest is worth a lot more than fifteen grand, when you consider the savings in lawyer fees. Think of the pay you'll be missing during a stay in jail. Let's go, finish what you started, I don't have all morning."

Sal Manfassi completed the check writing and said, "It's written, now what?"

"Write out a simple bill of sale for various personal items. The details aren't necessary; just say various personal items and the amount. Sam will sign it when he gets the keys to a functioning truck. By the way, have the oil changed and make certain a mechanic inspects the vehicle. We don't want Sam to get into something that's not ready to roll, do we?" Manfassi turned red while maintaining his silence. Cornier smiled and then said, "You're a generous man Mr. Manfassi."

"Detective Cornier, you've got to work with me. I just wrote a check that's no good. Try cashing it today and it'll bounce – when I transfer some funds – sometime after tomorrow, it will be covered. I don't have this kind of cash. I have to borrow the money. Can you hold the check for at least a couple of days? Okay? Please?"

"Sure, Sam will understand. You realize, of course, if you screw this up it can be defined as another element of fraud. And that means I'll be very angry and . . ."

"I need a couple of days, and it'll be in my account. Please trust me. Will you work with me?"

"I'm a very reasonable guy. You know that."

***

"Miss Archer, I have a problem. Are you up to a little working of the brain?" Sam Termine said as he approached.

"Sounds like fun. Is this going to be a long game?"

"That's what I'm hoping to avoid. Every minute that goes by means she is digging in deeper and finding her becomes more difficult."

"Oh Sam, let it go. You can't dedicate your life to trash. She's gone. Let the police find her."

"Miss Archer, I have to try. And besides look at the fun I'll have traveling and living in the sun."

"It makes me very sad to think I pulled you into this mess. Please try to forget her."

"You didn't do anything to me. Jack and Gail, they are the bad ones. They're the people – oh let's not relive any of that. I need you to help me think of a way to find her. From what I learned, it's possible she's in Florida. That's a big state. Here's the way I figured it. One, she probably changed her name. Two, she's working somewhere in the healthcare industry. And three, that's all I have."

"And what do you want me to do?"

"Tell me how to find a needle in a haystack."

Mary Archer smiled at her student and said, "Sam, you have to think of your problem in a different light. Use a tool to find your needle. So, what kind of tool would find a needle buried within a huge stack of hay? You know one answer."

Sam looked at his old teacher shrugged his shoulders and asked, "I do?"

"Think about it." She waited for a moment and then said, "A very powerful magnet will pull that needle right out of the hay. She's like that needle. You want to find her? Do it the easy way. Make her come to you Sam. Make her come to you."

"You make everything so easy. Why didn't I think of that?"

"You were too close to your problem."

"What else am I missing?"

"Design your magnet with great care. Remember a magnet works two ways. It can attract or it can repel. If you do it wrong, she will be pushed further away, and you will never find her." Mary lowered her head and said, "I wish I could convince you to walk away from this."

"Danielle Turner will be a good person to talk to if you have a problem," Sam said in an attempt to change the subject.

"I know what you're doing. Don't get cute. Stick to the subject. Sam I want you to be careful, please don't get hurt." She looked at him, and he grinned. Mary stiffened and said sternly, "I said to be careful, and I mean it."

"Yes Ma'am. Class is over, isn't it?"

"For me it's never over. You're always in my heart. You and all of my students are all I have. In my mind, it goes on and on."

***

Harry Benas walked down the hallway looking for Sam Termine. He found him in the recreation room and greeted him. "Hello Sam, how are you feeling?"

"Absolutely great. I'm almost there. I'm healthy and soon to be a free man. You can keep my wheelchair for someone who needs it."

Harry Benas smiled knowing the wheelchair didn't belong to him. It was the property of the facility and chose to ignore the comment. "Sam, we've got some clothes and things people leave behind. Can I interest you in any of it, sort of make up a little wardrobe of wearables?"

"No thanks. Mrs. Turner promised me a present of some new casual clothes. She measured me for size and said the next time I look the stuff will be hanging in my closet. The Turners are generous people. So no thanks on your offer," Sam said trying to sound sincere.

"The word's around. Looks like you stiffed Sal Manfassi for a couple of bucks. Congratulations, it isn't often Sal takes a hit. I enjoyed hearing about it. There's a certain joy a man gets when he can squeeze some green stuff out of a tight-fisted guy like Sal. Believe me, I know how that feels." Harry smiled and waited for Sam to query him on his secrets.

Sam looked at the man quizzically and then gave a simple reply, "Thank you."

THIRTY FOUR

Cornier waited an extra day before personally presenting the check to Sal's bank. He deposited it, in Sam's name, in a newly opened savings account. The money wouldn't earn any serious interest. He would have a debit card, checking privileges and access to nationwide ATMs.

The remaining issue was the return of Sam Termine's truck; and in proper functioning condition. Sal reverted to his obstinate manners, sullenly gave the detective the keys to the truck, and told him he didn't have time to run errands. If Cornier wanted something done he could do it himself. It took just a few minutes of verbal blasting, by the detective using very crude language, before Sal caved in. He consented to the servicing of Sam's truck and charging Belvedere's account. After a few more choice words by Cornier, Sal recanted and promised to cover the expenses.

The attempt to lull him into some collusion not only reinforced Cornier's dislike of Sal, it instilled an assurance he would squeeze the man a little harder.

The service started with an oil change, then a request to look for, and to comb out, all possible problems. An hour later although the truck showed it was in excellent condition, the brakes did exhibit some signs of excessive wear.

"Change them," Cornier ordered.

An invoice for Five hundred dollars' worth of service and parts restored the vehicle to excellent running condition. With the registration current and insurance in force, Sam's truck was ready to roll.

***

A good tall cap and some modest electrical work could convert Sam's truck into a camper. The dealer listened to the tale of horror, and of course he knew of the murder. Sympathizing with Sam's experience, he recognized the not-so gentle suggestion that he should help. A few caps were in stock, and Cornier told the man any recommendations were welcomed. Within minutes, they choose one with a coordinating color. Even though the shop was booked solid he took the keys and drove the truck into an open bay.

The pickup truck quickly became a camper. Upon completion, the dealer showed Cornier an invoice detailing the cost then drew a line through everything other than the price for materials.

"Just pay me what I paid for the cap. The rest is on me. Okay?"

"More than okay," Cornier responded. "I owe you one."

The man smiled and added, "And Mr. Termine can pay me when he's ready."

Cornier drove the gleaming truck home. He would leave the problem of bedding and accessories to Sam.

***

Sam's last days at Belvedere stressed the staff. The front office scurried to get his financial business in order. They had to reroute his pension and Social Security payments using direct deposit procedures to his new personal account. Cornier remained involved in the process and forced a special accounting of his monthly stipend. Since they were the fiducial agent for his finances, by law, Belvedere had to allocate a very small amount of funds for sundry items. Since these records were non-existent, Cornier demanded they pay him, in cash, for the few dollars allocated. Sal bristled at the constant drain of money towards Sam. Cornier's continual presence annoyed him. He hated the constant pressure and looked forward to the day Sam Termine left his care.

Sam's discharge records, signed by every professional within Belvedere, required a final approval by Sal Manfassi. For this discharge, Sal demanded Harry hand carry the document to everyone, including himself and when presented scrawled an illegible signature.

***

As promised, more so to Sal than Sam, Cornier arrived in time to act as Sam's surrogate. He reviewed the contents of a large envelope assured Sam everything appeared proper, shook his hand and wished him good luck.

Some of the ambulatory residents gathered in the hallway, bid Sam goodbye and watched as he, escorted by

Harry walked down the hallway. Sam waved a goodbye as he went past Sal's office; an office with a closed door.

They continued their silent stroll to the main door. Harry pushed it open, ushered Sam out and shook his hand goodbye.

***

Cornier prepared for Sam's re-entry into the world by renting a small furnished room. The rent was reasonable, payable weekly, and he could stay as long as he wanted. At Sam's urging, Cornier advised him on items needed to complete the conversion of his truck into a livable camper. Two weeks and a day after leaving Belvedere, Sam exhausted his to-do list. Now fully prepared, physically able, and mentally alert he could begin driving south.

***

Before he left the area, Sam had one social obligation. He drove to and entered Belvedere Manor, this time as a visitor. He strode past the general office area, waved a polite hello and proceeded to his former wing.

Some of the women were in the recreation room. They greeted him with spontaneity of shouts. Mary Archer, at the far end of the room, waited patiently while Sam worked his way chatting.

"Hi Miss Archer, did you miss me?"

"No Sam, I did not, because you're never out of my thoughts. I think of you and what . . ."

"Yeah," he said interrupting her. "I know what you mean. Although I've been very busy, I keep seeing you and – and Emma. I can't shake those terrible moments."

"Work on it Sam. Think of the beauty of the world and not – you know what I mean."

"I still stay awake all night. I lie down, and I can't sleep. I get up, exercise, and meditate, and things are okay for a while and then it happens all over again."

"You should talk to a good professional. They can do wonders if you will work with them."

"Maybe, someday, right now, I just want to get rolling."

"Give yourself some time to heal."

"I'm as fit and ready as I need to be. That's why I'm here today. I'll leave around mid-night. Since I can't sleep at night, I might as well take advantage of the light traffic."

"Sam, you need more time."

"I know my limits. I'll try to enjoy the ride. Maybe stop and see some of the sights along the way."

"When will you come back?"

"I have no idea. I might like it down there. Maybe make it my new home. Miss Archer, I don't like long good-byes. I hope you understand. Can I give you a hug?"

"Sam you can always count on a good hug." Mary Archer broke her usual calm and began to cry.

"Miss Archer, I don't want to remember you this way. Please give me a big smile." He walked to her, gave Mary a gentle hug, turned quickly and quietly sobbed, "Bye." He strode away before Mary could respond.

***

Sam could not miss seeing the huge roadside sign: WELCOME TO FLORIDA. He slowed down, rolled towards the welcoming station, eager to test their sincerity. They did not disappoint him. Unlike the other states he visited, Florida offered some free refreshment. A small paper cup full of grapefruit juice, then a sample of the orange juice gave Sam a wonderful feeling. He enjoyed the welcoming embrace by the good people of the State of Florida.

Walking around, while scanning the walls filled with brochures, allowed him to sense of the enormity and diversity of Florida. He grabbed a handful of items that seemed of interest; the friendly attendant gave him a map of the state. After hearing he drove a camper, she offered that camping sites were available throughout the state. He asked for advice on an economical place, pretty much in the middle of the state. She didn't directly recommend any, merely suggested some possibilities. There were three sites located between Daytona Beach, on the east coast and Tampa on the west coast.

That broad expanse made it far too big an area to explore; he arbitrarily circled one located right in the middle. Sam walked back to the dispensing machine to try another sample of the free liquid sunshine.

***

Sam opened the envelope containing a list of Lani's friends and relatives. Many lived in the major cities and others in some of the smaller towns in Florida. Lani enclosed a note, introducing Sam as a friend imploring the people on the list to help him. A review of the names and locales had little meaning other than he had a wonderful network. Sam pondered how to find them; and how could they help him.

***

Using a stub of a pencil, Sam marked what he perceived to be a reasonable route to the remote camping site; his immediate target. Then checking the town names along the way against the list of Lani's friends showed zero matches.

Driving on the local roads proved pleasant; he enjoyed the continual change in scenery. The reduced speed limit of the secondary roads gave him a chance to relax. He felt the release of tension created by the intense driving on the Interstate highways. Relishing the warmth of the sun as it penetrated his truck he welcomed its calming and therapeutic effect.

***

Sam rolled into the lonely and desolate campground. Since he wanted cheap, this place offered basic and fundamental camping. After parking his vehicle, he checked in, and quickly settled in for the night. Receiving his reward for the long periods of stressful driving he fell into a deep sleep. It pushed his troubled mind, and exhausted body, into a desperately needed rest. Before this peaceful night, Sam continually relived the gruesome encounter with Jack Tridon.

On this, his very first night in Florida, Sam enjoyed a restful night.

***

The strong Florida sun penetrated his window and danced with the shadows created by the leaves in the trees. The flickering of morning light alerted his eyes that a new day arrived.

The camping cap didn't give him very much vertical room. The best it offered: either sit up or be flat on his back. Sam stretched, sat up, wiggled out of the light-weight sleeping bag and exited his camper.

Keeping his food in two coolers worked. One for his non-perishable items didn't need any maintenance. He had another, albeit very small, for an occasional cold item. As a long time bachelor, he learned to use dehydrated foods and found them to be convenient and inexpensive. A box of powdered milk was cheap and tasted just fine. He also found eating meat every day too much of a luxury; he learned some of the basic principles of eating vegan.

Sam didn't enjoy eating the rudimentary meals he prepared on his propane-cooking stove. Most warm meals were cooked in one pot. The pot became his plate, and since he ate everything he made, there were no leftovers. On this trip, he ate just enough to keep going.

***

Sam anticipating he needed some stability, booked the camping site for a one-month stay. The campground clerk sounded like a cheerleader touting the wonders of the local town. It's just a short drive away and has a small library and a post office.

It took Sam fifteen minutes to drive to the town. The library proved adequate. The post office had a small box available. Sam grimaced hearing the minimum rental was three months. He smiled after hearing the low cost.

This little town appeared to be alive with its version of a supermarket, a no-name diner, and general hardware store. They, so far, escaped the assault of the forever expanding franchises. He found a nice town with friendly people.

***

The community library said they subscribed to newspapers from some of the major cities. He expected to see Orlando, Miami, and Tampa papers hung neatly on the current-day rack only to learn their big city subscriptions arrived in the form of an efile. And yes, he was welcomed to use their media center computer for two hours maximum.

The desktop computer performed just fine finding the address for the classified sections for each of the major cities.

He challenged the word processor software and printer by requesting a test copy. The machine racked out a nice letter quality sample.

He started to type:

Dear Advertising Manager:

Please run the following ad in your Help Wanted section. A money order for the indicated one-week rate is enclosed. As noted I intend to use a blind newspaper box number and request that you forward all responses to the above address. I've enclosed funds to cover forwarding of any mail. Please advise if you require any additional dollars for this service.

NURSE - RN OR LPN NEEDED FOR A PRIVATE ALL FEMALE HEALTH CENTER IN AN EXCLUSIVE SOUTH EASTERN FLORIDA LOCATION. PRIVATE EXPERIENCE A PLUS. EXCELLENT COMPENSATION PACKAGE INCLUDES GATED LIVING ACCOMMODATIONS. SEND A DETAILED RESUME AND A BRIEF NOTE DEFINING YOUR NEEDS AND REQUIREMENTS. PO BOX (please insert your newspaper's blind box number)

Sam individualized and printed three letters. He folded them with care and placed each in an addressed envelope. After calculating the fees for the three advertisements, he added a generous amount for the extra service charges then marked that amount on the corner of their respective envelopes.

The post office sold him the three required money orders and the postal clerk patiently waited while he carefully inserted same into an envelope. After weighing the three packages individually, the clerk indicated all were within the one-ounce limit.

***

Sam visited the library everyday reading the current issue of the newspapers. His little advertisement began to show within a day of each other; the published versions were verbatim, save the newspaper box numbers. His request for anonymity worked. Each assigned a newspaper box number giving him that added element of mystery. Though the ads looked good, when viewed on the diminutive computer screen, they looked small. Being buried within a multitude of other requests for nursing help made Sam believe he was wasting his time and money.

His post office box remained empty for an entire week. As far as he could determine no one responded. Sam wondered about the wording of the ad. Perhaps it wasn't enticing enough or maybe Gail simply didn't see it. Then he thought she could be in another part of Florida. Perhaps the newspapers he chose weren't available in her area. Or maybe Gail didn't read a newspaper. All reasons for failure flooded his mind. Since the professionals back home didn't have any success finding her what made him think his simple idea would work.

Sam, pondering his next step, decided to wait at least another week.

***

One day dragged on into the next. Without any nibble on his advertisement he began to lose hope. Sam needed some diversion.

Florida offered many different avenues of entertainment. Swimming and boating opportunities were plentiful. Golf courses existed everywhere. He didn't need nice and ordinary he yearned for some escape, some fantasy.

THIRTY FIVE

Enthusiastic families held the hands of tugging children. Their anticipation strained the arms of parents and when finally entering the Magic Kingdom they erupted with shrieks and peeps of joy. Their energy transposed into his body and he made an attempt to see everything. "The Pirates of the Caribbean" and "The Haunted Mansion" were exciting and required a second trip to make certain he did not miss a feature. The attractions suppressed the problems that compelled him to go to Florida. "It's a Small World" had him smiling and twisting his neck to see the little characters in motion. He hummed the tune of "It's a Small World After All" long after he left the ride. It was a great day, and Sam now understood why he paid such a huge fee for a three-day pass.

Sam didn't anticipate the possibility of such a high level of enjoyment. He stayed the entire day and waited with the crowd to witness the activities at the day's end.

Sam didn't want the day to end. He vacillated as to leave or not, looked around, found a bench and sat down.

The din of the crowd disappeared as he watched the people drift out. The night air still and quiet offered him some peace. He remained until the Park closed.

***

Sam strolled through the exit, ignored the train-like parking shuttle and slowly walked back to his vehicle. The joys of the Magic Kingdom made him want to see the rest of Disneyworld. He turned his eyes towards the sky, breathed in the night air and released a long sigh; he again thought about the business of locating Gail.

Though late he knew if he had mail that it would be sitting nice and safe in his post office box. Sam pondered the dilemma and mumbled, "I'll stay one more day. What's one more day? There's probably no mail any way."

***

Sam had no desire to drive all the way back to the campground. He drove into a few motels and received the same answer: No Vacancy.

The secondary highways surrounding the Disney complex had strips of motels, restaurants and souvenir shops. He rode up and down and then picked out a large Motel as a likely place to park. He located an open spot in the furthest row and across the way from the motel units. He parked in between a couple of other trucks and hoped the security people wouldn't challenge him.

Sam entered the motel lobby. The clerk ignored him as he became engulfed within a very boisterous crowd; a multitude he realized overflowed from the adjacent bar. Sam maneuvered past the partying throng right into the men's room giving him a chance to refresh and to take care of nature's call. The free coffee available in throw-away cups, made him feel very welcome. He thanked the uncaring clerk on his way out.

Sam waited outside for a quiet moment before entering his truck. His mini-camper filtered out most of the external noise; he wished for a comforting sleep. Although grateful for the wonders of the day, Sam yearned for the start of a peaceful night.

The joy of the day ended when his torment returned. Sudden flashes of the agony wrested away the pleasure of sleep. He twitched, jerked and sweated as he relived the last moments of Jack's life. The night droned on; he tossed fitfully; he made many futile attempts to shake the memories. Sinking into a troubled sleep finally came during the last few hours before dawn.

***

Sam's spent his second day at the Epcot Center. He marveled at its counter point to the Magic Kingdom. Epcot was pure adult entertainment; yesterday's fun was filled with childhood fantasy. Yesterday joy remained embedded in his mind as he approached Epcot with youthful enthusiasm. He again dashed about in a festive frenzy. He wanted to see everything. And the aromas of exotic food created an unknown desire. He always ate simply. Now the stimulation caused by the exciting food presentations made his eyes dart from one item to the next. He started hesitantly then approached each purchase with an explorer's anticipation. Savoring the first little item he bought from a food cart whetted his long suppressed appetite.

The atmosphere of Epcot and seeing people munching on treats amplified his desire to eat. He yielded to the temptation and began to splurge on food. He couldn't resist the exotic items offered by the foreign pavilions. Lunch in Morocco, a small dinner in Japan, and a creamy pastry from France made him feel the effects of his gluttony. The fullness of his stomach forced a slowdown in his gait. The sluggish feeling was a blessing since it gave him an opportunity to study the wonders of Epcot at a slower pace. The day flew by, and the peace of the evening cradled him with warm moist air.

The movement of the people slowed as they began to gather around the lake for the laser and fireworks show. It began with music blasting from the speakers and then augmented by the crack of the fireworks. Laser beams shot out from various locations and the pavilions became aglow with lights. Sam enjoyed the excitement and remained seated on one of the benches. He could see some of the glow. The spectacular lights and booming sounds had its appeal; he just wanted to watch the happy people. Sam had enough excitement for the day. He tried to relax through the noise of the show.

***

Sam trudged out of the park, pocketed his three-day ticket, and decided two full days at Disney World was his limit. He returned to his truck and started to drive back home. The nighttime drive was peaceful and he returned to the campground.

Sam parked, visited the toilet facilities, climbed into the truck and prepared for the night. He stripped off his two-day-old clothes and lay on top of his bedding. Within moments his full stomach rebelled against the prone sleeping position. For the second time in his life Sam felt the rush of acid reflux. The discomfort of his sudden heartburn made him sit up and he groaned in pain. Sam rubbed his torso in an unsuccessful attempt to quiet the internal hurt. The combination of unusual foods percolated within his system and forced him to leave his bed. He dressed and walked around the dark campground; he made his way to the office. The night clerk, asleep on the office lounge chair, awoke with the noise of the screen door.

"What can I do for you at this crazy hour of the night?"

"My gut's killing me. Got anything to put out this fire?" Sam said sounding desperate.

"Eating them fatty foods will get to ya every time. Go look under that there counter. I've got a few small bottles of that pink stuff. Take a swig and you'll be fine. It ain't for free."

"Thanks." Sam retrieved the small size bottle, read the instructions and broke the seal. He put the bottle to his lips and poured an unmeasured amount into his mouth. The stuff tasted chalky and coated his tongue. He tossed a few dollars on the counter, didn't wait for change, and left saying, "Hope it works."

"It'll work. Give it a few minutes and you can get back to bed. Guarantee it."

***

The potion took a bit of time to work its magic. Sam's gut stopped hurting and his heartburn settled down to a simmer. With the pain subsided his mind returned to his problem: How to find Gail? So far his advertisement did not yield a single letter. He began to think about the next group of cities to plant his baiting advertisement. Perhaps he had to hit the small town papers. If so that would make the job extremely difficult. His mental review of the geography of Florida mesmerized him; and the relief generated by the anti-acid allowed his body to relax. He fell asleep sitting up, slumped over and onto his pile of dirty laundry.

***

Gail Summun, now known as Emma Joslin, spotted Sam's advertisement. She read the ad and watched it reappear every day for the entire week. Wanting to respond immediately she tried to write a good resume. Tossing one after another knowing they appeared weak she thought she finally had a decent looking resume. It too got tossed after reviewing it the following day. Trying a new version, Gail inserted a higher level of experience. With each attempt, she realized it wouldn't impress anybody.

After reading it every day, for a whole week, the ad disappeared. A wave of panic hit; surges of anxiety smothered her when it failed to reappear. She knew she couldn't wait any longer. Gail decided to use a basic resume. It looked weak. Hopefully, the accompanying note would sell her abilities.

***

Gail's quality of life dropped dramatically since she left Belvedere. Her income, now miserably low limited her to very basic living accommodations. She purchased a small used car; it didn't look very good with its peeling paint; it ran okay.

A small inner city convalescent center needing people didn't ask many questions and ignored previous employment history. She appeared to be willing to do the minimum wage job and hired her on the spot. Gail started working concurrent with her application.

Although the tasks were demeaning and well below her training, abilities and experience, she had some income slowing down the drain on her meager resources. When she accepted the position, she knew working a forty hour week wouldn't cover her expenses. Toiling extra hours on the job became a continuum of drudgery. She worked seven days a week, without any relief in sight. That ad could be just the ticket back to sanity.

She thought a simple resume, handwritten, would be a huge impediment to get a decent job. It needed formality. It needed embellishment. Rereading the ad indicated private experience could be a major factor. That meant blending in elements of private and institutional practice. She decided to limit her resume to two long term jobs. Fabricating a history of years of employment as a private nurse sounded right. It had to have some sophistication. Caring for the mother of an unspecified well-known public figure fit the profile. Adding her current job showed a gapless employment history.

Gail penned the brief note explaining the lack of detail on the resume. They should understand that a patient's family insisted upon complete privacy and would demand non-disclosure of their name and location. Therefore, she could not divulge any other information. Since her current position was strictly temporary, the note highlighted, it should not be used as a measure of her abilities. She offered to work for a trial period, demonstrating her competence. Finally satisfied with its appearance, Gail mailed the resume and the brief note hoping she didn't miss the opportunity.

The newspaper's advertising department received Emma Joslin's letter, promptly placed it in another envelope and forwarded in the next day's mail. The post office did its job while Sam Termine enjoyed his visit to Disneyworld.

THIRTY SIX

The small post office received its bulk load of mail by late morning and usually distributed mail to box customers, if they weren't too busy, by mid-afternoon. Sam without any history of receiving mail didn't know their schedule decided to check his box at the end of the day.

Sam entered the post office, walked over to the wall of boxes. Before placing his key into the lock he glanced into the tiny window. He saw an envelope. Dropping his hands to his sides, he wiped the sudden flow of perspiration off of his palms and onto the sides of his pants. Sam pulled in a deep breath, inserted the key, opening the box gently. He withdrew the single envelope.

The brown business envelope, with a newspaper return address, felt thin. Tugging on the sealed flap proved fruitless, he tore off an end then ripped it wide open. A small white envelope dropped to the floor. It landed, address side up. Noticing the sender's name, Sam stared while chills ran down his body. Reaching down, he picked it up and held it to his chest. Tears welled into his eyes; he turned towards the wall trying to hide the emotion. It took a few moments for Sam to gather his courage.

Sam walked out of the post office not noticing his failure to re-lock the box. The door hung open; the key remained in place.

***

Sam jumped into the passenger side of his truck and closed the door. The envelope stayed in his hand and he gazed at the name: EMMA JOSLIN

"Gail Summun, you are one sick lady. How can you profane the name of that good woman? You violated her and now you steal her identity." Sam pounded the dash and said, "I found you Gail – I found you. No, no that's not right. You found me Gail. You found me. Let's see what lies you've concocted."

Sam gently opened the letter and tried to preserve all evidence of her existence. He removed the two sheets of paper from within. Both were handwritten.

Dear Manager:

I have the education, experience and desire to do all the tasks of a dedicated nurse. Employed as a private nurse for the past seven years I cared for an invalided woman. She is now deceased. My employment contract demanded that I remain discrete and hide all the pertinent facts of this position. Since I can't verify the majority of my experience, as shown on my resume, I am willing to work, without compensation, for two weeks, to prove my competence. My current job is classified as a temporary position. I can terminate this job with one day's notice. I am unattached, able to relocate and would enjoy the opportunity to live in southwest Florida. My address and telephone number are listed on my resume. Please call any evening, after 5 PM.

Sincerely yours,

Emma Joslin

***

"Well done Gail. Nice touch and it sure has me wanting to call you. Now the big question: is it really you?" Sam knew he was babbling; he felt he had to hear his thoughts; plan his next move. The various ways he could approach the respondent flooded his mind. His thoughts scattered while looking for a good method and then became frozen as he failed to formulate a reasonable plan of action. He wished for a good talk with Mary Archer. The hours flew by. He ate his supper because it was time to eat and not because he was hungry. The sun began leaving long streaks of waning light and soon disappeared. The cool evening air chilled his skin and stirred him from his complacency. He suddenly woke up to the fact he had to confirm that the woman using the name Emma Joslin was indeed Gail Summun. He reread the letter. She indicated her current job was daytime employment. It was time to travel and to see who claimed to be Emma Joslin.

***

Sam knew he wouldn't sleep; the excitement of finding Gail became overwhelming. He stowed his lawn chair, secured his things for traveling, closed the tailgate door, and jumped into his truck. The engine roared into life while the headlights glared and lit up the area. He concentrated on his planned route. His mind became absorbed with thoughts of the long drive, and he carelessly drove out of the campground. He wasn't thinking of the consequences and he threw up clouds of dust from his fast spinning tires. Sam couldn't hear the obscene words thrown at him by his sleepy neighbors while he quickly rolled out of the park. He headed south.

***

Sam chose to drive on the inland roads and ignored the major highways. He figured he had the advantage of traveling at night and the lack of traffic would be in his favor. The truck had a full tank of fuel and he knew he could travel the minor highways all night without stopping.

Initially the roads were somewhat busy. Now he was the only one traveling. He rounded the south end of Lake Okeechobee. At this unencumbered speed he could be in Gail's area within another hour or so.

The long drive, the excitement of finding Gail and the lack of sleep made him very weary. The desolate road didn't offer any comfort. He began to regret his decision to drive all night. Without any options Sam had to drone on looking for relief. A few vehicles traveling in the opposite direction perked up his spirits. Their presence indicated the world was coming to life. The absence of roadside businesses changed rapidly as he arrived on the outskirts of the city. Darkened mini-strip malls greeted him as he sped by.

He could see the lights long before he arrived at the small motel. It was an oasis offering both rest and food. A no-name pancake restaurant, attached to the motel, advertised all night service. The sleepy-eyed motel clerk said he had a room and didn't question his strange hour for check-in. He didn't even offer a smile when Sam offered him cash for a two-day stay. Having some pancakes and coffee would be welcomed but he needed to rest a lot more than food.

Sam set his tiny portable alarm clock for twelve o'clock noon and dropped into bed fully clothed. His fatigue robbed him of immediate slumber; he felt dizzy and lightheaded. Breathing in deep slow breaths brought the comfort he sought and he sank into a deep sleep.

***

He awoke with the gentle buzz of his alarm. Sam felt like he only slept a few minutes. The clock and blazing sun indicated otherwise. Sam took a fast shower passing up the opportunity to shave. Previously worn clothes were reused and he knew he looked a little shabby. Choosing to ignore his unkempt appearance, he walked towards the restaurant. Sam hesitated for a moment feeling a compelling urgency to keep going and find Gail. The urge slowly subsided when the continual pangs of hunger fought hard and caught his attention. The pancake restaurant offered a quick meal, and he welcomed its invitation.

Sam ate his breakfast while fully absorbed using his phone to find the best path he should travel to find his quarry.

Since he had both her home and work addresses he learned these were within seven blocks of the other. Due to the distance, he guessed she probably walked. She walked to work and then walked back home. If she did walk, there were a lot of possibilities, and he had to figure out which streets should be monitored. Then he thought she could be driving the seven blocks, and that would mean a plethora of other problems to consider. If he had the job, he'd opt to walk. Walk and save the cost of driving and to get some exercise.

He had to see the area. A slow drive through the neighborhood should give him some ideas on how to start.

***

Within thirty minutes, Sam arrived at a very small convalescence facility. According to Gail's resume, this is where she worked. As he drove by within the traffic, he noticed a tiny sign, with an arrow pointing towards the rear. It offered parking for visitors. On his second pass Sam judged, by the location of the building, on a busy street, with very limited parking, he needed another site for possible surveillance. He drove by the facility a few more times, just in case he missed something, and then proceeded towards her home.

The area subtlety transitioned from business to be residential. The traffic pattern changed from dense to sparse. It gave Sam an opportunity to drive, very slowly in her neighborhood of many identical looking homes. Driveways separated the houses and each led to a garage in the rear. Based on the size of the homes Sam surmised Gail either rented the house or sublet a room. Her car, if she had one, probably remained on the street. A few cars sat idle in front of several houses. He looped around and drove various routes trying to guess which way a person would choose to walk. There weren't any stores on any of the paths and the streets all looked alike. She could walk any of them to get to work, and most likely did just to get some variety into her life.

Sam saw enough. He located both addresses by driving around. Now his truck became a liability. It may look like many other trucks. The out-of-state license plates shouted a different message. He had to continue his exploration on foot.

Sam found a small strip mall about ten blocks east from her home. Parking away from the stores, he withdrew his phone, called up a map and reexamined the area.

Satisfied with his knowledge Sam pocketed the phone and started to walk back.

Home and work were diagonally away from each other, four blocks west and three blocks north. Wanting to travel the most probable route, though risky, Sam decided to start from her home. He checked his watch when he walked by her residence. It showed a few minutes after two o'clock. Gail's letter said she worked during the day. To him that meant she could be at the end of her shift at any time from now until five o'clock.

He had to imagine how she would walk the pattern and started by going one block west, then one block north then kept repeating the zigzag until he reached the facility. Checking the elapsed time showed the trek took twenty-one minutes to walk one direction. Since he set a very rapid pace, she could have walked a lot slower; the amount of her travel time could be longer. Varying his path and selecting alternate streets to simulate another zigzag trip home still took about the same time.

After walking the complete loop twice, he checked the current time: 3:50pm. Another route wouldn't significantly vary the time, plus he realized it was very close to 4:00pm. Gail could be on the way home right now. He had to be discreet; he wanted to be part of the scene or at best unnoticed.

Pulling the peak of his cap down formed a shadow over his eyes. A quick rub of his face reminded him of his stubble of a beard. His unkempt clothes gave him the disguise of a laboring man. Knowing Gail never saw him walk, he maintained his normal gait, striding briskly. He walked with a purpose; he had to get to work.

***

Gail, bored with her life, never varied her route going to and from work and home. Her chosen streets, always quiet and seldom used for casual strolling, were embedded in memory. On a few occasions, she saw a mother with children. Seeing a single man walking on these streets was unusual. She glanced about looking for the nonexistent service truck. Not knowing who he was, she sensed trouble. It made her heart race. He was still too far away; it didn't allow for any recognition. Although they were on the opposite sides of the street, she felt she had to avoid contact.

Sam saw her, at a distance. He wanted it to be Gail. He felt it was Gail. Anticipation turned to fear; his mouth grew dry. Biting on his lip drew some blood; he developed an urge to urinate. Sam's hands clenched as he fought off his body's reaction to the moment. The woman came closer as they both approached with a fast determined pace. Though the distance shrank quickly any recognition failed to come.

When she crossed the intersection, instead of continuing towards him, Gail turned at the near corner and within moments disappeared from his sight.

She was going in the wrong direction. If it was Gail it didn't make sense. He crossed the street, ran to the intersection and looked towards her new path. She was now ahead of him, on the same side of the street, albeit still traveling away from her home.

His eyes remained locked on the back of his quarry when she quickly turned her head. For Sam, it happened quickly, too fast to identify her. Since she had turned and looked directly at him, he knew she was very suspicious and wary of his intent. He had to do something and fast. The phone was in his pocket. As he grabbed for it, it flew out of his hand and hit the ground. He scooped it up and looking at the street sign and back to the phone hopefully conveyed a message: he was lost. Sam pocketed the phone and retreated. She turned again and watched as Sam strode away.

Whoever she was, escaped his amateurish attempt. It could've been Gail. To continue following the woman didn't make sense. Obviously the woman read his motives. As a novice, his approach for subtle surveillance failed miserably.

***

Sam very tired and heavy with anxiety walked back to his truck. His body rebelled and hit him again with a cramping urge to urinate. He tried to relax and overwhelm the sensation jumped into his truck and started back to the motel. The bouncing of the vehicle generated a pressing necessity; he squirmed and forced himself again to ignore the pressure on his bladder. Parking without regard to allotted spaces he jumped out and dashed to his unit. The pressure quickly changed to desperation as he arrived at the motel door.

***

Sam, believing he had vital information, punched in Detective Cornier number, waited and heard: "Sorry I'm not in the office. If you want a call back, after the beep, leave your name and telephone number."

***

The Six O'clock News announced its arrival with a blast of a vigorous theme song. It was time to call his prey. Sam yanked a tissue from the dispenser, rolled it into a ball and placed it under his tongue. His saliva wicking quickly dried out his mouth. He pushed the slick ball between his cheek and teeth and tried speaking. It disrupted his normal voice slurring his enunciation.

The television set obeyed the mute command. A few minutes past 6:00pm the phone rang in Gail's room.

"Hello," she answered. Her response was quick and so short that Sam didn't recognize her.

"Good evening," he said trying to sound professional. "Ms. Emma Jezlen?"

She wanted to laugh at his deliberate mispronunciation. "Yes I am Emma Joslin," she said correcting him.

"We received your letter in response to our newspaper advertisement. Are you still interested in our open position?"

"Oh yes! Thank you. Yes, I sent a resume and a note." Gail, dazzled by the call, started to sell herself, "Is it possible for me to meet with you? There's a lot more I can tell you about my experiences."

The excited words were enough for Sam. He recognized Gail Summun, and his face flushed with rage. "First, I'd like to introduce myself. My name is James Freely. I'm the human resource manager."

"Thank you for calling Mr. Freely. Again, can I meet you somewhere?"

"You're very welcome. Let me say I do want to meet you, and I will, as soon as possible. Your private experience is very exciting – at the same time a little troubling. That shroud of secrecy may be necessary so you'll have to convince me of your abilities when we meet – and that will be very soon. My schedule will put me into your area at the beginning of the week. Is it convenient to meet during some evening?"

"I can travel right now and meet you anywhere. Just name the place."

"No – no that's not practical. I'm in the facility and there are some very important matters needing attention. However I can tell you a little about this important position."

"Please – I want to hear about my future place of employment," she cooed.

Sam wanted to sink the hook. "We are a healthcare facility catering to people in the arts and other interesting professions. We are very exclusive and will only accept female clients. Let me give you an example. Actresses are very susceptible to substance abuse problems. They need help, and we offer them our love and our care. We're the best in offering comfort and always nurture them back to good health. Our staff must have the talent, energy and most of all the desire to help our clients. Some of our guests have to be supported day and night. It is not unusual to see some of them cradled by a staff member and both asleep on the couch. Do you understand our needs?"

A thrill drove through Gail as she envisioned the possibility of an ideal career. She took a deep breath and tried to contain her passion. "Yes, I do. And I am very interested in the job. I only wish it could be happening right now."

"Be patient. We need good help, and it could very well be you. I will call you next week. Can I count on your availability?

"Absolutely – your need and my job objectives are identical. I assume the pay is as good as the position sounds."

"The pay is extremely generous. It's substantial because we have important clientele demanding the best in care."

"I have your telephone number. May I have an address?"

Ignoring her question he asked, "Is it proper to call you at work?"

"For this job you can call me anywhere, any time. I hope I'm not killing my chances by sounding to enthusiastic?"

"Not at all, my associates and I will be very happy knowing we are close to adding a new professional to our staff. I will call you, very soon. No more questions please. I must attend to other business."

"I understand. I'll be waiting for your call."

"That's nice to hear. Goodbye for now." The phone clicked as the connection broke.

Gail threw up both arms in a victory salute and yelled, "YES! This one's for me. Get those dolls ready for some real care and what they really need: Lots and lots of loving."

Sam dropped the sweaty phone, withdrew the sloppy tissue from his mouth and threw it into the toilet.

THIRTY SEVEN

The grilled hamburger accompanied by a mound of crispy golden French-fried potatoes cooled while Sam dwelled on how to continue his pursuit. Finding Gail proved simple thanks to Mary Archer. Calling and failing to make contact with Detective Cornier was frustrating. The next step eluded him. Miss Archer's thoughts were always clear and to the point; his thinking seemed clouded without her direction.

Staying in the motel and eating meals in a restaurant, no matter how rudimentary, were costing more than he wanted to spend. Sam had to obtain some basic supplies. He had to get back to his simple way of living.

The evening sky twinkling and alluring lulled him into a moment of content. It didn't matter that the small strip-mall's parking lot was full he double parked until a car backed out giving him some space. Due to the narrow parking slots, he squeezed out of his truck while holding his door trying not to bruise the car next to him.

Sam, marveling at the brisk business in each of the mom-and-pop markets, entered the food store. From the outside, it appeared to be tiny, and once inside it proved true with the extremely narrow aisles and shelves loaded high with product. Happily they stocked the modest foodstuff that made up his usual diet. Roaming through, with a basket hooked over his arm, Sam concentrated on his shopping. He had to digest all the information on every single label before making a decision to buy. On occasion, he would gaze at the people within the little store. None were of any interest to him. Sam continued to examine items of interest. When a product passed his scrutiny, an infrequent occurrence, he placed it into his basket and moved on.

One person in the store did notice the basket toting man: Gail Summun. She too had been perusing the aisles picking up her basic supplies. Gail gasped when she saw him. He still had his gaunt-like appearance making him instantly recognizable. Without any question, this guy was Sam Termine. She, with her head down, pushed her tiny shopping cart to the far end of the aisle, abandoned it, and quickly exited the store.

Gail drove slowly until she located the familiar looking truck. The conversion to a camper made it look different. Out-of-state license plates confirmed her suspicion. But why was Sam here? For a moment she thought it could be an extremely unusual coincidence. Then the shock of realty hit her.

"That damned wonderful job," she said as she slapped the steering wheel. "It was a perfect fit – too perfect, and I wanted it – and I bit."

She fumed at the circumstances and her stupidity. The realization slammed into her. Then yelling she said: "Suckered me in and you almost caught me. NOW that I know you're here it's my turn to hunt you. Let's see where you're bunking my little sick friend."

Gail double parked and had to move a few times while she waited for Sam to finish his shopping. The wait tested her patience. "Come on, get out of there," she demanded while seated in her shabby little car.

Sam maintained his no hurry style of reading and rereading all the labels while Gail fumed with impatience. As her wait drew longer she thought about Jack, pointed a finger towards the store and said aloud: "You're walking around pretty good for a guy who was supposed to be on his back. You fooled all of us Mr. Termine. None of it made any sense, until now. You killed Jack. Sure it all fits. We thought you couldn't walk. Now look at you go. You killed Jack – you killed Jack – you killed Jack."

Her rage soared; she started to twist and grasped the wheel with sweaty hands. Gail's heavy breathing stopped when she saw Sam Termine stroll out of the store. His bag of food, small compared to the amount of time it took him to shop, made Gail spew out a few words of exasperation.

Following Sam would be easy. With the traffic flowing normally, Sam left first and Gail's vehicle eased into the stream of cars. Sam dutifully flicked on his turn indicator and turned into the open parking lot. Seeing his signal to turn, Gail slowed down, drove by the entrance and turned into the motel's exit driveway. She killed her lights, stopped her car and observed Sam maneuvering into a stall.

Sam stepped out, gathered his grocery bag and strode to the unit directly in front of his truck. With a flick of a passcard, Sam opened the door and entered his room.

Gail sat in her darkened car and smiled while saying, "Got'cha."

***

The moment after Sam plopped the bag of groceries on the desk his phone jangled an alert.

"Hey Sam, where are you?"

"I found her."

"Sam, where are you?"

"Florida, Miami."

"How do you know it's her?"

"Believe me, I know. I talked to her on the telephone. I'd know her voice anywhere."

"Tell me more."

Sam hearing skepticism in Cornier's voice said, "She calls herself Emma Joslin"

"Okay, you found her. What are you going to do? Nothing stupid I hope." Cornier rammed his words and not allowing Sam time to answer said, "You have to let us take care of her. No more following or telephoning, you know that – right?"

"Yeah I know. No more calling. What should I do?"

"Nothing, absolutely nothing, I'll be down – late tomorrow. I'll catch an early afternoon plane and – well let's see – I guess I can see you late tomorrow night, somewhere around nine or ten. Where are you staying?"

Sam gave all the details on the location of the motel. "You want me to pick you up at the airport?"

"No, just tell me what unit you're in?"

"Sixteen. I'm right in the front. This is a small place. I have two beds, so you can stay here if you want. It's nothing fancy. It's close to her."

"From what you're telling me, you're too close. You have to hide, both you and your truck. Can you park in the back of the motel?"

"There's no back, only a front. Why are you concerned about the truck?"

"Just the way I am. Always looking for – ah, forget it. I'll see you tomorrow night. Do you want someone to stay with you?"

"No way, I don't need any baby sitter. In fact, I'm just going to take it easy all day tomorrow. Sleep in and relax. I picked up a bunch of stuff to eat so there's no reason to leave. I'll be here whenever you get in."

"You're a good man Sam. Please take care of yourself."

"See you tomorrow."

"Right, I'll see you tomorrow." Cornier hung up the phone and immediately booted up his computer. The travel web site searched and displayed the multitude of direct flights to Miami. Within minutes, the printer dutifully copied the information, and he caught each page as it exited the machine. Cornier circled the most likely flight. He chose two other possibilities, just in case. He needed one more thing: permission from his supervisor to travel to Florida.

***

Gail, utilizing the narrow driveway between houses, stowed her car next to the homeowner's tiny garage. Satisfied that anyone searching for her car would have a very difficult time seeing it, she entered her home by its rear door. Although no one should be home, a quick walk through confirmed she was alone. Gail strode into her small rented room; a room with a single twin sized bed sitting beneath a window; a window offering a view of the backyard. Gail peeked out towards her car then pulled down the shade.

Still numb from the sudden appearance of Sam Termine, Gail slumped down into the bed. She covered her eyes; she pondered on her immediate future. Moving away, moving from the current drudgery would be easy to accept. She had to do more than run. Gail had to eliminate the trail.

She leap from the bed and stepped towards the armoire. Grabbing the larger of her two pieces of luggage, she flung it onto the bed knowing exactly where she hid the small pistol.

The small caliber gun looked tiny in her large feminine hand. Though trembling slightly, Gail removed the bullets turning them over in her hand. To her untrained eye, these appeared to be okay. She reloaded the magazine, pulled back the rack chambering a cartridge and pointed the weapon at an imagined target.

"There's a time to flee and there's a time to fight. Sam you came here looking for a fight, and I'm ready for you. I think you're a loner. There are no more surprises in your favor. And I owe you one for Jack," Gail said with a sneer to her words. She raised her arm held out the pistol and then said, "Bang, bang, Sam, bang you're dead."

THIRTY EIGHT

Cornier, without knocking, entered the Lieutenant's office, stopped just a bit past the doorframe, and asked, "Got a minute?"

The Lieutenant, while continuing to work, waved his hand in a don't-bother-me-now go-away gesture.

"How about thirty seconds?"

Lieutenant Gabriel looked up at the intruder and said, "What's got you all steamed up this morning?" He didn't wait for an answer and said, "Let's have it. Keep it short."

"I found Gail Summun. She's in Florida. There's a flight I can catch."

Gabriel looked at the Detective, shook his head, and smiled. "Sorry, no special paid vacations allowed. No Cornier, you can't go to Florida. If you know where she is, that's fine. Get the Florida guys to pick her up."

Cornier anticipating this response said, "That takes time. She could run – again."

"If you didn't hear me the first time, I said no. And they, as you know – and I know you know. They don't care – no one cares if we find her." He strung out his words to emphasize the issue. "You remember the press conference. Sorry Cornier. If you have good information get the . . ."

"Can I have some personal time off – a week or a maybe a few days?"

"See I knew you wanted a vacation. You want time off, okay. You can use some of your accumulated vacation. I'll grant you one week's leave for purposes of a needed vacation. You can start tomorrow."

"I need to go now," Cornier demanded.

"You go now and I'll consider all of today as a vacation day. And that is the best I can do."

"See you in a week."

"Oh, Cornier, the guys upstairs are not going to like what you're doing. Don't bring her back without going through all the wickets. You understand me?"

"Oh, I understand. I understand very well."

***

Cornier returned to his office and placed a call to a longtime associate. He met Bernie Gold years ago at a seminar on police procedures. They seldom met after that conference. Wanting to maintain a good friendship they communicated by telephone and when it became available, they switched to email. Today Cornier needed an instant link to his friend.

"Hello, Bernie. Cornier here."

"Wow, what have I done to receive a call from the Mounties in the north? How are you – you old flatfoot?"

"I'm coming down your way, and I need a favor. Well, make it a favor or two. My plane will be in around six. Are you available for a little breaking of bread and maybe a drop of the good stuff?" Cornier said with urgency in his voice. Gold's sensitivity picked up on Cornier's intense voice. It was direct, all-business, and there were no words representative of a friendly greeting. This was a serious contact; it immediately stimulated his interest welcoming the opportunity for some excitement.

"Perfect timing, the old lady's got a quilting club meeting tonight. And would you believe it's at our house. I want out. Old pal of mine, you've got yourself a party. What's your flight?"

Cornier gave him the three potential flights and said, "I'll call you with the final details."

"And, I'll meet you at the airport." Gold hung up the phone and smiled when he thought about the possibility of a little intrigue.

***

Gail worked her standard daytime shift. She tried to present a normal happy image though her blood was boiling with anticipation; she continually envisioned her encounter with Sam. The picture in her mind showed her heroic stance and her challenge to this intrusive man. She purchased the little pistol years ago and on occasions fantasized using it. It was easy to imagine the blaze of the bullet's path, glistening and searching for its target. She felt a rush of excitement as her thoughts worked the scene. Waiting for the potential violence made the day drag on. It seemed to go on forever, stole her attention and eventually corrupted her nursing skills. She made some medication mistakes ignoring the possible consequences. Gail or Emma as they knew her was just sloppy today, and she didn't care. She put in her time and knew this was the last time this place would see Emma Joslin. She and the name of Emma Joslin would disappear. Gail had a nice list of names. She dwelled on the thought that she might become Mary Archer.

***

Cornier used his official status to reserve a locked out seat on a direct flight to Miami. The reservation clerk tried to convince Cornier that the plane was over booked and it was impossible to secure a seat then yielded to his official pressure.

"Detective, please pray for me that I get a bunch of no-shows."

"You got it. I'm a guy who's good with a prayer. How's this one? Now I lay me down to sleep."

"Oh, oh, I'm in big trouble," she said.

Cornier concerned that his pressure was causing a major problem for the clerk said, "Look, I want to help. Who can I call? I'd like to get you off the hook. Just give me a name and number."

"No, no thanks. I think I'd rather stay with your first attempt to help. Your prayer sounded sincere." She smiled and shooed him away with a small wave.

Cornier gave the woman his card. "You may need MY help someday," he said emphasizing my. "If you do, please don't hesitate to call me. And again thanks."

***

The uneventful flight landed on time, and the plane parked at the assigned gate. It took some time for all the passengers up front to shuffle out. He tugged his bag out of the overhead rack, queued up, slowly worked his way off of the plane, and into a loud greeting.

"There you are, you son of a gun. I wondered if they gave you the last row or maybe the toilet. Got everything with you?"

"This is it," he said hoisting the bag up a few inches in demonstration. "How've you been?"

"Things could be better; I have to go with the mood of the day. Tell you the truth I've been hinting for an offer of early retirement," Gold said as they walked out of the terminal.

"You're too young to retire, or do you have something going on the side."

The two visited, talked about their careers and problems while continuing to walk. The unmarked car, parked in a no-parking zone was protected by the airport police roaming the area. Detective Gold flipped an off-handed salute to the man and said, "Appreciate the help. I owe you one." The airport cop waved back and smiled at the offer of a never-to-be-seen favor.

***

They drove a short distance to a roadside restaurant. It was located away from the main stream of traffic and offered them a good meeting place. A corner table in a quiet area awaited their arrival.

Before Cornier sat down he said, "I have to say one thing. This is a must and in no way negotiable, I'm buying."

"Okay, you're buying and I'm listening. First, we've got to get a little libation and sustenance, right?"

"Nice fancy words. Does that mean I'm in for a night of champagne and caviar?" Cornier said and waited for his reply.

"You know that's not my style. Beef and suds will be perfect. Maybe we can start with a couple of Scotches. How's that sound?"

The drinks and food were good. They ate and joked about their work and the crazy things that happened since they last saw each other. They felt the special bond of two men working in a difficult environment with their work demanding an effort greater than the weekly standard of forty-hours. They talked about the frustration of seeing the same individuals causing trouble and again walking the streets. The identical issues burned into both of their hearts: Picking up bad people and watching high price lawyers hold their hands and then lead them out into freedom.

Cornier told Gold about the Belvedere Manor murder, and the fraud, and then about Sam Termine finding Gail Summun. Both remained quiet while sipping their coffee. Then Gold said, "What do you want from me?"

"I'm way out of my district, and I have all the authority of a tourist. Will you help me bring her in and try to hold her on some kind of a charge? If I don't get her now I doubt I'll get another chance."

"Why can't we get an arrest warrant?"

"Politics, they don't want her back. I'm on my own nickel."

"Whoa! You really want me to put my neck on the line. Tell you what. Let's go see this guy Sam. I want to talk to him and get his drift. You know I'm not saying yes, and I'm not saying no. Okay?"

"More than okay, I want you to see him. Maybe he'll tell you more about these people than – Aw, let's go," Cornier said in frustration. "Here's the address and . . ."

"I know that area. This is my town, Detective. This is my town," Gold said proudly.

***

Gail put her small amount of possessions into her car. She put on a pair of latex gloves, looked over her room very carefully and tried to wipe down all the surfaces she envisioned she could have touched. When satisfied she closed the door, then remembered the toilet. She sat on the commode to see what she could touch then wiped clean everything in her range of motion.

Gail exited via the rear door, entered her car, peeled off the perspiration laden gloves and threw them on the car floor.

Now dark and almost 9:00pm, Gail pulled into the motel's exit driveway and parked at the far end of the small lot. She saw a light in Sam's unit leaking through the sides of the window curtain. To her, those lights announced he was in the room. She withdrew the small weapon. The pistol nesting in her right hand fit easily into her coat pocket.

***

While Gold drove to Sam's motel, they discussed some of the potential methods of arresting Gail. Whatever they did both knew it would be a difficult task holding her. Every angle had a major problem. Arresting her on a minor charge was easy; keeping her, for any amount of time, was most improbable. They both understood any lawyer, good or not so good, would, very quickly, get the woman released. They had to get some meaningful information from Sam.

They drove into the motel parking lot. Cornier noticed a car entered the property through the exit driveway and parked – next to Sam's truck.

"I think that's Gail," Cornier yelled.

A few casually parked autos blocked their access to go deeper into the lot. Gold, barely off the road, killed his engine. Both men leaped from their vehicle and started to run the distance to Sam Termine's room. They watched helplessly as the woman pushed on an opening door; then heard the gunshots. Both drew their weapons. They stopped at the partially opened door and hid behind the doorframe. Gold yelled, "Police. Drop your weapon."

Gail blanched seeing two guns pointing at her. Cornier rushed in and she immediately threw her pistol onto the bed. She held up her hands.

Gold, slightly behind Cornier, believing the woman surrendered, lowered his weapon. Cornier assumed a shooter's stance. While Gail's eyes flicked from Gold to Cornier and back, Cornier peered towards the lifeless body of Sam.

Then Cornier yelled, "Drop the gun – drop it – drop it." Gail, sans a weapon, could only respond to the demand by raising her hands higher. Gold recognizing Sam's intent, backed away.

Allowing Gail a few moments to taste fear, Cornier fired two quick shots into her chest. Gail Summon driven back by the impact of the body-destroying ammo, died with her eyes reflecting terror, her mouth agape in a silent scream.

Acknowledgement

I offer a special thank you to Michael Brown, Elizabeth Brown, and Leah Loffek, who continue to offer their expert reading of my working manuscripts. Most of their valued comments and suggestions were incorporated in the final version of this book.

I also offer many thanks to my family: To Chris, Jean, Terry, Matt, Carol, and all their spouses, I love them for their support in my writing endeavors. Chris, though departed, remains ever present in our hearts and mind.

The original *Grey Justice* manuscript gathered dust for many years because it was viewed as too dark by literary agents. It is now the prequel to *A Touch of Love*. Though its theme remains the same, encouragement and editorial efforts by my dear wife, Marie stimulated a complete rewrite removing the distained darkness. Marie's reading early versions of the new manuscript, with the many-many grammatical errors, and typos, exhibited a special love and dedication.

This novel, as with all of my previous work, is dedicated to my dear Marie.

About the Author

Frank J. Kopet, a retired Aerospace Corporation Division manager, lives with his dear wife Marie on the east coast of Florida.

Also by Frank J. Kopet

Justice Series
A Touch of Love

Tomorrow Series
Wait 'Til Tomorrow
Wait 'Til Tomorrow II
Wait 'Til Tomorrow III
Sarah's Tomorrow

Website: www.frankjkopet.com

Email address: fjkopet@hotmail.com

Made in the USA
Columbia, SC
17 April 2018